TEMPTED

"You have no reason to go, Miss Devlin," Braxton said, "and every reason to return here with me following the wedding."

"That is nonsense, sir."

"It is not nonsense. I wish to take good care of you. Beautiful care, in fact. You will want for nothing with me as your protector. You can be nicely situated for the rest of your days if you play me right."

Despite her inward preparations for this meeting, Tressa was shocked to hear the specifics. Protector, not husband. Nicely situated, not married. Play him right, not plight her troth.

"Stay with me." He held her tightly, pressuring her.

Finally Tressa peered up into his gaze. She was lost. His gray eyes filled themselves with her expression, spying out any least resistance.

"Stay with me," he coaxed, lowering his mouth to hers. His lips spoke both of a surface, silken seduction and of a deeper, more urgent press.

Her lips hinted at a possible capitulation. She couldn't believe how quickly she might give in to him. But at what cost?

BOOK YOUR PLACE ON OUR WEBSITE AND MAKE THE READING CONNECTION!

We've created a customized website just for our very special readers, where you can get the inside scoop on everything that's going on with Zebra, Pinnacle and Kensington books.

When you come online, you'll have the exciting opportunity to:

- View covers of upcoming books
- Read sample chapters
- Learn about our future publishing schedule (listed by publication month *and author*)
- Find out when your favorite authors will be visiting a city near you
- Search for and order backlist books from our online catalog
- Check out author bios and background information
- Send e-mail to your favorite authors
- Meet the Kensington staff online
- Join us in weekly chats with authors, readers and other guests
- Get writing guidelines
- AND MUCH MORE!

**Visit our website at
http://www.zebrabooks.com**

LADY MISTRESS

Anne Laurence

Zebra Books
Kensington Publishing Corp.

http://www.zebrabooks.com

ZEBRA BOOKS are published by

Kensington Publishing Corp.
850 Third Avenue
New York, NY 10022

First Printing: June, 2000
10 9 8 7 6 5 4 3 2 1

Printed in the United States of America

*For Larry
and for Catherine Lawrence Thompson
and Benjamin Lawrence Cohen*

Prologue

Lance Hall
Middlesex—1803

Even at age ten, Tressa Devlin knew Lance Hall was drab, hung about with something dreadful. Her Aunt Editha, invariably dressed in dark garb, was dull. Her uncle was, despite his quiet ways, the dreadful part.

Upstairs in his big bed, her grandfather, the Earl of Straith—ill for as long as she could remember—lay dying.

That was why Tressa felt she must see her own father, just this once. Buck Devlin. The very devil, as Aunt Editha called him, had come to Lance Hall that morning. From the nursery window, Tressa had seen him alight from his carriage in the front sweep. Right away, she'd known Buck Devlin was not drab.

No, he had guinea gold curls very like her own—the curls her aunt and uncle so despised.

The looks they hated, for she was the ''spit of him.''

At the book room door, and with the old house as dark as the midnight hour now being struck by the long-case clock, Tressa bolstered herself as she blew out her candle and set it on the hall table.

The crack of light showing from beneath the door would be enough for her to locate the handle and creep inside.

But just inside there was hardly any light at all.

The low fire barely burnished the gold lettering on the books, barely warmed the ruby-red luster in the glass and bottle on the desk. On the desk, the curls that were like her own mounted to a pile. Seated at the desk and bent over it, her father slept deeply, without a twitch or a snore.

Helplessly lured by the welter of curls, feeling in her soul for the first time in her life that someone like her existed, even as bad as he was, Tressa tiptoed as near as she dared.

Bad Buck Devlin.

And she was Bad Buck's daughter.

Hadn't she just been bad again, feeding the kittens in the barn at the home farm when she'd been told time and again not to? "We don't need so many kittens," Aunt Editha had told Tressa, while also telling her she was bad like her father. Yes, in a world so unlike them, she and Bad Buck were the same.

When the great paneled door to the room swung stealthily open, Tressa's heart told her to dash behind the nearby hearth chair. With its big wings and a tall back, it would be her friend and keep her safe from someone afoot at Lance Hall at midnight.

Her uncle, pale as a ghost, stern and tall and thin, moved quietly across the carpets toward the elder brother he continually blamed for their ruin.

"If Devlin's to take the reins here," he'd say quietly to Aunt Editha, "we're done up."

"We are," his sister would reply. "That father favors him and has spoilt him every day of his life has placed him beyond redemption."

"And now he's to be Straith. Mark my words, the house will be on the block before we're out of mourning."

Her uncle's words, like his quiet relentless footsteps, echoed in Tressa's ears. His shadowy figure passed her. At the desk, he fitted the dueling pistol he carried into her father's limp hand.

The subsequent raspy click, the flash and explosion, the giant swelling drift of dark smoke and the horrid odor, froze Tressa as she was. Only Aunt Editha, like a black crow in the doorway, her eyes locked to Tressa's own, stood out in the dreadful din.

Chapter One

London
June 1816

"Miss Devlin, is there someone in the street watching this house?"

Tucking the draperies closed where she'd made the barest crack so as to peer down onto deserted Pocket Street, Tressa Devlin turned. Smiling, she took Doro's elbow. As an extra precaution, she shielded the candle Doro carried as she ushered the younger woman out of the servant's chamber under the eaves of the small London house.

"I really don't believe that to be the case, Doro dear. No one's watching the house. I'm quite sure of it."

Though Tressa disliked lying to the younger woman, she kept the secret that resulted in someone's watching from down in the streets no matter where she was.

And here she'd thought she'd put the watchers behind her.

In the cramped hallway, Tressa opened a similar door which

let into another frugal chamber. She would rather have settled Doro into her own room behind the final door along the passage.

But that wouldn't do, not with the worry that marred Doro's nearly perfect features. Tressa had to address at least some of those worries before they went to bed.

Although the hour was late, it was nearly mid June. Outside, a long twilight surrendered to darkness. Like Tressa herself, Doro wore a plain nightgown beneath a voluminous cambric dressing gown. Doro's hair, dark as the oncoming hour, was braided, put up beneath her cap. Tressa's own thick blond braid swung at her shoulder.

Before Tressa and Doro were quite inside Tressa's tiny quarters, however, a banging at the front door downstairs froze them as they were.

"Oh, dear," Doro gasped. "Neither Robert nor Mudge are here."

"No," Tressa said, forcing what little smile she could. "But Mudge will be here shortly. Surely no one with truly nefarious doings would cause such a commotion."

An enormous ruckus that could bring down the very house arose, causing Tressa to straighten her shoulders despite her mounting trepidations. Her personal enemies were chill, lurking, and cleverly relentless. They wouldn't present themselves with such heat.

Tressa grasped her layers of nightclothes, whisked the candle from Doro's fingers, and marched down the stairs to the front door none of them had used in the two and half weeks they'd lived on secluded Pocket Street.

For the first time since the four of them had stolen through the rear door into the vacant love nest belonging to the Marquess of Braxton, a pool of candlelight floated along the front walls and down the first flight of risers, illuminating dust covered lumps of every sort.

While Tressa was aware Doro followed her—and not liking that at all—she gave the girl some credit. True, Doro had a gentle nature, but she was also strong and practical, accustomed to life's adversities. Doro would do whatever needed doing. Of that Tressa had no doubt.

On the landing, Tressa paused, the candle flame wavering between them, and gave husky orders to the tall, slender, eighteen-year-old girl.

"Remember now, you are Miss Sweet-As-Pie and I'm Miss Dear."

"Miss Dearie-Dear," Doro insisted, despite the noise shaking the front door.

Not wanting to stop and argue that point again, one that admittedly denoted Doro's affection for her, Tressa shielded the candle as she voiced her last precaution. "We are to act as if Mudge—er, Mr. Right—is in the house and likely to burst forth at any moment. We'll brave it out. Just follow my lead."

Upon reaching the entry, which was as cramped as everything else about the house, Tressa handed the candle to Doro. The girl had gone still at the bottom of the old oak stairs. Her candle flame, almost cringing in reaction to the sharp knocks, revealed an upright, Holland-covered monster and a walking stick propped in the corner. The continuing assault on the door, demanding and regular like the devil's own drumbeat, was punctuated with phrases uttered in the devil's own tones.

"I know you're in there! Open up, I say! I saw you at the draperies up in the attics."

Avoiding Doro's wide dark eyes, Tressa grasped the walking stick, only to put it down as she tried to get the lock open. It seemed a surprisingly shiny new lock for the age of the house. As soon as it gave way, she grasped the stick again, stepped back, and watched as an enormous male, dark and glowering, terrorized the fragile candle flame nearly to dying off. The moment his iron-eyed gaze collided with her own saucer-eyed stare, Tressa knew this Old Scratch must be the Marquess of Braxton.

Yes, if she was Miss Dear and Doro Miss Sweet-As-Pie, if

Robert had dubbed himself Mr. Wrong to Mudge's Mr. Right, before her stood none other than Braxton, the iron-eyed general. Fittingly, he'd been christened Hannibal.

Wondering why she didn't find their little company's earlier jollity so jolly anymore, Tressa became conscious of Braxton's hard eyes dropping to the stick in her hand.

"Never mind that, woman. I'm as angry as the very devil, but no one here will get a cracked head." His gaze searched the small entry. "Not with just the three of us."

"Oh, but you are wrong in that." The steadiness of her voice surprised Tressa. "It is not merely us, sir."

He snorted. "Then why the stick, eh? Indeed, call out your bruiser. I should like that. Otherwise, have done with it."

Tressa couldn't call out her bruiser. Her deflation must have shown in her face, along with other rioting emotions.

"Ah, yes," he said, all triumph as she set aside the cane. "Just as I thought—although there is a bruiser, as I understand it. Four of you in all, I hear. And a new lock that don't fit my damned key, and I own the place."

Unable to reply, Tressa allowed him the floor.

Not unremarkably, he took it.

"I'm only interested in my cousin, however. Where the deuce is the rascal? Surely not at Pounce's twenty-four hours a day—not with the pair of you here."

Tressa glanced at Doro.

"Well?" his lordship demanded. "Where is he? I have someone in the street holding my horse, woman. Robert and I need only a moment. Then I'll assuredly leave you to your . . . doings here, whatever those may be with two of you as fresh as summer peaches. Frankly, I wouldn't have thought Robert much interested in two."

Tressa was stunned by the gentleman's turn of phrase, by his train of thought. "He isn't interested, sir."

"He isn't?"

"Of course not."

"Well, that seems a damned shame, what with, as I say, the pair of you so obviously perfect for it. One dainty and fair, one tall and dark. 'Twould make for a very pretty featherbed jig."

Tressa swung away from him, toward Doro. "Miss Sweet-As-Pie, you will retire on the instant."

Doro remained steady, if also wide-eyed. "No, Miss Dearie-Dear, I will not leave you."

Reaching behind him, Braxton finally closed the door and heaved a sigh. "So much for making quick work of this. My poor Saracen will have to cool his heels, I see."

Tressa rounded on the man. "I cannot simply produce your cousin—I mean, Mr. Wrong—with the flick of a wrist, my lord. Indeed, I do not think I can produce him at all tonight."

"And where is he?"

"He is . . . is busy, sir."

"Yes, well"—Braxton's eyes turned iron gray again, visible even in the faint candlelight—"I say he has important business with me, and you shall conjure him up."

"I will see what I can do, sir—*if,*" she added with emphasis, holding her gaze to his, "you will guard what you say here."

With her mind more settled now, Tressa couldn't blame his lordship for thinking as he did. But that didn't mean he should continue talking as he was. Doro shouldn't hear such things. She herself couldn't make out the half of it. But the "featherbed jig," the intonations, the cast of his eyes were clear enough.

Squaring her shoulders, she assumed her most imperious stance and voice, despite his being the imperious one—the Marquess of Braxton, an iron-eyed general who'd never served a single day in the army.

He stood at least six feet tall, dressed in costly riding attire. His mulberry coat fit his broad shoulders like—well, if she were a London tailor, she'd want this man above all to wear the clothes she crafted. The coat was comfortable enough for riding, yet well-cut enough to be recognized for what it was in Town. His buff breeches were as tight as his coat and top-boots, his linens fresh and fragrant from the hands of his valet. His quirt, his gloves, and his hat were the best to be had, announcing his crisp dark hair, his aristocratic features, his large, well-kept hands, and his commanding stance and attitude.

Braxton was a man among men.

No wonder the house on Pocket Street, which was intended for his ultimate pleasure, all but quaked at his displeasure.

Knowing the house as she did now, Tressa found it hard to believe he belonged there. The house was simply too small to contain his size, too neglected, too . . . tawdry.

When had he been here last? And with whom? The questions startled her, but she knew they'd come again. Later, when she had time to recall him, picture him in her mind, the questions would stir. Braxton made that kind of impression.

She regathered her scattered wits. "Will you come into the sitting room, sir?"

He thrust one hand through his black hair. "Devil take it, I suppose I must."

"You must watch your language, sir."

He peered at her. "I am unaccustomed to my women telling me what I must do, ma'am."

"I well understand your usage of 'women' as opposed to 'ladies,' sir, and you may treat me however you will. But I ask you once again for the sake of my companion—"

"Your Miss Sweet-As-Pie? Now, there's an appellation that demands regard."

Goodness, Tressa hadn't considered that. Their little names for each other, concocted to keep who they were a secret in the neighborhood, hadn't seemed to carry the connotations his lordship attached to them. She and Robert, Mudge, and Doro, had had quite a time inventing them some three weeks ago when they'd planned their escape from Mayfair.

Still, even if they'd been who he thought they were, he, with his privilege, would be obligated to—

To do nothing. Braxton did and thought as he pleased, and everyone was supposed to give way. He was accustomed to people giving way in big and little matters. His every move spoke of his sway in his world.

She'd been in service for five years. Why couldn't she learn?

"So, my Lord Braxton," she said, "if you will step into the sitting room—"

"Since you know me, I have the right to know your name. Yours, too," he added, as Doro joined them, lighting their path through the shrouded front parlor to the rear sitting room.

There were only two rooms on the ground floor, the two bedchambers with accompanying dressing rooms on the next floor, two servants' quarters on the last.

"I don't know the house," he admitted as Doro's candle struck its light into a chamber that was obviously more in use.

As Doro went to light more candles—and Tressa to poke the coals back into what life they might regain—the table with its fabrics and sewing materials, the few uncovered chairs, and the single settee by the hearth were visible.

No, Braxton did not belong on Pocket Street. He was too large. Too fine.

Even so, after settling his accessories on a side table, he took the chair Tressa offered as she put away the bellows. She ignored the long stretch of his legs and the way he immediately uncoiled.

"Someone will be here shortly, sir, who can take a message to your cousin. But Robert might be unable to come."

"Is he tied to a bedpost?"

Since Braxton took unkindly to being thwarted, Tressa stayed as patient as she could. "He's not tied to a bedpost, sir. But as you must know, he is very conscientious, and he'll likely return only when he feels it's right."

"And this is why you call him Mr. Wrong, no doubt."

"No, my lord." Tressa's eyes met Doro's, then lowered.

"He must tell you why he chose such a name for himself. And now, if you'd like, we can offer—"

"Actually, I'm sharp set, and—"

Braxton interrupted himself. Tressa's bruiser, Mudge, had entered the sitting room and locked his wise old eyes to the marquess's equally astute stare.

So this is the bruiser, Braxton thought. Mudge was a large, somewhat older fellow, his hired investigator had told him. A difficult man to put in a box.

Clearly, the man was protective of the two females. And naturally, Braxton was not obligated to get to his feet.

Sweet little Miss Dearie-Dear, however, introduced them as if they were peers. Despite himself, Braxton stood and spoke. "I'm looking for my cousin, Mr., uh, Right. I'll have my say with him and leave, so you needn't come the ugly with me."

The man measured him calmly, not responding. His old but sharp eyes were drawn away only when Miss Dearie-Dear spoke again.

"If you could run a message to Mr. Wrong, we'd certainly appreciate it—that his cousin is here to see him, of course."

The man inclined his head, giving her his deference. "If you think you're safe, Miss, I'll go right along."

"Oh, we're certainly safe, Mr. Right. His lordship, however, was just saying he's hungry. If you'd stop on your way back at the Crown and Feathers again, we'd appreciate it."

"I've brought a meat pie and some ale. 'Tis in the kitchen, Miss."

"Oh, good, good." Tressa smiled. On turning to Braxton, she sobered somewhat. "I hope a pie and ale sounds all right to you, my lord. The Crown and Feathers makes a very nice savory pie, and we have bread and cheese."

"And some lovely plum cake," Miss Sweet-As-Pie interjected. "I shall make up a tray. If, that is . . ."

The chit's pretty dark eyes glanced from Miss Dearie-Dear to himself, Braxton saw. Those eyes, although less fearful now, still held caution.

"I can assure you," he found himself saying with some sincerity, "that Miss Dearie-Dear is entirely safe with me. I intend only to eat what you bring me from the kitchen."

"Oh, Mr. Right," Miss Dearie-Dear said, ignoring Braxton's jab, "his lordship's horse is in the street."

"I'll have Knobby take him 'round to the mews. Knobby will see to it."

"Old Saracen can be nasty," Braxton warned.

"So can we all," Mr. Right said softly, his meaning nevertheless plain.

Mr. Right, as the women called him, wasn't precisely challenging him. Mudge was rather stating that the females in his charge wouldn't go unprotected. While Braxton could muster mild admiration for that, the fact he'd leave as soon as he could comforted him more.

He wasn't in the mood to brangle. For weeks he'd longed to be shut of London, and, devil take it, after this one last distasteful duty, he'd be off to Devonshire and Cannongate, By Jove, he would.

Braxton found himself alone with Miss Dearie-Dear. He wondered what they might have to say to each other. She obviously meant to keep as much as she could from him. Just as obviously, more was going forward at Pocket Street than he could fathom.

In the abrupt quiet, he settled his eyes on her, a most pleasant thing to do. She stood before the meager fire, with him still at the chair he'd briefly used. They were a bit close, and he sensed her discomfort. The woman was ready for bed, and as conscious of that as he was.

Ready for bed, he thought. And so . . . desirable? Definitely. But sweet, too. Damnably appealing. So brave on first encountering him that he respected her. She appealed to him mightily, and in more than the sensual way.

Still, what could they have to say to each other? Above all, why did he feel the need to talk?

Could she be available to him? Right now? Tonight? No, she didn't have the look of the usual dolly-mop. But, by God, he wanted her. Oddly, he wanted her more than he wanted to leave for Cannongate.

"I should prepare a place on the table for the tray, my lord."

Scissors and pins and fabrics littered the top of the table in the center of the room. When she moved to clear a space, her nightclothes rustled, releasing the soft scent of lavender behind her.

Delicious.

A dalliance? He was definitely inclined. He could spend a few more days, although not under the same roof as his cousin.

And what of his cousin and this particular female?

Miss Sweet-As-Pie, younger—but not by much—entered with the promised tray. Immediately, Miss Dearie-Dear grew less awkward and instructed the gel in what to do.

"You must go to bed now, Miss Sweet-As-Pie. I'll wait the necessary few more minutes with his lordship, and then I'll come up, as well. It's late, and you've had a very long day."

Watching the pair carefully, Braxton assumed the prepared place at the table.

"Go on to bed, Miss Sweet-As-Pie," he said, taking in the appetizing spread. "We've come to our agreements, have we not? I've promised to be good to Miss Dearie-Dear, and I invariably keep my promises. Besides"—he shook out the napkin—"I have something to eat. Once I'm less hungry, I'll be more manageable."

He caught the exchange of glances between the women. He rather liked it that they took him in stride now. No simpering misses these. But not doxies, either, he decided.

They stood together, observing him as he took his first bite of the pie. Because it was good, he realized how hungry he was. He nodded at them once again, and they exchanged another communicative look.

So pretty together, he thought.

"And where do you sleep, Miss Sweet-As-Pie?" he asked, as if he'd inquired about the weather.

"*Go*," Miss Dearie-Dear ordered the girl. "Upstairs."

"But—"

"Upstairs. Right now. I'll be perfectly all right. Besides," she added with a glower in his direction, "you'll certainly hear me shouting from the rooftops if I'm *not* all right."

His ploy got him what he wanted. The younger girl went out, leaving him alone with his true quarry. He much preferred Miss Dearie-Dear, even if they ended in verbal jousting.

As he continued to eat, she began it.

"I told you to watch how you spoke in front of her."

He feigned innocence, now enjoying the crusty bread and melting butter. "And what did I say?"

"You asked her where she slept, and well you know it."

"An unremarkable question on the whole."

"Most certainly not."

"And where do you sleep?"

"I shall leave you to your own designs, sir, if—"

"All right, all right."

He surrendered by taking recourse in his meal.

Miss Dearie-Dear remained staunchly near the door.

"I'm sure," he said after a moment, "that I know where you sleep, in any case—up in the attic. And she, too. The question is where does Robert sleep?"

"In the male servants' quarters in the basement," she all but hissed.

"And Mudge?"

"You're insufferable."

He ate. Drank some ale. "Most interesting arrangements. It makes me wonder why, of course."

She couldn't seem to help being led. He liked that.

"Despite what you may think, sir, despite even what it appears, we're all decent people. You say you need but to speak to Robert and you'll be gone. Indeed, if that is all that's required, I shall excuse myself."

"You shall not."

"And, pray, why not?"

Purposely he pinned her with his gaze. "Because I own this house. I can have you put out on the street in a twink."

"And you would, too," she said.

He went back to his ale. "If I'm so moved, I will. I will, however, not be so moved if you stay with me until Robert comes."

"I will stay, sir, if you will watch your . . ."

"My what? My curiosity? Is it so beyond belief amazing I should find the circumstances here curious?"

She had no reply.

"Mudge I can comprehend, of course. He's a man of all jobs, hiring out for this and that. He works at the Crown and Feathers—for food, mostly. Back and forth from here to there. Not an easy one to put a finger to, though. Roots in the City, it seems. Good enough sort, I suppose."

"It's your watcher who's been in the street, isn't it?"

She spoke so coolly that he paused to peer at her.

She was quite a picture, standing there in her thick layers of cambric, observing him levelly and speaking to him as if she were his equal.

Deuced unusual in anyone, especially a woman. And all that innocent appeal, as well. He was more intrigued than he could like.

"And what else has your watcher told you, sir?"

"Nothing of you and Miss Sweet-As-Pie. You and Miss Sweet-As-Pie seldom leave the house, and only venture into the neighborhood on foot and veiled. Unfortunately, you remain a mystery to me."

She didn't so much as stir, not even blink one of those long, soft, golden-blond eyelashes. He quite liked her guinea-blond hair, her deep blue eyes, the dimple that winked at him as she spoke, that lovely, creamy skin. That delicious little body.

Still, she was all business, so he sat back on his chair and looked at her as good as he got.

"Robert comes and goes at Pounce's just blocks away," he said. "I know he's Sir Percival's friend, but I also admit I don't like it. I'd much rather he'd be here with you, no matter what is or isn't going on. Of course, I'd most prefer he was back in his rooms in St. James's. You must tell me, ma'am, what's going forward here."

"None of that is my concern. 'Tis yours to discuss with Robert, no matter how quickly you can turn us out if I fail to please you."

Fair enough. He'd deserved that thrust.

Fortunately, the door opened and Mudge entered, interrupting their standoff. After closing them in, the large man swept his hat from his head and met Braxton's gaze as calmly as did Miss Dearie-Dear.

"I'm sorry, me lord," the man said, "but I've spoken to Mr. Wrong, and he's unable to return to the house straight off. He'll likely stay where he is until after dawn."

Employing his napkin before placing it on the table, Braxton got to his feet. "So he's at Pounce's, is he?"

This pair also exchanged glances. Theirs, too, were quickly and solidly supportive of each other.

"I can't say where Mr. Wrong is, me lord."

"Easy enough for me to discover for myself," Braxton replied dismissively. "If, that is, I want to deal with that deuced bufflehead Pounce, which I don't."

In the ensuing silence, as Braxton stood deciding where his next move would take him, Mudge stepped to the table. Removing a key from his pocket, he laid it on the polished surface.

"I changed the lock, me lord."

Again the man spoke to Braxton levelly, even though he'd stolen into Braxton's house and was living there without charge, for God's sake.

"I didn't, me lord, want to leave the ladies alone without knowing I pocketed the key to tha' front door. Besides, the lock was too contrary to trust."

Grudgingly, Braxton nodded. He appreciated the responsibility in the man's actions. And his straightforwardness.

"I'll stand the bill meself, me lord."

Braxton grunted.

"But your horse, me lord, is in the stables and the lad will be needin' a coin."

When Braxton reached for his money pouch, Mudge went on. "And then there's the pie and ale, me lord."

Braxton grumbled as he dropped what was required onto Mudge's work-worn palm. "I could well charge you for sneaking in here, you know."

"Oh, but I've done this and tha' around the place, me lord. I'll be glad to give you an accounting."

Gazing into the older man's canny regard, Braxton knew he needed no accounting. Besides, this wasn't about money.

"You can valet me then, old man, because I intend to spend the night."

Miss Dearie-Dear, for all her steadiness up to that point, gasped.

Chapter Two

At his lordship's astonishing declaration that he intended to spend the night waiting for Robert, Tressa thought her wits might go wanting. Never was she so grateful that she and Mudge had, over their years together, developed a cooperation that would fall into place without her having to think.

In the little sitting room, right in front of the Marquess of Braxton, Mudge listed his intentions. The man was apparently receptive to the idea of valeting his lordship, and since the occupants on Pocket Street were accustomed to doing for themselves, Mudge sorted out what was necessary. He'd see to the washing up and to the hot water his lordship would need in preparing for bed. Mudge would also look after Saracen, settling the horse into the stables for the night.

Knowing that the bedchamber normally used by the master of the house was unprepared, Tressa offered to find candles and bedding.

"I'm afraid nothing can be done about the dust in general,

my lord.'' She faced Braxton squarely—indeed, calmly—for the surprise she'd experienced. "But I shall tend to the bed.''

He had an enormous and certainly perfectly staffed house in Mayfair. That he'd stubbornly stay the night on Pocket Street seemed ridiculous.

Worse, more work would fall to Mudge, whom his lordship plainly intended to pay. But she, because of her concern for her friend, would insist on helping. Bedding and candles, despite the curiosity that registered in the marquess's features, became her objective.

His lordship hadn't quite decided who she was as yet—doxy, seamstress, companion to Doro, perhaps now housekeeper—or, worse yet, maid of all work.

The marquess's gaze still measured her, even followed her, as it had done since his arrival. The idea that she intrigued him astounded her as much as it caused a frisson of . . . what?

She was unaccustomed to drawing the attention of anyone, particularly the opposite sex. She cleared her thoughts, nodded to the marquess and to Mudge, and then left the sitting room. She had only to look after what comforts she could for Braxton before finally retiring. Then she'd carefully consider what had happened to her tonight.

In fetching fresh bedding and candles—beeswax, for there were nice things in the house—Tressa felt a great relief. Free of the marquess and his dark gray eyes, she could catch her breath. She was a sensible person. Good sense, together with the needs involved in their days at the little house on Pocket Street, would soon have her firmly on her feet again.

Still, Tressa recognized another part of herself. At the age of eighteen, she'd been brought to London as a companion for the aging Lady Farronby. Though Tressa had taken her responsibilities seriously, she'd whiled away those little corners of time she'd had for herself in . . . well, not in daydreaming. She was too sensible for that. But she had, over the five years since, claimed bits and pieces for herself, reserving them for some daring, stolen time she would clasp to her heart.

She would always need to support herself. She'd recognized that and adjusted to it years ago. But this idea of having something exciting, something meant only for her to treasure in her mind and memory, was an idea that would not leave her alone.

The Marquess of Braxton was the first male to present her with the slightest suggestion that her "something" might be shaped into reality. On Pocket Street, she had her opportunity. She hung between the obligations she was leaving behind at Lady Farronby's and the equally certain life ahead of her, one that would require circumspection and a solid repute.

But here she was, briefly, outside owing anybody anything. Oh, she had duties toward Mudge and Doro and Robert, but those were duties of affection, a mere respite from what she *must* do, from what she *had* to do.

Did she have the sense to recognize her chance? Did she have the courage to grasp it and hold it close, if only for the moment? Was she—basically an innocent in such things— capable of attracting the Marquess of Braxton?

Indeed, was she being ridiculous?

After all, she was no longer an earl's daughter. She was a hired companion whose secrets were so dangerous that they could destroy her should she make the least misstep.

No, her "something" was meant only for the corners in her mind.

Carrying the fresh blankets, line-dried sheets, and the few good candles she was able to unearth, she entered the bedchamber the marquess would soon occupy. Heavens, she thought, lifting her light to pass it over the dark, paneled chamber, how could such a man spend a single night in this room?

The dust she'd expected covered everything. Here, as in the other rooms in the house, the furnishings were draped with Holland covers.

Tressa set her candle on the lump that was a table and went

straight to the bed. A veritable cloud of dust arose as she removed its protective covers. She finally opened a window.

A fairly reasonable mattress lay underneath, but no fresh featherbed, as he would certainly anticipate.

Trying to suppress the picture that stirred in her mind, a picture of the marquess actually lying on the sheets she would . . . well, she wouldn't allow herself to picture anything that could revitalize her dream of "something."

She'd save that for when he was well and truly gone.

In replacing the candles, Tressa found even more to ignore about the chamber, and again focused on the four-poster bed. She dusted it and the night table, finally returning to the waiting sheets and pillowcases. As she floated the first fresh-scented sheet into place, the door creaked and the marquess entered the room.

Usually as steady as could be, Tressa started.

"I beg pardon, Miss, ah, Dearie-Dear. I didn't mean to frighten you."

"You wouldn't have," she retorted, "if you'd waited in the sitting room. Mudge has not come up as yet."

She was embarrassed to be found at such an unladylike task, especially in her state of undress—not that she wasn't covered from head to toe, but preparing a bed in front of a gentleman simply wasn't done in the proper world.

Worse and worse, she suspected he'd sought her out precisely to embarrass her. No, to watch her make up his bed, an intimate thing to do. Tressa's heart beat a silly tattoo.

"I must say, my lord, I can't understand your staying here. There's absolutely nothing to be done about the dust, not tonight, anyway. You are but minutes away from . . ."

"From where? You know of me, don't you? You know I have a house in Mayfair."

She knew to guard her tongue, to keep her emotions from running away with her. She tucked in the sheet and concentrated on smoothing it, lit as it was by the buttery flicker of candle flames.

He edged closer, observing her with dark gray eyes. She knew better than to look at him in that seductive light. Beyond her embarrassment over their improper circumstances, she had personal embarrassments that befuddled her—the fact that her heart, her body itself, seemed to respond to his mere presence.

"I'll be fine here," he finally said. "I don't wish to miss Robert yet again. From what I understand, he's hardly here except to sleep. Makes me think he's more than keeping company with Percival Pounce. He's in the man's thrall."

"I told you, my lord, I will not discuss your cousin with you. It's not my place."

Tossing her blond braid over her shoulder, Tressa floated the next big sheet onto the first one, straightening it as she walked around the bed. Truth be told, she wasn't a chambermaid, and she wasn't doing very well. She'd merely wanted to save Mudge what tasks she could, but now Braxton had come to shred her nerves.

Although he didn't follow her step by step in her erratic moves around the bed—its heavily carved head and footboards made her work awkward—he did manage to position himself so she couldn't ignore him.

Buttery candlelight painted him, as well.

"Besides," he said, his voice low and relaxed, "I'm tired enough to sleep almost anywhere. I've been preparing to leave London for days now—have, in fact, closed Braxton House and sent most everyone to my estate in Devonshire, including my valet and groom. Racking up at the Clarendon and using their staff. Down to just the necessities."

Yes, she thought, beautiful necessities like mulberry coats that fit to perfection, boots with the soft gleam of finest leather. He smelled of leather and polish, of expensive soap and sweet water. He suited to perfection her taste in what was fine, the very prince in her dream of "something."

"You're not speaking to me," he murmured, having gone still at the foot of the bed, hovering above the buttercream smoothness of the sheets.

She worked at stuffing a fat pillow into a case. "I have nothing to say, sir."

"I like hearing your lovely voice. You have perfect elocution."

She didn't reply. Her heartbeat, though, must have resounded in his ears as it did in hers.

"Who are you, Miss Dearie-Dear?"

She spoke tersely to his suggestive murmur.

"Miss Dear will do, if you must address me at all."

"I do indeed mean to address you—by your given name."

"As I said"—she plucked up another pillow, struggled dreadfully with another case—"Miss Dear will do."

"Perhaps I might suggest a compromise." He eased around the foot of the bed, lifting a large hand and placing it on the carved post. " 'Haps I might call you dearest."

"That would sound silly."

"Not to me. In fact, it would seem quite natural, I think."

Although the room was thick with Braxton's suggestion, a silence built between them. Tressa concentrated on the pillows that looked like fat, white pullets nesting along the headboard. The sheets, though a bit askew, were creamy, butter rich. She plucked open a thick blanket.

His lordship wouldn't sleep beneath a fine counterpane emblazoned with his family crest on this night. Plain but clean blankets and sheets—those were her obligations toward him. Surely Mudge would come soon.

"It don't at all matter to me, you know."

His voice, the lowest, most comforting murmur she'd ever heard, ebbed around Tressa. With little jerks, she tugged at the blanket. But she couldn't help asking, "What doesn't matter to you, my lord?"

He cleared his throat and fixed his eyes on her. "That you are love-begotten."

Her astonishment forced her gaze to meet his even as her fingers stilled.

"Love-begotten, sir?"

"You have left me to my own reckonings, Miss Dearie-Dear, and—"

"Miss Dear, sir."

"—Miss Dear. The way I see it, you must certainly be love-begotten. I'm simply informing you it will make no difference to me."

Tressa peered at him. In the diffuse glow of the candles that rendered him even more handsome, his eyes even more dark and commanding, she chanced connecting with his gaze.

He shrugged one large shoulder somewhat speculatively. "Well, you must be love-begotten. As we all know, the love-begotten are beautiful."

Tressa shook herself mentally, ready now to sail around this mountain of a man and have done with it. "I hope you will be comfortable, my lord. If you'll excuse me, I—"

"I will not."

"Then I'll leave."

He stood as he was, making it impossible for her to go around him without appearing craven. Her cheeks heated. Worse, she was angry with herself. Why did she find him so enthralling? Why wouldn't her heart stop its foolish, tripping beat?

If Mudge's arrival hadn't been imminent . . .

"I see, sir, you will use any means, any compliment, to have your way."

"I'm not complimenting you. I'm telling the truth."

"In calling me love-begotten, you're leading me into admitting whether or not you've guessed aright."

"No, I'm not." He appeared quite firm on that score. "You can only be love-begotten."

She folded her arms across her chest, challenging him while

also trying to appear less confounded by the fact that she remained in her nightclothes. They, too, had assumed a fragile, buttery allure in the soft light.

Since her stance demanded he proceed, he did.

"Your elocution, your grace, your use of words eliminate the possibility of your coming from the theater. Though actresses are trained in suchlike, the qualities aren't ingrained in them as they are in you. On the other hand . . ." He let go the bedpost and actually paced a bit away, elaborating on his deductions. "You are here, which means you cannot be a lady of quality, either. No, you were born on the wrong side of the blanket, and your father likely loved your mother well enough to have you gently reared. When the time came, you were found a position somewhere—again reflective of your father's concern, something like companioning some old woman somewhere. You're much too lovely to have been considered for a governess. Would have wreaked havoc in a household where males were present."

Tressa swallowed hard. He was far off the mark, of course, but close enough to give her a chill. Because she didn't reply, he paced a bit again, still continuing his clever, intricate ruminations.

He'd been more than watching her that night. He'd been studying her.

"The question is," he said, piercing her with something more like his general's iron-gray gaze, "what happened to you? How did you come so far afield of your little niche in the world? My guess—the best guess—is that you fell in love. You're obviously meant for loving, and when you chose this fellow over security . . . well, when he left you quite insecure . . . indeed, I should like some time alone with this loose fish. Alone with a horsewhip, that is."

Tressa was so flustered by this story—well, not by the story; these were common enough occurrences in his world. But that he applied such sordid doings to her, that he saw her as some fallen creature . . .

"So," he said, facing her, "if I'm not precisely on the mark, I'm close enough, am I not?"

"If you will excuse me, my lord, I should like to retire now."

"I do not excuse you. I repeat: I am close enough in my deductions, am I not?"

His tone was not accusatory. It was low, even sympathetic. His grievances were with the man who supposedly ruined her, perhaps even with the father who had abandoned her after her fall from grace.

Tressa felt a welter of emotions. Mostly, she was tempted to smile. Then, thank goodness, she did smile. In the end, her sense of humor did not desert her.

"There," he said, all pleased as Punch. "I'm glad it's clear between us."

"What's clear between us, sir, is that you are quite inventive and formidably judgmental."

He stiffened at that.

She smiled fully this time. "Obviously, you've been called judgmental before, and I don't think you liked it any more then than you do now."

She'd ruffled his feathers. "It's only natural I've been called judgmental. A man in my position is forced to make judgments. And to be damned sure, they're good ones."

Robert had spoken of his cousin often enough for Tressa to know the marquess was one of the biggest landholders in England. But Braxton's responsibilities were not limited to Devonshire or even to England itself.

Over the generations, family interests had taken the Wexbys to the West Indies, to America, to India, even to the Far East. Braxton was not merely a gentleman of the first stare, but prodigiously wealthy.

"Making judgments is what I do, ma'am. I need to know if

a tenant will do well, both for himself and for me. I need to understand that any single land steward in my employ will be level-handed in thousands of transactions, big and small. Yes, I make judgments, and it's a damned good thing I have the talent and inclination to do so. You can't imagine the number of people who depend upon my willingness to take on the . . .''

Tressa saw she'd been given a glimpse into the true Braxton. She hadn't thought about the vastness of his responsibilities, the very weight of them. A man with less will for his duties could mean the desperation of innumerable others. That she understood all too well.

"So, sir, I say again I hope you are comfortable here tonight. I'm sure Mudge will be most helpful."

Tressa's eyes still held Braxton's deep gray stare. She began to feel she couldn't drag herself away. The gentleman exuded such power and strength and capability that she simply couldn't help being drawn to him merely by the force of will expressed in his iron-gray eyes.

But more than that mesmerized her.

That he watched her, that he openly desired her and hoped to make that clear to her, that he'd be considerate of her, that he'd give her an equal standing in this one regard, that she, in a way, held her own sway over him in the power of his desire for her . . .

Desire tricked his eyes, and it confounded her ability to see anything else, to think about anything else.

He moved toward her quickly, as if he'd read her thoughts. She was such a small, fragile pray that he caught her to him easily, gripping her with an urgency that eliminated any last chance she might have had at reasoning.

His body was powerful. His big heart hammered beneath her slender fingers. Layers of fine fabric separated her fingertips from his warm chest, but this first contact with him—with any man—aroused something sleeping inside her.

Peering into his eyes, which pled with hers, she saw, even more amazingly, he was her prey.

"Don't resist me now, my dear." His words were a rasp. "It's time to throw caution to the wind. We shall be all pleasure together, and I pledge no pain at the end. We shall run away to bliss."

Surely he spoke of that stolen time for which her own heart had yearned. That "something," as she'd considered it so often, seemed to lurk in Braxton's gray eyes. But then he closed his eyes and, unbelievably, settled his mouth on her lips.

At last, she'd been kissed.

And, oh, the wonder of it. His lips coaxed hers, cajoling her. Braxton could take her to bliss. His mouth was firm yet pliant, obviously practiced in an art of which she was ignorant. At the moment, she wanted nothing more than to revel in his regard for her. He believed she could match his expertise with an experience of her own. He thought she could carry *him* to bliss.

She despised her ignorance.

She shunted that ignorance aside and, just that quickly, decided to do her best. The moment she lifted her hands to his shoulders, the moment she applied her own pressure to his lips, he groaned.

He came back at her double force, treating her as if she, too, pleased him, as if she knew how to participate, as if she'd said she would participate wholly.

The wonder of his desire for her fueled her own blossoming desire. The pressure of his lips on hers, the stunning realization she could give him his desire, catapulted her into someplace unrecognized in herself.

Oh, the shock of it, that he took her more tightly into his arms and, groaning, opened his lips over her lips, savoring her as he would a peach.

Tressa thought she'd die of her cascading emotions, of her thousand little awakenings.

She pleased Braxton.

She could transport him to "something."

Her body could, somehow, run away with his to bliss. But how was this to happen? And how was he not to guess her ignorance?

She had no choice but to do as he did. What better teacher than the marquess's lips? Who could tutor her better in parting her own lips, in slanting her head, in a determination that matched his?

When he held her tighter, as though he would drown her in his powerful warmth, she slipped her arms around his neck, clasping herself to him with all her might.

His groan was her signal she'd done well.

With his mouth, he opened hers, coming into her with his tongue in such a way that bedazzled her. She never would have imagined it.

Then, with a fierce peck to her lips, he pulled away enough to plunder her with his want-heavy eyes. All thick as fog they were, and laden with desire—desire for her.

"Let's run away to bliss," he whispered, obviously wanting them to be clear, and just as obviously meaning the buttermilk expanse of waiting linens.

Barely above the answering thrum in Tressa's every vital part, she heard sounds from the dressing room off the bed-chamber.

Mudge had arrived.

Sanity returned. Tressa pulled away, and Braxton reluctantly let her go.

She needed time to consider her actions, far more than the hour or two she'd had since they'd met. She couldn't capitulate to him or to her own awakenings, without some consideration.

Looking at his lordship while uselessly smoothing her night-clothes, she saw he read the swift changes sweeping into her.

"I must go," she said, her eyes pinned to his.

"You will come back to me," he stated.

"I cannot."

"In no more than a quarter hour."

"No, my lord."

"If you do not come back to me, I'll come find you in the attic."

Cool, clear reality struck Tressa. "Oh, but Miss Sweet-As-Pie's room is next to mine. The walls are paper-thin, and she would hear. No, my lord, I will not allow her to be tainted by—"

"So we are back to that." He spoke mockingly. "Miss Sweet-As-Pie."

Tressa couldn't imagine that the heat of only moments ago had abruptly ended in this chill—she and Braxton at a draw in the rich yellow light, all cool disagreement.

"You will come back," he commanded. "If you don't, I'll come find you."

Not ten minutes later, Tressa sat at the top of the attic steps, clasping her knees to her chest and making herself small and quiet.

She had to think. She had to stay vigilant.

Keeping her eyes on the risers that marched down to the middle floor of the house, she watched the familiar, well-used space as it was transformed to an oddity by the candle flickerinq beside her. Her nightclothes would suffer from her sitting on the dusty floor, and she felt as if she'd worn them for ages. They'd definitely eaten at her confidence that evening. One simply did not get caught in one's nightclothes in untenable circumstances.

That she was thinking about her commodious nightclothes demonstrated how her wits kept scattering. She had to think. If she went to bed, Braxton would find her. Whether in her little room or near his buttery expanse of sheets, she'd give in to him.

Playing general to his general, she chose her best ground for taking her stand. He'd come—she knew he'd come—but he wouldn't find her ready to be convinced by him right there under her own sheets. At the top of the stairs, she could hold firm. With Doro nearby, they'd be forced to keep their voices down or be discovered.

The very fine Braxton would not wish to be discovered in a backstairs brangle.

Not a minute later, his lordship appeared at the bottom of the risers, his candlestick in hand. She recognized her advantage, reflected in his brief surprise at finding her as she was.

Like a general, however, he recovered well. He lifted his flame toward her, illuminating his own toughly chiseled features. Amazingly, the light also exposed his bare upper torso. Having no night things of his own, he'd wrapped his blanket at his waist and tucked it in. It formed a cylinder around him, a creamy encasement revealing his bare toes on the floorboards below.

Obviously, he still believed her to be experienced in amorous doings. In fact, she tried to appear as if she wasn't agog. She set her chin.

He rapped a long finger, pointing at the old oak planking on which he stood. "Come down here," he mouthed, rather than whispered.

He had some concern for Doro. Tressa had to admire him for that, and for the decision he continued to leave to Tressa herself. He would not take her against her will or even against her wishes, but she knew not to let him get too close. The man had the ways of a wizard.

"Come down here," he repeated.

She shook her head.

Exasperated, he shifted his weight. His candle flickered; his eyes blazed a cool warning.

"I shall come up if you don't come down."

She brazened it out. "No, you won't. It will make too much noise."

"Don't underestimate me, my Miss Dear."

"I understand you, sir. I hold your honor in highest regard."

That seemed to confound him.

Again, she could have smiled.

He was torn between wanting to charge her position atop the hill and this mention of his honor. A dustup on the backstairs he had no taste for.

Dragging in a fierce breath, he welded his eyes to hers. Then, slowly, he let the wind hiss from his chest like breath from a great hot dragon. After one more moment, he withdrew. Tressa could only thank heaven he was a gentleman and that he hadn't been able to get within inches of her. She would have been sure to surrender then, and they both knew it.

Fresh from her victory, Tressa remained as she was, allowing the single picture she would never want to forget. Unclothed, Braxton was as impressive—as beautiful, really—as he was dressed to the nines.

His shoulders were broad, ending in thick, smooth, powerful knobs. His chest was sculpted and, amazingly, covered in hair as dark as that on his head. She'd glimpsed nipples buried like bronze coins in that hair and his navel riding just above the creamy blanket. The flare of his hips left her with a thousand conjectures.

This picture of Braxton at his most elemental, wanting her above anything else in his fully appointed and peopled existence, she'd cherish forever. Here, she found, she possessed a taste of her "something." One day, she'd recall how the Marquess of Braxton had desired her enough to—

His candlelight barely preceded him as he appeared again at the bottom of the stairs. While Tressa hadn't dismissed the possibility of a second skirmish, she had drifted from her post.

Righting herself, she engaged his eyes when he stepped into view. His appearance hadn't altered, and she had all she could do not to capitulate merely to the look of him.

Yes, nipples like hers—vulnerable like her own?—formed

the centers around which the dark hair of his chest swept in whorls. When she forced her eyes to his, she saw the ground she'd lost by indulging her fascination with his body.

Encouraged, he whispered, "Come down."

She managed to shake her head.

He managed to read her weakness.

Bending, he placed his candlestick on the floor of the open doorway. Cautiously, he put one big bare foot on the bottom riser, then his other on the next. He rose toward her slowly, both of them listening for any noise that would disturb the peace. While the risers creaked under his weight, they didn't sound the call she hoped for.

As he drew stealthily nearer, Tressa felt her eyes grow large. His eyes filled with anticipated triumph. She couldn't seem to get up and run. She couldn't stand against his slightest touch. She could barely resist that sense about him of a red-coated soldier closing in with his unsheathed bayonet.

And then, thank goodness, a riser cracked a warning that halted Braxton's advance. He hovered, absolutely still for a moment, listening to the house and watching the war of emotions in Tressa's own expression.

He tested the stair again. It cracked so loudly he dared not use it. Nor the next, which also gave a long, drawn-out creak. Placing his hands on the third step up, one shy of her position, he stretched so close she could read his face, drink in the span of his fine shoulders as they supported his great weight.

His smile pierced her heart—a soft smile, a smile of regret and surrender.

"You win this one, Miss Dear," he whispered. "I lay my colors at your feet."

By that he meant her barely slippered toes, peeping from her nightclothes under her clasped hands at her knees. He bent, a feat that demonstrated the power in his body, and revealed the top of his dark head. Spanning a length of the stairs, he suspended himself so as to quickly drop a kiss on the tip of her toe.

She wanted to call out all the white flags she could, but he lifted himself away before she made such a fool of herself. Skillfully, he righted his bulk, then turned to pick his way down to his waiting candle.

At the bottom again, he drew in a deep breath and looked up at her. For all her rioting fancies, she hadn't stirred.

"I'll not be able to sleep," he said softly. "Pray come to your senses and change your mind, Miss Dear."

He moved off, and she watched as he and his light disappeared. Tressa felt disappointment as keenly as she felt her triumph.

She also knew not to rest on her laurels. She settled in for the night exactly where she was. If he came back—and he well might—he'd find her ready to defend what scant virtue she had left. Her memory of Braxton's nakedness she wouldn't indulge again—not until he was safely gone to Devonshire.

Chapter Three

Hannibal had never spent a worse night than that on Pocket Street. He'd thought Miss Dear would come to him, or if she didn't, that he, by hook or by crook—even by creaking staircase—would charge her bed.

But Miss Dear hadn't come, and he hadn't charged.

Well before dawn he'd been up, pacing the kitchen sunk halfway below ground level. Mudge had repaired Braxton's toilette, fetched him a steak and a light ale from the Crown and Feathers, and left him with coffee and newspapers at the rough-hewn servants' table. A small coal fire glowed on the hearth despite the bright June morning, and Hannibal watched the rear door of the little house as if he might miss Robert's entrance.

Robert wouldn't be expecting him, and the best thing about his stay here was that he'd shocked Miss Dear. Shocked her. Then, well, she'd softened into the sweetest, most desirable little bundle he'd ever held.

Rattling his paper, he adjusted himself on his straight-backed chair and addressed the column he'd started thrice over.

Enough of the agonizing. Enough of wanting Miss Dear. He'd nearly had her. She'd nearly complied. But she'd escaped. Like a well-matched foe, she'd taken her position at the top of that deuced noisy staircase.

Enough is enough, he reminded himself, grateful when his cousin came in the door. The boy was surprised to find Hannibal at the table, newspapers at hand.

"Cousin Braxton?"

"None other," replied Hannibal, ready for this second foe, but abruptly aware of the weariness behind his cousin's surprise.

Twelve years separated them, and he and Robert were definitely aware of the age difference. Hannibal had been appointed Robert's guardian when Robert was at Eton. They invariably related with decorum and respect, but Hannibal felt he didn't know the boy personally. What bound them together was the fact that they were the last of their line. Robert would marry and produce the next generation.

"I cannot like this business with Pounce," Hannibal said, sure as soon as the words were out that he'd taken the wrong tack.

Robert, tall and slender, with light brown hair and ascetic features, apparently mustered what regard he could by going to warm his long, pale fingers at the tiny fire.

"Sir Percival has been very helpful to me, Cousin Braxton."

"Rackety pack of artistic types, this Pounce and his set. I suppose he encourages you to defy my wishes in this portrait painting you've mentioned. Really, Robert. We discussed this and you agreed to give it up."

Because Robert kept his face averted, Hannibal pressed on.

"Three weeks ago, on your birthday, you and I made ourselves plain. We decided that though you missed the Season by a wide mark this year, next year you will set your mind to it and find a proper wife."

Robert didn't reply, didn't even glance at Hannibal. That aggravated him as much as if the boy had ranted at him. "You are my heir, Robert. We agreed you are indebted to that fact."

Still no response.

Hannibal held his temper and plunged ahead. "Your friends claim they haven't seen you in St. James's for at least three weeks. While I can understand how a young fellow can need this sort of thing here on Pocket Street, I—"

Robert all but rounded on Hannibal. "On that you will go no further, Cousin Braxton."

Hannibal was surprised at the heat in Robert's brown eyes. "What?"

"You say, 'this sort of thing here on Pocket Street.' Indeed, I'm sorry to have taken advantage of you in coming here without permission. I owe you an apology. But you will be remiss, sir, if you misjudge our arrangements here."

Robert seemed to recall himself and lose a bit of his heat. Even so, he went on.

"When Mudge—I mean, when Mr. Right delivered the message that you were here last night, he said you also met Miss Dear and Miss Jupe."

"Miss Jupe and Miss Sweet-As-Pie are one and the same?"

"Yes. And you must not let our little names for ourselves mislead you, either. I understand what they might cause you to think, but they were more for keeping our true identities from being known in the neighborhood."

"A pretty piece of work," Hannibal said, all judgment.

"A *necessary* piece of work," Robert retorted.

"Necessary because of me? Because I might find you?"

Robert's usually pale cheeks reddened. Still, he faced Hannibal squarely. "I intend to marry Miss Jupe."

"What?"

"She is a very fine person. Miss Dear is here to chaperon us until we marry and leave for Italy."

Hannibal couldn't believe his ears. "And who's this Miss

Jupe, this very fine person, that you must marry her on the sly and run away to Italy?''

"I knew you would not accept her, sir. But you must not blame Doro for any of this. It's my doing. The others, Miss Dear and Mr. Right, are here only out of the goodness of their hearts and to support Doro and me.''

"Start at the beginning of this, Robert, so I can make some sense of it.''

"It's not necessary that you understand. I don't expect you to. I will not be dissuaded, so there is no need for explanations. Indeed, if you truly knew me, sir, you would accept whatever I had to say without question. If you ever listened to me, you'd know I never say anything that isn't true or honorable.''

Narrow little Robert—quite tall now, actually—puffed out his chest and peered at Hannibal with tired brown eyes. Hannibal lowered his voice to its most powerful.

"You are a boy, scarcely one and twenty. You've had rum notions before, what with your wish to go off to Italy and paint or some such twaddle. Indeed, I thought you'd given up that idea.''

"I haven't.''

"So what is it I'm to believe now? That you are to marry Miss Jupe and paint to your heart's content?''

"Precisely, sir. You have little control over my purse strings anymore and are no longer my guardian. We are the last of our family and I should like to remain in good standing with you, but I know it is not to be. And so, sir, if you cannot accept what I am telling you, I must bid you farewell—with my best wishes, of course, and with Miss Jupe's best wishes, too. Neither of us has wanted it to come to this, but obviously it has.''

Hannibal found he could murmur only, "Well, well. Pretty kettle of fish.''

Already more off balance than he wanted to admit, Hannibal

was drawn to the two women, who entered the kitchen only to excuse themselves with pretty blushes. Miss Dear and her charge turned as if to go back up the stairs, not wanting to interrupt his conversation with Robert.

But Hannibal also knew not much more could be said without some rethinking. He got to his feet and, bowing to the charming looking pair—and Robert, of course—bid them good morning.

"Pray, you must stay," he said. "While I'm unsure as to whether I'm the host, or you, Miss Dear, are our hostess, we can certainly all breakfast together."

"You have not yet eaten, my lord?"

Miss Dear's cheeks flushed a lovely pink despite her steady tone and gaze. She remembered the events of the night before as well as he did. She also knew where they stood. She may have refused him, but she had also kissed him very, very enthusiastically.

"I have, in fact, had breakfast," Hannibal said. "But I'm comfortable here, and shall enjoy watching you have yours. You, too, Miss Jupe. And you haven't eaten, have you, Robert?"

There. He'd nicely gotten them over the awkwardness, although that didn't seem enough for Robert. His cousin went to lift Miss Jupe's hand for a light kiss.

"I have, my dear Doro," he said, as confident as you please, "just told my cousin about us. I should also like to introduce the pair of you. If I may, sir," he added, turning to Hannibal for his permission.

What could Hannibal say, particularly with Miss Dear watching, her deep blue eyes taking it all in?

"I should be pleased to meet your . . . er, Miss Jupe, Robert."

Fortunately, that seemed good enough, and cordial formalities were exchanged.

"You must be quite hungry, Robert," Miss Dear said. "You look exhausted. Sir Percival kept you at it all night long?"

In dove-gray attire, and with her blond hair properly arranged beneath a proper cap, Miss Dear tied on an apron. Doro Jupe, looking every inch the innocent in a green ensemble with rather nice trimming here and there, did the same. As a pair, the women doubly fascinated the eye. Miss Jupe appeared somewhat younger, but was taller and had dark hair and eyes which contrasted with Miss Dear's fairness and her graceful yet influential manner.

"Precisely what is it Sir Percival keeps you at all night, Robert?"

Hannibal's sardonically posed question didn't sour the routine that went forward around him as he resumed his place at the table. Sending him only a slightly repressive glance, Miss Dear followed Miss Jupe in and out of the larder.

Miss Jupe set about making toast over the coals with a toasting fork and a few slices of the loaf he'd enjoyed the night before. Miss Dear took a chair adjacent to his, and, with quick efficiency, began removing the starry green tops from plump strawberries.

Robert hovered around Miss Jupe as he replied to Hannibal.

"I've been assisting Sir Percival for a few weeks now— organizing his study and papers, copying his most recent writings—"

"His drivel, you mean." Hannibal's interjection earned him another quashing glance from Miss Dear. "From what I hear," he insisted, "the man writes only drivel."

"He's paying me," Robert stated.

"Robert and Doro are watching their expenditures until they're ready to leave," Miss Dear added proudly, as if to bolster Robert's bid for independence.

With the war with France over for exactly a year now, the continent was more and more open for travel. Robert could well get away for two or three years.

"I hope your calculations are feasible, Robert." Hannibal spoke nonchalantly enough. "These are expensive doings—marrying, running off to Italy. Better than anyone, I know your financial situation, and I can't imagine Sir Percival paying enough to make up what you'll need."

Robert, thin and plain, but also calm and intelligent, seemed heartened merely by Miss Jupe's nearness. "We'll manage, sir, Doro and I."

Hannibal glanced back at Miss Dear. She sent him a triumphant little look, then got up to set her lovely creation of freshly prepared berries on the table. Again, Hannibal was conscious of the smooth routine exhibited by those around him. A surprising harmony, even a sense of closeness, knitted them together.

Actually, it quite amazed him. Pink and yellow flowers were added to the table, as well as pretty blue-and-white china that apparently went with the house, silver cutlery, thick cream for the strawberries, fresh butter for the toast, and more of Mudge's delicious coffee carried from a true surprise, the new wood stove that Mudge had heated that morning.

It was comfortable—cozy, even, in a rustic sort of way—if one didn't mind the dust in the corners. The three others finally sat down and, after grace, addressed themselves to their meal.

"You must tell me, Miss Jupe," Hannibal said, "how you met my young and very eligible cousin."

At Miss Jupe's ferocious blush, Robert grew defensive. Miss Dear addressed Hannibal with a starchy stare.

"It's I, Cousin Braxton," Robert announced, "who will explain how we met. There's nothing to be ashamed of. I used to go regularly to Lady Farronby's to play cards of an afternoon. I went with her grandson, a good friend of mine, and we often played with Miss Dear, who made up our fourth."

"Ahhh." Hannibal purred. He was getting what he wanted now. "Miss Dear—a companion, no doubt, to the old dowager before she died. When was that?"

"Her ladyship died," Miss Dear said, "mid Season of last year. I still miss her."

"So say we all," seconded Robert.

"Miss Jupe"—Hannibal pressed of his cousin, who hardly ate a mouthful—"also played cards with you and your young gentleman friend, his esteemed lady grandmother, and her companion?"

Hannibal heard the nastiness in his question.

Not surprisingly, everyone at the table went still.

Only Robert spoke—as calmly, if also firmly, as ever. "Doro was in service then. Lady Farronby spoke nothing but well of her, and I soon learned she is a fine person. From the first moment I saw her, I considered her very beautiful."

"And so deliciously willing," Hannibal interjected.

When Doro hung her head, Robert got to his feet and reached his hand to her. "We'll excuse ourselves now. Miss Dear, I hope you'll forgive us."

"No need for forgiveness, Robert," Miss Dear announced, her eyes speaking volumes to Hannibal. "I'm excusing myself also."

With that, the three of them left Hannibal to his newspapers and a table with a very pretty, uneaten meal.

By mid afternoon, Tressa simply had to get away from the house. She loved to walk, and she walked, walked, walked all the way to the old Cupid's Tea Garden.

Pocket Street was, as the name indicated, a small street of a few close houses. Nearer the bustle of the inn where Mudge spent so much time, the Crown and Feathers, shops of every sort were interspersed with high, narrow houses.

Still, even veiled, it was unusual for her to go to the tea garden without Doro. North of their own neighborhood, with its busy mews and even a quiet churchyard, she passed the inns of court, ancient Green Lion Square, and questionable little nooks and alleys.

On this bright, somewhat cool summer day, she wanted nothing more than to forget the intruder at Pocket Street. The house was *his*, and they'd been living there without *his* knowledge and permission, but ...

Well, he'd soon be rid of them. Ever since breakfast, when Braxton had crushed Doro's feelings and driven a knife through his cousin's heart, Robert had been out and about, finding temporary rooms for them while she and Doro packed.

Braxton had disappeared.

Since they'd been unable to locate Mudge, he hadn't had his say in their quick decision. Still, Tressa was certain Mudge would go where they went.

Faithful Mudge. What would she do without him?

Of course, now they would pay the rent they'd avoided by sneaking in the rear door on Pocket Street two and a half weeks earlier. Their best reason for having sought refuge there after having fled Lady Farronby's house in Mayfair had been precisely because they hadn't had to pay.

Still, it would be worth it to spurn the Marquess of Braxton and walk out before dinner. But that probably wouldn't affect him, in any case. He had his hotel, and soon he'd leave for Devonshire.

Oh, yes, Tressa had heard about Braxton from Robert—about the marquess's wealth and responsibilities, his enormous seat called Cannongate right on the wildest of seacoasts, his commanding ways, his iron-eyed gaze.

Opinionated. Judgmental. Bullying. Unkind.

Tressa wanted to think of Braxton negatively. She wouldn't recall him as she'd seen him just last night at the bottom of the attic stairwell or beside the buttery surface of his sheets.

Fortunately, even through the fluttering veil that complimented her conservative dove-gray pelisse and bonnet, Tressa anticipated her approach to the tea garden. Black railings topped a high rusticated wall behind which lush green trees could be glimpsed. Urns announced the entrance. Just inside, one found oneself standing beneath the long elegant sweep of a colonnade which overlooked a formal pattern of walks, shrubberies, and gardens.

The tea garden was beginning to show signs of dilapidation, but its proprietor fought the fast decline of such places as his bravely, and it remained an acceptable amusement for all but those of the highest echelons, particularly if, as a lady, one was chaperoned.

Indeed, without Doro by her side, Tressa felt quite on her own. Doro, however, had needed to rest. Having had the opposite reaction to the marquess's rudeness, Tressa'd had to walk.

At the Cupid's Tea Garden, walking was the norm—or, rather, strolling beneath large overhanging trees, meandering along well-kept gravel paths with clipped hedges. Here one encountered the nods and smiles of others who also enjoyed the day.

There were flowerbeds surrounding a clear, spring-fed pool, honeysuckle-covered arbors for taking refreshments. At the center, Cupid, his bow in hand, ruled a fountain where respectable London citizens, City matrons, half-pay officers in bright coats, and even artists from Sir Percival Pounce's set could enjoy the veil-like spray drifting on soft breezes.

Tressa liked the tea garden, the eddying murmurs of conversations, the sense of really being in London.

That the tea garden took on an entirely different appearance and purpose at night she hardly considered. Should she guess some young woman who passed her wasn't a genteel visitor but rather a strolling damsel, as she'd heard them called, she paid no heed. She'd grown to believe that the garden was what one made of it. For two and a half weeks, she'd reveled in the freedom she knew would not come again soon.

Her hard-won peace was suddenly cut up at seeing Braxton striding toward her along the gravel path. Intolerable! The way his eyes met hers, even through her light veil, told her he'd come specifically to find her, and he'd been searching for some time.

"This is beyond reason ridiculous, my lady."

He confronted her on the path so as to stop her without having anyone view them from either direction.

Not that she feared him. She didn't.

His use of "my lady," however, caught her off guard, setting her heart into a flurried beat.

"Where or when I walk, sir, is none of your concern. In fact, I was quite enjoying myself and nearly recovered from this morning's piece of work until you appeared. Allow me to pass."

"I will not. I'll allow you little more than to climb into the hired carriage I have waiting."

"You have no right to make such demands on me, sir, and I will not do as you say and be at your mercy—if you have the least mercy, which I doubt."

Tressa would have preferred stalking off at that point, but he'd again positioned himself so she was unable to without drawing the attention of a couple who'd turned into their alleyway and nodded at them pleasantly.

Showing a slight deference, Braxton removed his beaver hat, but his scowl remained firm. Obviously, he'd returned to his hotel, because he wore a forest-green coat with black lapels, buff breeches, and brown topboots. Worse, he smelled wonderfully of fresh linens, particularly in the bright summer sun that set them whitely ablaze before her eyes.

The day, the surroundings, were at odds with their designs as he set his hat back on his black hair and broke their impasse.

"If you will, my lady," he said, more levelly, "I have a carriage waiting."

"And I, sir, have no need of a carriage. I have come for tea."

He grasped her elbow. "So we shall have tea."

The rhythm they set up rapping along the gravel path seemed to repeat the pulse in Tressa's veins, the race of her thoughts.

Braxton escorted her without saying a word. Past Cupid's fountain, he guided her to a secluded arbor, positively draped in honeysuckle and so sweet smelling as to suggest heaven itself. The dappled shade and the ribbony sun shafts on the white table linens mocked Tressa's mental state.

Rather than sitting across from her, Braxton edged in beside her, so close as to make her feel she could not maintain her collected demeanor. A waiter appeared immediately, obviously recognizing her as a regular despite her light veil.

Braxton ordered tea for her alone. Then, removing his gloves, he placed them on the table along with his black, silver-headed cane. Perfectly polished, its silver glinted and its blackthorne gleamed.

His accessories, she thought. *Always so fine, like him.* A picture of him wrapped in a blanket but naked to the swell of his hips caused her to blush.

She had to force the picture out, had to ignore even the leafy bower in which they sat. She had to stay sharp.

"And so, my lady," he said, once the waiter had left Tressa's little china teapot with its delightful accompaniments.

"You must call me Miss Dear, sir."

His gray eyes, holding the cool regard of a general, fixed on her. "I must call you Lady Tressa. You have a title of your own."

"I do not."

"You are the niece of an earl. Straith, in fact." Braxton seemed sobered by what he'd evidently uncovered about her since that morning. What hubbub might he have raised by inquiring about her? She'd been long forgotten, and she needed to remain that way for safety's sake.

"I'm Bad Buck Devlin's daughter, sir."

She'd never voiced that truth. Now, however, she said it directly into the marquess's stare. "My father never succeeded to the title. He died the same night his own father died, and his younger brother became Straith. I have never made any claims, either on a title or my uncle."

Tressa felt proud in making her announcement to Braxton above anyone else, though she could never admit such things again. Indulging her pride could rouse the sleeping giant she'd already toyed with merely by having run away to Pocket Street.

"You must call me Miss Devlin. Those few who know me are accustomed to knowing me as Bad Buck's daughter. Although they don't speak of his ruination and passing to my face, I'm sure those things are mentioned outside my hearing. Old scandals never really die."

"What in the devil can Straith be thinking to have left you unprotected?"

"He and my aunt found me a position with Lady Farronby because, once I was eighteen, they said I needed to support myself. My father's profligate behavior left them barely scraping by at Lance Hall, and they had no funds for a Season or for a dowry. Besides, my father's demise—especially the means of his demise—can hardly recommend me as a bride."

"Nonsense. The Devlins have some of the finest blood in England."

"Blood tainted by my father's madness, my lord—or so it's said."

Finally taking her eyes from Braxton's, Tressa poured her tea, concentrating on her smooth movements, the aroma of honeysuckle, and the sweet warm steam.

Yes, she was quite proud to have recalled hell while sitting with Braxton in this heaven.

"For five years, sir, I've led a useful, independent life and paid my own way. Lady Farronby became my good friend and gave me the little freedoms I have grown to protect."

At that, his lordship dropped his eyes to the teacup meeting her lips.

"Little freedoms that allowed you to include this man who abandoned you," he murmured.

" 'Tis you who claim there was a man, sir." She smiled. "Your story about my being love-begotten and having had a man of my own . . ." When he turned his hard stare on her, she knew he disliked that topic. "Let's just say I prize my independent life. My walk here today, the freedom to get out and walk, means a great deal to me and would not be allotted to Lady Tressa. No, you must call me Miss Devlin now. Mudge and Doro and Robert will be comfortable with that again. That is, sir"—truly, how could she have forgotten?—"if you see any of us after today."

He grew visibly agitated, rapping his fingertips on the table. "I intend to see a great deal of all of you. I have apologized to Miss Jupe and to Robert for this morning's fiasco. It was unfair of me to accept Miss Jupe's introduction only to cut her. No matter how I feel about her unsuitability for Robert, that was wrong of me."

Tressa was both gratified by his admission and upset. "You are too harsh, my lord. Doro is—"

"I will not hear it now. I have apologized and they have accepted my apology. The four of you are no longer leaving Pocket Street, and I am, in fact, moving in."

"Moving in?" That Tressa was shocked by this rang clear.

"I must evaluate the situation," he said, "and how better than to spend some time with my cousin?"

"You mean how better to dissuade him."

"We are talking about the breeding of my heir, Miss Devlin, about the begetting of a marquess with a great deal of responsibility. Robert's barely been up to the task. Although he's clever enough when he applies himself, I have a deuced hard time *getting* him to apply himself. 'Tis I who must keep an eye to the next generation. Even you must admit Doro Jupe is hardly the one to breed my heir.''

''I admit no such thing. Indeed, I feel quite the opposite.''

''I know, I know. I've heard enough on that head for one day.''

Tressa could see no matter how much she was prepared to sing Doro's praises, the marquess wouldn't be pushed on the subject. Besides, Tressa had a lingering fear that had to be addressed, even within the secluded, honeysuckle-fragrant bower. Looking at Braxton, so handsome—if also still disgruntled—she wondered how she should present the subject around which all her terrors centered.

He was so worthy. For all his evident experience in the world, her own experience would seem foreign to him, even ugly. He was extremely intelligent, and he would begin to have his own questions if she didn't approach him carefully.

''Today in Town, sir, whom did you question with regard to me?''

He peered at her, his gray eyes steady. She could trust Braxton, if no one else. It would simply put him in danger if he'd heard too much.

''I asked an old school fellow of mine, one who's reputed to be knowledgeable in such matters, if he knew who'd been the Dowager Lady Farronby's companion. It took him a while to recollect, in fact. Fortunately, he's the soul of discretion. He also knew about''—regret rode oddly but quite wonderfully in Braxton's gray eyes—''well, about your father. I'm sorry about his suicide and how it affected you. All the more reason, you see, to think ahead to one's heirs.''

''Why don't you simply marry and have your own children?''

Here was something he wouldn't discuss. His eyes, his expression, the set of his whole body so close to hers on the arbor bench, declared she shouldn't encroach.

''I will not marry,'' he stated simply. ''All along, it's been agreed between Robert and me that is his to do.''

Braxton grew remote, and Tressa had finished the tea she'd insisted on. "Let me say, my lord, that despite your admirable apologies, I'll be vacating as soon as I can."

He seemed stunned. "You will not."

"Oh, but I shall. Indeed, it's likely Mudge will go when I go, so you'd best be prepared."

"But Miss Jupe needs a chaperon."

"On Pocket Street? Hardly. Besides, Bad Buck's daughter is a less than proper chaperon for Robert's Miss Jupe."

"Your suggestion, ma'am, is ridiculous, and unfair to Miss Jupe."

On that, Tressa had to agree. Still, even with that single good reason for staying, she could not remain on Pocket Street.

Looking at Braxton, who peered at her demandingly, she said, "Well, we shall see. They are soon to leave, in any case."

"And so we shall go," said Braxton. "But I must also ask you, ma'am," he added, as he assisted her out of the arbor, put on his hat, and pulled on his gloves, "never to leave the house again on your own."

"No," Tressa quietly declared, when he took her elbow and escorted her toward the sweep of the colonnade. "I will not be moved on the matter of my small freedoms, sir."

"And I will not have you unsafe. Should you like to walk, I will accompany you."

Tressa would say no more. The day remained too lovely, and she had too few precious moments before their return to the house.

For all their backstairs intimacy, she and Braxton would behave with every propriety in front of his cousin and Doro. All the more reason for Tressa's shock when Braxton spoke softly.

"None of what happened this morning would have happened if you'd come to me last night. I was in agony and hardly slept a wink. You must certainly come to me tonight so we can both go on happily. Our bedding will put us in tune, and late at night we can talk things out. Nay, do not peer at me with such shock in your lovely face—which I can see even through your veiling, my sweet Tressa. You know what I say is true. We wish to bed together. There's no denying it, and so it shall be.''

Chapter Four

That Lord Braxton had spoken to Tressa so openly about wanting to bed with her had shocked her. That he'd read her own desire shocked her even more—shocked her so much, in fact, that she hadn't been able to reply to any of his subsequent and less indecent attempts at conversation in the carriage on their way back.

Fortunately, she hadn't had to deal with him beyond that. He'd left her at Pocket Street to return with Mudge to the Claredon Hotel to fetch his things. After settling into the master chamber, he'd gone to dinner with friends. The household had heaved a sigh of relief.

Tressa, however, had begun to recognize some very important factors. Females considered open to pursuit were treated differently than ladies of quality. While Braxton insisted she'd remained a female of excellent blood and breeding, because she had for the past five years earned her own way in the world, she was vulnerable to his advances—advances for purposes clearly outside marital bonds, the latter of which she could have expected if she'd stayed under her uncle's roof.

As Lady Tressa, and if her father hadn't ruined the family financially, she might have met Braxton in society and been considered a good match for him. He might have courted her and been all that was correct—if, that was, he hadn't disliked the idea of marriage.

Her mind still awash with his outrageous proposition, she finally went to bed wondering how she and Doro and Robert would rub along with him. To think he again occupied the bed he wanted her to seek out, just a story down from her, resulted in a fitful rest.

By late morning on the following day, she was on pins and needles. Although they all had managed an early morning routine in which they had avoided one another, he barged into the little back sitting room where she worked on the last of the gowns she and Doro had made as a part of Doro's traveling trousseau. The table was cluttered with Tressa's efforts.

When he recognized he'd found her alone, he started off in that shocking way again.

"Tressa, my desire." He closed the door behind him, and came into the peachy light flooding through the windows overlooking the walled garden. "I waited again last night. Fortunately, I was tired enough from the night before to have fallen asleep without too much agonizing."

"Your agony, sir, moves me not one jot."

"How could it? Otherwise you wouldn't leave me to agonize."

Really, Tressa thought, not looking up from her handwork. The man was blunt beyond belief. Nor could she believe all gentlemen pursued women, even outside of polite society, in the stunning manner he employed. He'd known her scarcely thirty-six hours, and he spoke to her as if she'd surrendered to him that first evening.

Tressa, my desire.

"And where is Miss Jupe?" he inquired, standing over Tressa and plucking up a pink satin ribbon.

"She has the headache, sir. Since she never has headaches, I'm quite convinced you're the cause of it."

If he could speak frankly, so would she, whatever her mood and without guarding her tongue.

The man was insufferable.

He was also freshly appointed and as mesmerizing as ever. Stealing a peek at him as he stood pulling the fragile-looking pink ribbon through his long masculine fingers, she saw he wore country clothes again—a skirted riding coat done up in a beautiful shade of sage green and Buckskins which fit him like his own skin. His topboots, which Mudge had probably seen to, gleamed.

The fresh unique scent of Braxton trailed like tendrils of some male magic into the small room, forcing her to his will— the iron-eyed general, tugging a pink satin ribbon through his fingers.

Was that all it took to send her reeling?

Somehow his simple act unraveled that part of her he blatantly held as his objective. She could almost feel the ribbon pass sleekly through his strong fingers. It seemed elementally female and he the epitome of virility.

Resettling her skirts on her chair, clearing her throat, and focusing her attention on the fine hem she stitched, Tressa warned herself inwardly. She pledged herself again to Robert and Doro's cause, but also realized she had to consider her own plans for leaving. She couldn't afford to indulge the emotions that arose in her in Braxton's company.

Pink ribbons! Hmmph!

Braxton let the ribbon slowly settle onto the sewing pile at Tressa's elbow and walked to the mantel over the fireplace. Like almost everything in the room, the large portrait above was dust covered, and Tressa had placed a small cloth carefully over the clock on the mantel.

Braxton twitched the fabric away. "Aha," he murmured, as if not surprised by the subject of the statuary which supported the slightly tarnished silver clock.

Tressa heaved an exasperated sigh, forcing her eyes to her needle and thread. Braxton swiveled to look at her.

"I suppose you've seen this."

"I covered it, my lord, and I'd appreciate it if you'd cover it again. We must think of Doro. Indeed, none of us much wants to consider the environs here."

" 'Tis a rather clever piece," he said. "Haven't seen one quite like it before."

He urged the little display to work as it chimed. Tressa didn't need to peer up and observe. Beneath the clock's face, a heavily draped bed was wrought with a man and a woman lying flat on their backs, side by side. When the clock chimed, the mattress flipped over and the man reappeared atop the woman.

Though the figures remained largely hidden beneath the bedclothes, it was one of the innumerable pieces in the former owner's collection of curiosities which were downright embarrassing to the average viewer.

Tressa, however, did not blush or blink an eye. Even when Braxton lifted the dust sheet away from the painting above the clock, just enough to get its gist, she remained impervious.

"Well, well," he murmured.

"It's all of a piece." She sounded prudish even to her own ears and couldn't avoid her next clipped remark. "The painting revolts me."

He shrugged. "Isn't so very out of the common way in these situations. Merely one more satyr pinching the nipple of one more—"

"You need not recall it to me, sir."

"I'm surprised you've had a look at all, Miss Dear. Have you examined what waits beneath every dust sheet in the house? Considering the great number of dust sheets, it must have taken you some time."

"This is not a subject I wish to discuss, my lord."

Tressa laid her handwork on the table and faced the over-weening man, determined to get on with the important business of the day.

"What we must discuss here, sir, is Doro. You've told me you apologized to her and to Robert and that you intend to consider the matter of their marriage."

Braxton stiffened, ever the general when it came to his duties. "What we are talking about here, Miss Dear, is the breeding of my heir. I say again the likes of Doro Jupe hardly qualify."

"You will not consider her as Robert's wife?"

"I will not."

"Why, then, have you decided to move in here with us if your mind is so closed? Oh." Tressa almost sighed on comprehending the obvious. "You remain determined to change Robert's mind."

His lordship didn't reply. He merely clasped his hands behind his back and settled himself. He was firm in his decision.

Tressa's heart could have broken. Surely no one could go against Braxton. Still, she would try, no matter what it could cost her personally.

"Doro Jupe is a very fine girl, sir."

"It doesn't matter."

"It would if you'd just listen. You don't even know her."

"I've already admitted to being what I consider a good judge of character, Miss Dear."

His hard stare, his even harder demeanor, warned Tressa to go no further. When she decided to speak anyway, Braxton spoke over her, surprising her with the slight change in his features.

"However," he said, still commanding the quiet room and dazzling sunlight, "I will prove I can also listen to reason. Pray say what you've attempted to say before concerning Miss Jupe."

Tressa rose to her feet, taking the moment to evaluate Braxton's powerful masculine face. He seemed attentive. His eyes certainly didn't leave hers as she squared her own shoulders and began at the beginning.

"Doro Jupe is a country solicitor's daughter from my neighborhood in Middlesex." Reading the accusatory dimming of those gray eyes, she rushed along. "Because her mother died when Doro was young, she had a governess who taught her the basics. When Doro was fifteen, however, her father died, leaving her in a penury that surprised everyone. The Dowager Lady Farronby, my employer at the time and a neighbor in Middlesex, had Doro sent to her. Doro has a good heart and is very brave and hard working. The Dowager Lady Farronby and I appreciated her very much, and by just looking at her anyone can see why Robert has fallen in love with her."

Braxton emitted a sour little snort.

Tressa fired her declaration in reply. "Robert loves Doro, sir."

Again he snorted.

"Over the last pair of years, Doro has worked hard to make herself worthy of Robert. She reads very prettily, and her deportment and behavior are beyond reproach. She talks of nothing but your cousin."

"What young gel wouldn't want to be a marchioness?"

"Oh, sir." Clearly, Tressa disparaged him. Still, just as clearly, she wouldn't give up. "How easily you say that. How easily you sum up a life that you, with your privilege, are unable to comprehend."

When Braxton remained still, his eyes moving over Tressa's features, she knew she wouldn't win by striking at his heart. It was invincible. His head ruled his heart, exactly as it ruled his life.

"If you hadn't preached to Robert on his birthday three weeks ago," she announced, taking a harder tack, "none of this would be happening at this pace. You who precipitated our exit from Lady Farronby's. You who brought us to this pass. Robert had not considered himself anywhere near ready to marry Doro.''

Braxton seemed aghast, but not at Tressa's points.

"Preached to Robert?"

"Yes, *preached* to him. Everything he's heard time and again. He has his reasons, you know, for calling himself Mr. Wrong. You've told him he must marry. He must beget your heir. He must be Braxton one day."

"I did not preach, ma'am. I never preach."

"I cannot argue that. But did you listen to him?"

When his lordship opened his mouth only to shut it, Tressa plunged on.

"After you left him that night, he came to the Dowager Lady Farronby's house in Mayfair. We had barely passed the year of mourning for her and were still a skeleton staff of Mudge and Doro and I, waiting on the new Lady Farronby's wishes for the house. Over tea in the kitchen, Robert explained what had happened. He told Mudge and me he wanted to marry Doro, not that Mudge and I were precisely surprised," Tressa admitted. "What did surprise us was your ignorance as to Robert's wishes."

"Robert didn't explain his wishes."

"He didn't explain about wanting to paint portraits? He didn't explain about wanting to go to Italy in preparation for doing so?"

"He did not."

"Not that night," Tressa scoffed, "but numerous times before, no doubt. Still, he stayed in school and worked hard at his books to please you. And were you pleased? No. You only gave him more orders."

" 'Tis my place to do so."

"It's also your place to understand Robert, to listen to him once in a while."

"You go too far in telling me my place, Miss Devlin."

"You go too far in telling Robert whom he can or cannot love, sir."

"I tell him only whom he cannot marry."

"He will marry Doro no matter what you say. The question is, will you forfeit the single family member you have left—someone who will, as I understand it, become Braxton in your place—because he brings to you a fine young woman lacking only in her bloodlines?"

" 'Tis done all the time."

"Yes, but will *you* do it, sir? Does blood really mean all that much to you?"

" 'Tis more the order of things. We each have a place, Miss Devlin, and we must abide by the order of things."

"Robert and Doro will never listen to words like duty and order when they have the word love."

"I say again, what is love?"

"Love will carry Robert and Doro far away from you forever."

When Braxton went silent, when he continued to stare at Tressa, she felt her knees wobble. She didn't know how much longer she could hold her eyes to that iron-gray gaze. She was grateful, even swallowed hard, when his lordship finally lowered his gaze, and, with his hands still clasped behind his sage-green coat, paced a bit away from her.

"What would you have me do, ma'am?" he asked, much to Tressa's amazement. "Just give in? Tell Robert to marry whomever he will?"

"No. Not whomever. Doro."

Braxton cast a gray glance at Tressa over his broad shoulder. "You think so much of her to have gone head to head with me?"

"I do." Sensing that Braxton was actually reconsidering bolstered Tressa in every way. "Truly, sir, you need only know Doro, give her a chance. Sit with her, sir. Talk to Robert and her."

"Dinner tonight, perhaps?" he murmured.

Torn between triumph and the possibility of losing all, Tressa whisked along. "I'm afraid the house isn't set up for dining in, sir. We all do for ourselves at dinner. No cook, remember? But certainly taking tea would not be beyond our doing. Doro could serve, with Mudge's assistance."

"Tea, you say?" Braxton rubbed his chin. "Seems little enough."

Tressa could feel her own smile breaking out like victory.

Cautioning her with an upraised hand, Braxton turned and walked to her. "Now, now, I'll have no words of gratitude, Miss Dear."

He stood over Tressa, making her knees go watery. Seriously, quickly, he spoke to her, so close now that the sunlight shafting in the window revealed the smoothness of his freshly shaven face, the thickness of his lashes, the gray of his eyes.

"I want other things than gratitude and lawyerly arguments from you, my clever, sweet desire."

His sudden alteration, the fierceness of his quiet statement, bemused Tressa to the point that she feared the weakness in her limbs might pitch her forward, up against Braxton's bright, country-scented linens. She had the strangest urge to rest her battle-weary head on his broad shoulder, to nestle her cheek into his sage-green coat and drift for a moment in the fragrance that lingered in the folds of his perfectly tied cravat. She wondered if the warm male flesh she'd seen that night on the back stairs—

The clock beneath the cloth on the mantel released a final chime. It performed its little trick beneath the cloth, then revealed itself—male and female now lying side by side facing up—as the cloth slid to the hearth rug.

"When we meet again in here for tea, Miss Dearie-Dear"— his lordship plucked up the cloth and covered the supine cou- ple—"I'll be thinking of you, wishing we were thus satisfied together. Truly, my sweet desire, you must put us both out of our misery. Soon.''

Hastily, Tressa excused herself, barely making it to her little room in the attic, where she finally sat on the edge of her mattress to regain her strength and senses.

Braxton remained intent on his purpose, no matter what he said to Miss Devlin. Entering the busy mews behind the house, he nudged his big black horse toward the small stable, satisfied that things were sorting out to his advantage despite the unexpected time involved, the patience required—merely necessities in getting Miss Devlin into his bed.

After the bright sunlight of the mews—for the day had stayed surprisingly clear—the interior of the stable seemed extra dark and quiet. He led his favorite but nervy mount inside and squinted his eyes.

It smelled like any stable, a smell to which he'd been long accustomed. Now that Mudge had taken a hand and hired a boy to help clean it, Braxton thought it would do.

As his eyes adjusted to the dimness, he made out the boy— no more than a street urchin, really—forking through the fresh bedding of straw in one stall.

Braxton had sized up the youngster as clever, even savvy, and he knew the display of busyness was meant for him to see. Still, if the boy continued to do as he should, Braxton would continue to flip him the little coins that made the youth's bright blue eyes even brighter.

''Hallo, Gov','' the boy of about eleven or twelve called, catching his coin easily and smiling equally as easily.

''He'll need a good walking out and brushing,'' Braxton said. ''But take care. I haven't nearly used him up.''

''Oh, I know to keep me eye on ol' Saracen, Gov'. We're good friends now, but I watches him all the same.''

Braxton hesitated, observing as the boy took the horse and

spoke to him. Murmuring encouragingly, if also roughly, he got Saracen out of his bridle and into a halter fairly easily. Though from the metropolis, the youngster seemed to have a natural affinity for horses, one Braxton knew couldn't be taught.

Fortunately, Saracen appeared to like the boy, and that would mean safer handling for the much smaller, lighter youth. The skinny boy, garbed in a ragamuffin imitation of a young gentleman, would be no match for the large black should the animal get it into his head to do something about his attendant.

"Mr. Right says you come over from the East End every morning," said Braxton.

"Aye, Gov'. Tha' I do."

"You can make a place for yourself here, you know."

"So Mr. Right tells me, Gov'. But I've got me friends back home."

Braxton imagined that meant the boy slept with other boys with whom he'd grown up in familiar doorways, getting their food any way they could if they hadn't been able to hustle a coin or two that day.

Even so, Braxton liked the unabashed way the youngster spoke to him. While he knew not to trust him one jot, he thought they'd rub along well enough. Mudge had said the boy was ready to earn any coin and had been delighted to work with a fine horse like Saracen, no matter how limited the time element.

"Your name is Knobby Knees, then?" Braxton inquired, ready to move to the house, but catching the boy's glance up from the girth he uncinched.

"Just Knobby now, Gov'. Used to go by Knobby Knees, but I'm gettin' too old for that name, me thinks. Becoming a man, with such a good place an' all. In fact, me lord, have you heard the name Hill afore?"

"The name Hill? Of course I've heard it."

"My name's Knobby Hill—er, Charles Hill."

"Charles, eh?"

"But the important part's Hill, sir. Hill."

Braxton understood that the urchin was trying to tell him something other than his name. Unfortunately for the boy, Mudge entered the stable, sending the youngster a stiff look for what he saw as the youth's impertinence.

The older man, equal to Hannibal in size, seemed to be everywhere on Pocket Street, keeping a close watch on things. Hannibal liked that and certainly admitted the man was good at seeing to him personally, but he and Mudge remained on cool terms.

Nodding, Braxton uttered his final words for the boy. "Take care with Saracen, Knobby."

"Oh, I will, Gov'. Never fear on that head."

Outside, Braxton opened the gate in the high stone wall and entered the large garden at the rear of the house. He'd won the house at the card table not two months before, and it had stood empty since. The garden, with its summerhouse and small reflecting pool, was a riot of color that soon would be out of control.

Red, white, and purple berries shed by the mulberry tree and a feast for a dozen noisy birds squashed under his boots, annoying him. If he'd be staying for any length of time, it would have been worth it to hire a couple of gardeners.

On down the short flight of stairs, he entered the kitchen. A flurry of activity greeted him, with three pairs of eyes finding his gaze in surprise and even disappointment. Miss Devlin, Doro Jupe, and Robert were obviously involved in preparations for the tea over which Miss Jupe would preside. Hannibal was unwelcome.

"Go on with what you're doing," he urged. "I'll not mind at all."

They were uncomfortable with him there.

Good.

"I'll wait in here while you get ready," he said for emphasis. Even more unsettled glances among the trio made him feel better and better. They were truly nervous. He would play his advantage.

"Couldn't you wait, sir?" Miss Devlin said. "I mean, upon seeing you enter the stable, Mudge carried up warm water to your dressing room for your convenience."

"Indeed," he replied. "Normally I would retire after the busy afternoon I've had away from the house. But on this occasion—on this special occasion," he added for Miss Jupe, "I'll simply wait until you are ready."

Right away, he had to wonder if Miss Devlin did not read his purpose aright. Those beautiful deep blue eyes of hers sent him a narrow glance.

"Perhaps, sir," Robert said, settling the better china that went with the house on a silver tray, "you might make yourself comfortable in the sitting room. It's quite prepared."

"No, no," Braxton insisted, "I'll wait to go up with the rest of you."

Poor Robert, Braxton thought. *Tall, narrow, and wren-brown Robert, trying to protect his pretty Miss Jupe.*

She herself was flushed red to the cheeks, although otherwise pale. Braxton almost felt sorry for the gel, who was no more than eighteen. While she carried on bravely enough, arranging the cakes and sandwiches on more fine china, she was quite in awe of him. Once again, he relied on his advantage.

Yes, he felt sorry for her. Well, a little. But she presumed too much, aimed too high in tossing her pretty cap in Robert's direction. Robert would recover. He was but one and twenty, and one recovered from these attachments easily.

Not ten minutes later, all were assembled in the sitting room, including Mudge, who appeared stately and wore white gloves. Like the rest, he was grave, of course, facing the circumstances seriously. Hannibal, feeling his power in the situation, remained decided.

Miss Devlin continued to send him sharp glances. Robert's solid brown gaze never wavered from the object of his adora-

tion. Miss Jupe set herself to her task at the tea table while
Mudge stood sentinel at her shoulder.

Since the larger table, including its sewing paraphernalia,
had been cleared away and stood against the wall, the party
was able to take chairs in comfort. The other tables blossomed
with vases of flowers and shone with a fresh polishing.

Miss Jupe, looking the perfect picture of a lady in a pale
blue gown and with her dark hair nicely arranged, poured her
first cup of tea from the recently rejuvenated silver pot. The
initial cup was intended for Hannibal, of course. She peered
levelly at him and asked quite prettily, "Will you have sugar,
my Lord Braxton?"

"No sugar, thank you, Miss Jupe. Just a touch of whiskey."

The poor girl froze, and everyone else went momentarily
quiet. Braxton swelled with satisfaction. Now the chit didn't
return his gaze so squarely.

"Whiskey, my lord?"

"Yes. Fetch the gel some whiskey, will you, Right?"

"See here, Cousin," Robert said, all but jumping to his feet.

"Pray, sir," Miss Devlin began, running over Robert's stiff
plea.

Mudge, however, performed best of all. Taking the cup and
saucer that steamed and rattled in poor Miss Jupe's fingers, he
set them on the small table.

"There is whiskey, me lord, in the cabinet in the front parlor.
I will fetch it, sir—if, tha' is, you wants it."

Braxton gazed into the canny old stare of a man who'd face
him as an equal, no matter what the stakes.

"No, er, Right," Braxton replied. "I detest whiskey, come
to think on it. And tea, as well. I'll have the plain cake."

With that, everyone resumed their places, although still on
guard. Miss Jupe cut his piece of cake; Mudge delivered it.

Tea went on.

Even so, Braxton knew his tactic had unsettled Miss Jupe.

She poured and spoke with less confidence, rattling the cups and saucers as everyone was served.

On the final cup, one for herself, Braxton had an unexpected stroke of luck. That morning he had fingered the still covered clock on the mantel to see it turn over the sculpted mattress on which a couple were suggestively portrayed.

Much to everyone's surprise, the clock sighed, ratcheted up, and performed its little trick again, sending the cloth that covered it fluttering to the floor.

Miss Jupe, unseated merely by the unexpected sounds in addition to already being unnerved, spilled a bit of her tea onto her skirts. Standing up and staring at the growing blotches on her new blue gown while Mudge swept a cloth over them, she drew all eyes to her distress.

Both Robert and Miss Devlin were on their feet, trying to locate places for their tea things and stepping forward as Mudge next removed the still sloshing cup from poor Miss Jupe's fingers. Swiveling as smoothly as you please, Mudge again covered the clock.

Taking in everyone with a horrified expression, Miss Jupe rather amazed Hannibal by not bursting into tears and dashing from the chamber. Instead she collected herself. Speaking calmly, her fine eyes passing from one person to the next, she addressed them all.

"Pray, you must allow me to apologize. And you must, each one, accept my gratitude. My dear Robert," she said, focusing sincerely on him, "for being so convinced that I would do for you. My sweet Miss Dearie-Dear for sacrificing so much in staying with me to help make me better fit for my dear Robert. And Mudge," she added just as warmly and turning to the soldier who remained by her side, "for all your good will and staunch support. We must admit now, dear friends, that we've done our best and failed. Help me set our lives back on their proper courses. Although Lord Braxton has not been so unkind as to say I'm not lady enough for his cousin, we know his lordship is right in his opinion, and we must stop this.''

''But, Doro''—Robert bolted to his feet—''no.''

Employing as much dignity as any lady of Braxton's experience, Doro simply left the room.

With a few quiet words, Miss Devlin advised Robert to allow Doro some time alone, and everyone left the sitting room. They abandoned Braxton, who stood at one of the windows and peered out onto the ragged garden, leaving him quite, quite alone in his triumph.

He didn't feel the better for it, but it was done. His worst concern now was that Miss Dearie-Dear wouldn't allow him within ten feet of her.

Chapter Five

Perched on the second to the bottom riser in the small entryway with her candle beside her, Tressa fingered her conservative dove-gray skirts. She wished she had something suitable to wear, something dignified, even stunning, that would bolster all that she wished to throw at Braxton's head.

Alas, the dove-gray would have to do.

She waited. She fidgeted.

The manner in which his lordship had treated Doro that afternoon at tea had been beyond anything Tressa could have imagined. Braxton knew the awe he inspired in most people, the great power he wielded. That he had used it to trample an innocent creature told Tressa things about Braxton she could not like.

Worse, Tressa believed he'd hardly given the situation more than the necessary consideration that would get him his way. That was all the man wanted: His way, without a care as to how he had affected Doro—and Robert, too.

Following tea, Doro had retreated to her room. Once she'd

convinced Robert to go on to Sir Percival's, Tressa had had a talk with the girl. Calmly, Doro stood firm in her determination to break it off with Robert. She insisted he would go on to Italy and she would go on to another position, perhaps in a shop.

Tressa's blood boiled.

She would make Braxton understand the pain he had caused if she had to—

Tressa heard a carriage enter the street. Braxton had dined out as usual, and his host had sent a carriage for him. Rising and picking up her candle, she heard him call good night to the coachmen and then the rattle of his key in the lock.

His surprise when he opened the door and found her registered in his every inch.

Tressa's initial reaction was to blot out the absolutely wonderful way he looked in dark evening attire, even following his night with friends and at this late hour.

"Miss Dearie-Dear," he said, cautiously.

His cape swirled darkly as he removed it. He placed it in the crook where the banister met the newel post. Popping his hat on the post, he propped his cane against it. His gloves ended on top of the cape, everything ready for Mudge to find come morning.

"Needless to say, you're waiting for me," he murmured, "and I can guess the subject you wish to discuss. By your stance and the way you have all that lovely hair tucked up beneath your sober cap, you wish to ring a peal over my head like my old nanny used to do."

"I am not your old nanny, sir."

"Thank God. As I've been plain as pikestaff in telling you, I want you for other purposes."

"We shall have none of that kind of talk, my lord."

"No, I'm sure any consideration of being my little bedmate has flown out the window."

"Such a consideration was never in the room."

He smiled his smallest smile. Still, it went to Tressa's heart like a knife.

"That one won't wash with me, my desire. You've shared my kisses, remember? I certainly do."

Tressa couldn't reply without lying.

"So where shall I take my caning?"

"I will not fall for your diversions in this instance, my lord. I am intent on sticking to the point."

"To having your pound of flesh?"

"To having Doro's pound of flesh."

"So have it, my sweet, and good luck to you. I'm not too happy about the matter myself."

Tressa felt thrown off. In going tooth and nail with Braxton, she knew to beware a savvy, practiced adversary. She lifted her candle, indicating the staircase. "If you will follow me, my lord."

Puzzlement entered his handsome features. Still, he inclined his head deferentially. "I will follow you into hell, my sweet. Could it be I'm not under fire after all?"

"No. You are definitely under my fire, sir."

At the landing, Tressa lighted their way to the back stairs.

Braxton climbed the creaking stairs behind her, obviously recalling that first night when he'd come to her wrapped in a blanket and had been defeated by the popping and groaning of the very risers that popped and groaned now.

"Will we not awaken Miss Sweet-As-Pie?" he inquired sourly.

"I doubt, sir, that after what you've done, she will sleep well for weeks to come."

At Tressa's own door, Braxton paused, grasping the latch and sending her a hopeful, questioning look.

"Not in there, sir."

She opened instead the door leading into the front room, the one which looked down on Pocket Street. Earlier, Tressa had carried up what candles she could, including the branch of work candles, and she began lighting them with her own candlestick while his lordship closed the door. He took in the few furnishings, then waited quietly.

As the small, dingy room came into definition, the reason for her bringing them there was also revealed. On the wall, Robert had hung, both for safekeeping and secrecy, the portrait of Doro he had recently finished.

With some satisfaction, Tressa watched Braxton's expression change as he peered up at Dora's lovely illuminated face. Her cloud of dark hair was crowned by a wreath of wildflowers. The gentle warmth of her gaze as she met the gaze of the viewer was riveting. Her simple white gown emphasized her willowy figure. In truth, the simplicity of it in total was so stirring that even Braxton was momentarily taken aback.

Tressa played her advantage. "Robert loves Doro and she loves him. Here is your proof, sir."

After a minute more, he dropped his gaze from the picture, as though Tressa's proof was too obvious to deny. "What do any of us know of love, Miss Devlin, particularly when we are so young? I did my duty today. While I'm not proud of the means I employed, I did what had to be done."

Tressa gazed at this immensely appealing male, a capable man who remained sure of himself. He was the best of what his society produced, the epitome of the dutiful gentleman, a blessing in so many ways to so many people.

Oddly enough, Tressa saw he believed what he said. Even more oddly, and for all she'd waited that evening to blister him with her tongue, she spoke more wearily than anything. Suddenly she was just plain exhausted by that day's emotions.

"I don't think you believe in your duty, sir."

He peered at her as if her wits had gone wanting.

"You don't believe Doro will not suit. You are no slave to convention, no matter how harshly you took your stand today. You would decry Doro's origins, but you are also basically a fair man. Do you believe her blood is any different than yours or even that of the Prince? No, in what you did today, you were more interested in having your way, as usual.''

''That's nonsense.''

He turned serious. He looked at her with such aloofness, gathering his great height and retreating from his earlier light cynicism, that Tressa's own smile sneaked across her lips.

''No, sir, you cannot deny it. You aren't driven by convention, and especially not by society's opinions. Otherwise you wouldn't be here. You wouldn't be so comfortable in making do here, even in doing so much for yourself. Mudge has told me how you shave yourself, bathe and dress yourself, tie your own cravats, even shine your own boots. He says you're satisfied with whatever he brings for the meals you take here, and that you never complain. He says you show concern for the little boy you've hired to help in the stable, and that you—''

''Mudge says too much.''

Truly, Braxton's assumed starchiness caused Tressa's soft, unexpected chuckle. She'd been so angry with him and now she was halfway to funning him. Why did this man affect her unlike any other person in her life, with so many conflicting and deeply felt emotions?

''No, sir,'' she said, knowing she must leave as soon as she could, ''you weren't concerned today with the order of things. You were merely being a great, horrid bully.''

He stared at her as if she'd struck him.

She couldn't help it. She smiled. ''There. For once in your life, you have the truth from someone, and not at all gently given.''

''Should you have been any more gentle, ma'am, I'd be flat on the floor.''

Wonderfully, amazingly, Braxton smiled at her as if she were his equal and he respected her as such.

Tressa thought she herself might end up flattened on the floor.

Grasping his hands behind his back, revealing the white of

his cravat and shirtfront and waistcoat in contrast to the darkness of the rest of his attire, he relaxed somewhat.

"No," he admitted, "I'm not one to believe a person's life should be dictated by his blood. I've known too many gentlemen of supposedly the finest blood who are the lowest of the low. Still," he added, "I am against the marriage."

"But why?"

"They're too young to realize what they're getting into. Being leg-shackled to someone, unable to get away under any circumstances short of mutual poisonings . . ."

"My goodness, what a horrible view of matrimony you have."

"I have a perfectly reasonable view of marriage. For years, I was daily witness to the marriage between my parents, who held such a choking hold on each other's throats that they would not let loose even to separate."

"That's not the normal marriage, surely."

"And how would you know? Believe me, there are more cold marriages and more hot marriages, like that of my parents, than you can imagine. The way we arrange our unions guarantees the worst."

"But Robert and Doro—"

"Are somehow different?" he scoffed.

"With Robert and Doro we are not talking about an arranged match."

"I know, I know. Two lovebirds who have me to defy."

"How jaded you are, my lord."

When Braxton didn't deny this last evaluation of him, Tressa almost began to feel sorry for him.

"Know you nothing of happiness, sir?"

"Happiness?"

"You claim to know nothing of love, but we are talking about happiness when we speak of Robert and Doro, their present and future happiness. About, God willing, years of happiness. No matter what comes—and there will be unhappiness—Doro and Robert will have each other. Down through the years and adversities, they will simply look at each other and know that, in one aspect, they are happy. Without each other, sir, they will never be truly happy.''

Braxton gazed into Tressa's eyes.

He looked so long she thought she must drop her own gaze. Finally, though, he turned those storm-cloud eyes to the portrait of Doro. He didn't say anything, and Tressa wondered what he could be thinking—if he'd actually listened to what she'd said.

At last, in the small dingy room full of candlelight and beguilement, Braxton moved toward Tressa, his gray eyes pinning her where she was.

"And what about our present happiness, Miss Dearie-Dear?''

No, his mind, she saw, ran in only one direction. But it was a riveting one, especially as he hovered over her, all dark, suggestive, seductive desire.

He stroked her cheek. "You are so very lovely when you smile at me.''

Tressa quivered in anticipation.

The man was practiced in seduction, not in love. He bedded for pleasure, not marriage. He was quite plain on all that.

She'd have to take him at his word.

Finding no resistance from Tressa, he smoothed her cheek and spoke softly again in the glowing quiet.

"You are so very lovely in your sober little cap and with that wonderful honeyed hair all but hidden.'' He edged closer, his mesmeric whisper drawing her eyes to his.

He was a wizard of seduction, and Tressa wanted to be seduced.

"Your eyes are so deep and dark I can never be sure what you're thinking. When you smile, I'm relieved—although I do believe your smiles are as much a surprise to you as they are to me. Yes, yes,'' he said, gathering her into his arms, "I like your smile. I want to make you smile with such bliss that I'll know you've never known quite the same sated, sweet joy. You must come away with me, Miss Dearie-Dear, to my bed.''

Tressa wavered enough to let him catch her up more tightly against his masculine warmth. The scent of country washing assailed her.

If she were to stop him, she had to do so now. Was she capable of turning him away with a light smile and remark? Or even with a firm rebuke?

She could muster neither.

She'd have to keep up with this practiced lover. He believed her to have had at least one lover of her own. The first time he'd kissed her in his bedchamber as she'd made up his bed, she'd imitated whatever he'd done.

Now, evidently sure he'd be welcome, he brought his mouth to Tressa's with a sweet slowness, as honey is brought to ripe berries. The idea that he'd practice his wiles on her, that he found her desirable enough, thrilled Tressa. Every new realization, as part of her grew more enthralled with him and part of her measured her enthrallment, thrilled her again.

Her recollections were quite right. His lips were soft and firm, heated and dewy and honeyed.

"You are so very delectable," he murmured between kisses, voicing the term she sought for.

Delectable, delicious, like summer berries and honey.

She could kiss him over and over, and she was sure she'd never tire of it. She wondered, though, how long it would be before he lost interest. How would he tell her? How would she know?

He seemed to find her returned kisses good enough. She could have gotten lost in them, in his growing heat—and in her own.

He was leading her somewhere, coaxing her on to . . . to bed.

Tressa pulled back. The expert in him recognized her hesitation, and went all-out to overcome her doubts. His seduction turned from honeyed and languorous and delectable to more urgent, more decided. The part of Tressa that had been thinking could no longer think.

Ever more lost in the delectable heat, she fired back with her own kisses, a whole variety she had learned from him. When he slid his tongue into her mouth and groaned, she experienced a frisson of surprise, then recognition.

He was possessing her, pushing her toward the ultimate possession . . . in bed.

Tressa leaped at the idea. She yearned for his claim on her and longed to see his body again, his nude upper torso with its thick dark hair and bronze nipples, his narrow waist and puckered navel.

"I'm so glad, my desire," he whispered, "that I'm the first to kiss you in the French manner."

"In the French manner?" she barely replied.

"With my tongue tasting your sweet mouth."

"And how do you know that you're the first to kiss me in the French manner?"

"Because, sweetings, I felt your surprise at my taking your mouth thus."

There was little he wouldn't know of her, read of her, if their intimacy continued. She wondered again if she could carry off her great ignorance in amorous affairs.

Still, his next kiss, again in the possessive French manner, sent her careening onward.

The picture of him from that night when he'd sought her at the bottom of the back staircase formed in her mind, running away with her senses. He, too, seemed to be losing himself in her efforts.

Emboldened, she slid her hand beneath his dark evening coat into the warmth and fragrance of his linens, past his waistcoat and into his shirtfront, into the very heat beneath. She traced his nipple through the cambric, small but hard like a pebble.

"Good God," he gasped, as if she'd shocked him.

In her search for this remembered bit of his flesh, she'd forgotten him as he was now. She'd been so centered on her quest that his response seemed to come from far away and so unexpectedly as to shock her in turn.

He peered down at her, his gray eyes amazingly full of passion. Holding her wide-eyed gaze, he stroked her breast as she had pressed for his.

A downward thrust of heat, so intense as to awaken that long sleeping aspect of her, jolted through her. She removed her pressuring, seeking fingers from deep inside his coat, but he did not take his hand from where it molded her breast. He kneaded her there, fondling her, again stirring that thrusting heat.

She'd urged Braxton to a threshold she couldn't cross. She had no idea where they'd go next. She only knew she wasn't ready.

"W-we must not," she said, her voice unrecognizable to her own ears.

"Not here, but—"

"Not at all, s-sir."

His tone was incredulous. "What?"

"I'm sorry," She pulled away from him. Somehow, she still had her feet under her, and they took her to the window where she was accustomed, late at night, to standing and watching the street.

She dared not look back at Braxton, and was grateful he didn't follow her. He was too incredulous, likely. She'd clearly surrendered, even inadvertently pursued. She'd been the first to touch him in an intimate way, and he'd been shocked.

No wonder he remained incredulous.

"I simply cannot, sir."

"Certainly, ma'am, after that you can tell me why you cannot. It's not that you don't want to."

Still at the window, Tressa absently nudged aside the drape. "No," she admitted. "I want to, I suppose."

Braxton spoke from behind her—cynically now. "You *suppose*? You're right in that, by the very devil."

"You must forgive—"

"Forgive? I want to know why. It's Doro and Robert, isn't it? If they were to leave Pocket Street, you'd stay with me here, wouldn't you?"

Tressa was abruptly distracted by the slightest movement in the street down on the corner.

A watcher!

Clearly, even this late at night, somebody was watching the house.

"There's someone in the street, sir," she managed, despite her sudden fear.

She heard the perplexity in Braxton's barked, "What?"

The watcher had caught sight of her in the window, lit from behind by numerous candles.

Braxton was quickly by her side, pushing away the drape and looking down. He, too, saw the man, who was little more than a silhouette.

His lordship's testiness readily ran from one subject to the next. "That's just my man," he said, tersely.

Tressa couldn't believe her ears. "Y-your man?"

"It's obvious word hasn't gotten down to him that he doesn't need to be here anymore."

"Are you sure, my lord?"

Obviously, Braxton wanted to get back to the former topic, to ignore the man in the street. Then he read how shaken Tressa was. "He makes you afraid?"

"No, I . . . I'm not afraid."

Either she was good at playacting or Braxton was ready to explode with his frustration—or, perhaps, he sensed her fear more than she thought.

In any case, he pivoted from her and his aborted seduction, striding to the door of the small room.

"I'll see to him," he ground out over his shoulder. "And

you, Miss Devlin, put out the candles and go to bed. We've both had enough of thwarted wishes for one day.''

Tressa stayed at the window for as long as she dared. She watched as Braxton exited the house, crossed the street and had a word with the man who stepped out of the shadows.

In plain view, he was a nondescript fellow, no one to be afraid of, just a man earning his pay by keeping an eye on the marquess's house and cousin.

Even so, she lingered in the window even after she'd blown out all the candles except her own and Braxton had shut himself back in downstairs. The street was empty, but she shivered with dread just the same.

That man in the street hadn't been her uncle's watcher. Joe Legg was his name. Joe Legg hadn't caught up with her yet on Pocket Street, but she was certain he was trying to do so. Both Joe Legg and her Uncle Straith had to be mad as fire at her.

Going on a month now, for the first time in her life, she hadn't been under their thumb.

For three days, Tressa couldn't seem to rid herself of her renewed dread.

With Braxton's arrival, she'd been somewhat diverted from her worries about her Uncle Straith catching up with her. In truth, only Braxton's powerful personality could have caused such a lapse. But seeing Braxton's man watching the house had sobered her.

She'd been additionally sobered by Braxton's advances and by her own reactions. While he had cooled to her since their encounter in the attic room, she couldn't get the man out of her mind any more than she could stop Joe Legg, her uncle's watcher, from haunting her thoughts.

That no one noticed her soberness, was not, as it turned out, surprising. The surprise arose from the new direction in which Braxton was taking his cousin Robert and even Doro.

After that night in the attic when Tressa had shown Braxton Robert's portrait of Doro, his lordship had reversed himself. Tressa couldn't believe she had effected the change in the iron-eyed general, but he *had* reversed himself.

The next morning, Braxton had called the young couple into the sitting room and evidently given them his blessing. Tressa had walked to Cupid's Tea Garden early that morning and hadn't been present.

Still, Doro's recounting had been so riddled with wonder and relief that Tressa knew Braxton had done an excellent job patching things up.

Ever since, Robert and Doro's joy had filled the house, making little else recognizable, and Tressa was glad for that. Inwardly, she rejoiced along with them.

Still, she couldn't help an outward quiet that hid her mix of emotions. With Braxton's reversal, he and Doro and Robert were becoming a family, and she had no part in that.

Standing in the second-story window overlooking the burgeoning garden, she saw Braxton below, talking to the couple. She couldn't hear what they were saying, but Doro, seated on one of the benches at the front of the octagonal summerhouse, smiled a soft, pleased smile as yellow primroses, blue columbine, and pink peonies rioted around her. Robert, who stood next to his older cousin and who was habitually sober, all but grinned as he nodded and plucked the petals from a daisy.

"His lor'ship," Mudge said from behind Tressa as he finished the polishing needed on Braxton's bed, "must be making more amends, I'd say."

Smiling slightly, Tressa pivoted into the bedchamber with the fresh sheets she carried. "I'd say he has enough amends to make to keep him busy."

"A family engagement ring for Miss Doro," Mudge recounted, "a special license, a wedding in the bishop's chambers come tomorrow morning, and a tidy sum as a wedding gift tha' will take them back and forth to Italy in comfort.''

"And don't forget his offer of carrying Doro's portrait to Cannongate with him when he goes.''

"To hang in the main drawing room, so he says.''

"It will look wonderful—and very right—in his main drawing room,'' Tressa declared. "I'm so happy it's all turned out well.''

"And I, too.''

She peered at her old friend, who hesitated in the streaming afternoon sunlight. After the morning's rain, it was becoming another lovely summer afternoon.

"Yes,'' Tressa said, "I know you're happy. You've done Robert and Doro a great service over the past month.''

"An' you, as well.''

Tressa sighed. "And now it's time, my good friend, for us—''

"For us to disappear again. Mr. and Mrs. Swallow stand ready to hire you once you're finished here. We'll have to leave the house well before dawn again, before even the street hawkers are out. You'll be safely hidden in the City, Miss, my old stomping ground.''

"Thank you, Mudge, for finding my new post.''

"Not nearly so fine as in Mayfair with the Dowager Lady Farronby, but a companion to old Mrs. Swallow, the mother of a newspaper writer.''

"And you, Mudge?''

"I can always find meself a situation, especially in the City.''

"Somewhere near to the Swallows', I hope.''

"I'll always be nearby, Miss. As long as you needs me.''

Tressa smiled, precisely so she wouldn't burst out crying at this solemn, sincere pledge on Mudge's part.

She and Mudge had become acquainted at the Dowager Lady Farronby's. When the dowager died, the staff shrank to just Tressa, Mudge, and Doro in the large closed town house. The three of them had grown quite devoted to each other.

At Mudge's discovery of the regular guard that was kept on
Tressa from the streets, he'd wanted to do something about Joe
Legg in particular. Mudge had no regard for the barrel-like
spy.

Even so, Tressa had never explained to Mudge, much less
anyone else, the reasons behind the guard her uncle had insti-
tuted. Everyone who knew her story simply believed Buck
Devlin had taken his own life by his own hand, not that he'd
been murdered in front of her very eyes.

Tressa had never told a single soul the truth she and her uncle
and her Aunt Editha kept buried. Tressa especially couldn't tell
Mudge and endanger him. The elderly man, with his knowing
old eyes, simply recognized Tressa needed his help and gave
it without question.

And so, with a soft smile, Tressa reverted to their favorite
shared subject. "You will not leave me, Mudge, for anything
short of warm weather and sea breezes in your hair?"

"Not for anything short of *hot* weather, Miss. Hot days and
warm nights would be good for me old bones."

They laughed. Mudge's bones were as strong as his devotion.

Tressa moved toward the bed to dress it in fresh sheets.
"We'll leave, then, once Doro and Robert are well and truly
on their way to Italy."

Chapter Six

Tressa floated the large fresh-smelling sheet down over the mattress. She was getting better at making Braxton's bed, and she knew when he quietly entered the room.

Mudge had gone along to other business, and Tressa finished in the well-kept, darkly paneled, darkly furnished bedchamber. She didn't glance up from her work when Braxton raised a hand to a bedpost and, relaxing, observed her.

"You look like the perfect sober little nun today," he said, evidently not entirely meaning her understated garb.

Tressa didn't reply.

He edged around the bed, forcing her to look at him.

"How wonderful it is to know you're not a little nun, but a beautiful, fiery woman."

Tressa blushed, but kept working.

Today Braxton was dressed in tight-fitting, light drab pantaloons with Hussar boots. His blue coat was closely fitted, more for Town. As usual, his linens were just from the laundress, the whitest of whites. Mudge had mentioned the name of Braxton's tie, *de Voyage*—simple and comfortable, executed by his own hand.

"Tomorrow is our big day," he ventured.

"I must admit, my lord, you've done well by Robert and Doro." Speaking stiffly, Tressa shook out the next sheet.

She should simply walk off and let him deal with the old monster of a bed!

But, no, he'd only call Mudge.

He pressed in on her. Even though his hands were folded behind his back, she knew he was closing in on her, waiting to get what he wanted.

This was to be a seduction, she thought. They were alone, secluded. The house was quiet. A window overlooking the fragrant garden was open, letting in the dizzying air. A bumble-bee buzzed just outside, quite impressed with seeing himself in the glass.

Even the day conspired against her—lazy, lovely, silken.

"Just why," he said, "they invariably have weddings so early in the morning I'll never understand."

Tressa merely tucked in the sheet, then marched around the mattress as he languidly followed. He pressed on.

"After the ceremony, a private wedding breakfast with just the five of us. And then you, as I've been given to believe, going off in a hackney carriage to your next post."

Tressa didn't tell him that things had become more compli-cated for her than that. She and Mudge would wait a few days at the Crown and Feathers before leaving one quiet morning. The Swallows would be ready for her three days hence, and she and Mudge had decided a short secluded spell at the inn and a quick dash to the City should likely foil any gains Joe Legg might have made in finding her.

There still were no signs of him at night in the street near the house. But he and her uncle would never give up on finding her. She remained her uncle and aunt's worst fear in the commission of their horrid deed, and Tressa couldn't grow lax and forget that.

"Where is your new post, Miss Devlin?"

She'd known he'd be curious.

"Evidently," he pressed when she didn't answer, "not even Doro and Robert know where you will be."

"I'll let them know when I'm settled, sir."

"When will you let *me* know where you are?"

"I have no need to let you know."

When she delivered her little retort, Braxton blocked her from going back around the bed.

She was forced to face him.

"You have no reason to go, Miss Devlin, and every reason to return here with me following the wedding."

"That is nonsense, sir."

"It is not nonsense. I wish to take good care of you. Beautiful care, in fact. You will want for nothing with me as your protector. You can be nicely situated for the rest of your days if you play me right."

Despite her inward preparations for this meeting, Tressa was shocked to hear the specifics. Protector, not husband. Nicely situated, not married. Play him right, not plight her troth.

His tone remained silken, but his words shocked.

Even more shocking was Tressa's reaction. She yearned to say yes. Worse, he knew her weakness. He'd plumbed her wantonness. She didn't dare let him take her in his arms.

But of course he did—urgently, before she could get around him. Firmly, quickly, as if she might escape.

"Stay with me." He held her tightly, pressuring her.

Finally Tressa peered up into his gaze. She was lost. His gray eyes filled themselves with her expression, spying out any least resistance.

"Stay with me," he coaxed, lowering his mouth to hers. His lips spoke both of a surface, silken seduction and of a deeper, more urgent press.

Her lips hinted at a possible capitulation. She couldn't believe how quickly she might give in to him. But at what cost?

After their interlude, would she be able to find the threads of her real life again? It was crucial that she did, of course, and not merely because she needed the financial security with which he teased her. She needed to keep herself—and now Mudge—safe.

Braxton, however, aroused in her a stronger need than the one for safety. Just where this need had come from, Tressa couldn't imagine. She'd always been so sensible, so resigned to her lot.

His lips, so firm, so soft, were seduction itself. His scent beguiled her, even in the fragrance of the afternoon. The bumble-bee buzzed vaguely now. The sun surely shone through the window more softly.

All was Braxton.

Tressa's heart beat. Her breathing failed. She became a wanton, warm and willing. She confirmed Braxton's beliefs about her. She wanted what he wanted.

He pivoted with her, plunging them into the fresh sheets as if into a refreshing pool. With his heavy body, he half covered the whole length of her so she couldn't get away. Her arms went up around his neck. She smoothed her hands over his broad shoulders, caressing him, rather than pushing him off.

Oh, she did enjoy touching him, seeing him.

She had the makings of a mistress, and he'd known it from the start. Now he awakened her to it.

His hand curved along her waist, smoothing up to her breast. She arched her back. He kissed her in a rhythm that drummed her body into being. He set up such a chorus in her that she lost herself in the swelling warmth and music, the pure sweetness of it.

He placed his leg over her legs, the weight of it wonderful and claiming. He would soon devour her, somehow take her into himself. His hand slipped to that throbbing desire building between her legs. Again he knew her body better than she did. He read what it needed and understood how to fulfill its needs.

His stroking, seeking fingers at the apex of her legs would drive her mad with yearning, even through her skirts and petticoats.

"At least," he breathed into her ear, "we can please you one way or another, can we not?"

"Sir, we must not."

Yes, she had murmured those words. Some little part of her sounded sensible.

"We must not?" He lifted himself and smiled—actually smiled—into her eyes.

His gray gaze was as soft as a dove's breast.

"We must not, sweetings? Must not what? Get undressed? No. We'd end up here all afternoon and evening if I were to see you nude. But we can dally, can we not?"

"Dally?"

"You haven't dallied? My, my, I have so much to teach you, and I'm so very glad I'll be your instructor. I should have thought . . . and so we shall dally. We shall accomplish a great deal, even clothed."

When his smile turned to kisses again, Tressa felt herself sinking into the mattress, ready to learn about dalliance. But something in her simply could not succumb.

He was a wizard who worked magic with his hands. He gathered her skirts, his wicked hand slowly advancing up her stocking, past her knee, toward her garter and naked thigh. She couldn't seem to breathe.

He lifted her skirts, petticoats and all.

Lightskirt.

She'd overheard the term recently at Cupid's Tea Garden. One young man had been speaking to another, describing one of the equally young females as a lightskirt.

Tressa herself was a lightskirt. Braxton would make her one. He was certainly treating her as one.

Somehow, the pleasure he gave her didn't dispel the sudden inward accusation. *Lightskirt.*

When Tressa wiggled enough, Braxton rolled off her and let her sit up. His great gray eyes burned between the pleasurable haze she'd put there and an emerging displeasure.

"What is it?" he asked, coming to a seated position as Tressa left the sheets altogether. "Did I hurt you somehow?"

"No." She fumbled, endeavoring to regain her senses and arrange her clothing. "You didn't hurt me."

"You don't like it that Robert and Doro are still in the house. I thought you wouldn't. Tomorrow, after they're off to Dover, we'll be on our own here."

"You assume too much, sir."

When he eyed her, she blushed. She had to. She'd given him reason to assume anything.

He stood up, tugging his waistcoat taut, hardly mussed at all. Dalliances with one's clothes on made one a rumpled mess. But only in her case, of course. Braxton remained as polished, as controlled and calm as ever.

"Stay with me," he said.

Tressa shook her head. Knowing that to remain, to uselessly brush at her skirts and listen to him would be her undoing, she left as quickly as her legs would carry her. She couldn't even afford to wish him well and say her good-byes.

In fact, Tressa could only walk, walk, walk in the lovely summer afternoon. As quickly as she could, she headed for Cupid's Tea Garden. She slowed as she entered Green Lion Square, finally crossing the street and attaining the garden with its high, deep-green palings.

The square was an old one, its once grand houses now growing dilapidated. The plane trees in the garden were thick and deep, the gravel paths invaded by clumps of grass and weeds, the benches peeling paint and seldom used.

Tressa found it refreshing, a bit of greenery she needed. She'd been reared in the country, and the nearly abandoned garden in Green Lion Square took her back not to Lance Hall, but to the countryside.

Finally, she could draw a full breath again. Finally, she could think. Could she become a lightskirt, a mistress?

No, she couldn't.

But could she live with and even love Braxton, if only for a short while and without him loving her?

There was a difference between the two, although only she would recognize it. He would see her merely as his mistress. He'd treat her well. From what she could tell, he treated everyone well, with the same regard he demanded for himself.

There was much about him she could admire and even love.

Wasn't this precisely what she'd always dreamed about, an opportunity to grasp that "something" despite the names she'd be called? In any case, when she left Braxton, she'd also leave behind the names and resume her respectable life.

Tressa fully recognized this opportunity. A man like Braxton would never come again.

At the gate in the palings and deep in thought, Tressa experienced one of those silly occurrences where she and another woman played with allowing the other to use the gate only to accept the turn they were offered and nearly bump into each other.

"I do declare," the girl of about Doro's age said, laughing, "we shall knock each other down with our politeness."

Tressa needed the light moment.

She knew the young woman was, in fact, a mistress, currently under the protection of Sir Percival Pounce. Naturally, the girl was pretty and fashionably dressed, if also exhibiting some exaggerated notions in her garb. She had ginger coloring and bright green eyes that added to her youthful attractions and her open manner.

All along, Tressa had known she would miss Doro. Here was another eager face smiling into hers, even with Tressa's veil between them.

"You are Miss Dear of Pocket Street," the girl said.

Tressa was thrown off balance. Invariably veiled outside the house, she had rather thought she moved through the streets unnoticed and definitely unnamed.

Miss Dear of Pocket Street.

"Naturally," the girl continued, not at all encroaching but brightly curious, "everybody knows you are a lady, ma'am. The question is," she pressed boldly, delightfully, "are you also one of our sort? Like my friends and I, you see. A mistress, I mean. To Braxton. You must pardon me, but we have all been quite at odds in deciding."

Tressa chuckled. "I do indeed pardon you," she said, evading the rush of inquiry and conjecture.

She was surprised, then, as the girl fell into step beside her, not a bit put off as Tressa resumed her pace along the flagway.

The girl wore a lovely walking costume and bonnet, suitable for any London Miss in her first Season—except for the color. The ensemble was too bright a green for a debutante, overly decorated with common frou-frou.

Tressa had picked up quite a lot on her walks, and knew the gel simply went by the name Ambrosia—as colorful a name as the girl herself.

Yes, Tressa knew enough of the demimonde which operated around her to understand there were all sorts of lightskirts, from strolling damsels who circled the tea garden, particularly at night, to glamorous, well-recognized females passing from one notable protector to another, gathering themselves fortunes and lending a certain panache to their keeper's repute.

There was society, and there was the gentleman's world outside of society. The ladies governed society, the gentlemen and their mistresses, the half world. While each world recognized the other—was even curious about its doings—never, never did those worlds meet.

How could I, Tressa wondered, *ever be a mistress and remain a lady*? How could she expect Braxton to continue seeing her as the latter when she became the former? Was a born wanton, however, ever really a lady? Never had she recognized herself more clearly as Bad Buck Devlin's daughter. Maybe it was all in the blood.

So deep in thought she forgot that Ambrosia still walked beside her, Tressa was called back by the girl's chuckle.

"I can see you don't wish to discuss yourself, ma'am, and I appreciate that. I have things I don't tell my friends, not even my sister, Lottie. Have you heard of my sister, ma'am? She calls herself Lotta Delight, which I think sounds too vulgar. It was Lottie who was with Sir Percival first and who introduced him to me. These days, she's off with Willby to Paris—if, that is, you can imagine Lottie—er, Lotta—in Paris. Of course, she'll laud it over me for weeks after her return, but she was nice in lending Sir Percival to me, so I can't complain much— not that she didn't ask me to do her a favor in return. Which she did . . . but, well, I've sworn not to talk about that."

"Then certainly you must not," Tressa said.

She sounded like an old maiden aunt, and she knew it. But her mind still hadn't settled on the answer she sought.

"An' then, there's the lovely Miss Doro Jupe of Pocket Street," Ambrosia announced. "We've quite decided she's a lady for certain sure. Robert Wexby comes regularly to Sir Percival's and closes himself in the book room. Now, there's a true gentleman—who, of course, never speaks to me beyond the polite, which is well enough as far as I see it. Indeed, he is the best of gentlemen—and now to marry Miss Jupe come tomorrow. She must be the luckiest of ladies."

The girl's eyes glowed, much as Doro's had of late.

Females had such tender hearts, no matter what their echelon, especially when they were merely eighteen or nineteen or so.

Still, Tressa was amazed at what Ambrosia knew about the circumstances on Pocket Street—not that Tressa shouldn't have expected some gossip. There always was gossip. She'd merely hoped because they worked very hard at protecting their privacy, that—

"There across the street," the youthful Ambrosia was saying as she pointed to one of the high, narrow town houses, "is Sir Percival's. I've quite decided I don't need a walk in that gloomy old garden square, no matter how much Sir Percival wishes me out from under his feet. I have, though, enjoyed your company, my dear, well"—she chuckled—"Miss Dear. I hope you haven't minded that I walked with you. I don't like being alone, you see, and my only choice of company is Sir Percival."

Tressa gazed into the open regard of this . . . this young girl, really, who called herself Ambrosia for all the blatant reasons. Tressa could not like what she was thinking of the demimonde now, and especially of Sir Percival Pounce.

The old bounder.

He had a title, of course, and a fortune. But he lived in shabby Green Lion Square while his family carried on respectably in Mayfair and at a seat in Kent.

He considered himself a writer, and because other lesser lights of the literary world had found reasonable accommodations in Green Lion Square, he lived there, too. He enjoyed, even headed up, a set of artistic types—Bohemians, as they were called in Mayfair—who wanted to live more freely—indeed, irresponsibly with young vulnerable mistresses like Ambrosia and her interchangeable sister, Lottie.

Tressa wondered what Ambrosia's real name was, even as the girl's green gaze grew bright. A grand carriage had entered the square, pulling smartly in their direction. Tressa recognized the woman set like a jewel in the pink, satin-lined open barouche, displayed for all to see.

The Moon and The Stars—an actress, a mistress, a beauty, a woman who had attained much in her thirty-some years. She currently resided with the Duke of Exnor in a nearby love nest.

Ambrosia obviously admired her.

The girl's snapping green eyes tracked the equipage from

its chestnut horses, who wore high pink plumes, to the pair of footmen at the rear, dressed in gaudy pink and green and silver livery, the green and silver being Exnor's colors.

In fact, Tressa waited quietly by the girl's side until the carriage and four disappeared, down to the last jingle of its harness.

Surely, The Moon and The Stars was Ambrosia's ideal, the very example for her life. Tressa could read the excitement lingering in her pretty face when she turned to Tressa herself.

It was evident the girl carried a genuine admiration for Tressa, as well. Her expression filled with it as she spoke.

"In case you don't know, ma'am, my name is Ambrosia. Food for the gods, you see. I do hope you will speak to me next time we meet. I should so like to talk to you, Miss Dear, and I promise next time I will not pry."

"Yes, Ambrosia, I should like to walk with you again. And you must certainly take good care of yourself in the meantime."

"I surely will, ma'am." She giggled. "You sound like me old mum."

With a lively step, Ambrosia crossed the street and, upon reaching its other side, turned to wave at Tressa before disappearing into the town house.

Suddenly realizing it was growing late, Tressa set a smart pace back to Pocket Street. As she entered the little close, she was surprised by the harness jingle, the grave shine, of another fine carriage. A closed town coach with a darkly matched pair, four attendants, and crested doors, barely squeezed into the tight space.

Another of Braxton's friends had sent a coach round for him so he could come and dine. The Earl of Sleet.

Tressa hadn't realized it was that late.

In the doorway of the little house she found the marquess, dressed in his fine evening attire. Mudge waited nearby with his lordship's cape, gloves, cane, and tall hat. Braxton was pacing and very testy.

"Where in the devil's name have you been?" he asked—all but barked, really.

Mudge shifted his weight uncomfortably. The tall, dust covered object in the small entryway hung over them, surely listening. Tressa was surprisingly calm.

"I walk regularly, sir. I have explained that before."

"Robert has gone to finish at Pounce's, and Doro has been waiting to share her final meal here with you."

"I am sorry for keeping her waiting. I will hurry along to her and explain."

"And what about explaining to me, ma'am? I have not felt I could leave until your safe return."

"You needn't discommode yourself on my account, sir. As I say, I walk, and I shall continue to walk."

She swept past him, on up the stairs to remove her bonnet, to wash and find Doro. She threw her remarks, quite confidently, back at him as she went along.

"I shall stay with you, sir."

"What?"

Yes, that had nicely thrown him off. She turned to send him a collected gaze as she also removed her dark gloves, finger by finger.

He appeared incredulous.

A little smile sneaked across her lips. "Indeed, I'm glad you're here, Mudge, and that it is just we three. You and I have three days, have we not, Mudge?"

"We have, Miss."

"If you don't mind, I should like to spend them here on Pocket Street. In fact, I would think his lordship would be glad to have you stay, as well—if you'd like to."

Mudge didn't even glance at the marquess. He dipped his head toward her, up where she stood several risers above them.

Braxton simply remained as he was, measuring her with his general's eyes, his irritation draining away.

"So you will stay with me," he repeated.

She met his gaze levelly. "For three days."

"The devil. It will be more than three days."

She lifted a shoulder. "We shall see. I shall make my own decision. On that we will be most clear, sir. We are equals in this house, and I walk regularly. I walk when I wish and for as long as I wish."

Grabbing his hat and putting it on his head, Braxton signaled to Mudge that he was ready for his other fine accessories.

Tressa turned away just as brusquely, continuing up the stairs. She was serene now. She'd made her decision. For good or for ill, she would stay with him for three days.

Braxton had had mistresses before, of course, but none he'd thought to live with, none he'd spent time with out of bed.

Lately, he hadn't been very comfortable about how he generally thought of the females he bedded. Because he never, never courted ladies for marriage, nor even took unhappily married ladies for his most private pleasures, he didn't give females much thought beyond fair treatment and a clean break.

Since he'd met Miss Dear, he'd been thinking more seriously about his ways with women. He had to admit it made him uncomfortable to think Miss Dear would be treated the same way, although not by him.

But in all events, that would be weeks, months, even years off—after their parting. This business of a mere three days was nonsensical.

The royal dukes had mistresses who were more like wives than their own wives. They lived together openly in long relationships and had numerous children with them—not that Braxton wanted to compare himself to the royal dukes. A worse passel of jackanapes he'd never seen.

Still, still, still, she would stay with him. For a week now, he'd thought of little but having Miss Devlin—Miss Dear— and he would make it all right. He was a man who did things as they should be done. She would be safe with him, now and in the future.

To go to Rundell's would be to announce his mounting of a mistress. Instead, Braxton went to a jeweler he used in these situations. Braxton was ushered into a tiny, well-lit room behind drawn dark velvet draperies.

The elf-like man within, the jeweler's glass apparently affixed permanently in his one eye contorting his features, greeted Braxton in hushed tones. Pulling out a tray and unfolding a velvet cloth, the man revealed bright stones in all shapes and sizes and colors, enough to bedazzle even Braxton.

"A diamond, you say, my lord?"

"A very special diamond. Something fine, but not as pretentious as these things usually are."

Quickly, the man located the perfect stone, discussing it with Braxton as they took turns examining it, turning it over and over.

They discussed price—inordinate.

They discussed how it should be set—delicately.

"It will be very pretty, my lord, and for you alone, it will be done in time for this evening."

Braxton nodded.

"And the family stone, the lovely emerald you brought to me just days ago to be cleaned and checked—did it please your little bride, my lord?"

"Yes, both my cousin and his fiancée were quite pleased with the ring."

"And the wedding ring?"

"Yes, that as well, thank you. The ceremony went off beautifully this morning, and they're on their way to Dover."

"And you not even hours later purchasing the best yellow diamond I've ever had the pleasure to see. I know you'll be happy with it, my lord. And your lady, too."

"It is to be kept—"

The odd little man nodded, lifted a finger to his lips, and

spoke even more quietly. "My discretion is as reliable as my service, my lord. You will have your special yellow diamond this afternoon."

"I appreciate your trouble."

"My man shall arrive late today in plain dark clothes. His little package will be in his pocket. No trouble at all. No notice taken."

Chapter Seven

Tressa watched a little man in dark plain clothing exit the hackney carriage in Great Crow Street, just steps before it could turn onto Pocket Street. That someone would visit Pocket Street was unusual. That someone would pay off the jarvey in an almost clandestine manner in Great Crow Street and seek out Pocket Street in a hurrying, scurrying sort of way made her heart sicken and her pulse race.

Picking up her pace and tracking after the man, Tressa told herself to stay reasonable. It wasn't Joe Legg, and it was broad daylight. Her uncle's watcher had never pursued her, even spoken to her. He'd merely observed outside Lady Farronby's at night.

Besides, she followed the scurrying man with his surreptitious glances, not the other way around.

When the fellow turned and mounted the steps at Braxton's love nest, Tressa's inner reassurances collapsed. She couldn't think, couldn't breathe. Rather than contend with this creature on her doorstep, she quickly opened the dark green gate that stood between Braxton's house and the house next door. Stepping into the confined, coolly shadowed passage between the houses, she heard Mudge answer the door.

Catching her breath and getting her bearings, she realized the pair had little to say to each other, and the man was soon hurrying away.

Surely Mudge, she thought, still trying to calm herself, would have noticed any danger. Mudge had had a few verbal encounters with Joe Legg while trying to chase him off, and would be attuned to any threats now.

After a short while, somewhat more calm, Tressa walked to the gate that led into the garden, on around to the stairwell, and down into the kitchen.

In the same finery he'd worn to the wedding that morning—gray kerseymere pantaloons, a blue coat with gilt buttons, and tasseled Hessians—Braxton peered at her.

The kitchen was amazingly abuzz with activity. He stepped away from it, coming to grasp her arm where she stood, still veiled and ready to go all aquiver again.

Really, she had to get hold of herself. She wasn't in any danger.

She'd decided to remain on Pocket Street. Despite the wedding that morning, despite the fact Doro and Robert had gone on to spend perhaps years away on the continent, she'd decided to stay with this man for three days.

"I'm glad you're finally back," he said, disapproving of the long walk she had taken. "As you can see, we're in the middle of fixing dinner. I've borrowed a cook and his assistants from a friend who will not need them for the rest of the summer. The fellow is, quite naturally, upset about putting together any sort of impressive meal under the circumstances."

"I don't require an impressive meal."

Tressa allowed Braxton to usher her up the stairs and past

the open doorway into the sitting room. Though the room was still thick with Holland covers, the table was nicely made up with a large vase of hothouse flowers in its center.

"We shall have a cook, ma'am," he said, "and I feel damned fortunate to have gotten this fellow so readily. He's touchy, but he's sure to settle in. Best of all, he's accustomed to being discreet.

"Also," he continued as he hustled her along to the front staircase, "Mudge has found two young females to come in and help with the cleaning. They've taken apart your bedchamber—"

"*My* bedchamber, sir?" Tressa halted just shy of the risers.

"The bedchamber accorded you here," he said firmly, obviously trying to coax her on to the second bedchamber in the house, the one for the mistress.

In the entryway, however, Tressa was reminded of the little scurrying man who had been there only minutes before.

"Mudge answered the door to a man, and I was wondering—"

"A man?" he queried, not wanting to be diverted.

"Yes, Mudge—"

"Oh, indeed. A delivery, no more," he said dismissively, taking Tressa's elbow to move her toward the stairway.

She felt as if she were being led to the gallows. She'd never so much as peeked into the mistress's bedchamber, and she didn't want to see it now. Why couldn't she continue on where she was, in the tiny bedroom on the third floor?

Obviously sensing her reluctance, Braxton spoke to her in a decidedly lowered voice as they mounted the risers.

"You are to sleep with me from now on, ma'am. I'll have us be comfortable. The master's room, as you know, is dark and severe. Why use it when we can have a more comfortable room for only the cleaning?"

At the top of the stairs, Braxton walked Tressa directly toward the single open door. Straightening her backbone, she prepared herself.

Much to her astonishment, the bedchamber was not what she expected. Sunlight flooded in, illuminating a richly appointed yet tasteful room in mellow shades of biscuit and straw and pale yellow. The bed was huge, with an overlarge tester and drapes in pale velvet and white lace.

The coarser influence that lurked beneath the dust sheets in the rest of the house was absent here. A gilded cheval glass, a dressing table skirted in lace and velvet and topped by another thickly carved and gilded looking glass, indicated that the room was meant for a female. Little gilded chairs upholstered in straw-colored silk floated upon a carpet woven in greens and tans and pale yellow.

Tressa struggled to acknowledge the young maids and their bobbed curtsies and shy glances.

"You're doing a good job of it," Braxton told them, setting them back to their tasks. Finally releasing Tressa's elbow, he added, "They'll help you bring down your things when all is in readiness. Mudge is even now locating a lady's maid for you."

With that, his lordship left Tressa.

Also murmuring her appreciation for their efforts, Tressa bid the females a good day and scurried away. On up the back stairs, she let herself into her now familiar cubbyhole of a room.

In deciding to stay with Braxton, she hadn't considered the embarrassing practicalities. Without his arms around her, without his general's eyes to mesmerize, without his kisses to carry her away, everything felt riddled with something less than fine.

The day had started with such joy—with Robert and Doro's great happiness and legitimate relationship—but had turned . . . tawdry? Frightening? Ridiculous?

She couldn't say. She wished she could turn back, and she didn't know how to do that without arousing Braxton's ire. It seemed he wouldn't be thwarted in his designs. If she asked him to slow down and simply be her friend for a while, to simply talk to her and enjoy their company, which she longed for . . .

Liar, she scolded herself, *you want more than to be Braxton's friend.*

Besides, there was nothing else to be but his mistress. Braxton would never consider a woman as a friend, and he certainly wouldn't take a wife.

In the long lavender twilight, Braxton threw open the two windows in the sitting room. Outside, little balconies overhung the garden that sent up a wild and heady fragrance.

Not at all as a garden should be, he thought, but most sensual, a treat to run away with the senses on this balmy evening.

Letting his gaze drift over the small back sitting room, he realized he couldn't expect perfection in a single day. Not with just himself, Mudge, a temperamental nodcock for a cook, so little help, and so much to be done.

The table, however, with its flowers and china, its cutlery and napery, its little gift in silver paper reflecting the candle glow, looked fine. The scent from the garden, the gentle rustling sounds, would help mellow those things he'd been unable to change—the dust sheets and what they hid; the lack of a good cleaning.

He could only hope the room would suit his Private Fancy well enough. He'd managed to remove the painting above the hearth in which a lecherous satyr pinched the nipple of an innocent maiden. He himself had taken it down. Unable to find a replacement for it, he'd left the wall bare.

Moving to the mantel, he fingered the single object he would not remove, the clock. He rather liked the clock's naughty little trick, and the room needed a good timepiece, which the clock, with its bedding couple, had proven to be that day. He'd checked it off and on as he did now, toying with the suggestive display and rusty chime.

Miss Dear. Finally, at last, he and Miss Dear.

At her soft knock on the door, he clasped his hands behind his back, stood like a sentinel guarding the fireplace, and called, "Come."

That morning she had worn something other than her characteristic gray skirts to the wedding, something that, evidently, she and Doro had sewn. She wore the same gown now. It was conservative, tight at the neck and long in the sleeves, covering her like a little virgin, but it was also soft and blue—a lustrous shade that brought out the deep blue of her eyes, the contrast between her thick dark lashes and honey-colored hair.

The latter, of course, was tucked up under her cap, also new and remarkably smothered in lace. With her hands folded in front of her, she appeared serene, if additionally pale.

She didn't look like a mistress.

Tonight she was Lady Tressa, through and through.

Braxton felt a slight qualm, which he immediately quashed.

Forces in him urged him onward to the beginning of something he desired as he'd never desired anything else. For this liaison, in fact, he had sacrificed his say in the woman who would likely breed his heir. For this ladylike beauty, he'd lost track of his regulated life.

Looking at her, feeling as he did, he knew it would be worth it. People would say he had everything, and he did. But the truest pleasure he reserved for himself was the choice of his mistress. This time, he would possess his ideal.

Tressa Devlin had the appearance he preferred.

Tressa Devlin had a grace and intelligence he admired.

Tressa Devlin looked him squarely in the eye and spoke her mind to him.

Yes, he'd enjoy her to the fullest. He need only convince her to do the same.

"Good evening, Miss Dear," he said.

He would protect her identity by not using her name. In any case, Miss Dear suited her. Even Miss Dearie-Dear suited her down to the ground, although she avoided that name.

"Good evening, my lord."

"Pray, sit here by the fire. It's a small one, just enough to allow us some light, to lend us some intimacy and warmth. As you will note, there are few candles in the room."

She sat as he wished, her skirts offering a small sigh, no competition for the lazy, suggestive drone from the garden and the oncoming dark.

"We'll have dinner soon. Despite his ups and downs today, I'm happy to report that the cook has said he will stay at least one more day in our dreadful dungeon of a kitchen—if I let him redesign it according to his wishes."

"He asks a lot, my lord."

He bent toward where she sat, speaking softly. "You must no longer call me my lord, my dearest. We are to be as intimate as two people can be, remember?"

"I suppose I hadn't considered it." She blushed nicely. "I mean, I hadn't considered what I might or might not call you."

"You must call me Hannibal."

She looked taken aback. "Oh, surely not. I should think Braxton will do."

"No, it will be Hannibal. I'm already sacrificing a lot in using my Christian name."

"Sacrificing?"

"Terms such as my desire, my heart, my life."

"Oh, my. I thought mistresses gave only their bodies, not their hearts—certainly not their lives."

"So we shall settle on my desire?"

"No, we shall settle on Hannibal, if we must."

"Hmm," he murmured, moving to the table. He plucked up the little box and gave it to her.

"The delivery we spoke about this afternoon," he said. "The one that seemed to upset you."

She lowered her head to the gift. "I wasn't upset, sir."

"My desire."

"Hannibal."

She slid aside the silver paper, then opened the box. Pausing for a moment, she tilted the velvet-lined container. The diamond inside picked up the flames from the fire and scattered them like candle flicker into the chamber.

"Ahh, yes," she said, again softly, but surprising him.

He'd expected praise, gratitude.

" 'Tis called whore's fare, as I understand it," she said.

He unclasped his hands and assumed a stiffer stance. " 'Tisn't whore's fare."

"I thought I'd heard the term."

"Where? In Lady Farronby's drawing room?"

"Of course not."

He couldn't hide his feelings of slight. " 'Tis a yellow diamond, ma'am."

"Very beautiful, no doubt."

She stared at it.

He stared down on the fans of her lashes lying on her sweet, soft, pale cheeks.

"If you don't like it—"

"I do like it. Who could not?"

"Indeed, who?" he asked, all sarcasm.

She replaced the lid. "I thank you, sir."

"My desire."

"Hannibal."

"You will not try it on, then?"

"Oh, should I?"

"You are to wear it."

"Rather as Doro wears the emerald, I gather. Or is it more akin to a possession like the wedding band itself? Sir."

He inhaled deeply.

He walked to the window and stood looking out at the garden, unseeing. "I certainly intend to possess you, Miss Dear. You will not put me off."

"I don't intend to put you off."

"There will be a contract to consider. My solicitor is drawing it up even now under the name of Miss Dear. I hope you will see it as generous enough."

"I'm sure it will be—although, of course, I'm not an expert in such matters. Nor will I be here for longer than three days so as to need to agree to your contract."

Ignoring her point, he pushed on with his.

"Under certain conditions, there will be servants, a carriage and horses, and another house in the country, with you eventually holding the deeds to both that house and this one."

"My, my, you take my breath. I do indeed recognize your generosity. But you also use the words 'under certain conditions.' "

He turned to her, wondering why he liked it when she faced him as an equal, as she did now when she spoke back to him.

Still, frustration roiled in him. He hadn't envisioned verbal fisticuffs on their first evening together.

But then, she was a lady. She had her pride. He could appreciate that.

He faced her just as squarely, trying to stay patient. These matters had to be discussed, and it would be good to get them out of the way.

"Exactly what 'under certain conditions' means, ma'am, involves the matter of time. The longer we are together, the more will become permanently yours. You will accrue a large sum of money that will allow you to maintain the standard of living to which you will become accustomed."

"To maintain this standard of living, whether or not I am living with you? As I say, I shall be here but three days."

Damn, but this was uncomfortable.

Why in Hades had he started down this path tonight in particular? He wanted, *needed*, other things. He'd waited aeons to possess this woman, and here they were, her little dagger at his throat.

His dagger was ripe for thrusting elsewhere.

As if Hannibal didn't think they had differences enough, the clock on the mantel huffed up, chimed the hour, and flipped over the couple on the mattress.

Clearly Miss Dear saw the man atop his lady, even with her quick glance at the again peacefully ticking contraption. Her deep blue eyes focused on him, sending darts of disapproval for using the contrivance.

Without planning to do so, Braxton stepped to Miss Devlin, grasping her hands and pulling her up into his arms. The small box on her lap tumbled to the carpet as he, not at all intending to, lowered his mouth to hers, urgently.

There. That was what he wanted—her soft mouth beneath his, even if in surprise, open so he could plunder it, rob its sweet treasures with his tongue, his rough, ready kisses taking her before she could defy him any more.

Here was where he'd subdue her. He'd ravish her with kisses until she couldn't think, couldn't talk back. There was no denying she reveled in their kisses as much as he did.

She would make a glorious mistress, lady-born, with a wanton heart, and too honest, too brave, to deny it.

Stopping abruptly and lingering over her enough to see the muted surrender in those dark blue eyes, he released a satisfied grunt and grasped her by the hand. She came along readily as he took her to one long window, stepped over its low sill onto the balustraded balcony, and assisted her behind him.

Without letting her get her bearings on their little perch overlooking the voluptuous, rioting garden, he again pulled her into his arms. Tonight he'd meant to persuade and please, but he plagued and plundered. He couldn't help it.

Now, now, now, his body beat as a drum.

No more yearning for the myriad delights this woman offered merely by existing. "I want you now."

His words sounded so husky and deep with desire he had to repeat them.

"N-now, sir? But there is dinner—soon, certainly."

"We shall feast on each other."

She peered at him, perhaps a little quizzically. But scant illumination reached the balcony, and her eyes were so very dark and deep as to be unreadable—as dark and deep as the garden, and equally seductive. He and Tressa could have been in paradise itself, set down by Aladdin's carpet.

The musical sounds, the rhythmic drum, the thick, dizzying mix of aromas, the muted, after-dark colors, the faint dappled light—paradise.

He could have taken her on the balcony standing up, he was so ready.

His seeking fingers quickly discovered that the lady wore light corseting. But above the lacings and through the rich fabric, he found the lush give of her breast. All of her, every inch, was yielding to him, slowly and against her better judgment.

She wanted him, but she didn't want to want him.

He set to changing her mind. He plied her soft breast, covered it with his hand as he covered her lips with his mouth.

"Now," he whispered urgently, "now, now."

She arched her back responsively, balancing against the thick stone handrail. He smoothed his fingertips to her waist, then down to her round bottom.

"You are perfect," he said. "Perfect for me. You suit my taste for grace and delicacy. I love your honeyed hair. I long to see it let down, to sift it through my fingers. Now. It must be now, or I shall go mad."

He pulled her into his arousal.

She seemed to pause, to quiver as she sought his face, his

expression, his eyes in the frail light from inside. Her stillness was like a secret she hid from him, and he wanted to know all her secrets. He wanted nothing withheld from him—not her body, not her thoughts, not her conversation, not her very soul.

"Satisfy my hunger, sweet desire."

"I daresay," she whispered back, "we'll lose your temperamental cook if we do not eat his meal, especially after the difficult day he's had."

He bent over her, following her as far back as she could lean on the balustrade. She smelled teasingly of lavender, putting all the flowers beneath them to shame.

"I really don't want this to happen, this first time for us, on a balcony. But you decide—quickly, here and now, with a leisurely supper to follow, or soon, in a freshly made bed, with my finding something for us to eat afterward from the larder. I promise."

Her deep blue eyes searched his, seeking a reply.

"Upstairs," she managed.

"Aye." He released her and stepped slightly back. "We'll save the balcony for when we are more practiced with each other."

"For when there is no dinner on its way," she replied, obviously gathering herself, but still pluck to the backbone.

"We shall surely insult the cook and lose him."

"Sounds as if he's an uncomfortable sort to employ. Certainly Mudge, with his wide acquaintanceship and vast knowledge of these things, can find you someone better."

"No doubt." He sighed. He felt too pressed to dally any longer. "And now you must go abovestairs and let your lady's maid assist you. And here," he added, removing a silken pouch from his inner pocket and tucking it into her palm. "I never go without."

Again, she had almost an air of puzzlement as she searched his eyes. Then she smiled, a slight, surprising smile.

" 'Tis actually a good way to rid oneself of a tiresome cook."

His heart warmed to her brave smile and remark.

"You must also let me help you pick up your ring from the carpet before you go, my desire. The next time I see you, I expect you to wear little else."

Plucking up her blue skirts, Tressa fled up the stairs in such a hurry she almost flew on up to the third story before realizing she was now housed in the mistress's bedchamber on the middle floor, across from his lordship's quarters.

Reaching the closed door and knowing she had to collect herself because her new lady's maid waited within, Tressa stood a moment to catch her breath.

She hadn't understood half of what Braxton had said to her in the sitting room, especially on the tiny balcony, but she'd understood enough to keep her heart racing for days to come. She'd clearly understood his kisses, his boldly admitted intentions.

He meant to possess her.

Soon.

Inhaling deeply, not wanting to waste a moment's time in trying to prepare herself, she entered her room. If she allowed herself to admit it, it was indeed lovely, quiet and soothing despite its subtle opulence and hidden messages.

At this hour, the gilding appeared almost light itself, shining from the mirror frames, from the huge and heavily draped tester bed, even from the scattering of little chairs.

The middle-aged woman Mudge had hired for her arose from a chair and curtsied. After an exchange of greetings, Tressa placed the small silken pouch and little box Braxton had handed her onto the bedside table and gave herself over to the woman.

As quiet and soothing as the chamber itself, she helped Tressa out of her clothes and into a plain nightgown with full sleeves and a bit of lace at the neck. It was Tressa's best, but far from what would be expected in this place, farther still from Braxton's stated expectations—his wish that she wear nothing but the yellow diamond.

Trying to ignore her blush and relax, Tressa sat at the fanciful dressing table with its large mirror. The maid unpinned and brushed out Tressa's hair. Instead of braiding it for the night, she let it drift down Tressa's back to her waist. Indicating the warm water that waited in the dressing room, the woman withdrew, assuring Tressa that if she needed her, Tressa had only to ring her bell.

Tressa understood few, if any, of the temporary staff Mudge had hired would stay the nights on Pocket Street. This was a temporary situation—three days, despite Braxton's wishes.

After waiting just a little longer—endeavoring not to think about Braxton, of what was to come—Tressa at last rushed to the night table and the two packages there. She'd surely do as his lordship wanted and slip on the ring. But most of all, Tressa wondered what the little pouch contained.

Opening the drawstring, she released onto the polished table a collection of small dried sponges with strings and a vial. Even more perplexed, she uncorked the vial and cautiously sniffed it.

Vinegar.

She couldn't imagine what this unusual second gift could mean.

''I never go without it,'' he'd said.

It must be for him, then, she thought. Something he'd use and had merely wanted her to bring abovestairs with her.

But that didn't make sense.

She had no time to consider the odd assortment. Stuffing the sponges and vial back into the pretty little pouch, she decided to leave it on the table where he'd find it.

Finally, she again opened the box and slowly slid the ring

on her finger. Despite hoping desperately that it wouldn't fit, she found it did. Unaccustomed to its weight, to its awkward feel on her hand, she perched on the edge of the mattress behind her, holding the ring up to the lights in the room.

It caused no little awe in her, performing as it was supposed to do. Sparkling. Impressing.

Unfortunately, Braxton found her thus, fully impressed. After a soft but shocking rap, he swung in through the door, closing it behind him.

No longer in fine attire, nor in a blanket with a bare torso, he came toward her in a flowing silken dressing gown of midnight black. It swished around him, opening and closing, barely secured at his waist with a braided silken rope and gold tassels.

Unable to drag away her eyes, Tressa caught glimpses of his legs, his thighs, and his bare feet. The opening above the rope with its swinging tassels revealed a slice of his chest not quite large enough to display his nipples, only his dark, thick hair.

Tressa hardly noticed he carried a brandy decanter and a glass, one in each hand. Those he finally indicated by setting them on the nightstand next to her.

"I thought you might like some brandy. I surmise it's been some time for you, or at least you've done this little enough to need some liquid comfort. Of course, you made a good show of it in the sitting room just now. But . . . well, here it is all the same."

He walked around the room pinching out the candle flames.

"Not," he stated, "that I'm saying you shouldn't be nervous. You simply must let me know so I can be of help." He pinched out the final flame, except for those by the bedside, and blew on his fingers. "I'm quite prepared to slow down now. But talk to me. Have some brandy, please."

He stood for a moment, his dressing gown going silent, his

bare toes reminding Tressa that he wasn't an iron-eyed general, but a man about to bed a woman he didn't really know.

He was being thoughtful. His eyes told her so.

Did she dare tell him? No.

She'd kept up with him before, pleased him several times. She simply wanted to grasp the moment and stay courageous. Her ignorance, her innocence, wouldn't last for long before they'd be done with, without his knowing.

She was three and twenty. She'd decided.

Concentrating on the moment, Tressa admitted to herself that Braxton was beautiful. He *was* her desire.

"So," he said softly, "you're wearing more than my diamond, I see."

She smiled. "The ring's quite lovely . . . Hannibal. I'm sorry if I seemed less than respectful when you gave it to me. And I hope you don't mind"—she indicated her modest nightwear—"the gown, but I was . . . chilly."

He also smiled. "Chilly, eh? My little lady mistress." He stepped nearer, near enough to pick up her hand and, bending over her where she perched on the bed, to kiss it.

"My beautiful, perfect mistress," he murmured. He gathered her hair at her shoulder. "With her flowing, honey hair."

He bent to kiss her eyelids. "With her night-sky eyes."

He kissed her mouth. "With her sugared lips."

Her cheek. "With her spring-cream skin."

He touched her breast, waiting puckered beneath her nightgown. "With her breasts exactly fitted for my hands. I've longed to see," he added in a whisper at her ear, "the color and shape of your nipples."

His nipples.

Bronze and small, tucked into his dark hair. Yes, she longed to see his nipples, too, to touch them without a shirt between them.

With nothing between them.

Yes.

Sighing, Tressa fell back on the mattress, with Braxton following her down. He pursued her with his lips, this time softly, sweetly.

Chapter Eight

In his bed, Tressa had thought to be lulled into some dream of bliss.

As it was, she entered a shattering rush of pleasures she wanted to explore but could not. There were too many. They followed one another too quickly—Braxton's delicious warmth encompassing her, his wondrous weight pressing her into the soft, freshly laundered sheets, his desire, bald and unrestrained despite his evident attempts to coddle her.

Tressa, who had been raised a lady, had been taught never to peer at a man too long, especially not in a personal manner. With Braxton, she wanted to fill her eyes. She wanted to drink him in, to absorb his power, his strength.

His muscles were evident, hard beneath his silk gown. He was so different from her that she wanted only to look at him. But before she could, he'd moved on, taking her chance.

His kisses ranged from slow and tender to intense and deep and demanding. He'd abruptly recall himself only to lose control of his passion, over and over.

Tressa became the very center of his focus. As much as she couldn't believe it, she exulted in it. Whether his kisses seared her hungry soul or awakened her long sleeping body, she enjoyed them, learned from them, endeavored to return them.

When he got up from her to hover at the edge of the mattress in the candlelight, she read the passion rampant in his eyes— passion she had put there, passion she could feel unbridled inside.

Slowly, in the golden light, he untied the tasseled cord at his waist and let it slip to the floor. Slower yet, mating his eyes with hers, he let the midnight-black silk also slide to the carpet.

Boldly naked and as beautiful as a well-honed warrior, he claimed her with his iron-gray eyes, daring her to claim him, too.

For the first time, she faltered, blushed, and glanced away. She couldn't look at the manhood he wanted her to see. Worse yet, to disguise the cowardice which could only form in the heart of a virgin such as herself, she scrambled under the covers and sat bulwarked against the pillows.

Before he could join her back in the bed, however, she stayed him by wiggling enough to pull her nightgown over her head. But cowardice still ruled as she remained under the white, crisp sheets and pale yellow coverlet.

Flinging back the bedclothes, Braxton joined her. He grasped her to him, mercifully acknowledging her modesty by throwing the covers over them again. Even so, they were well and truly bedded together, she thought, feeling Braxton's—er, Hannibal's—nakedness along her own nude and heating body.

Just like the couple on their mattress under the clock face.

Soon Hannibal would be atop her.

Unaccustomed to touching another person, Tressa was skin to skin with Braxton, flesh to flesh, heartbeat to heartbeat. His kisses again escalated, taking her ability to think and tearing at her every reserve. She clung to him, seeking his heat, his nakedness, the odd combination exhibited in his smooth skin and the dark hair that gently abraded her flesh.

She wanted to truly, deeply grasp the moment, weld every move, every kiss, into her memory. Her "something" had come and would go, but she yearned to store it in her heart.

His hands stroked her, measuring her curves, plumping her breasts, arousing her nipples.

"They're pink and perfectly round," he whispered of those suddenly extremely sensitive and alive bits of herself.

Ducking beneath the covers, he seemed to study them before she followed her instincts and tugged the lace-edged sheet over them.

"You must have pink diamonds next time." His dark head reappeared from under the sheet, his generous mouth smiling. "Round pink diamonds set in earbobs so I can see them and recall your Christmas-candy nipples."

He lifted himself to kiss her lips, then to whisper to her once more. His gaze held hers with a gentle yet urgent warmth.

"And your sweet pink-candy blushes, too. By the very devil, I like pink, sweet candy called Tressa. But also by the devil, my Pink Sweet, I'm feeling cocked and ready to fire. We'll make it quick for me, then give you all the time you need, eh?" He spoke close to her ear. "All night for you after I'm off and can concentrate again."

He hung above her, obviously expecting a reply. Tressa nodded. She thought surely he meant to get atop her now, and readied herself to enjoy his warmth and weight, to try to understand what he'd meant by a pistol going off.

She shivered at the idea of a pistol going off.

Mistaking her shiver, Hannibal did in fact slide atop her.

"I'll warm you. Never fear."

She didn't. She reveled in the pleasure she read in his handsome, softening features. It delighted her that she had pushed him beyond control and concentration.

He locked his eyes to hers, nudged her legs apart with his

knee, and settled himself more comfortably, more seriously, into the natural harbor her body made for his.

He rocked against her delightfully.

She watched his eyes close, then drift open again, foggy gray with desire. That part of him she had only glimpsed was between them and very hard.

And then she wasn't sure what happened.

Somehow his hand got in the way and pierced her so as to make her cry out.

It had been so delightful—then suddenly so sharply painful that tears welled in her eyes.

Just as quickly, he was off her, out of the bed. Standing in the candlelight, he examined that part of himself that was surely the pistol. Then he looked back at her on the sheets.

He peered at her, incredulous.

"There's blood. You're a virgin, damn and blast."

Tressa came up on her elbows. "I-I . . ."

"Did you manage the sponge, by God?"

"The—no, I . . ."

"Thank heavens I didn't seed you. I never, never go off without a sponge."

Tressa didn't think she'd ever seen anyone more angry than Braxton was. But his anger was controlled—by his incredulity, likely.

"Here." He jerked back the covers, exposing Tressa on the sheets. "Let me see."

She reached for the top sheet, tugging it back to her. "See? See what? There's nothing to see."

"There's blood on me, ma'am, and it can only have come from you. What I know about virgins can be put in a thimble. Let me see."

"No." She curved around the linen and held it tight.

He pulled it away. "Let me see, I say. I came at you like a bull, for God's sake. I've certainly ripped you apart."

"I'm just fine, and there's little to no blood. Women must survive this quite nicely all the time."

Staring at her, he was the cold, hard, iron-eyed general. With an exasperated huff, he dropped the sheet and turned away from her. She covered herself properly.

He plucked up his dressing gown and wrapped himself in it tightly before securing it with his tasseled tie. Then he started to pace. Each time he came in her direction, he sent her a dark glower.

"I can only thank my stars I didn't seed you."

She didn't reply.

"And what of this fellow, this one with whom you had a brief liaison?"

"There was no fellow."

"But you said—"

"No, *you* said. You wove that little tale about my having someone."

"But why didn't you—"

"Set you straight?" Tressa warmed to her subject. She could feel the heat in her cheeks again, only this time she didn't blush. She was as angry as he was.

"I tried to tell you, but you wouldn't listen. You made your little judgments about me, told your little story, and seemed quite satisfied in it no matter what the truth might have been."

He didn't like her reply. He pivoted away from her to pace again, the sway of his dressing gown reflecting his extreme agitation.

"A virgin," he grumbled. "A lady." He said it as a nasty word.

"I am no longer a virgin, my lord." Tressa spoke stoutly. "And ladies do not make their own way in the world."

He kept striding, unanswering.

There was nothing to be said. She wished he'd go and be done with it.

"So," he declared, stationing himself beside the bed and

tightening the tie at his waist to ensure his decency, "you must do me the honor, ma'am, of accepting my hand in marriage."

If Braxton had thrown a bucket of horse trough water on her, Tressa couldn't have been more stunned. Her mouth opened, but she spoke nary a word. Even thoughts wouldn't form in her mind.

"You are a lady, Miss Devlin," he ground out. "You are a virgin."

"But you, marry a lady who's no longer a lady? A virgin who's no longer a virgin?"

"I felt your maidenhead give way. I have bloodied us both."

"With blood tainted by scandal and madness. By my father's . . . suicide."

He lifted a shoulder. "Your bloodlines are older than mine, finer than mine. Unquestioned before Buck Devlin. He must have been the exception to prove the rule."

"But you don't want to marry."

"I do things I don't want to do all the time, Miss Devlin."

"But I don't want to marry, either."

"You want to fetch and carry all your days, no doubt."

He twisted his words into purest sarcasm.

The gaze he sliced at her cut deep.

"I," she said, "appreciate an independence even you can't claim."

Again he ripped her with cynicism. "Independence? When you're tied to one old woman after another? Better to be tied to me. Once I have my heir off you, I will leave you be."

"But we'll end up as your parents did, at Cannongate, firing rockets at each other as we are now."

Shrugging again, he turned away from her.

"No," said Tressa. "I have the right to refuse you and I do so, clearly and definitely."

When he walked to the door and grasped its handle, Tressa's heart plummeted. He never would have guessed, though. Her blood was up. Her courage returned. From her place beneath the covers, despite being naked, she held his hard gaze.

"Then I bid you good-bye, ma'am. If I had seeded you, I would drag you to the nearest anvil in Scotland. As it is, I will apologize and bid you farewell. You may remain here the three days you have left before going on to your new and unidentified post. But if you wish to move into temporary accommodations such as the Crown and Feathers, I'll gladly pay the shot."

With that, Braxton, like a general, left the room and firmly shut the door.

Late into the evening, even as midnight approached, Tressa waited for Braxton, sitting on the front stairs in her plain night rail and dressing gown with her candle beside her.

A determination she'd never known kept her there. She would see him, would talk to him, no matter how late it got.

The night before, he'd begun to make love to her only to discover she was a virgin. All that day, as if to demonstrate what he'd said, he'd avoided her. He'd meant his final good-bye.

Oddly, though, he hadn't left for Cannongate.

While Tressa had long ago given up the idea of marrying— marriage was something she seldom thought about, really— marrying remained impossible.

Braxton would be the only man she'd ever know intimately. For Braxton's own safety, marriage was impossible. For fear her husband might learn his secret, her Uncle Straith would destroy her husband—and then destroy her.

No, marriage was out of the question.

However, a small part of that "something" she'd always dreamed about could still be realized—if, that was, she could stay strong and face Braxton, no matter how embarrassing it might be initially. If she could stand up to him and say her piece, becoming his mistress would be the easy part.

Admittedly, she'd played a role in his having been misled. When he'd woven a story because she wouldn't tell him her real story, when he'd assumed she'd had at least one male partner and she allowed him to assume that, well, she'd had a role in misleading him.

His shock at finding her a virgin had been most evident in his handsome features and his general's eyes.

Last night he'd desired her. Desire had marked his features and eyes, had colored his voice with a soft rasp.

Candy pink, he'd called her nipples. Like Christmas sweets.

He'd been taken with her, and surely that could be the case again. She wanted, with all her being, for it to be so.

From Mudge, Tressa had learned Braxton had hired his own carriage that night. Because they hadn't eaten the cook's meal the evening before, the temperamental man had quit, leaving the kitchen particularly quiet after the stir he'd caused.

But Tressa knew the cook's exit had little to do with Braxton's having gone out. The long-case clock struck once and lightning scoured the sky almost simultaneously, but she heard his lordship's coach above the driving rain.

Tonight, he didn't call farewell to his coachman. After the splashing sounds of the equipage faded away, he didn't walk through the front door, either. Worried on top of being anxious, Tressa unlocked the barrier only to discover Braxton on the other side, key in hand, somewhat in a muddle.

If he was surprised to see her, he didn't let on. He was drenched, of course. When he came into the small entryway, its dust covered hulk still vigilant in the corner, he dripped rain from his black evening cloak.

To see Braxton less than immaculate struck Tressa as odd. He removed his cape terribly inefficiently, and dropped his hat so that it rolled on the black and white flooring. She met his eyes in the light of her candle.

"Foxed," he said belligerently. "Best stay out of my way, Miss Devlin."

"I need to talk to you, sir . . . Hannibal."

Leaving his outerwear in a less than neat pile on the banister rail, he walked to the hall table and attempted the tinderbox Mudge had left for him.

Scant hope of managing that, Tressa told herself, watching him for a moment. To see the more than competent Braxton this way struck Tressa as odder and odder.

"Pray, sir . . . Hannibal. Let me light our way up."

"Naw, naw," he said. "Can light my own cursed candle."

So he was still angry.

She plunged ahead, painfully observing him as he struck the flints, waiting for the cotton-wool inside the box to catch fire. Finally, she grasped her opportunity.

"I'm sorry about what happened last night. I apologize for allowing you to think I—"

"Go to bed, Miss Devlin. 'Pology accepted."

"But I want . . ." She ended up exasperated. "Let me light your candle with mine—although I'm sure you'll set the house afire in your state."

"Haven't been in this state for years and years," he said loftily. "All of a sudden it jus' made cursed good sense."

"Yes, well, you're at a point where you're making little sense at all, and I've decided to carry the candle. You'll have all you can do to get yourself up the risers."

When she removed the tinderbox from his fingers, he straightened and gazed measuredly at the stairs. Knowing she watched, he was sure to make a good show of it. Indeed, tugging straight his white marcella waistcoat, he addressed the stairs with some normalcy.

But it cost him. By the fifth riser, he abruptly stuck out his hand and grabbed the handrail.

Tressa, who was ahead of him with the candle, glanced at him. "I daresay you won't recall anything I have to say come morning. But I should like—"

"And I should like to take you to my bed and strip you of

those deuced nunnish nightclothes. By the light of the blaze they'll cause, I'll make mad love to you." He peered at her as levelly as he could. "But I won't. Promised myself, so I won't."

Lightning flashed. By the time the thunder rolled away, he and Tressa had reached the middle-floor landing, where they turned into the passageway between their bedchambers.

"That is, in fact, my point, sir . . . Hannibal."

Slowing in front of his door, he peered at her quizzically.

"Your point, Miss Devlin?"

"I've decided I want to be your mistress—for the rest of the summer, if you'd like."

"Can't do it. Promised myself. Don't ever, ever break promises. Besides, virgins ain't mistresses."

"I'll warrant every mistress was a virgin at one time."

He peered at her, obviously trying to take her point or come up with his own.

"Promised myself. You're a lady."

"I think I'm best suited to decide my own future, Hannibal."

He opened the door to his bedchamber. She followed him in with the candle.

When she moved to the candles at his bedside, lighting them one by one, he surprised her by falling across the mattress, face down, clothes on and all.

"Hannibal?"

When he snored as a reply, she blew out his lights and left the room.

Even so, she remained determined.

Hannibal entered the stable fairly early the next morning. He had quite a head and felt he had something important to remember, but he was anxious to get away from the little house. There was no cook to serve him breakfast, and he needed something on his stomach, or at least, a bumper from the Crown and Feathers.

Feeling irritated enough because he'd barely managed his toilette with starchy old Mudge grumbling about, he saw Knobby was eager to talk. The boy was working out well in the stable, but he had a tendency to trap Hannibal with his light talk and bright blue eyes.

The boy, in fact, seemed to be trying to make a point with him here of late. He was likely a whore's whelp, of course. Street urchins usually were, and he'd asked Hannibal several times if he wasn't familiar with the name Hill.

"Ya see, Gov', me mum's name was Bet Hill. Do you remember a Bet Hill?"

"Bet Hill?" Braxton's mind was foggy enough. "No, I don't recall a Bet Hill, Knobby."

"Elizabeth Hill," the boy declared, his unusually bright blue eyes riveted to Braxton's less sure gaze.

"If you'll fetch Saracen, Knobby—"

"Sure thing, Gov'." The boy seemed disappointed nonetheless. "He's all ready for ya, Gov'."

Bet Hill. Bet Hill. The name rang through Braxton's brain until he reached the inn. It seemed familiar, but he couldn't place it. Besides, he didn't want to place it. He had too much of importance on his dish. If he hadn't feared for Miss Devlin's safety in being alone for the next three days, he would have left for Devonshire.

As on the evening before, Braxton ordered a carriage and went out. Tressa, dressed in her plain nightclothes, sat in the small entry with a candle, anticipating his return. She remained stubborn about speaking to him when he made some sense, and since he'd avoided her all day again, she waited.

In this case, it was well after two when he came in, his dark evening attire swirling around him like threatening weather.

"Foxed," he announced, as she got to her feet.

"I'll light you up. You may not recall, Hannibal, but last night—"

With his outerwear in a haphazard pile on the banister, he addressed the staircase as he had the night before while also interrupting her.

"If it was mine to do, I'd have you out of those cursed nightclothes in a trice and under me in my bed."

"Yes, so you said last night. Indeed, there's nothing to hinder you, Hannibal. As I told you, I'm ready to become your mistress."

They'd attained the top of the stairs, and he stopped to peer at her. His gray eyes were decidedly unfocused, and when it seemed he might fall backward down the stairs, Tressa grabbed his elbow and guided him toward his bedchamber.

"Do you understand me, Hannibal? I'm prepared to be your mistress."

"Can't," he said, mulishly setting his jaw.

"I know you've promised yourself you won't, but—"

"Promised myself?"

Now, he was truly puzzled.

She ignored his puzzlement, as well as her own perplexity.

"Can't bed you," he said. "You're a cursed lady. Want to, but can't."

They'd reached his room. Once again, even with her help in lighting his way, he closed in on his bed, fell across it, and was immediately fast asleep.

With a sigh, and knowing she had only one more day and evening before she had to leave for the Swallows', Tressa also went to bed.

"Mudge?"

Braxton stood in the all too bright morning light pouring in through his dressing-room window. He was endeavoring to shave himself without cutting his own throat while also managing to keep his blasted head upright.

The retainer, who moved about picking up after him, glanced at Hannibal disapprovingly in the shaving stand mirror.

"Aye, me lord?"

"You know where Miss Devlin is going, don't you? I mean, in her new posting."

"I do, me lord."

"I don't suppose you'd be willing to tell—"

"No, me lord."

The old bogey.

Hannibal knew the man was loyal, and he was glad for that. To a large extent, he even trusted Miss Devlin to the sturdy, reliable fellow's keeping.

But Hannibal was unaccustomed to being unable to earn a fellow's regard. This man, with his wise old eyes and numerous fine qualities, simply wouldn't be won.

Not that Hannibal wanted to win him away from Miss Devlin, either. He didn't. He simply didn't want . . .

Well, if he hung on for one more day, she'd be gone to a place he knew nothing about. Then he'd leave for Cannongate.

He'd forget her.

"Mudge?" Finally finished with his razor and wiping away the last of his shaving soap with a hot towel, he forced the elder man to meet his eyes in the glass again. "What of this boy Knobby?"

"What of him, me lord?"

"What do you know of him? How did you come to hire him?"

"He's just a street boy, me lord, like so many others. He hung about at the Crown and Feathers, talking with the ostlers and doing what they'd let him do when they were busy. They said he had a natural hand with the horses, and when you needed someone like tha', I spoke to him. Seemed very glad, he did, to have the place. Has he done something amiss, me lord?"

"No, no, nothing amiss. He merely mentioned his mother's name was Bet Hill. She's dead now, I think."

"Don't know anything about the boy but what I've said. Nor about his mum, me lord. If you want me to have a talk with the lad—"

"No, no, I can talk to him. We won't be long for this place in any case."

"No, me lord, not long at all."

Tressa didn't catch sight or sound of Braxton all day on her final day at Pocket Street. Mudge told her he hadn't seen him either, not since he'd left that morning. The only indication of any intention on his part to return were the possessions in his rooms.

"Still," Mudge had said, "he could well have his things collected by someone else or even abandon them altogether."

After waiting on the stairs with her candle until nearly three of the morning, she went abovestairs and lay across her bed. She and Mudge were packed. They planned to go to the City, to the Swallows', before even the hawkers were out, the better to fool Joe Legg.

They'd wait until a decent hour, of course, to present themselves to the Swallow family.

She'd lie down for a while. Evidently Braxton wouldn't return while she was there, and she needed her reserves to vacate the little house.

Her "something" had indeed been brief, but also a treasure she'd always remember and keep close to her heart.

The mistress's bedchamber on Pocket Street had become oddly her own over her short stay there. In the light of her single wallowing candle, the soft solace offered by the chamber embraced her. The sounds from the garden below, its sweet mixture of scents, had reached their most mellow. The large cheval glass reflected her flame in its gilding, a reminder that past occupants of this room had examined themselves in its surface.

Goodness knew what else it had witnessed. She couldn't imagine any of it, and her own chance had come and gone.

Abruptly, a thump interrupted her sadly drifting thoughts. Braxton closed the door downstairs, then made his way up.

Wanting to dash to him before he entered his bedchamber, she had everything she could do not to grasp this final opportunity to speak to him. She might find herself reduced to begging.

Listening, listening to the old house with which she'd grown so familiar, she heard him at her door, saw the handle turn.

From across the room, he peered at her on the bed.

"Awake?" he whispered.

"Yes."

"Foxed."

"I'm not surprised."

He came in and closed the door. Making straight for her bed, he fell on it as she'd seen him do two nights in a row onto his own. Fortunately, he must have left his candle in the corridor, else they'd have been alight.

Tressa couldn't help her quick small smile. She gazed at him, lying full out and wholly dressed—although somewhat rumpled for Braxton—along the bottom of her mattress amid a welter of sheets.

She expected to find his gray eyes already shut, to hear him snore. But his gray eyes were slitted, intent on her.

"Been at the jeweler's all day and night. Hanging over him, drinking, while he did what I asked."

His fist opened and out tumbled a pair of earbobs. Tressa picked them up. They were delicately fashioned, perfectly round, beautifully faceted pink diamonds set in gold drops.

Pink candy. Whore's fare at its finest.

"Stay with me," he murmured when she looked at him.

Smiling softly, she nodded. "For a while."

He seemed relieved, if not exactly satisfied. He heaved a heavy sigh.

Again she thought his eyes would close and that would be the end of it.

But his voice next sounded far off. His gaze slid away from her face.

"Cursed awful, terrible thing, Tressa. I think I have a son out there. A street urchin. On his own for years now. Barely getting by."

Tressa was so shocked she didn't know what to say.

Braxton continued, almost pleading with her—Braxton, a man who didn't plead.

"Must promise me if I get you with child, you'll let me know as soon as you know. We'll marry and make it legitimate as soon as may be."

This promise she couldn't pledge. She couldn't marry him and endanger him. She'd ensure she didn't have a child, just as he wished.

Her failure to make him this last promise drifted into a silence, a silence that comforted nonetheless.

Finally, as she watched, he gave in, closed his eyes, and, slept—deeply, immediately, as he had the former two nights when he'd been inebriated.

Still stunned and saddened despite knowing she'd be with Hannibal for a bit longer, Tressa placed the earbobs on the nightstand beside the ring box. She covered herself and Braxton as best she could, and blew out the light.

She couldn't marry.

No more than he would.

But for now, as the dawn crept in, Braxton slumbered at her feet.

Chapter Nine

Slowly, Braxton opened an eye. For a moment, he didn't know in whose bed he slept. It had been a long time since he'd been with a woman.

Miss Dear.

Lifting his head, he saw it was indeed her bed he shared, only in a peculiar manner. He'd slept like a stone on the sheets at the bottom of her mattress. Her sweet curves were outlined above him. Her head, with its grand sweep of honey-colored hair, rested on the bolster and pillows.

Carefully pushing himself to a seated position, he felt cloth-headed. He hadn't been foxed in years, and for three days in a row he'd been drunk as a wheelbarrow.

He remained dressed as he'd been yesterday, and the crocheted covering Miss Dear had thrown over him slid to the floor. He still wore his boots, and his beard was rough. His knot, although askew, rode beneath his chin.

He was exactly where he wanted to be, with the woman he

wanted to be with, and he didn't want to recall anything else about the night before or even the last three days.

Miss Dear had agreed to stay with him, and he was prepared to deuced well enjoy it to the hilt, despite her neatly packed bags sitting by the door.

He'd start, of course, by remaining as he was and drinking in the look of her. She was an innocent, and he wanted to embrace her as such before he taught her otherwise.

It would be his enormous pleasure to introduce her to . . . he didn't wish to consider that, either. He'd concentrate instead on the present and what they'd have together. Anything beyond the now, anything beyond the walls of the house on Pocket Street, he'd close out of his mind.

He wanted Miss Dear too badly to allow it to be spoiled.

Carefully, Braxton eased up from the mattress, his eyes still locked to her sleep-flushed face. In removing his boots, which wasn't a quiet job, he realized she slept soundly. Tugging himself out of his coat as he stood over her bed in the dazzling sunlight, he saw her silken blond lashes didn't so much as flutter.

Unwinding his cravat brought him to his own sleep-warmed skin while he longed for hers, but she was bundled up in a coverlet, her dressing gown, and voluminous nightclothes.

Waking her sweetly, undressing her with every care, was all he desired. He'd never possessed a woman who was completely his from the start. While he'd hardly considered that idea in the past, it pleased him immensely.

With Miss Devlin . . .

With Miss Dear . . .

Nude at last, Hannibal gingerly lifted the pale yellow coverlet and settled beside her. He'd wanted her since he'd first seen her, her loveliness, her innocence, her satiny inner self.

* * *

Tressa found herself awakening to what had to be the bright
heart of a summer's day. The sun was ablaze, illuminating the
bedchamber, gilding it with light. It caught in the velvet drapes,
turning them to mellow golden shafts. It pierced the lace, scattering it across the bed in a rich, shadowy pattern.

The garden, with its own leafy green laces, its colorful tiny
blazes of red and orange and yellow, surely burned under the
same sun, sending up fragrances steamy and deep.

But it wasn't the sun's afternoon heat that aroused her. It
was Braxton's heat. He had the sun's fire in his fingertips, the
very fingertips that stroked her cheek. He bore the heat of desire
in his gray eyes, and it burned into her.

Not fully awake, not expecting this so soon and especially
not in bright daylight, she heard her own voice, soft and thick
from resting.

"Surely, sir, everyone's up and about."

He smiled. "And not a single one matters."

"But Mudge and I were to leave."

"And now you will not."

"I must at least speak to Mudge."

"If anyone knows what's afoot here, my little Miss Dear,
it's Mudge."

Tressa's thoughts settled uncomfortably around her original
complaint. "But this is broad daylight."

"My sweet Miss Dear, you are a mistress now, and mistresses
have rules by which they abide that are different from those
the rest of us follow."

Tressa had the sense his lordship half teased her. Still, she
struggled with the circumstances. She'd expected evening to
fall before she saw him again, had thought there would be
another dinner and preferably good conversation.

She hoped to be courted and convinced by this man, not to
suddenly find him next to her, the very summer's heat, naked.
Naked beside her, and breathing his sultry summer's air in
every word.

"So, your first rule, ma'am, is to be prepared for whenever he's . . . er, inclined. With you, of course, you need but appear, and he's certain to be . . . er, inclined."

Tressa was as bedazzled by Braxton as she was by the mellow heat. He was halfway funning her. Wasn't he?

She stared across the pillows into his eyes—so close, so gray, so thickly lashed.

"Of course, it's best for *him* when you want *him*, too."

This *him* was Braxton. That Tressa knew.

"It would please him if you liked his body, although naturally he's going to like yours far better. You must train yourself to look at him, not to shy away when he's naked, which he'll likely be a good bit of the time. You must also learn to tantalize when you're in his company, especially in bed."

He said this as an insinuation, moving his hands beneath the silky, sliding coverlet. Not surprisingly, he worked at the closings on her nightclothes, mercifully leaving the coverlet as much in place as possible.

"You must understand I intend to save your blushes when I can," he said, "and, I'm concerned about this day's growth of beard. I promise this won't happen to your flawless skin again. But you must, if you will, sit up so we can remove all this clothing."

Tressa slowly rose to a seated position. So did Braxton.

He smiled again, making quick work of tugging off the dressing gown and night rail, consigning them to the floor as Tressa replaced the puffy coverlet. The sensation of its delicious smoothness sliding, whispering along the length of her body, awakened every inch of her own shameless heat.

"I've soaked one of the sponges with some vinegar," he said, causing a rush of blood to her cheeks.

His consideration reached her as surely as his heat. The iron-eyed general had all but vanished, leaving in his place a considerate lover, as gentle as any new groom.

That he needed to explain the use of the sponge to ensure

there would be no child was embarrassing enough. That he had to describe the workings of her own body heightened her coloring to what would surely become permanent. That he was the one to insert the sponge—reassuringly, tenderly—resulted in a quick, surprising turn of emotions in Tressa.

Beneath the pale, sighing coverlet, he became her lover again and her thoughts readily followed. That place in her that he caressed with his fingers fixed itself in their minds. Their union, something akin to the night when he'd taken her maidenhead and had left her, recoiling with shock, solidified as their mutual goal.

Tressa desired Braxton, too.

She couldn't deny it, and he read her well.

Matching the sculpted wall of his chest to her soft, giving breasts, he mated his lips to her lips. His hands brought her into his hard male part between them. Now she understood his signal.

She guessed he might be more ready for their mating than he wanted to be as her instructor. The fire was back in his touch and in his gray eyes. His glance was a little dangerous, warning her.

Heat-drenched, he settled on her, seeping into her very skin, her pores, possessing her. His lips prowled over her face and throat, downward to her breasts. He tasted her there—one nipple, then the other. He sucked her, laved her with his tongue.

Teaching her. Teaching her.

She was made for more than just herself.

She was made for him and his pleasure. In return for that pleasure, he lavished a like pleasure on her.

She melted under his relentless heat. She merged with him. His heat became like a second skin to her. His eyes seared hers, sapping her will. He blanketed her with long, hot kisses. He claimed her, made her his with the fire in his touch.

For Tressa, there was no longer a question of modesty, only

the mellow blaze. She kicked at the coverlet and let it slip away.

He became her covering. He became her lover between her legs. He became one with her, taking her not with pain, but with the brilliance of the sun.

She reveled in being made his.

She exalted in the intense joy she gave him when he suddenly swayed above her, peering down at her, all male satisfaction. He collapsed onto her, kissed her, then rolled off her. Breathing heavily, he turned his head on the pillow to peer at her, his eyes welling with a soft gray passion.

"Now that that's done, we shall have all the time in the world for your pleasure, sweetings."

Tressa forced herself to remain as she was, as naked as a babe, exposed to his gaze and slick from his heat. "I'm quite pleased already."

His bark of sudden laughter told her she'd said something amiss.

She deplored her ignorance. She determined, then, to learn from this amazing instructor of hers. She'd attend to him closely. She'd hang on every word, each physical nuance.

She'd become his true mistress, the woman of his pleasure—such a mistress as he'd never forget, just as she'd never forget him.

When he fixed his eyes to hers, she saw something resembling tenderness again. He rolled back in her direction and began to stroke her, but not with the same fire in his touch.

Oh, he was an expert. She knew enough already to grasp that. Briefly, she wondered about the women he'd bedded in becoming such an expert.

He knew, it seemed, precisely where and when and how to touch her, knew about her own body, about her desire, about her deepest, most unattended core.

She'd be his best mistress ever, all right.

In doing so, she'd close out the other women, both those

who had gone before and those who would come after her. She'd also forget that brief, regretful mention of a baseborn son, one Braxton had likely just discovered.

Fortunately, it was easy to forget.

Braxton was bringing her to brilliant heat again—in this case, the heat in herself. The wizard worked his fingers just so, at a particularly swollen, achy spot between her legs she'd never known.

He kissed her.

He coaxed her.

He carried her to the heat.

She gasped for breath, felt wildly that she must step over a precipice and fall to . . . to what? At the precipice, instead of falling, she took wing and flew up to the very brilliance of the sun itself, up and up into the immense satisfaction expressed in Braxton's dove-soft gray eyes.

They'd spent two days in bed. They'd made love as often as comfortably possible, doing nothing else but what was necessary to stay alive. Braxton had treated his Miss Dear as if she were a young wife.

He wanted to lavish all he could on her.

She was everything he could want. While she kept something of herself to herself, she gave the rest wholeheartedly, generously, sweetly, innocently.

To pick up even the barest threads of his life went against his grain. But for fear of wearing Miss Dear to the bone—and himself, too, of course—well, because he wanted to drape her in diamonds and lay gold at her sweet little feet . . .

Noting his own half smile in the shaving mirror in his dressing room, Braxton turned to Mudge to accept his gloves, hat, and cane.

"I hope you're satisfied here, Mudge."

The fellow merely nodded, keeping his distance through a formality he refused to drop.

"I appreciate all you've done, especially in finding a cook and hiring Rosemary for Miss Dear. Rosemary is precisely what we need for her."

"Since Rosemary worked for Miss Lovelace, the woman who lived here just before we came, I thought she'd sort out well, sir."

"Once again, you are right, Mudge."

Mudge waited, obviously wondering why Braxton didn't hie himself off.

In wanting to lavish what he could on Miss Dear, he'd had all he could do to talk her into a trip to the modiste.

"So, Mudge," he said.

"The carriage has just come over from Mayfair, me lord. It's in the street."

"Yes, but I want to ask you . . ."

Feeling completely unlike himself, Braxton forced himself on.

"As I've told you, Knobby informed me his mother's name was Bet Hill. Since hearing the name again, in fact, I've recollected that I was with a Bet Hill—Elizabeth Hill—some dozen years ago."

Mudge appeared decidedly uncomfortable. He shifted his weight, but listened nonetheless.

"In recalling this Bet Hill, I also remember she was a good woman, one who, I think, would have considered her boy more than just another cast-off. In other words, I'm thinking she might have had him baptized if she could have."

The man's wise old eyes held Braxton's as he nodded and said, "I see, me lord."

"I can't say what parish church she might have attended, but I thought you might have an idea as to where—"

"Aye, me lord. If I were you, I'd check the open register at the Church of St. George's Wells. 'Tis a very old church, abandoned by its parish and reopened to serve those tha' feels they need such a place, but who might not be accepted anywhere. St. George's might have a record of the lad's birth date. Don't know of anybody else who keeps such records, and they've been open now for a long time.''

"Thank you, Mudge, both for your help and your discretion.''

"Aye, me lord.''

Funnily, Braxton recognized how much he trusted this man without having much in return from him.

They'd been having breakfast—in bed, of course, something Hannibal had run down and fetched from the larder, no more than fresh milk and strawberries, bread and butter—when he'd said they must go out to the modiste's, the jeweler's, and the shoemaker's.

All of them special vendors, naturally, discreet and accustomed to serving those who relied on discretion.

Tressa had been shocked.

"Vendors for mistresses alone?'' she'd inquired.

"Indeed,'' Hannibal had said. "Where there's money to be made, my sweet, it's made.''

Tressa hadn't wanted to go. She still didn't.

The sweet summer's day did not beckon her out to the shops. It called her, perhaps, to a little dalliance in the overgrown garden, or to a walk with Hannibal up to the tea garden and then to her room again.

Truly, she was a natural mistress. Worse, she reveled in learning what Hannibal had to teach her. She wished no more than to be with him. She enjoyed his conversation as much as she did his beautiful, warm body.

Unfortunately, he'd had his way.

He found her ready and waiting in the little entry. As he

came down the stairs, she could view him fully, and he looked as wonderful in his clothes as he did out of them.

Beneath the highly polished boots, she knew, his feet were large, nicely arched, and well kept. She'd heard, from some mention on one of her walks, that his balustraded calf was the envy of numerous London gentlemen. His knees, from which swung the silken ties of his yellow breeches called Inexpressibles, could have been sculpted. As she also could easily picture now, his thighs were thick and powerful from the riding he did.

His belly was flat, his navel neat, his bottom rounded yet trim. The waist beneath his waistcoat could be easily spanned by her arms and hands as she nestled her cheek into his broad, warm, deeply shadowed chest.

His arms were a delight when they enclosed her. His hands, now in tight-fitting dark gloves, were also suitable for the sculptor's chisel and hammer. His shoulders, smoothly fitted by his blue coat, were broad and simply lovely, her favorite part of him—if she had one. His back was muscled, corded with strength.

No doubt about it, his dark hair shaded a noble forehead. His gray eyes beneath dark eyebrows could arrest with a single glance. His nose, aristocratic and with great distinction, marked him as a Lord of Braxton, or so she'd had it from Robert.

In a word, the marquess was perfection. There wasn't a single thing about him she didn't like, and that included that amazing part of him she hadn't fully examined as yet—that part that could be hard, then soft. The part that gave them both such pleasure.

Yes, she was fast outgrowing her modesty. But that part— well, she'd get around to being comfortable with it. She was his mistress, and she intended to be the very best he'd ever had or would ever have.

For now, he seemed satisfied, and he was very good to her. Too good to her.

Taking her elbow, and with a slight, respectful tip of his hat, he ushered her through the front door as Mudge closed it behind them. They were off to the modiste's. Braxton's own crested town carriage—sleek and black, with a dancing, matched pair of bays and two attendants who kept their eyes from her—waited.

"Thought I might as well have it sent round," he said as a liveried footman dressed in gold and black assisted them with the steps.

Like everything that belonged to the marquess, the coach was the latest in fashion and comfort, and remarkably kept.

"Just one coachman and footman, though, so we'll have to let them do their business while we do ours in the shops. They'll have to keep moving, circling the block, and we might have to wait a minute or two. John Coachman will need the footman, so we won't have anyone to carry for us."

"There won't be so much—"

"There will be quite a lot. I want you to have whatever you wish."

"But I don't wish."

"And I say there are two more rules you must note, my sweet Miss Dear. Firstly, a man wants to bring his lady-love . . . well, things. He wants to dress her according to his taste, and he wants her to like what he gives her."

"I've hardly had an opportunity to wear the ring and earbobs, my lord."

Tressa well knew Hannibal had been disappointed by her reactions to the diamonds. Whore's fare, she'd called them, and well they were. She had a point, too.

He could hardly expect her to wear diamonds to bed, and that's where they'd been for the last pair of days and nights.

"Besides, diamonds, especially the ones you've chosen, hardly go with my wardrobe."

"And thus the new wardrobe, ma'am."

Tressa allowed him his points, as well. She focused on the

sights outside the open windows. London streets, crowded with all sorts of people, on foot and in a wide assortment of conveyances, made for a busy, noisy scene.

"Aren't you afraid, sir," she couldn't help asking, "that someone will recognize you out and about with me, particularly in your own carriage?"

"'Tis summer, and London grows more light of company every day. Besides, we will stay clear of Mayfair and the shops most frequented by anyone who might recognize me. Except, that is," he said, smiling at her—nay, grinning at her—"for one surprise I shall not discuss."

Since she shared the forward-facing banquette with him, she could view him in every detail. Simply sharing a carriage with him privately, much less sharing the same seat, was unheard of in the polite world. As it was, though, she was additionally veiled. From the outside looking in, she would be named for what she was—Braxton's latest paramour.

Most people who knew him would be surprised he'd remained in London. But most would recognize he'd taken some time for himself and his most closely held, if not entirely hidden, pleasure, his mistress.

Braxton had obviously mounted a new mistress, it would be said, this one unknown to all the world.

Tressa could have shivered. Whereas she was as sure as Braxton that most of his acquaintances, if they did happen to spy him, would leave them alone, she had to consider again what possibilities they were opening for Joe Legg and her uncle.

Not many, she honestly supposed.

She and Braxton would remain in parts of London where she wouldn't normally be found. Anyway, she was as much in disguise as ever. She wore her veil, a thick one this time, and Braxton accepted that.

Mistresses, better mistresses, regularly wore veils. Even

ladies wore veils upon occasion. Absorbing the activity in the streets through that very barrier, Tressa posed her question.

"And the second rule, my lord?"

"Hannibal. You must use Hannibal."

"Even when outside the house?"

"No more my lording, my sweet. I'll use Miss Dear when in the hearing of others. You may use sir then. But no more formalities, for heaven's sake. We're past the formalities, are we not?"

Tressa blushed, even after two days, even beneath her veil.

"And what's this second rule you were speaking about, sir?"

"The basic rule in being a mistress is to accommodate yourself to what *he* likes, to what *he* wants."

"You are alluding, I suppose, to the fact that I refuse to sign your contracts."

"It is precisely for your future security that I've had the contracts drawn up."

He was exasperated with her again, and she could understand why. They'd gone round and round about her refusal to sign his contracts.

"I want no security aside from what I earn for myself, my lord."

"Hannibal."

"Hannibal. I want my independence. If I wish to leave Pocket Street, I shall simply leave. If you wish me to go, you have only to say so. That's the agreement I want between us. One of equals."

"But I've agreed to that, too. I'm merely interested in your own good. Anyone will say the contracts are—"

"Most generous. I understand that, and I thank you. But I will not sign them."

When Tressa heard his frustrated huff, she kept her gaze to the view outside the windows. They'd arrived at the modiste's, the establishment of Madame Henri.

* * *

"Gunter's! For ices? But Gunter's is in Berkeley Square."
Braxton smiled smugly at Tressa's exclamation.

Across the parcels that separated them on the carriage seat—
the other seat was full, as well—she stared heatedly back at
him.

" 'Tis my surprise," he repeated. "A little birdie told me—"

"Who's this birdie?"

"Doro, in fact. She told me you quite like the ices at Gunter's.
You and the late Dowager Lady Farronby enjoyed them frequently during an afternoon's carriage drive, and you brought
back ices to her ladyship's house for the staff. A very nice
treat, I've heard."

"From a wonderful lady." Tressa's eyes followed the familiar scene as the carriage drew nearer and nearer to Berkeley
Square.

Torn between wanting to see the graceful old square again,
between the idea of having an ice and the knowledge that they'd
enter the very heart of a summer afternoon's society, Tressa
glanced at Braxton.

Despite her veiling, he read her dismay.

" 'Tis quite all right. I've given instructions to park the
carriage on the edges of the activity. If it proves too busy, we'll
drive on—which I doubt will be necessary today."

"But it's a lovely warm afternoon."

"Not overly warm, however. Pleasantly warm, with no real
need for an ice unless it's your favorite treat whatever the
weather."

He appeared too pleased with himself for Tressa to insist on
returning to Pocket Street. He had all the confidence of his
station, and she wondered if she shouldn't just allow him to
prove how far his consequence would take him.

At all events, the vehicle was entering the long rectangle,
crowded shoulder to shoulder by dignified houses on all sides,

known as Berkeley Square. The garden at the center was particularly touted for its fine plane trees, which cast their dappled
shade on what standing carriages there were.

Funnily enough, Tressa felt as if she were returning home
after a long time away.

Not trusting her mix of emotions, she remained as still as
she could, watching as the carriage was carefully edged against
the garden side of the street, not at all far from Gunter's.
Surprisingly, there were few other vehicles despite the lovely
day. She clearly saw the sign that designated the confectioner's,
the Pot and Pineapple.

Braxton was much too pleased with himself.

Tressa reverted to her window. The waiters hurried back and
forth from carriages to shop, balancing trays of ices and cold
drinks.

For a moment, she yearned simply to relax and enjoy herself.
She was veiled, pressed back into the corner of the carriage,
almost holding her breath as a waiter approached the door
Hannibal opened.

Cream fruit ices made from a secret recipe: peach for her;
the most expensive, pineapple, for Hannibal.

"See?" Once the waiter rushed off to fetch their order,
Hannibal smiled at her again—nearly grinned, actually. "We're
perfectly safe. Hardly anyone to notice us. 'Tis the single place
a gentleman can take a lady on his own, in any case."

"But I am your mistress," Tressa said in a hoarse whisper.

He chuckled. "You are a lady."

Devil take it, as he himself would pronounce it. He had the
bit between his teeth and he'd bolted. They should return to
Pocket Street, ices or no ices, even peach.

Soon Gunter's man returned, and Braxton received their
treats into the carriage. Passing the peach to Tressa, he sat back
with his pineapple, blatantly savoring it. Confronted by the
problem of having to lift her veil every time she took a bite,
Tressa managed nonetheless.

And, oh, it did taste wonderful, just as she remembered.

Braxton's smile taunted her yet again. "I was right, eh? Well worth it, and little bother at all."

As if on cue, trouble arrived in the form of a youthful female voice calling his lordship's name just beyond the carriage door that stood open.

The footman, who'd evidently been warned to keep a watch for them, moved to close the door. Braxton, however, moved faster. Shoving his treat into Tressa's trembling fingers, he all but vaulted down from the carriage, allowing his man to shut it behind him.

Tressa shrank further into the corner, still able, however, to peek at the woman. She was a young married lady of fashion, Mrs. Venetia Toussand, better known as Tia.

Tressa knew something of society, and Tia Toussand would be known to almost anyone. The Toussands, heirs to the Tevor-Tait fortune and the title that accompanied it, were very popular—or at least as Tressa understood it, Tia was.

Vibrant, with auburn hair and brown eyes framed by her beautiful violet-covered bonnet, she faced Braxton, unabashedly smiling at him. Her little side glances might have searched out the situation within the marquess's vehicle, but when Braxton focused on her, the lady beamed.

"Mrs. Toussand," he said, evidently not knowing the lady all that well.

"Braxton. And here we all thought you'd gone to Cannongate."

"I'm on my way. Soon."

"Aha," she murmured, reading the situation precisely.

Braxton, who was apparently discreet about the mistresses he mounted and enjoyed, had his current demimondaine out on a summer's day in Berkeley Square for ices.

Mrs. Toussand grinned in a tolerant, if also teasing, sort of way. "We live here on the square, you know, and I'd love it if you'd come for dinner. There are so few people left, and even Sandy's going down to the country in a few days. My husband in particular would appreciate an opportunity to know you better.''

''Your husband's repute, ma'am, is for being as much of a recluse as I am. I'm sure Mr. Toussand must be as tired of dinner parties as I.''

Tia Toussand's animated expression brightened. She wasn't at all embarrassed by the arrangement she had with her own husband. ''Poor Sandy. He longs for his diversion away from the dinner parties—and I don't mean merely the country air, sir.''

Braxton smiled and tipped his hat, breaking off the conversation. Again, Mrs. Toussand took no slight. With a final close look at the quiet carriage, she went on her way.

Braxton returned to the vehicle. No longer full of derring-do, he watched as Tressa placed their half-eaten ices on the tray the footman next ran to the confectioner's.

Soon after, they were out of the square. For the first time Tressa, and probably Braxton, was deeply aware of their circumstances.

They were man and mistress.

Their relationship was something of which their world disapproved, no matter how common it was, no matter how lightly Tia Toussand and her set might regard it.

And while Tressa could be sure Braxton was ashamed neither of her nor their relationship, she experienced her doubts with renewed dread.

Chapter Ten

Hannibal found the Church of St. George's Wells up one of the narrow lanes in the stews of Seven Dials, not very far from Pocket Street. It was an old church, distinguished by intricate brickwork, checkered by once white stone.

Tenements crowded around it, cutting out the overcast, milk-white sky and late morning warmth. Its recently swept stone steps gave him reason to believe he'd find a caretaker, and he did, a large lanky man by the name of Dodd.

Inside the edifice, it was even darker. Dark wooden benches, a dark hammerbeam roof overhead, offered scant comfort as Hannibal followed Dodd down a side aisle past the altar.

"A very old church indeed, me lord. The wells is under a trap door, just beneath us. Used to be medicinal wells, drawing those who were in need from all around. Mostly dried up now, though. Mostly we serve the females from around here, those of a certain ilk, if you know what I mean. Our benevolent society keeps us open."

Dodd led Hannibal into a small side room, this one also well swept and dusted as high as Dodd and his broom could evidently reach. A few plain pieces of furniture were scattered in the space, which was oppressively airless.

"Just the open register there, me lord."

Dodd indicated a large book resting on a table beside a collection box.

"You're welcome to sit and look through it, of course. Can't read meself, and can't afford no candles in the daylight. But I'll be glad to open the door here for you. Let some light in, I'd say."

"Thank you," Braxton replied, gingerly sitting on the creaking chair and addressing the book.

The door Dodd propped open lent a bright rectangle of white light and the noises of the stew—dogs barking, a child crying, a man hollering.

Dodd left quietly. Once Hannibal settled himself, he dropped what he'd brought for the coinbox into the slot. Without a candle, the spidery entrances in various fists, especially the ones from a dozen and more years ago, were difficult to decipher.

About to give up after an hour or so, Hannibal finally came across the name he sought—Charles Hill. Anxious to see the date, he growled with disappointment to see it obliterated by ink blotches.

Turning over the page, he held it up to the light. Nothing revealed the date. Only the birth dates before and after gave him any indication of what Knobby's might have been. No christening date was to be had, either.

"Quite a shame, ain't it, Gov'?"

Surprised, Hannibal peered up at the doorway. A youngish man, no more than a silhouette because of the bright white light behind him, lounged in the door frame, his beaver hat cocked down to shade his eyes as if masked.

He was a dandy—or at least he had aspirations to his own brand of dandyism, garnered from the secondhand shops.

"I beg your pardon?" Hannibal said, at his most starchy.

"I say it's a shame Knobby's name got blotched that way. But the boy's yours, Gov'. I can guarantee he's yours."

Already in unusual circumstances and with his mind awhirl, Hannibal calmly closed the register and stood up to brush his coat.

"And who are you?" he inquired coolly.

"My name is Daniel Quick. I was Bet Hill's friend, and I was here the day she put the boy's name in there. It meant a lot to her, it did, just having his name writ down like that. She said it made him official, a real person. A real gent like his da' was—like you, Gov'."

"And you, Daniel Quick?" Hannibal sounded doubtful. "How do you come by my identity and the fact that I'm here?"

Against the light, and even lazing in the doorway, Daniel shrugged his shoulder. "I keep an eye on the boy. Promised Bet I would. Saw you leaving Pocket Street and thought I'd trot along behind you. Had a bumper at the pub just down the way while you found the name. Knew you'd find it. Knew you'd see."

"See what?"

"Tha' the boy's yours, me lord."

"I see no such thing, my man."

Hannibal plucked up his cane and popped on his hat. When he neared Daniel Quick, the fellow tugged down his beaver, ensuring his face remained largely in shadow.

Still, Hannibal saw enough to know the man felt his threat. Just for emphasis, Hannibal rhythmically applied the gold ball on the end of his cane to his cupped and softly gloved palm.

It thudded quite nicely.

"I'd better never see you around Pocket Street, Daniel Quick. Not even to visit the boy."

With that, Hannibal left the cramped room, calling to Dodd that he was finished at St. George's Wells.

* * *

The sky was overcast, but Tressa knew it wouldn't rain. Hannibal had gotten up that morning and left her, which he hadn't done before. Something weighed on his mind, and she wondered if it had to do with nearly being revealed the afternoon before by Tia Toussand.

For all their physical intimacy, even for the time they spent in each other's company, they didn't discuss anything personal. He hadn't mentioned the possible little boy of his, and she would never tell him about her Uncle Straith and Aunt Editha's wicked deed against her and her father, Bad Buck Devlin.

But that was the way it was with kept women and their keepers. In the end, it was the physical intimacy for which the man paid.

Another heavy lesson learned.

Feeling she must take advantage of Braxton's absence, Tressa decided on a long walk. She was accustomed now to meeting Ambrosia along the way, particularly as she passed through Green Lion Square and by the town house of Sir Percival Pounce.

Tressa rather wondered if the girl didn't have much to do but watch for her, then catch up with her in a rush, tying her apple-green bonnet ribbons as she did now. With her gingery hair in fly-away tendrils and her shawl thrown over her shoulders, she looked no more than a girl.

In some ways, Ambrosia was as young and innocent as Doro. In others, she was far more knowing than Tressa. Tressa especially wondered if the girl was content with Sir Percival Pounce. Obviously for him, the relationship was strictly about his own physical needs. He was an uncaring man—a bounder, as Hannibal called him—and he used Ambrosia for his own pleasure.

Forcing a smile for the girl, Tressa remained as neutral as she could. Ambrosia was quite enamored of the type of life she lived, and she accepted it for what it was. She and her sister had been introduced into it, Ambrosia had explained to Tressa, when they'd been in their early teens—by their own mother, no less, a kept woman herself.

The girl's bright green eyes shone admiringly into Tressa's at their exchanged greetings. Pacing along the garden's palings in Green Lion Square, Ambrosia fell into step with Tressa.

"Did you hear about The Moon and The Stars?" Ambrosia inquired, obviously anxious to relate the latest on-dit circling the half world.

How funny, Tressa thought. The half world easily patterned the polite world in its pecking order, its maneuverings to end on top, and its need for gossip.

The Moon and The Stars was a rarified beauty who'd reached the pinnacle of success by capturing a duke, but who'd also had a difficult climb in the theater.

Godiva, of whom Tressa regularly heard but had never seen, was the aging doyenne of the demi-reps. In retirement now, she had a predilection for heavy gaming that made her salon a meeting place for almost any sort of gentleman and Cyprian.

Miss Lovelace, the woman who had preceded Tressa at Pocket Street in living with Mr. Bennett-Hayes, was compared to Tressa herself. Obviously, she was a lady who'd somehow fallen from grace. After Mr. Bennett-Hayes, she had taken up with Lord Brampt.

And then there were the Ambrosias and Lotties, young girls, some of them chosen on display as opera dancers, some servants ruined by the very gentlemen who were supposed to protect them.

And on and on, down to the low women who had fallen so far as to live on gin.

Tressa shuddered.

She could never be a true whore, taking on any man who desired her. That was precisely the security she'd passed on in refusing to sign Braxton's contracts. He'd wanted to ensure she'd never fall any farther than she wished, if at all.

Still, she wouldn't sign his contracts.

She was grasping for her "something." She'd attained it, actually, and she'd return to her respectability. She'd never want another man except Braxton, not even a husband.

Was she falling in love with Hannibal?

She shuddered again.

Therein lay the most important lesson. She refused to become attached to a man who wouldn't attach equally to her.

"So what I'm saying, Miss Dear, is that if you receive a book delivered to your door by Sir Percival's footman, you must look inside for my message."

Tressa peered at Ambrosia.

Truly, she hadn't been half attending, and she did what she could to piece together what the girl had just finished telling her.

"You say"—she gazed into Ambrosia's unusually serious regard—"that Robert Wexby left a few books at Sir Percival's while he was working on his book room. You might one day wrap one in brown paper and send it via Sir Percival's footman, and I'm to look for a message inside."

Ambrosia smiled, but not happily. "Yes, you've got it just right, Miss Dear. Thank you so much. I'm not really supposed to tell what my sister asked me not to, but I don't know anyone else I can trust, and the time is drawing near when I shall have to act . . . to do something."

Yes, the girl hadn't disclosed anything but a possible message at some point.

"So you're saying"—she prodded delicately—"Sir Percival is watching you, that sometimes he doesn't let you go out when you wish to go out."

"Yes, although that's not so much the worry, for I really don't know what to do about my sister's request, even if I could go out whenever I wish." She bit her lip. "Aside, that is, from prostrating myself at Godiva's feet, I suppose. Oh, but I've already said too much," she insisted, looking at Tressa with pleading green eyes.

The last thing Tressa wanted was to become involved in Ambrosia's—and particularly Lottie's—problems.

"I'll simply watch for a message, and if you tell me you're in trouble, I'll contrive to do what I can. Will that promise satisfy you?"

Appearing most relieved, Ambrosia beamed.

Tressa's thoughts naturally ran to Hannibal. He could certainly have a word with Sir Percival, if it came to that. Tressa wouldn't mind asking him, and Hannibal wouldn't mind doing it. To be sure, it was a gentleman's duty to keep other gentlemen in check.

After looking into what few ideas he had for discovering more about Knobby, Hannibal returned to the house on Pocket Street late in the afternoon. The milk-white sky had grown more gray during the day, and occasional light rain fell only to cease and leave everything spattered with large round spots.

Over their brief time together, Hannibal and Miss Dear had discussed what might be done about the house to make it more comfortable for them however long they stayed. The kitchen had been freshly cleaned and whitewashed, and the cook Mudge had hired satisfactorily installed.

The middle floor, with its two bedchambers and dressing rooms, had been finished some days ago, thus leaving the main floor, the back sitting room, small entry, and front parlor to be dealt with.

Hannibal wasn't surprised, then, upon entering the front hall to hand his accoutrements into the keeping of the new footman Mudge had taken on.

The girls Mudge had in to clean were also there, along with a pair of carters who were filling the covered wagon outside.

The latter were in a rush, hurrying to carry off the framed oils and bits of statuary connected to the house before it rained again.

Satyrs with wood nymphs, a large, undulating female nude, and a scene of purest bacchanalia sat about, freed from their dust sheets. A swan being ridden by a cupid, nicely worked in marble, waited half-covered in its draperies, very suggestive indeed.

In the center of the activity, Miss Dear, aproned and dressed in conservative gray, directed the goings on. Like a misplaced governess, she rid the premises of some terrible to-do enacted by misbehaving charges.

Miss Devlin and Miss Dear were beginning to separate in his mind, and Miss Devlin did not belong on Pocket Street. Even so, she appeared comfortable with her doings. She wasn't averse to turning her own hand to a task or two, and the smudge on her cheek appealed to him in a tender way.

In fact, he felt a great deal of tenderness toward her. He'd introduced her to her circumstances with as much care as possible, but the demimonde remained what it was. As he had learned that afternoon at St. George's Wells, women and children paid a high price for what gentlemen regarded as their right to pleasure.

"You are quite busy, I see." He neared her, lifting her hand to kiss it in greeting, but also to draw her attention away from the busyness to him, to what they were becoming to each other. He needed merely to see her and he desired her, even with others around, especially when her large, subtly lashed, deep blue eyes engaged his.

"My dearest," he whispered over her hand.

She held his gaze for a moment longer, softening. Then, recalling herself and what was afoot, she tugged away her fingers as a lady would. That she was a lady fired him as much as knowing he could have her soon—if not soon enough.

"We're making progress, sir." She rubbed the back of her

hand along her flushed and dewy cheek, obviously conscious that it might be smudged and wanting to please him enough to wipe it away.

He smiled. "Yes, I see. The carters are Mudge's acquaintances, no doubt."

She also smiled. "And glad to have our artwork merely for hauling it away."

"You are happy to see the back of it, I'm sure."

"I've been quite shocked, sir, to see it so plainly at all."

He followed her gaze, as a voluptuous lady who flirted with a leering Pan, perched and piping on a rock, was hauled off by two burly men.

"Mr. Bennett-Hayes," Hannibal said, "would be brought to tears to see his collection meet this end. The devil knows who will enjoy it next."

"Well, Mr. Bennett-Hayes should not have gambled and chanced losing the house and its contents to you. Indeed, I'm surprised you—"

"I know. I didn't want any of it. But we were in one of those awkward situations where I had to accept whatever he had as payment. Debt of honor, you know. It taught me not to game with anyone but my friends when possible. I hardly ever game, in any case."

"And alas, Mr. Bennett-Hayes, gone. And his Miss Lovelace, too—although I understand she is a woman of great gentility. And now I also consider her as having nice taste. Without Mr. Bennett-Hayes' collection of art—and I use the term lightly—I can see her choices for the soft colors in the draperies and walls, her liking for suitable upholsteries."

"And how do you know to attribute the pleasing decorations to Miss Lovelace?"

"Because Rosemary, who is now my lady's maid, was her lady's maid, and she liked Miss Lovelace quite a lot. Rosemary also a lady, and also fallen from her place."

He disliked hearing such a comparison, but he didn't say anything.

He and Miss Devlin were following the carters. They carried the last of the artwork through the small entry and down the front steps. Mudge and his cleaning people, even the footman, was disappearing. It grew late, and Hannibal paused when Miss Devlin indicated the large roped and still draped hulk occupying the small entry.

"They say this is too big for them, sir, although they might be able to take it later."

"What is it?"

He, as well as she, could see the breasts disclosed through the Holland cover.

"Goodness knows. There's a knife there on the side table for cutting the ropes. I thought we should have a peek at it, then decide what to do about it."

"Mayhap," he said, still smiling and fetching the knife, "we could take a hammer to it ourselves. We can break it into small enough pieces, both to make it more easy to remove and to rid us of our feelings for it."

His delight laughed delightfully as he addressed the ropes, slicing through them with a sharp knife and letting them fall. A quick tug of the dust-filled cover revealed a marvelous white marble statue of a lovely Venus.

"Oh, my goodness," she exclaimed, looking up into the appealing face of the diaphanously garbed beauty. "How could Mr. Bennett-Hayes have had the taste to add this to his collection?"

Hannibal chuckled. "He must have won it while gaming and felt too embarrassed to refuse it."

Her happiness enchanted him as much as the bit of soot smudging her cheek. "Oh, we must keep it, don't you think?"

"Yes." He spoke softly, catching her gaze as they realized she used "we" as naturally as she breathed.

Quickly, she blushed and glanced away, evading that

moment's intimacy. Before he could capture her for a kiss, she led him back through the male haunt of the front parlor into the sitting room.

"We are finished in here," she explained. "If, that is, you approve."

Standing there, with her gaze running over the now very nice room which was divided for a place to eat and the traditional hearthside seating, her mood shifted as she took in the mantel.

"Oh, except for that clock! They left without taking that dratted clock."

He burst out laughing, then went to enfold her in his arms, as he'd been wanting to do all along. "We'll leave the clock as it is."

"Oh, but—"

"And"—he stayed her with a kiss—"in return for keeping the dratted clock, we'll bring down Doro's portrait from the attic to fill the wall space above the fireplace. That way, we shall each have something we like, one standing by the other and nicely sharing the same place. It will speak well of *us*, don't you think?"

She peered up at him and smiled again. "There will never be anyone here to see it but us, so I can easily relent. I simply dislike looking at Doro's near downfall with any approval."

Hannibal liked the feel of the woman in his embrace. Just standing there, holding her loosely against him and smiling down into her eyes, made him surprisingly content—just talking to her, just sharing the house with her.

Just sharing his bed and body with her.

It all seemed so right, somehow.

They both liked each other, and yet they were strangers.

Pressed to possess her again, privately in their own clean and cozy and flower-filled sitting room, he knew he need but coax her. Intending to cajole, he set his lips to hers in a suddenly demanding kiss.

He didn't know why, but a desperation to claim her seized

him. He pictured them together indefinitely. He saw Pocket Street and the summer as merely the beginning.

He also knew, however, that she was expecting to go and that she had the independence to do so. He wouldn't know where she was. He wouldn't know if she was safe. He'd have no way to protect her from the world.

She was elusive. She didn't perceive them as "we" and "us." Sponges soaked in vinegar didn't invariably prevent children. As he'd seen that day, lone women and their offspring didn't fare well.

He needed to keep her close. He needed to mark her with his ownership. Then she'd never go.

His kisses didn't invite, they claimed. His hands didn't entice, they demanded. Vaguely, he thought he was a little rough with her.

Opening his eyes, imposing a bit of order on himself, he found her luxuriantly abandoned and unfocused in his arms. He wanted to act the brigand to her surrender, to ravage her with deep kisses, to maraud with his rapacious tongue.

Her skin was ivory.

Her cheeks glowed with a natural rose stain.

Her blooming red lips aroused his most virile wants.

Grasping her hand, he took her to one of the open windows, out on the little balcony above the garden. Below them, colors from delicate to savage ran as wild and rampant as his heart. Like the garden, she was lush and sweet and growing unrestrained.

The first large raindrop to fall on them plopped on her forehead. Grasping her to him, he licked it away. He lapped the next and the next from her forehead, from the side of her nose, causing her to chuckle softly.

He closed off the burble with his mouth, kissing her again and again, until she pulled slightly away and leaned into the stone handrail. With rain pattering around them, making unruly music in the lush greens below, she invited him with her secret-dark eyes to love her.

She couldn't know precisely how yet, not out here, but she knew he'd know. That she invited him in an open sort of way struck his most elemental core.

The lady wanted him as he did her, perhaps urgently, desperately. She trusted him to take her, here, clothed, in the madly dotting rain.

Stunning her obviously as much as he did himself, he inhaled deeply, then lifted her hand and bent formally over it.

"A true gentleman, my sweet, never makes love to his lady with his boots on. If you will, we'll have dinner and go to bed properly."

Tressa knew Hannibal was as confident and comfortable in the nude as he was fully turned out. After their dinner together, which had been pleasant, although he'd seemed to have something on his mind, he told her to let Rosemary attend to her, then wait for him in her room.

She'd been taken aback by his formality, as much as she'd been taken aback that afternoon on the little balcony when he'd put off their bedding.

Because he'd worn his boots, he'd said.

She was further taken aback when he joined her in her chamber, dressed in a nightshirt, slippers, and a magnificent dark brocaded dressing gown with muslin folded at his throat.

Again, he was all in state, like a new husband with a lady wife, like a man who was concerned about his bedmate.

Considering their last few days, the way he'd all but plundered her virtue, she was quite put off.

Could he be trying to tell her he was already tired of their arrangement? Disappointment she couldn't have imagined swept through her, surely showing in her eyes as she observed him from her seated position in front of the pillows.

"Is there something you wish to tell me, Hannibal?"

Best if they face this head on, she told herself, watching him hover in the thick folds of his garment over the nightstand on his side of the mattress.

"Tell you? No, not particularly."

"Is something wrong? I'd rather we be honest with each other, you know."

"Yes." He smiled sardonically. "Equals and all that."

She felt worse and worse. He looked very much the general, but perhaps not entirely iron-eyed. Something bothered him, very much.

"I think it might be best," he said, fingering the little box with the yellow diamond tucked inside, "if I were to sleep in my own chamber for a while."

"Yes, I see. You know, then."

"Know what?"

Tressa blushed. "My monthly. I'm to have it soon."

"Oh."

He didn't seem to have known. He had to understand much more about these things than she did, however, for she knew nothing at all.

"This will be good," he said. "We can ensure that it comes. We play with fire here, you know."

She rather thought he intimated something about the baseborn son he'd mentioned that once.

But such a matter was not a concern for them. She was learning to use the sponges and intended to be faithful to them. She felt relief almost. She looked at him from under her lashes.

"So you're not displeased with me, Hannibal."

He peered at her as if far away. "Displeased with you? But why?"

"Because you . . ." *Because you would sleep in your room*, she wanted to say. "Because I . . ." *Because I . . .* she didn't know.

Obviously reading her perplexity, he relented from his general's stance. He dropped down on the bedclothes, stretching in her direction so he was near enough to stroke her cheek.

"How could I be displeased with you when you're everything that suits me, everything that pleases me—everything I want?"

Tressa returned his close stare.

His face was near but shaded. The candles burned on his side of the bed. On her side, the cheval glass stood, mirroring the corner of the big tester and its pale yellow velvet curtains. Inner curtains of lace cocooned them, adding more shadows and emphasizing the mysteries that lay between them despite their being in bed together.

His fingertips stroked along her jaw, then reached into her thick hair. His hand curved at the base of her neck as he pulled her mouth to his for a kiss.

"By God," he whispered, "I want you. I can't help myself."

The lofty general, Tressa thought. He couldn't help himself when it came to her.

How much that pleased her.

This striking, arresting man was hers for now, and she wanted him as well. She wanted him in this bed, not asleep in his. She also wanted to tell him, but she felt too shy.

She could only show him.

Slipping her shoulder out of her nightdress, she caught his eyes in a way that thrilled her. He went still with attention, then leaned to press his lips to the rounded knob.

"You're so soft, like white lilies. So sweet to the touch. So delicately scented."

He stood briefly, long enough to pull off his nightshirt, kick out of his slippers, and extinguish the candles.

Except for the half summer moon shining through the window across their bed, all became shadows in the dark. The pale yellows and gilding disappeared in blue mist and bright silver. Hannibal's body transformed into a hard heat, demanding, coaxing, then lapsing into commands again.

He wanted her beyond his general's control, beyond his

ability to contain his wanting. Gladly, Tressa sensed his shifts as he struggled with himself.

In the cloak of darkness, he came to her as a heated, heavy warrior, unruly and untamed. His hot hands stripped her of her nightgown, his searing lips beat at her thoughts. Any trouble between them retreated into the shadows, disappeared into his absolute power over her.

She submitted to her wanton self.

In the silvery light, he rose above her, to his knees between her knees.

The lunar wizard.

The dark pelt of his chest repeated his shaded eyes, his night-sky hair. From the cant of his head, she knew he peered down on her bare and atop the sheets, now waiting, waiting for his sorcery.

Now he would stroke her. Now his eyes would watch as his hands worked their enchantment. He formed and reformed her breasts. They stood out in the single strip of bright sterling light, filling his warm sorcerer's fists.

But then he shifted again. Now he plied her, hot and urgent, rather than with sweet firm strokes in silver blue. He occupied the rich darkness beside her, all heat and power and desire for her alone.

This time he demanded her woman's core, the dampness that formed inside her, pooling for him. She was glad he claimed her there with his warrior's ways. In the dark, his fingers deflowered her again, briefly, gently, then exacted, dictated, that she spill her ecstasy into his heated palm.

Again she gave him what he wanted.

He groaned.

And again she gave.

He was atop her, warrior and wizard joined, demands and sweet devilry.

He plunged into her, setting her awash on a silver sea. He rocked. He plummeted. He fell into her. He was hers.

Exhausted and replete, he covered her body with his, fixing his head into the crook of her shoulder and neck. He breathed deep content into her ear.

Barely lifting a hand, she claimed complete victory. Her fingertips just nudged into the damp curling edges of his hair at his vulnerable nape.

Chapter Eleven

Hannibal slept like a stone, Tressa not at all.

Oh, he stayed in her bed as she wished. He cradled her in a warm embrace. He breathed his man's heat into the air. She had pleased him, no doubt. She felt close to him. But she could not sleep.

Slowly, inch by inch, she did the unreasonable. She edged out of his arms and crept from the bed. Standing over him, she slid into her straw-colored dressing gown and peered down on him, putting him away in the lavender of her memory. In the half moonlight, spread across her mattress, he unfolded into a relaxed position that reminded her of the sack of Troy.

Her warrior, her wizard, brought low by her.

Turning abruptly, she tiptoed away from the blue-silver light and beckoning security toward the door. There she twisted the handle, again by degrees, disturbing him not one jot.

In the corridor, she found a cooler sanity. Her relentlessness increased. Mudge and the new footman were lodged in the basement. Her lady's maid, Rosemary, had a cot in Tressa's dressing room, and Tressa swept by that carefully.

She hadn't been watching for a watcher lately, and the idea she might discover one in the quiet street outside the house had been preying on her.

If Joe Legg had located her on Pocket Street . . .

She'd have to scurry away some late night. Soon.

Up in the attic room, the one at the front of the house where Doro's picture had hung, she went to the window that lent the best view of the tiny neighborhood. Inhaling deeply, hoping against hope she wouldn't spy anyone, she nudged a slot between the draperies.

There didn't appear to be anyone. But sometimes it took a lot of standing, a lot of checking, to catch just the precise moment when Joe Legg would be checking on her.

She hadn't seen his barrel-like figure, shadowy and lurking but otherwise nondescript, for weeks. She'd left the new Lady Farronby's nigh onto three weeks before Hannibal had arrived at Pocket Street searching for Robert. She'd been with Hannibal a little over two weeks more.

Still no Joe Legg.

She was surprised he hadn't discovered her whereabouts as yet. Her Uncle Straith missed no tricks and had to be astir with anger and fear. Out of fear, her uncle could kill.

Shuddering, Tressa tugged her dressing gown more tightly around her, even dared to part the dusty drapes a crack more. With her candle blown out, she stood largely in the dark. In the street, a flambeau burned, glowing in a wide flickering circle. Beyond that disc, blue half moon light reigned.

If she was to see anything, tonight would be the night for it—clear and moonlit after a day of odd skies and occasional goose-egg raindrops.

A sharp noise from behind her startled her more than anything she might have glimpsed from the window. She shut the draperies quickly against the light cast by Hannibal's candle. He entered, wearing only breeches and heavy socks, his puzzlement exaggerated by his masculine features. His weight caused the old floorboards to creak.

"What, my sweet, are you doing up here? 'Tis scarcely midnight."

At Tressa's hesitation, he locked his eyes to hers.

Above all, she didn't want to answer his questions. She'd be forced to lie.

"What are you doing?" he pressed, his gaze growing harder.

Although she didn't open them again, she turned back to the drapes. "I-I couldn't sleep."

He set down his light and came to chafe her upper arms from behind her. His bare chest at her back, his capable hands colored her thoughts despite her worst fears. Braxton would always exercise more power over her than good sense, and she had to beware of that.

"What a shame," he whispered softly, kissing her ear. "I thought you slept as deeply as I did."

She didn't reply.

"Why are we staring at these old curtains? Are you thinking of replacing them? Of refurbishing this room, as well?"

"No, I . . . yes."

Her first lie to him.

He dropped his comforting hands from their reassuring contact. He was no man to lie to, no man to fool.

His voice grew low and doubt-filled. "I've caught you here before, looking down on the street. As I recall, you were upset by the fact a man I'd hired still kept an eye out there. Obviously, you're worried someone's watching."

She couldn't reply.

What could she say without lying again?

Nothing.

Exasperated, he brushed around her, puffed out his candle and threw open the draperies. Standing beside her in the dark, he searched the pavement.

He murmured, heavily, "Who's out there?"

In the mix of moonshine and the flickering light of the flambeau, the street lay quiet.

No one, she thought to say. That would be honest for the moment.

But then Hannibal stiffened. Placing his hands on the sill, he leaned close into the glass.

"Who is that?"

Tressa's heart dropped in her chest, then started to race. Leaning close to the glass, she swept the street with her gaze. Barely perceptibly, a slouched male figure in a high beaver hat formed from the shadows into her view.

But the man wasn't barrel-shaped.

No, this man confused her.

He had the attitude of a ne'er-do-well. Even in the shadows and from this distance, she could read that, even with her thoughts tearing around in her mind, even with him dressed fairly well—or so she judged.

"Daniel Quick," Hannibal breathed beside her, his heat clouding the glass in front of his face.

He swept out of the room. She heard him on the stairs and tried to follow, but it was too dark. Giving up on lighting the candle before she started, she returned to the window.

She heard Hannibal barge out of the front door, then saw him plunge into the street. Obviously surprised, the silhouetted figure across the pavement froze for an instant as Hannibal shot toward him.

Tressa could barely imagine what it would be like to see such a figure, half-naked and in his socks careening toward one.

Hannibal's big hand just missed grasping the cloth of the man's coat before Daniel Quick dashed away. Passing through the pool of flambeau light, the fellow barely escaped. Hannibal entered, then exited, the brief light himself.

The pair disappeared in tandem from Tressa's sight somewhere out into Great Crow Street, evidently heading in the direction of the Crown and Feathers.

Daniel Quick, not Joe Legg.

But another watcher nonetheless.

Any consideration of wearing only stockings on his feet and nothing else beyond his breeches was lost in Hannibal's mad dash after Daniel Quick.

Out on Great Crow Street, an occasional lamp marked the way in the warm, dark night. But the lighting was haphazard, nothing in comparison to that of the West End.

Still, Hannibal careened on, determined the fellow would not escape him.

Just as Hannibal suspected, Quick was making a beeline for the Crown and Feathers. The inn was well lighted, with a private coach getting under way in the inn yard. A low wall surrounding the yard showed as a shadowed barrier beyond which torches beckoned invitingly.

Even above the growing harshness of his own breathing, Hannibal discerned the low din of voices, the general to-do generated no matter what the hour at the rambling Elizabethan hostelry.

When Quick vaulted over the low wall, Hannibal did, too. Feeling his own strength and stamina and likely surprising his quarry with his determined pursuit, he closed the gap between them.

The dapperish fellow lost his hat when Hannibal caught him by the back of his collar. Turning him, Hannibal threw him up against the timber-frame wall of the building, very nigh to an open diamond-paned window.

"Blackguard," Hannibal muttered, controlling his breath as Daniel Quick stared, openmouthed, directly into Hannibal's face. "Surprised I'd go to the trouble of chasing you down, eh?"

No small commotion erupted, both within the taproom itself and just around them, as the ostlers gathered in curiosity.

Hannibal would have preferred another venue, of course, and was relieved when Mudge emerged from the front door. Tall and solid and obviously having some influence at the Crown and Feathers, Mudge calmed the circumstances by telling everyone to clear the way so he could see to the business.

When the man's wise old eyes found Hannibal securing Daniel Quick against the inn wall, Hannibal almost could have smiled at his dogsbody's brief amazement.

Still, no one else would have recognized what Hannibal saw. With every degree of collectedness, the elder man rapped his orders with a certitude they'd be followed.

"Aye, go on now," Mudge said. "All of you. I'll see to the matter, an' we'll have some privacy for it."

Needless to say, there was a good bit of grumbling about missing a fine show. But eventually only Mudge remained close enough to Hannibal and Quick to actually hear what might be said.

At that point, Hannibal shoved Daniel Quick into the wall even harder. Placing his forearm threateningly into the man's throat, he caused a squeak in Daniel's voice box. Fear opened the man's eyes to saucer-size as he stared into Hannibal's gaze.

"I told you I'd better never find you on Pocket Street."

Mudge latched the nearby window he'd just closed, its pattern of red and green light glowing grotesquely on their little scene.

"Caught him meself one night, me lord," Mudge added, matter of factly. "I warned him off, as well. Seems the fellow don't listen very close."

Hannibal felt Daniel Quick shudder at the idea of two equally large men having at him in the privacy of their little corner of the inn yard. Mudge appeared ready to follow Hannibal in anything he might do or say, and Daniel Quick's eyes switched back and forth from one to the other.

"So, Daniel Quick," Hannibal said, "it's been decided you

don't listen very well. I'd say it's time you talk. Why were
you outside my house?''

Hannibal felt Dan Quick's hard swallow against his forearm
and let up enough to allow the man to speak.

''I come by to see my boy,'' he grumbled.

''By your boy, I suppose you mean Knobby,'' Hannibal said,
greatly relieved to hear this news of the boy's parentage. Daniel
Quick had fathered the boy despite what he'd said at the Church
of St. George's Wells.

''And why,'' Hannibal pressed, not showing his relief,
''would you be standing out front at my house when the boy's
bedding down in the stable now?''

''I wanted to be sure you was in the house, Gov'. Didn't
want to run into you in the stable.''

''So you're here strictly to see the boy?''

The man appeared both puzzled and still a bit belligerent.
''I'd come during the day, but, like Mudge says, I've been
chased off then, too.''

''And you're the one who's put Knobby up to his doings?''

''What doings, Gov'?''

''Don't play innocent with me,'' Hannibal ground out, tightening his hold against the man's throat. ''You've put the boy
up to coming 'round to me as if he knows I'm his papa.''

''But he knows you ain't, Gov'. I swear it.''

''He may know it, and I thank God he does, but you're
putting him up to no damned good, and I don't want you around,
got it?''

Before Quick could reply, Mudge added his threatening
stance and voice to the matter by thrusting his face into the
already close pairing of Hannibal and the still hatless, hapless,
Quick.

''We've got a good boy, here, Quick. We don't need you to
ruin him. How he ever stayed so good, what with his ma dying
and you putting him up to tricks like this one with his lordship,
is beyond me, but his lordship and me is here now. We say

you don't see the boy no more. Either you don't see him, or you''—he shook his fist in Quick's face—''don't see at all, understand?''

Despite what little bravado Quick mustered by squaring his chin, Hannibal sensed the man's fear. He was just thinking Quick was well and truly scared off when Mudge put paid to the business by speaking in lower tones and especially for Hannibal's ear.

''He's known as Cocky Dan, me lord. Word has it he had something to do with some missing revenues at the Little Theater in Porridge Lane.''

''I didn't have nothing to do with the theater take in Porridge Lane,'' Cocky Dan said as Mudge went on, even more lowly, even more threateningly.

''His name's connected with another bit of missing money at the linen drapers on Great Crow Street, no more than half a block from here, me lord.''

''I never,'' Cocky Dan insisted, his eyes shifting and giving him away.

''So,'' Hannibal pronounced, releasing his hold with a final jerk. ''You'd best be off and lie low, Cocky Dan.''

Mudge, who'd picked up the fellow's hat, propped it on his head for him.

''You best stay clear of us, too—particularly of the boy, or you'll learn what for.''

Without a word, Cocky Dan Quick darted off, disappearing into the night beyond the inn yard.

Mudge, upon looking down at Hannibal's stocking feet, gazed up again. He gave him a respectful, almost warm, look as he offered his first real contact as one compatriot to another.

''Best get those feet of yours into a warm soak, me lord. Luckily, we have water on the stove. Can have it ready for you in a trice.''

* * *

Back at the house, Hannibal admitted the bottoms of his feet had to be seen to. Still solicitous, even jovial in going over their victory at Cocky Dan Quick's expense, Mudge fetched a straight-backed chair from the servants' table in the kitchen. Setting it in front of the hearth, he placed an enamel basin at Hannibal's feet, then went on to enliven a small fire.

While Hannibal removed his stockings and did his examination, the elder man brought water to exactly the right temperature in the large basin and added some salts.

"Are they bad, me lord?"

Hannibal peered up as he carefully slid his feet into the water. "A couple of bruises and abrasions, but nothing bad."

Mudge seemed to admire Hannibal all the more for his battle wounds. Going back to the stove with his kettles, he nodded appreciatively.

"You did us all a justice tonight in bringing Cocky Dan to book, me lord. He's a slippery sort who seems to slide by with his doings."

"So you did agree that he's put the lad up to pestering me?"

"Oh, no doubt about it, me lord. Always coming around, looking for the coins you tossed the boy and badgering him for his part, although he never did nothing of the sort in front of me. Nor would the lad complain about him, either. A good lad, sir. I'm especially glad you hobbled Dan Quick for Knobby's sake."

Letting the warmth of the water soothe him, Hannibal sighed heavily nonetheless. Cocky Dan obviously had smudged the open record of Knobby's birth date at St. George's Wells.

"Yes, well," he said, "in time I suppose we'll see what I accomplished tonight. These sorts don't give up easily."

"No, but Cocky Dan already has too much against his accounts to do anything but—like you told him—lie low. At least he won't come round here and bother the lad anytime soon.''

''As for that, I intend to ask the boy if he'd prefer to come with me to Cannongate and work in my stables there. That way, we'll well and truly separate him from Cocky Dan and I'll be able to keep an eye on him in the bargain.''

''Tha's very good of you, me lord.''

Again, Hannibal read positive, even comradely signals in Mudge's glances.

He reverted to his feet. ''As I say, only time will tell. Perhaps the boy won't be separated from his father or from London and his friends in the East End.''

''If the boy has one scrap of sense, which I know he has, he'll accept your offer, no doubt.''

Hannibal's next subject ran from his tongue rather than arose from forethought. Even so, he realized the subject was of utmost importance to him.

''Miss Devlin is watching the street at night, my good fellow. I don't suppose—''

''On that score, I cannot reply, sir.'' In fact, Mudge appeared regretful. ''I know she watches from the windows—has done ever since I've known her, even at Lady Farronby's. And while she halfway admitted the fact to me one night when I ran across someone actually keeping an eye on the house from the streets, and even heard about this blackguard asking quiet questions regarding Miss Devlin's comings and goings at the house, she won't confide in me about her precise problem. She just simply won't, sir.''

''And this blackguard, did you actually discover him observing from the street?''

Mudge nodded. ''I did. Name of Joe Legg. A real brute of a man and highly disliked. I managed to chase him off that night, but I couldn't uncover any more about him.''

''Not even where he comes from, or who pays his shot?''

''Nothing, me lord.''

The name coursed through Hannibal's mind. Joe Legg. Joe Legg. It meant nothing to him. It meant everything.

"And has this Joe Legg been seen around Pocket Street?"

"No, me lord. That I know for certain sure. I've been keeping an ear to the ground on that one, and there's been nary a whisper of him."

"So he doesn't know she's here. Did she so positively elude him in leaving Lady Farronby's and coming here?"

"Aye, she did. I mean, *we* did. Left Farronby House in the middle of the night and came here directly. Informed Miss Doro and Mr. Wexby that we was eluding you, of course."

Without the least embarrassment at this admission, Mudge went on. "Brought all our things by hackney carriages I hired. Some friends of mine on the sly. Lost this Joe Legg altogether. Certain sure. Still, he's not one to underestimate, nor one to discount. My tangle with him taught me that. He's smart and cold and thoroughly in his man's pocket. It's no wonder Miss Devlin fears him and the man who pays him. I fear for her, and I don't fear much in this life anymore."

"If you see him, let me know straight off. I don't want him hanging about."

"Certainly not, me lord."

If Tressa heard any of their discussion, she showed no evidence of it on entering the kitchen, tidily wrapped in a new pale dressing gown, her honeyed hair bundled at her nape. Only her own deep worry showed in her dark blue eyes and lovely features.

Yes, even with other matters on Hannibal's mind, she could take his breath, merely appearing *en déshabillé*.

"Are you all right?" she inquired of Hannibal, her eyes resting on his feet in the basin.

"He'll do," Mudge said, endeavoring to relieve her. "He'll do, Miss Devlin. Don't you fret now."

Obviously knowing no more to say than that, Mudge bid both

Miss Devlin and Hannibal well and retired for what remained of the night.

Left in the stillness of the now clean and cozy kitchen, Miss Devlin clasped her hands in front of her. Uneasy as well, Hannibal peered down at his feet in the cooling water.

She kept a secret from him, and that ate at his insides as nothing ever had.

She looked vulnerable, especially in her reluctant approach to him, in the way she opened her inevitable topic.

"That man you chased, you said his name was Daniel Quick."

"He's Knobby's father. I asked him not to visit the boy here anymore. When he came anyway, I decided to clarify things with him. You needn't worry, though. Mudge and I definitely made our point, and I doubt he'll be down in the street ever again."

Hannibal waited in the stillness. She had every chance to tell him now, and he wanted her to, more than he could say.

But she didn't.

He got up from the foot bath. Barely looking at her, he dried his feet.

She'd cut him. She'd hurt him. It angered him.

He spoke coolly.

"I mentioned once that I feared I had a baseborn son, and I've been thinking that son was Knobby."

"Knobby Knees?"

"But he isn't my son. As far as I know, I have no other children by anyone. I've certainly been careful enough that I shouldn't have any."

Going to the mantel, he leaned against the shelf, studying the fire. He didn't know why he was telling her this—perhaps to engage her confidence; perhaps to tell her a truth about himself because he desired her truth so badly.

"But the point is," he continued, "I believed Knobby could have been mine. He's about twelve years old, and I was with

his mother for several weeks. I was young at the time and in
my cups a good deal in those years. I've since learned, however,
that I shouldn't drink, largely because I tend to disremember
things. I do and say things I lose track of, and I dislike that
very much. But, in those days . . . well, I was with his mother,
a woman by the name of Bet Hill. She's dead now."

Those lovely blue eyes clouded with questions.

"You made love to her," she said to be clear.

"I bedded her. There's a difference between loving someone
and merely bedding with them."

"I suppose she was very beautiful."

He turned back to the gentle fire. "She probably was, but
I don't recall."

"Because you drank in those days."

"Because I've been with numerous women since, and, quite
honestly, I don't remember." His tone grew harsh.

He felt embarrassed by what he'd admitted. Though he'd
never considered the number of women he'd lain with in the
past, he'd begun to do so lately. Despite himself, despite what
almost any gentlemen would declare was well within the
bounds, he'd become uneasy with something he'd taken for
granted.

Numerous women.

Any woman he wanted.

All treated well, of course, but . . .

Tressa struggled to understand. "You don't recall Bet Hill
at all?"

"No."

"Yet you were intimate with her. As intimate as we are."

Hannibal didn't reply.

She still sought to comprehend—bedding someone, yet not
remembering.

"Knobby has such distinctive blue eyes. Did Bet Hill have
such eyes?"

"I don't recall."

He was *not* doing well anymore. *Not* patient. *Not* helping her grasp something he himself no longer understood.

He didn't want her to hear about, much less understand, a world he was beginning to see for what it was. The world of gentlemen and their mistresses—of gentlemen and their carelessness.

"And so," he said stiffly, "now you see why we use the sponges, why we await your monthly, why we don't want you carrying my bastard child. Surely you also see why you must sign my contracts and accept the lifelong security they offer you. If you will do that, we can bed together indefinitely, whenever and however we want, for as long as we want, and we'll not need to worry. Whatever happens between us, you and our children will be secure."

She seemed aghast.

Her lovely mouth formed a soundless oh of amazement. She shook her head no, then said it.

"No. I shall not sign. But what do you mean in saying children in the plural? In intimating months—nay, apparently *years* of being together?"

Hannibal inhaled deeply. Folding his hands behind his back, he turned from the fire and assumed an imposing stance as he faced Tressa and her questions. He believed in defending his actions and taking his blows no matter what.

That the person who delivered those blows was sweet beyond his bearing, desirable beyond his control, was bad enough. That she also desired him nearly pushed him outside of reason.

Occasionally—even now—her dark eyes coursed over his naked chest.

They'd been lovers fewer than six days, and he'd kindled a passion for her that now approached wildfire. He tended her capacity for passion most carefully and was driven mad at the mere suggestion of it, especially since he'd become its object.

He wanted her.

He wanted to use her passion to close the subject and put everything but them and their seclusion from their thoughts.

But she had a secret.

She kept it from him, and it drove him insane.

Still, he faced her levelly, even when her dark eyes helplessly drifted in the direction of desire.

"What I mean, ma'am, in stating that we could be together indefinitely, is exactly that. As a peer, I have my obligations, and I will continue to see to them. For you, I will live a minimal public life and tend to my duties on my own. When in London, we shall live largely as we do now, in seclusion. When I go to Cannongate, you may come with me, but only on the sly. I shall not be able to receive anyone who would be insulted by our relationship—that meaning almost anyone but my closest male friends and their mistresses. Doro and Robert will have my heir, and the line will pass through them. But I will live with you and have the children of my heart with you."

"Illegitimate children."

" 'Tis done all the time. They will be as fine as anyone's children and raised just as well. They will be educated and taught to make their own way, a way I'll prepare for them and oversee until I leave this earth."

"And you and I?"

"And you and I will live together as man and wife without the papers and ceremonies that would tie us together no matter what. You should rather like that, I'd think," he added, sounding cynical even to himself. "You'll be free to leave me, to sneak off in the night, whenever you wish."

She was so shocked, she obviously couldn't reply.

He drove at her with more cynicism, disguised in a flippant tone. "As I say, 'tis done all the time, ma'am. So, pray, begin to understand what we do here as sophisticated people. Even you must see I am offering you the best of these kinds of circumstances merely to be with you and yet preserve your independence. I have given you the choice of marriage, but you chose this.''

Those dark eyes he loved so well focused on him, full of confusion and shock.

And he burned inside, knowing she still kept her secret from him.

He bowed formally, then made his way toward the door.

''We shall sleep separately, ma'am, and await your monthly. Every good night to you, Miss Devlin.''

Closing himself away from her, both physically and mentally, only stoked the fire in his belly.

Neither of them had mentioned her secret, nor the watchers she feared—the watchers he now feared as well.

Chapter Twelve

"Thank you, Rosemary."

In the gilded looking glass above her dressing table, Tressa met the shy gaze of her lady's maid. For the first time, Rosemary had done her hair, and Tressa patted the still upswept but definitely softer style appreciatively.

She looked entirely different, and yet she liked the difference. She hoped her smile communicated that to the obviously fine lady's maid, who bobbed a curtsy, then went on with her chores.

Standing before the glass, Tressa also examined her new morning gown, one of several garments delivered in discreet unmarked boxes from the modiste, Madame Henri. Cut from cloth the shade of dusty old gold, the gown was unlike anything she'd ever owned. While the modiste had known better than to push Tressa too far from what she was accustomed to, she'd dressed her neither as a young miss nor as a mistress.

No, she'd garbed her as a youthful, fashionable woman of quality, someone showing a bit of dash.

Tressa liked it.

But she also noticed the paleness of her complexion, the unusual drabness around her eyes. She hadn't slept a wink.

The night before, down in the kitchen after his footbath, Hannibal had assailed her with such a barrage of confidences and insults and cynicism she still hadn't recovered.

She wished they could quietly and agreeably discuss each point he'd made, the better for her to understand them all. Still, she'd understood enough to have decided how she'd respond.

She'd thought of leaving, but she wouldn't leave. She wouldn't cry craven and sneak off into the night as he'd said she would.

She would stay. Hopefully, over the next few days they'd discuss what he'd said more calmly and arrive at other conclusions than confusion on her part and anger on his.

She'd concentrate on her best reason for approaching him over his breakfast in the back sitting room downstairs. They hadn't had breakfast together as yet, and she understood the new cook, together with Mudge and his equally new footman, were instituting a schedule to include household meals.

So be it.

Turning from the mirror with her new hair style and her new determination, Tressa saw Rosemary had made up the bed. Tressa's predecessor, Miss Lovelace, had asked that the big tester be dressed afresh each day, and the air was redolent with the scent of country-washed linens.

The bed reminded Tressa of the fact that she'd slept alone and hadn't liked it—had hardly slept at all, actually.

Her monthly had come, and that was important to Hannibal— likely, she'd realized, because it would signal she hadn't conceived. Her ignorance about the workings of her own body aggravated her. She decided to focus on putting together what information she gleaned from Hannibal as best she could.

Armed with enough to approach him, to make what amends she could, Tressa left the efficient Rosemary and went down to the sitting room. Early morning sunlight flooded the chamber through the windows that were opened to the garden below, letting in the sound of the new gardeners Mudge had hired taming the now familiar outdoor space.

Hannibal sat at the polished table with his breakfast and newspaper. Mudge bustled about, and the footman, without much to do, stood watching. The footman was a nice-looking, well-built fellow with blond curls that reminded Tressa of her father's.

Mudge's greeting brought Hannibal's eyes from his reading and the young footman to attention.

"Would you like something to eat, Miss Devlin?"

Tressa's own unexpected smile matched Mudge's delight. The man was in alt. Everything was obviously running to his satisfaction, and that included her arrival in her new finery.

"I'll not have anything but tea," she replied. Hannibal stood by the table, acknowledging her, as Mudge ordered the young man off to fulfill her request.

In fact, there was quite a nice to-do until she was settled across from Hannibal, with a vase of fragrant white roses and blue forget-me-nots close by. Mudge and the footman left as smoothly as glass, and she was alone with the man from whom she expected some apologies.

He wasn't about to apologize, though. She read that clearly.

He remained a bit on his high ropes as he drank his coffee and she toyed with her teaspoon. He was fresh from his toilette, her wicked wizard, a delight to her sight and as delicious to smell as white roses. She also recalled the vision of him last night in the dark, running in the streets, her warrior bedmate, confident without his clothes.

What lay ahead would not be easy, despite her determination, despite his close if covered perusal of her hair and her gown. Indeed, she thought it was a very approving study on his part, and her wish that it could be better between them spurred her to speak.

"I want to tell you, my lord . . . Hannibal, that my visitor has come."

She blushed, but she also kept her gaze to his.

He seemed puzzled at first. Then the light dawned. "Oh, your visitor. Well, good."

Because his iron-gray eyes fell away from hers, then drifted to his open paper, Tressa reverted to her tea. She also let her eyes, if not her mind, drift to the portrait of Doro, now hanging above the mantel, looking as stunning there as it would anywhere, to the silver clock with its naughty couple, now side by side and replete on their mattress.

She wondered if the man held the woman's hand beneath the covers as Hannibal had held hers when recovering from their loving. He'd been happy with her. More than happy, and wanting to prolong his contact with her all the while his great beautiful body took the repose it needed.

Tressa wanted those times again. Above everything, she wanted to stay with this man as long as she dared. Then she would go. And, yes, she'd likely sneak away with Mudge in the night.

"I beg your pardon, Hannibal? I'm afraid I was woolgathering."

"I said this missive arrived from Calais this morning, a last message of gratitude from Robert and Doro for my help and all that. They had a good crossing, but there's also"—his eyes briefly, intently, met hers—"a request that I send the new direction of your position. They say they miss you and want to write."

"I see." Tressa dropped her eyes to the letter that lay between them.

He was still angry with her. He wanted to keep his distance despite his politeness—and he was all politeness.

The iron-eyed general had returned.

"Since you've come down," he added, reinforcing her deductions, "I will inform you that I don't intend to be here for either luncheon or dinner. I may not, in truth, return for a few days. But you will, of course, be perfectly safe with Mudge.''

Tressa decided to meet his announcement with a nonchalance to match his. ''Yes, of course. I'll be perfectly comfortable.''

''Good.''

Getting up from the table, he executed a brief leg and left her.

He wasn't about to make it up with her and talk about the night before. Perhaps her monthly disgusted him. In any case, she'd have time to think, to wonder where he was, to pine for him late at night.

In the end, though, she owed him. She lied to him, kept secrets from him, and she knew he was too intelligent not to understand that and resent it.

Worse and worse, as the day wore on and Tressa lingered about the house, fingering the things in the front parlor with which she wasn't so familiar, Hannibal didn't return.

She ate alone in the sitting room, happily attended by Mudge and his footman, a young sturdy fellow, she discovered, by the name of Bates. At Bates's brief absences, she and Mudge stole their usual easy conversation. Mudge was full of talk about his lordship, about how he'd skillfully handled that rascal, Cocky Dan Quick.

Of course, Tressa didn't need any more convincing that his lordship was quite marvelous, indeed. She needed only his lordship's arms around her in her bed that night. But that, too, Hannibal withheld by not returning to Pocket Street.

By dawn, and again without having had much sleep, Tressa decided she would not act the part of some die-away miss. Her best remedy was to walk, walk, walk.

As Tressa exited the gate in the palings surrounding the overgrown garden in Green Lion Square, she wasn't surprised to see Ambrosia coming toward her, evidently again escaping the house of Sir Percival Pounce just down the block. What did surprise Tressa was the girl's unusual lope in her direction.

Ambrosia's pretty, yet sober features, her near state of . . . well, her shawl was askew and her ginger-colored hair billowed from beneath her bonnet, which cascaded with innocent, if all too many, open-faced daisies.

Already guilty of not having given the girl more than a thought since last seeing her, Tressa's concern for her rose another peg. Sir Percival was apparently watching the girl's comings and goings—perhaps on occasion even keeping her in when she would have gone out.

Tressa also recalled Ambrosia's puzzling suggestion about possibly sending a paper-wrapped parcel containing some book Robert had left behind in Sir Percival's study. Ambrosia had told Tressa to look for a note inside.

Thoroughly disgusted with her own secrets and what they were doing to her life, Tressa didn't wish to be included in Ambrosia's clandestine affairs. Still, Tressa also felt a strong sympathy for the girl who dashed up to her, so obviously happy to see her and so out of sorts as to cause concern.

The girl's worries, however, were quickly overbalanced by her great dawning smile.

"Oh, Miss Dear, you look so very wonderful. I was watching for you from my window, hoping I'd see you. But when you went in at the garden gate, I almost didn't recognize you for your lovely new ensemble. A walking costume, of course." Her bright eyes examined Tressa's every inch as the pair paused on the shaded flagway, outside the square's treed center.

"Oh, Miss Dear, it is so beautiful. I absolutely adore the color lilac. And the profusion of embroidered lilac ribbons . . ." Her green eyes lifted to Tressa's veiled face. "Your bonnet is lined with the same shade of lilac silk!"

Tressa chuckled. "It is."

She would have liked to lift her veil and show the girl her

bonnet lining, but she dared not. In any case, Ambrosia didn't expect to have a full view of Tressa's face, and went bubbling on.

"Oh, it is ornamented with a smart black feather, just so simply! Truly, Miss Dear, I should love to be exactly like you. The really finest of us in our tradition have a signature, and yours, of course, is that you are so like a lady. I should love to have such a fine signature—to be so serene as you and now so fashionable, and yet so understated. I do quite like you, Miss Dear."

"And I quite like you, Ambrosia."

Tressa didn't know whether to smile or weep. The girl's valueless aspirations tore at her heart. She wished better for Ambrosia than what the girl spoke of as "our traditions," as if the traditions of the half world were worthy of observing.

Once again, Tressa was struck by the combination of youth and innocence, of experience and the tawdriness of that experience. Tressa couldn't help wondering what sort of trouble with Sir Percival was diluting Ambrosia's enthusiasm.

"So," Tressa said, "shall we walk to Cupid's Tea Garden and take tea? My treat."

Not surprisingly, the girl's eyes sneaked to the town house, down the block and back. "No, I shouldn't go that far this afternoon. But if you wouldn't mind walking around the garden, I'd like very much to accompany you."

Tressa smiled. "Around the garden, then."

It didn't take long for Tressa to discover that the usually talkative Ambrosia was quiet indeed. Pondering something, no doubt. Trying to find words, mayhap.

Ambrosia started talking on a rush of words, as if she'd tried and failed to hold them in.

"Oh, Miss Dear, I am quite unable to keep my sister's secret. I must tell someone, and I do believe you are the most wise, most reliable, person in my acquaintance—not that I don't have two nice friends of my own sort and near my own age like my own sister, Lottie. But they . . . oh, I simply cannot tell them anything Lottie has asked me not to. And besides, my friends are hardly in any better position than I am at the moment.''

Tressa was accustomed to seeing the young girls, so easily caught up in the half world, walking together and talking, obviously comparing their experiences, their mentors, their men. It was a cruel world, and one hardly knew it until one was well and truly caught by it, never to get out again.

After being ensnared, a few females prospered, like The Moon and The Stars, who often drove by in her fine equipage flying its ducal colors. But most of the Lotties and Ambrosias grew not too much older, falling like stars and burning out.

Tressa decided she must listen to the girl and, if she could, help her despite her own numerous problems, the likelihood that she wouldn't be in the area much longer, and even that she didn't know Ambrosia that well.

"Are you familiar, Miss Dear, with the gambling salon owned by Godiva?"

Even Tressa had picked up tidbits regarding the retired whore—closer to a courtesan, really—who ran a high stakes gambling hell that attracted all sorts of participants. Every one from the Duke of Wellington to cits and their mushroom sons rubbed elbows at Godiva's, including available women of every kind. Godiva's was more than a den for those who craved high stakes.

Tressa's heart tripped in its beat.

"My sister met her current keeper at Godiva's," said Ambrosia. "It depresses me to admit it, but Lottie is most drawn to games of chance, as is the man she has now. I've told you how they are in Paris, gambling there for a while. And she has left me with Sir Percival, and I . . ."

Because they were on the opposite side of the square where the views from Sir Percival's town house would not find them, Tressa took Ambrosia's arm and urged her to a bench so they could sit, somewhat in privacy.

Tressa removed a handkerchief from her reticule and offered it to the girl, who dabbed at her few tears and heartily blew her nose. Wadding the new lace-edged bit of fluff into her fist, Ambrosia plunged on.

"When Lottie was with Sir Percival, she kept her little box of jewels in the room I have now. In the drawer, she has told me, at the bottom of the wardrobe. But before Lottie left Sir Percival, they had a great row—not that they didn't have great rows regularly. Well, Lottie suspects Sir Percival took her jewels before she could quite get away with her new protector. She thought she'd arranged it well enough with Sir Percival, for I was to take her place. But then, just as she was packing, she discovered her box was gone. Truly, she didn't know what to say or do—whether to go or stay and find it, so she asked me to find it. I was to search the house high and low, which I've done, of course. In fact, Sir Percival has caught me, and said I must behave myself or he will do something horrid. He watches me now, and sometimes won't let me come out."

Tears over the days of worry and mistreatment at the hands of Sir Percival again threatened in Ambrosia's eyes. Availing herself of the handkerchief, she took the moment she needed to compose herself and start over.

"The problem is, you see, my sister lost quite a lot at Godiva's, and the debt is still owing—close to coming due, in fact. Lottie has asked me to find her jewels and take them to the moneylenders so as to pay Godiva on time. It's a debt of honor, you know, and simply must, *must*, be paid or Lottie's name will be ruined and she'll never have a protector again—not a good one, in any case."

Ambrosia's watery eyes sought Tressa's pleadingly.

"Oh, my good Miss Dear, I don't know what to do. I've searched Sir Percival's house thoroughly, although now he watches me most closely, too closely for me to search anymore. Still, I haven't found Lottie's little container and I'm so worried. Even if I should discover the jewels, Sir Percival will keep me from the freedom I need to go to the moneylenders and then seek out Godiva. She's said to be an absolute tyrant—one minute coldhearted, the next hot as fire. She simply must be paid, Miss Dear, and soon.''

Ambrosia swallowed hard, obviously pressing to the end of what she had to say. ''I have a ring of my own, set with a sapphire. I thought I might take it and bargain with Godiva. When Lottie returns from Paris, she'll surely be able to pay all that needs paying. I need only convince Godiva to wait, to not besmirch my sister's name, and in the end all will be well, even if I can't locate her jewels. Do you think Godiva will listen to me? They say she loves only her money.''

Tressa didn't know what to say. Ambrosia was in a position she hardly could comprehend.

''It seems to me it would be in Godiva's best interest to wait for the money your sister owes, rather than not be paid at all.''

''And to keep my sister from ruin?''

Tressa nodded. After all, the girl had turned to her as a sympathetic, listening ear. Tressa couldn't do anything for her, and she couldn't bring Braxton into the matter by seeking his advice.

No, Tressa had no idea what to say. Taking Ambrosia's arm, she urged the girl to her feet. Pressing her to her side, she walked with her, offering her the creature comfort of her presence.

All the way to Sir Percival's, the girl daubed her eyes and nose. Then, squaring her shoulders, she readied herself to go back in.

With a few words, Tressa and Ambrosia parted. Tressa waited across the street until the girl disappeared inside the front door. She simply couldn't imagine what could be done. She hoped Ambrosia knew that and would look to her again only as a caring listener.

Ambrosia's was a tale one could hear as easily in the polite world as in the half world. Debts of honor. Where was the honor?

By evening, Tressa realized she wouldn't see Hannibal that day, and she went to bed early. She hadn't slept well for the last few nights. Lying in her draped tester bed, she thought she'd sleep no better this night.

She worried about Ambrosia, but her mind took up her own worries, too. Pieces of Hannibal's revelation, delivered on the night he'd chased off Dan Quick, would not leave her alone, even two nights later. His speech had been so unexpected and so full of the unbelievable.

He felt they could be together indefinitely, living a secluded life outside his public one and even having children. It seemed incredible. To live with him would be all she could desire. He'd make the sacrifices he must to be with her. She'd be as secure as any woman could be. He'd have, as he'd said, the children of his heart with her. It would give her everything she could wish.

Everything but his heart.

And therein was the problem.

Tressa admitted her ignorance on understanding how to satisfy Hannibal and the workings of her own female body. She knew little about clothes, had been basically sheltered from the world for most of her days. But in one aspect she was growing clearer. She was losing her heart to Hannibal. She'd probably always love him. To live with him, within the bonds of marriage or not, without his loving her in return would be too painful to bear.

Knowing she mustn't get any deeper into the morass of unrequited love, she began to think about leaving Hannibal. She'd clutch what days she could to her heart and live them as fully as possible, but she also started to examine the end of her time with him. For the most unexpected reason of all, that of loving him too much, she would go.

Having reached her conclusion, having faced it, brought her great sorrow. But it also brought her resolve and something other than fanciful wishes that could not come true. Above all, she must keep the man she loved—yes, she loved him with all her being—safe from the man who would murder him should he suspect Hannibal shared the secret of her father's death.

Uncle Straith would take no chances with another person's having knowledge of his deed. That Tressa should find a husband and confide in him would not be countenanced from the moment Uncle Straith discovered she had Hannibal, married or not.

No, the more Tressa turned her hard truths over in her mind, the more valuable the days she would steal with Hannibal became. She would grasp them and hold onto them forever, but she'd protect them by ending them as soon as possible— as soon as she could bear to let them go. As soon as she could bear to let him go.

Surprisingly, her abrupt clarity on so much that had been plaguing her allowed her to fall into a deep, restorative sleep. All the more reason for her grogginess when she awoke to Hannibal, in full evening dress, coming none too quietly into her room. With a candle he carried serving as their only illumination, he closed the door and stood looking at her as she tried to shake off her sleep.

He was beautifully garbed in a black silk coat, white starched linens and waistcoat, black pantaloons and pumps. The very precision of his garb, the way it fit his wonderful body, made him all the more formidable. His haughty stance, his general's eyes, warred with his slight waver and lightly slurred speech.

"Foxed," he announced, almost proudly and as a warning for her.

"What else?"

Her surprisingly chipper reply, as she sat up among her pillows wearing one of the new nightgowns from Madame Henri, riveted his dark gaze in the pale candlelight.

His eyes coursed over her, probably in spite of his wishes otherwise. Rosemary had bundled her hair quite attractively for bed. The nightgown was extremely delicate, made in a French nunnery with which Madame Henri did business.

Indeed, Tressa felt confident in her obvious appeal to Hannibal, and was happy in that. She remained firm in her decision to leave him, but her decision also freed her to enjoy what little more they would have.

She let him feast on the sight of her hair. She waited so his dark eyes could savor the slight tremble in the cobwebby fabric she wore. Her merest breath or movement, even her heartbeat, was emphasized by the gauzy cloud.

She waited for him to decide whether to take her or not. She wanted him to, but she had her visitor, and he could not like the mess of that.

His eyes lifted from the tightening responsive nubs of her nipples, clearly showing through the tender gown and its fine embroidery. In a hush of anticipation at her body's open invitation, she knew he wavered. He was as drawn to her as she was to him, almost beyond their individual resistance. She thought he might have cast everything that stood between them to the wind, but he didn't. The general won out.

He gathered himself on a deeply inhaled breath. He straightened his shoulders and cleared his throat. "I demand a compromise, Miss Devlin."

"A compromise, sir?"

"My greatest concern is that you be safe."

"Safe? In what way?"

"In every way, dash it."

The iron-eyed general's control wasn't so firm after all.

She smiled. Just a little.

"Devil take it, woman, I will not stand by and let you have your deuced independence at the damned expense of your bloody safety."

"Nicely put, sir."

He plunged on. "You will, therefore, no longer leave the house without accompaniment. You may walk, but not without either me, Mudge, this new footman Bates, or even Knobby. You may go to the shops. You have your fittings with Madame Henri, and nothing will keep you inside."

"Indeed not."

"But you will, by the very devil, not go anywhere unattended. Do I make myself clear, ma'am?"

"You most certainly do, sir."

He nodded, brusquely.

Her attitude seemed to take some of the wind from his sails.

He bowed from the waist, wavering just the least bit. He obviously meant to bid her an equally brisk good night, but briskness was not within his physical abilities.

Throwing back the light summer coverlet and springing from the bed, Tressa grasped his candle just as it tipped in his hand. She carried it to the nightstand, then turned to face him. She knew the whispery fabric of her gown had to glow pale yellow in the light behind her. She saw Hannibal's eyes trace the silhouetted shadow of her body as it responded to him, almost blossoming like a flower.

She could feel it was so, just as he could see it was so.

It bled pink into her cheeks, puffed yearning into her lips, ripened her breasts, swelled between her legs. She was beginning to know her body because this beautiful man had awakened her to its nuances.

Watching in the stillness, blossoming for him, she drank in his dark, rapacious gaze. But she was thrown off in the end.

Hannibal started for her—apparently had the will for taking her—but veered away instead, managing the few steps to the bed. As on other occasions, he launched himself toward the mattress, ending flat on his stomach and all but asleep within seconds.

Once again, Tressa's sudden smile served her best.

"So much for my wiles, I see. Thank you, sir, for setting me straight. I was beginning to get too big a head, to be sure."

Doing what she could with his heavy body, so totally

weighted against her, Tressa worked for a few minutes at removing his shoes. Finally resorting to her scissors, she snipped what she could of his cravat to loosen it, and he groaned as if somewhat relieved.

Aside from that and throwing the plush coverlet over him, she could do no more. Blowing out the candle, she climbed into bed and snuggled into him beneath the fragrant satin.

For now, they would sleep.

Her independence would be curbed, but they had an agreement that would allow them some peace during what time they had left.

Early the next morning Tressa was jostled awake rather rudely from the sweet sleep she'd enjoyed. She and Hannibal hadn't moved at all, warmly snuggled into each other, curled at the bottom of her mattress.

But Hannibal was abruptly awake, pulling away from her and drawing her eyes. He seemed disturbed at having found himself with her, especially cuddled so comfortably, and he stood up stiffly, thrusting his hand through his black hair. Next he fingered his brutalized cravat, then tugged it away from his neck in disbelief.

Recollecting himself quickly, as a general should, he stared down at her as she came to a seated position under the still warm coverlet. Once again, his eyes coursed over her diaphanous attire, her softly gathered hair. Once again, she read his struggle, then his victory over himself.

"You and I, ma'am, must reach an agreement," he demanded, his cravat wadded in his fist, his beard a shadow on his face as he stepped into his evening shoes.

"An agreement, sir?"

"My greatest concern is your safety. Especially with the watcher situation you refuse to explain to me. And so, ma'am, you will not leave this house without—"

"Without the accompaniment of either you or Mudge or Bates. Or even Knobby—or perhaps more than one of you at a time."

He looked rebuffed.

She smiled, jauntily for so early in the morning. "Yes, I understand our agreement."

His eyes dropped away from hers, absently taking in his formal attire. "I see we have discussed this."

She laughed. "Last night. And I see, now, how you tend to be forgetful when you have . . ."

His eyes dared her to accuse him of having had too much to drink.

Again, she laughed.

His eyes, helplessly, were drawn to her in the bed, in her delicate yet somehow demure French nightgown.

"You, I take it, still have your, er, visitor," he posed, lowly, as both a question and a suggestion.

"I do," she said softly. "But today should see the end of it."

He nearly snapped his heels before marching toward the door. "I will leave you to your rest, then. It's been deuced difficult, but I've managed to this point to leave you be until it's done. I'll see you tomorrow."

Tressa did see him the next day, but just barely into it.

Shortly after midnight, he again appeared in her bedchamber when she was half asleep. He slipped under the covers with her, garbed very properly as a husband in a nightshirt. He took her into his arms and cuddled with her warmly. At her ear, his breath soon turned soft and at last relaxed in sleep.

Chapter Thirteen

Tressa awoke in a flurry of regret and confusion. She was sure Hannibal had come into her bed, slept with her warmly and sweetly in a nightshirt as a husband might. But when she awoke, there was no hint of him.

A sudden fear gripped her that perhaps it was over between them. He'd stayed away from her so much over the last few days and nights—supposedly, as he'd admitted, for her own comfort during her monthly. But she suddenly felt unsure, even in the pale orange glow of a beautiful dawn.

Without throwing a shawl over the thin rich veil of her nightgown, she rushed out of her bedchamber, barefooted. One of the good things about a mistress's house was the discretion exercised by the servants, and she felt free to fly down the front staircase to the little entry.

She had to find Hannibal.

There he sat, as big as you please. He was swathed almost formally in his dark brocaded dressing gown, with crisp linen tucked at his throat. He was freshly shaven, and his slippered feet were crossed as he relaxed with his coffee and newspaper in the large, masculine, overstuffed chair in the front parlor, traditionally the male haunt in the little house.

Now highly polished and clean, denuded of its art collection and with the pale, nicely paneled walls available to the eye in the equally pale early morning light, it had become a respectable place for Hannibal to sit, although this was the first time she'd seen him there.

He peered up in surprise as she swept in, straight from her bed and a little off-kilter in her thinking. Still, her emotions ran high, and she needed to confront him.

"Hannibal, am I or am I not your mistress?"

"My sweet?" Puzzled, he stood up, still grasping his newspaper.

"I need to understand."

"Understand what, sweetings?"

"You stay away for days and nights, then come to me to cuddle. But when I awake, you are up and about, reading and drinking coffee."

"I've told you," he said quietly and, she rather thought, genuinely perplexed, "that I've been respecting your condition over the last few days."

"But you've been upset with me, too, I know."

"Some, I must admit. But since you won't share your secret with me, we've come to an agreement I can live with."

"But you've tamed the garden. You no longer buy me jewels."

"I was of the impression you didn't like the diamonds. You certainly haven't worn them—not that I want you traipsing about on the streets wearing them and getting knocked over the head. But you did, sweet, call them whore's fare, as I recall. Then, as to the garden, I believe you and Mudge . . ."

Tressa began to pace in a small circle in front of him. She felt all a-dither and didn't know why. She only knew she must get to the bottom of something.

"You came to me in a nightshirt," she accused. "Like a husband."

"Once again, out of regard for your condition."

Her elegant gossamer nightgown whispered between them. "It's my new clothes. You don't like them. Perhaps I look silly in them—or you like me better as a little nun, as you so often say."

He laid aside his paper. "Nonsense. I don't understand what this is about."

"It's about the fact that you don't treat me as a mistress." She pivoted to face him, then began her fretful display in front of him, half muttering to herself. "It's about that dratted dressing gown you're wearing."

Face to face with him once more, she saw his perplexity grow. "My dressing gown? This one? I'll have you know, ma'am, this gown cost me a pretty penny."

"Yes, but where is," she insisted, unreasonably, "the black silk gown you wore when I first came? The silky one that swished like murky water, that you wore barely tied, as if you could be uncovered in front of me? You haven't been treating me like a mistress, but more like a . . . like a dratted wife!"

He lifted his thick dark brows as if he'd finally discovered her problem and found it exasperating. Coming to her, he grasped her to him in an embrace that took her breath. Indeed, she breathed in Hannibal, his freshness, his shaving soap and sweet water.

After her pique, she thought she might swoon. She wanted so badly to be in his arms, to be the object of his ardor, that she might die with relief.

His kiss proved he wanted her. His arousal was quickly potent between them, barely kept from her in their morning attire. She loved this lover of hers, and couldn't bear not being with him. One day, she'd have no choice but never to see him again.

Hiding her sadness, Tressa threw herself wholeheartedly at

Hannibal. With her own hunger, she turned his kisses voracious. Tugging her back with him toward the big chair before the hearth, he worked himself free of his heavy dressing gown. His voice was husky when he spoke, his gray eyes thick with passion and challenge.

"Will you be taken, ma'am, here on the carpet in the middle of your abode, like a mistress?"

"I will. I will."

She threw her arms around his neck, wantonly embracing his nakedness. She kissed him as thoroughly as she could on tiptoe. He sanctioned her reach by willingly inclining himself toward her. He let her kiss him.

For the first time, she became the aggressor. He seemed to spark to her need for him. She kissed him in all the variations he had taught her, dropping the last few on his throat and then his upper neck.

She sought the bronze nipples in the thick pelt of his chest hair. When she kissed each one in turn, he threw back his head and groaned with pleasure and surprise. She took his nipples as he so often did hers, first with great care and reverence, tantalizing each one, coaxing its response until both were like hard pebbles. She sought his deep dark hair with her fingertips and savored the warm, hard muscles of his chest beneath.

Slowly, she slipped downward, kissing him and seeking his navel with her tongue. She became fully aware of his man's part, throbbing now, waiting and ready. She had only a peek at it, though, before Hannibal grasped her upper arms and pulled her up for his kisses.

He took his turn as aggressor, heated and expert and beyond resisting. He removed her featherlight gown so she stood naked against him. He rubbed her with his maleness, watching her eyes as she watched his.

His gaze turned light as a dove's wing and soft, so soft, with desire.

Tressa felt her power over him as a great pleasant wash of

delight. She was his mistress. She pleased him mightily, no denying it, no questioning it.

Slowly, he lowered her to the carpet, now piled with her nightgown and his brocaded robe, and centered her on the pile. He followed her down as a rampant pursuer.

"I cannot like abrading your skin on this carpet," he whispered. "Are you comfortable on our clothes? Or would you rather I take you upstairs?"

She stared up into his eyes. "I cannot like knowing you've loved other women on other carpets. I cannot like knowing that you stared, like this, into Bet Hill's eyes, and have forgotten their color, as you will mine."

He hung above her, a giant brought up short in his giant's doings.

She wanted him. Why had she said that?

"I've never loved any other woman on a carpet," he said. "And the reason I can't recall any of those other women is because you have blotted them from my mind. You are the most beautiful woman I've ever seen. The most lovely in every way, and I've had all I could do over the last few days to keep my hands off you—to keep my member outside of you."

With that open admission, he plunged his male part into her. Usually, he came into her only after preparation, after fingering her, testing her preparedness. In this case, though, he thrust into her and she was fully ready. Soft and wet from her monthly, she received him to his hilt.

He drove into her roughly, coming and going, his eyes riveted to hers in a matching, savage joy. There were no kisses now, no compelling strokes, no tenderness. He took her hard in her womanly softness all the way to her waiting completion.

This was what she'd needed to prove, she realized, her breathing as rapid as his. She needed him beyond his control, raw and ravenous, both of them at their most elemental. From this place on the floor, with him rising above her and going still in his ecstasy, they would build anew.

Tressa well and truly became Hannibal's mistress, the soft receiving part of his male virility.

At last replete and sprawled beside him on the carpet, she turned her face up to his. "You mustn't get angry now, Hannibal, but we have forgotten the sponges."

"You know my opinion on that head, sweetings. If I get you with child, you must surely stay with me, if for no one's sake but that of the child. If you don't wish for a child"——he caught his breath, his gray eyes locked to hers——"you must ensure you are using the sponges. My seed is in you, now, though, and we have a whole month until we shall see again. Frankly, I'm hoping to fill you with my child so we can both be happy."

Be happy, Tressa thought, vaguely collecting her thoughts as she nestled her head into Hannibal's chest. If it could only be so simple. But reality would soon return. She kept forgetting what power Hannibal had over her, even more than cold murderous reason.

"So it's a surprise, is it?" Tressa laughed, peering at Knobby, who perched on the backward-facing carriage seat across from her and Hannibal.

"His lordship says it's a surprise," he replied in delight, his remarkably blue eyes openly admiring of his lordship.

This afternoon, Knobby looked like a little gentleman in his fresh coat, breeches and gaiters, crisp white shirt, and knotted, red-spotted tie.

"Shall I guess what the surprise is?" she inquired teasingly, as the lad's eyes again sought his master's indulgent regard in this matter of a surprise for her.

She and Hannibal had made love on the front parlor carpeting that morning, thus solidifying their joining as gentleman and mistress. Of course, he still saw her as a lady, but he also made love to her now with the gloves off, and she reveled in it.

Knobby's presence in the vehicle clearly cued her in to this surprise, but he was too innocent to have surmised that as yet. He was simply all excitement, his blue gaze alight.

"And so I shall guess," she said, stealing a glance at Hannibal, "that you and his lordship are taking me to Hyde Park so I may walk on this lovely afternoon."

The boy chuckled at her guess. "Has nothing to do with Hyde Park, my lady. Or with walking."

"And speaking of walking," Hannibal interrupted, albeit gently for Hannibal, "Knobby knows he's to walk with you whenever you ask."

Hannibal all but lounged, for a general, in his corner of the carriage, the picture of sartorial splendor. He wore white corduroy breeches and the white-topped boots made fashionable among the riding set by Brummel. His coat and his waistcoat were a light-colored brown mixture. His neckcloth, in the shade she knew was called Russian leather, was tied in the Horse Collar, what else?

He carried a quirt rather than a cane, and his hat was a slouched affair that rode low over his eyes. In a word, he was all the crack, and Tressa recognized it despite his relaxed, even soft demeanor.

"Aye, my lady, I likes to walk, and I'll be happy to keep you safe."

"My own white knight," Tressa said, smiling at him. "But see here," she added, "we are talking about my surprise, remember?"

She peered out the carriage window as if ruminating, watching the busy London metropolis.

"Where could we be going for this surprise?"

"To Green Park," Knobby blurted out.

"To Green Park?" She acted all amazement. "But Green Park is so uncivilized compared to the other parks in London. Why should we be going to Green Park? Perhaps to see a bear—a big wild one."

Knobby's eyes widened, seeking Hannibal's face. "Are there

bears in Green Park, Gov'? Can't be good for the 'orses, bears can't.''

"Oh, it's to do with horses, is it?" Tressa laughed, causing a great dismay in Knobby's youthful features.

He looked at Hannibal as if he were sorry for ruining the surprise. Tressa reached across the space between the two luxurious banquettes and patted his tidily gloved hand.

"Actually, I'm funning you. I thought all along it had to do with a horse. After all, you take care of his lordship's Saracen. So what's it to be? A he or a she? And what color? I take it you've already seen this surprise horse.''

Still unsure as to how much more he should say, Knobby looked at Hannibal. At a nod from his lordship, he freely spilled the whole tale.

"She's most wonderful—a not too large but very fat gray mare with big dapples on her rump. Blossom's a great goer, but she's also as sweet as can be. Very easy handling. Like his lordship says, she's just right for you, and I'm to ride with you when his lordship can't, although, a groom from Blossom's stables will ride with us, too. We're to go to Green Park in the carriage, like we is today, and stay right in the park so we don't see nobody. His lordship's bringing me along now so I can explain everything and we can be clear.''

"And you have seen Blossom, then?" Tressa asked, smiling, first at Hannibal, then at Knobby.

"I've seen her two times, my lady. Come with his lordship, I did.''

Knobby seemed proud of companioning with Braxton. They made quite a pair, she could see. Perhaps that was her biggest surprise of the day—Braxton and a street urchin obviously spending time together at his lordship's instigation.

"But Knobby has other news," Hannibal said.

The child's eyes positively glowed. "I'm to go with his lordship and Saracen to Cannongate when the time comes. I'm to leave London behind, and work in the Gov's stables. But mostly, I'll see to good ol' Saracen, who likes me through and through.''

Tressa couldn't help but look at Hannibal.

He spoke her unvoiced concern.

"Knobby and I have had a talk, man to man.''

"Aye, my lady. Man to man. I'm to bid my friends a happy farewell and go off to the country, far away to Cannongate where there's a great sea just by.''

Hannibal and Knobby had obviously discussed all of this.

"And, Knobby,'' Hannibal added, "is very bravely to also bid his father, Daniel Quick, a hearty farewell. He won't be seeing him until we return to London. Even then, Knobby's to stay away from Dan Quick and to beware his doings.''

"My da' was the one to put me up to playing a hoax on his lordship. I was to act like I was his son instead of Dan's. It got me more coins from the Gov'. But it also was an untruth, and untruths hurt people, so I'm not being untruthful ever again. Not even if me ol' da' asks me to. Not even for coins. I'm to go to Mudge or to his lordship, and they'll help me if I need it. But I don't think I'll need it anymore. I'm growed now, making a man's decisions and talking man to man with his lordship.''

Man to man, Tressa thought, smiling at Hannibal.

It was quite wonderful, really. Hannibal wielded such power in his daily life, and he used it to the best of his ability. It was good to be able to admire the man one also loved.

"Well, I'm very happy for you, Knobby,'' she said. "Taking care of Saracen and going to Cannongate. And I'm happy for you, too, my lord.'' Her eyes engaged Hannibal's gray gaze. "You have a very special worker in your employ.''

"I do,'' he agreed.

Tressa thought her eyes might well with tears.

Fortunately, the carriage had reached what was apparently a small private stable on the edge of Green Park. On days when they'd had really long carriage drives, she and the Dowager

Lady Farronby had chosen Green Park for its seclusion. It was less used, more natural, than the other London Parks. On this sunny afternoon, one would have sworn one was in the country.

Hannibal soon helped Tressa down from the carriage. Knobby walked around, stretching his legs as if he owned the place. A small stable, busy with grooms and rife with the pleasant aspects surrounding a nicely run country stable, waited for their inspection—not that the sojourn there was to be relaxed.

Too excited for words and knowing where to find Blossom, Knobby led the way, with Hannibal and Tressa barely keeping up. Horses, known for their curiosity, swung their heads over stable doors and around their attendants, taking the measure of the newcomers. Some snorted disapprovingly and shook their heads. Some stretched their soft muzzles, hoping for a treat.

Some seemed especially cautious about the fluttering veil Tressa had lowered, the one that suited her French carriage dress and bonnet in cerulean blue.

Finally, they reached Blossom's stall, where Tressa and the horse were introduced by Knobby. He launched into such a listing of the horse's fine points that Tressa had to chuckle.

"We've hired someone to teach you to ride, to start with the basics," Hannibal said, having allowed Knobby and Tressa the bulk of the conversation while he stroked the horse in her stall. "You haven't ridden much, I take it."

Tressa knew he listened closely when she told him anything about her past, which she did rarely. Still, it was such a lovely day and he was doing her such a wonderful favor that she kept smiling.

"When I was eight, in fact, I rode most regularly. In secret, of course. An old groom at Lance Hall taught me to ride on the sly. But once my uncle and aunt found out, they turned him off and turned me over my uncle's knee. I haven't ridden since, I'm afraid. You needn't worry, though. The groom said I had a good seat—although, come to think on it, he was likely proud of his student and told me those things because he was fond of me.''

"So," Hannibal said, "we shall see then, shall we not, Knobby?"

The lad grinned. "I believe she's a natural, sure enough, Gov'. I'll bet me next meal on it."

"You don't wager anymore, remember?" Hannibal reached to jostle the boy's shoulder.

"Just a manner of speech, Gov', just a manner of speech."

Hannibal laughed, causing even Blossom to perk her ears. Tressa thrilled at the rare sound.

She was so taken that she didn't notice a horse and a rider coming upon them until the last minute. Tressa thought the dashing newcomer, Tia Toussand—aboard an incredible beast of satiny red and enormous energy—very brave.

Tia Toussand was small, but apparently so strongly willed and forward in her manner as to make one catch one's breath. No one, Tressa could be sure, simply came up to Braxton. But twice now, Tia Toussand had done precisely that, first in Berkeley Square, when they'd had ices in front of Gunter's, and now.

Tressa had to admire the fashionable, attractive, auburn-haired sweetheart of the *ton*, who was only a few years older than she. If things had been different, Tia Toussand might have been Tressa's friend.

Fortunately, Tressa could also thank Rosemary and Madame Henri that she herself appeared entirely à la mode in her cerulean ensemble.

"Good morning, Braxton," the woman called, capably reining in her mount. "I didn't know you kept horses here."

"Only this one," Braxton replied.

He moved from beneath the overhang of the stable block so as to position himself between Tressa and Mrs. Toussand. As Hannibal's veiled mistress, Tressa became invisible in public, if she was seen at all. Ladies especially were supposed to ignore mistresses, even should one run into her husband escorting his latest doxy about Town.

Which had to be dismaying for the wife, Tressa thought. More and more, she saw the embarrassments engendered by this strictly male world of gentlemen and their mistresses.

"Perhaps if you were to stable another horse here for yourself, the three of us could ride together sometime," Tia suggested, proposing even more outrageous behavior. "Or mayhap you could use a horse of mine. I'm known for owning very spirited horses."

Truly, it was brazen enough to invite Braxton to ride. But to also include his errant company ... well, it was beyond belief and also beyond explaining.

Still, Braxton remained all confidence and simply nodded. "Perhaps."

One didn't cut such an influence in society as Tia Toussand, and Braxton certainly had to wonder, as Tressa did, what the woman was about. Her repute could bear as much damage as anyone's—except Braxton's, possibly. But to be seen in the company of his mistress, even in the wilds of Green Park ... it simply wasn't done.

To top it off, Tia smiled and fingered the tip of her jaunty hat, easily riding out her great horse's sidestepping indication that he was more than ready to be off.

Leaving with her own groom following at a distance, she did at least obey that dictate. She'd take to the bridle paths with an escort. But also, as Tressa did to the flagways, on her own terms and for her own exercise and well being.

Sighing and watching the woman go—as his lordship and Knobby did, as well—Tressa had to admire Tia Toussand for the independence she stole from her husband and household— and from the polite world, despite her high position.

"So we shall go," Hannibal said, turning back to Tressa and Knobby. "We have a sidesaddle to fit and riding costumes to order. But first"—he smiled at Knobby, including Tressa with a communicative glance—"I understand a few milkmaids keep milch cows here in Green Park. 'Tis said the maids make the best syllabub, and I should like to try it."

"Silly what?" chimed in Knobby, causing both Hannibal and Tressa to laugh.

" 'Tis a treat," Hannibal explained to the boy. "A sweet. We shall see what you think, but don't expect syllabub on just any ride in Green Park. It has a bit of wine in it."

"Oh, but," insisted Knobby, "surely seeing Blossom is better than any treat, Gov'."

Braxton locked his eyes to Tressa's as he took her elbow. "We shall see, my young fellow. We shall just see. But I may indeed create a problem for myself here in future."

Late in the afternoon, when Braxton's carriage finally pulled up in front of the house on Pocket Street, Tressa thought everyone involved was relieved. They'd had a long afternoon, and Knobby and Bates, who'd ridden on the back of the vehicle as footmen, quickly hied off to the rear of the house as the equipage pulled away on its return to Mayfair.

Yes, Tressa liked it that the servants largely left her and Hannibal alone. She particularly was pleased when he let her into the quiet house on his own. Inside the small entry, which had polished up like a jewel with its white marble statue of Venus and its black and white tile, she paused at the gilded hall table to remove her bonnet and veil, her gloves and reticule.

Hannibal, she noted out of the corner of her eye, tossed his slouched hat to the banister post, then laid aside his quirt and gloves with her things. When he bent to work at removing his fine topboots with their immaculately white tops, she slowed to watch him in surprise.

That he tossed those aside, then shrugged out of his coat and began unbuttoning his waistcoat, riveted her.

"Are you going to take a nap, Hannibal?"

"No." His eyes met hers levelly, just as his voice also sounded frank. "I'm going to teach you to ride."

Half thinking that he was making light as he always did, Tressa chuckled. But her chuckle faded at the sight of Hannibal standing in the entry in his stocking feet and untying his cravat, which landed on the black and white tile.

Around them, the house was hushed. Late afternoon light barely penetrated the shuttered windows. Only a pearly shaft from the entry struck into the masculine study.

Hannibal had made love to her on the carpet in there that morning, beside the big, brown overstuffed chair and its accompanying table fronting the hearth.

As he tugged off his stockings, then worked at getting his shirt unbuttoned and free of his breeches, her heart began a madly tripping beat.

"T-teach me to ride, sir?"

With only his breeches on, and those gaping open, he grasped her hand and led her into the quiet, much darker study. Just as she suspected, only the opalescent shaft of light from the entry shone inside like a milky beam, softly illuminating the large brown armchair.

For some reason, she swallowed nervously. She couldn't imagine what Hannibal meant. And then he swept her, fully clothed, up against his naked chest.

"You did say ride, did you not?" she inquired.

He locked his gaze to hers. "To ride me."

Only Hannibal himself could outweigh Tressa's confusion, her sudden rush of emotions. He'd made love to her that morning, and yet he apparently intended to do so again.

But to teach her to ride *him* and that she remained dressed . . .

She understood only his sudden, searing, wanting kisses, his huskily uttered words.

"Madame Henri knows her business, by Jove. To dress you in that color, the same color as your eyes, has driven me wild today. The French call that color *bleu celeste*. Sky blue. And your eyes . . ."

He kissed her again, full of desire and building her desire as one would build a fire, stoking her, stroking her, breathing sweet passion into her like a great bellows.

"Sky blue," he whispered, his hands smoothing over her gown in intimate places—at her breasts, her bottom, her thighs, and around to the joining of her legs.

She caught his fire so quickly she thought she'd run rampant, too. The oddity of her being clothed and his being naked—for he'd let his breeches slide to the carpet—remained her only puzzlement. He usually wanted her as naked as he.

Still, she ran her hands over his heavily muscled flesh, the smooth curves and bulky maleness that were becoming so familiar to her, so necessary to her happiness.

She glanced into his gray eyes, then closed her own. She smelled his unique fragrance, the faded tones of sweet water and soap. His dark beard abraded just a bit, a reminder of his virility and her fragility. She reveled in the contrasts between them and yet the neat fit of them, too.

"Now, my sweet," he whispered, close to her ear. "You shall mount me and ride, as free as the wind."

Taking her to the big chair in the opaline light, he sat down.

He pulled her to him, intimating that she should put one foot, still in its dark jean boot, between his thigh and the large rounded arm of the chair.

When she lifted up her leg to do so, he immediately ran his hand beneath her cerulean blue skirts and her white petticoats up her white silk stocking, past her garter decorated in yellow buttercups, and along the warmth of her thigh. He sought for the dampness that surely dewed between her legs.

He slipped his longest finger inside her, moaning at her body's immediate and natural response to him.

"Sweetest nectar," he said lowly.

The mother-of-pearl light behind him cast his eyes in impenetrable shade. Still, Tressa knew he observed her, studied her like prey, waited for her completion so he could take his. When he intimated she should step up onto the chair by placing her other booted foot on it in the same manner, she did so, depending on his strong hands to balance her.

She couldn't imagine his desire for their odd positions and opposite states of dress until he coaxed her down to sit on his knees, facing him. Then it all materialized in her mind. Her bare bottom meshed with his bare thighs. His erection stood, waiting between them.

She blushed ferociously.

Still he pinned her with his gaze in the off-white light.

He lowered her onto his stiff and upright manhood and settled her cerulean skirts around them in a great soft sigh.

"You'll ride astride and without a riding costume. But you'll surely ride, my sweet, nonetheless."

With that, he encouraged her to lift from him, to test the feel of him inside her as he was. It was a tremendous, liberating feeling. She was free to move as she wanted—to post, as it were. Free to pleasure him and herself precisely as her feelings, her senses, directed her.

She experimented just a little.

She pleased him.

She experimented even more.

He liked that even more.

She used his smooth wet shaft to stimulate herself, to love him as she'd never dreamed. His eyes were dark pools in the dark depth of shadows. She was surely lit to his gaze.

She set up a cadence, and he sighed.

As if riding, she slowed her tempo and closed her eyes. Then she sped ahead, spurring his enjoyment.

"Ride me, ride me," he said, in rhythm to her lilting gate. "Set us free."

She took them to her completion, feeling it come and then come again. Out of breath, she responded to his expert hands

as he urged her to lay back along his thighs and let her head
and now unbound hair drop over his knees.

He watched her.

She spread her arms in purest flight through the pearl-like
light.

His fingers, at that little place between her legs, brought her
to one more ripple of pleasure, and then he took his own. She
sat up on his lap to hold him close to her bosom, within the
veil of her fragrant hair.

Light like pearls.

Bleu celeste.

Hannibal's male scent and warm male fulfillment shrinking
inside her.

Surely this was heaven.

As if he remained as in tune with her pleasant drifting
thoughts as he did with her body, he spoke lowly into her ear.

"We shall change Blossom's name to Sky, and only you
and I will know why."

Ten minutes later, his member slid from inside her. Only
then did Tressa realize that for the second time in a day she
hadn't used the little sponges. He'd left the choice of using
them to her, and hadn't mentioned them.

Indeed, she suspected he was seeding her, deeply and pur-
posefully. He believed getting her with child would keep her
with him.

How could she not want to let him?

How could she wait another month to know if he had succeeded?

Was it too late to begin using the sponges?

She thought if she asked him, she wouldn't get the answer
she needed, but the one he wanted her to have.

Chapter Fourteen

The next day started out perfectly, lazing in bed with Hannibal, languidly making love after snuggling through the night and remembering to use her sponges.

Over breakfast in the sitting room, he received a message that necessitated his carriage being brought over from Mayfair and his going to his man of affairs. Something about the purchase of Blossom, now Sky. Something about expenditures here of late, including Tressa's extensive new wardrobe.

All those diamonds she didn't wear, she was sure.

With Hannibal gone, Tressa took the time for a long toilette with Rosemary. Coming down the front stairs in an azure gown, she hoped its color would live up to the color she'd worn the day before, the color Hannibal had called *bleu celeste,* the one they'd enjoyed while she learned to ride in the big chair in the study.

Blushing as furiously as she had on the occasion itself, Tressa watched Mudge answer the door to the delivery person from

Madame Henri's. She assisted him with the numerous plain boxes only to have another delivery arrive at the same time.

The second man was Sir Percival's footman, a man Tressa knew Mudge would recognize from when he'd carried messages to Robert at the Pounce residence. The small paper-wrapped parcel the man brought indicated Ambrosia likely had sent her message, and Tressa grasped the parcel in such haste as to cue Mudge in to its importance.

Unperturbed, he closed the door, ready to call Bates to move the piles of discreet dark boxes now lining the sidetable and lower risers up to Tressa's chamber. Instead, he peered pointedly at the package in Tressa's fingers.

Tressa and Mudge were too close for Tressa not to understand that concern, rather than curiosity, motivated Mudge's pause. They had a private moment, and that usually meant exchanging confidences.

"It's nothing to worry about, Mudge." She tore a bit of the brown paper away. " 'Tis simply a book Robert left behind in Sir Percival's book room. I've met the new mistress at Pounce's, and she told me she might return this. There might be another, in fact, and I'd appreciate it if you'd notify me the minute it comes."

Tressa reddened. She was lying, and they both knew it. She detested lying, especially to Mudge.

She lowered her lashes shamefully. "I'm sorry, I can't tell you what's afoot with the girl, but you needn't worry, Mudge. I can assure you of that."

"I'm here if you needs me, Miss," he said, moving back into the house to call Bates. "I'll send the boxes up in a bit."

Tressa took advantage of Mudge's kind dismissal of the matter and rushed up the stairs to read Ambrosia's note.

No, Tressa wouldn't involve Mudge any more than necessary. She'd already dragged him into too many of her own problems, and this problem was Ambrosia's.

In the quiet luxury of her room, Tressa perched on the edge

of the bed and tore the paper from the book. Sure enough, a letter fell onto her lap.

Unfolding it and beginning to read the long pages, she saw how difficult this would be. Ambrosia spoke well, but wrote badly, and her untidy scrawl and disjointed sentences threw Tressa off.

Evidently Ambrosia, to show she was in earnest, had taken her own little sapphire ring to Godiva, the owner of the gambling salon, and had asked her if she wouldn't wait on Lottie's return from Paris for the payment of Lottie's debt. In a messy patch, Ambrosia described Godiva's reaction as nothing short of explosive.

Not only would Godiva no longer wait on the money owed her, but she increased the amount owed to an astronomical sum. Ambrosia, obviously distraught, wasn't clear as to what she wanted Tressa to do.

In going to Godiva, the girl had also raised Sir Percival's ire. He'd caught her coming in when he'd told her she couldn't go out. Now he was watching Ambrosia so closely that she couldn't even turn to her friends for solace.

Only Tressa knew about the deep coil into which she'd sunk.

Inhaling deeply, Tressa forced herself to consider what could be done. Immediately, she saw only one answer. She would pay Lottie's debt and relieve Ambrosia.

Fortunately, she thought she had the means to pay it. Frankly, she couldn't care less if she never saw the money she could raise from her own whore's fare. She disliked her diamonds from Hannibal that much.

Without thinking farther than that, she changed into one of her old conservative gowns and veils, then gathered what she needed for a trip to the moneylenders—not that she'd ever been to the moneylenders, but almost anyone in her area would know the block on Stump Street where they could be found.

Getting to Stump Street would require hiring a hackney carriage, but her plans fell so neatly into order that she had no time to worry. Hannibal was away, and while he was instituting a guard on her, that guard was not so efficient as to take note of her leaving the house unescorted.

She was able to go without anyone's noticing out the rear door, through the garden, and past the stables into the mews. From there, she reached Great Crow Street, where she located the two or three hackney carriages that regularly came and went at the Crown and Feathers.

Using pin money Hannibal himself had handed to her, she was on her way to the moneylenders in Stump Street without any trouble at all.

Hannibal arrived home on Pocket Street, finding it interesting he considered the little house *home*. He couldn't think of anywhere he had lived or stayed that had been more like a home.

Oh, naturally, many places available to him were finer, but—

Getting down from his crested coach with his footman's assistance, he was about to bid its attendants a safe journey back to Mayfair when Knobby appeared, coming around to the front of the house through the narrow passage between the neighboring dwellings.

That the boy popped up as he did was remarkable enough, but that he seemed reluctant to approach Hannibal was odder still.

"Aye, boy?" Hannibal called to him, staying the coach with a hand.

" 'Tis my lady, Gov'." The boy was out of breath.

Hannibal's heart assumed a deeper thud, thud. How unusual, he thought, concentrating on the boy. "Your lady? What's amiss with her?"

"Nothing's amiss, I don't think. But she left, and I knew someone was supposed to go with her, so I tagged along behind her, trying to catch up. She was walking fast, Gov'. Up to the hackney carriages just this side of the Crown and Feathers.

Never did catch up with her, I didn't.'' He wet his lips with his tongue. ''She tossed a coin to the jarvey afore she climbed in and was gone.''

A hackney carriage. That, too, was strange.

''Did you hear where she was going, boy?'' Hannibal got back into his own carriage, indicating their direction to the man on the box and the speed to use.

''No, Gov'!'' Knobby hollered as Hannibal's vehicle sprang away. ''Didn't hear where she went!''

At the hackney stand near the Crown and Feathers, Hannibal got down from his coach before it completely rolled to a stop. A pair of chattering jarveys relaxed with their clay pipes, observing as he bounded toward them.

''Did you see a lady hire a hackney carriage here? Just moments ago, likely.''

They both nodded, quickly commenting on the relatively unusual sight they had just witnessed. Evidently, a very fine veiled lady had gone off unattended no more than minutes before to Stump Street.

Already knowing what that meant and what she was about, Hannibal felt relieved. But he also felt bile in his throat.

Within moments, he, too, was trundling on his way to Stump Street. London traffic had never seemed more exasperating, and he hung in his window, wanting to yell orders up to his perfectly capable coachman.

What in the devil could she be doing, going out on her own to Stump Street?

Those answers he had for himself.

No matter how much he might possess the woman physically, she eluded him with this damnable independence she so closely guarded, the independence that could land her in any sort of trouble.

That she was going to Stump Street meant she was visiting a moneylender. That meant she needed a certain unknowable amount of money. There his reasoning stopped.

Still, his mind plunged on to his worst fears.

Tressa had a secret. That was all he knew. But what was involved was so serious as to drive her from their bed, to stand at windows in the dark of night, to watch for a watcher in the street.

Joe Legg.

Hannibal already had hired someone to track down Joe Legg, but so far there'd been no sign of him. Under the guise of visiting his man of affairs not above an hour ago, Hannibal had been given a report with no good news. No progress made in finding Joe Legg, in learning who he was, or in discovering whom he represented.

What Hannibal did know from Mudge, for Mudge had once chased off the man, scared Hannibal. Joe Legg was a bad sort, and that meant Tressa's troubles must be bad.

Surely, Tressa's mad dash out of the house while he was away had to do with her secret. And to go to a moneylender was as dangerous as all the rest.

Hannibal experienced a fear he'd never known in his life. Trapped inside his carriage, he willed the traffic to clear and wished for Tressa's safety.

His worst anxiety, though, arose from the very independence that had been honed by her evidently long-guarded secret. If he pushed her too hard, she'd leave him. In the middle of the night and without a word, she'd disappear, and likely he'd be unable to find her.

And if she were carrying his child?

Therein rested the fears Hannibal couldn't seem to consider yet. Something in him was shifting, and he wasn't ready to grasp it.

He only knew he must find Tressa. He had to look into her deep blue eyes again and know, at least for this hour, this day, she fared well.

* * *

The sign of three balls.

Tressa knew she was in the right part of Stump Street when the driver stopped her hackney carriage within sight of several shops on both sides of the block, each displaying the sign of three balls. At least one had three balls crudely painted on a wooden plank. Others had nicer representations. A few more had actual balls suspended in triplet above their doors.

Behind the dusty windows, with their barrages of every kind of item, lay mysteries she couldn't imagine. In truth, her mind was awhirl as to which shop she should choose. Moneylenders inspired little confidence.

Climbing down from the hackney carriage, she walked around to pay the jarvey. On thinking again, however, she asked him to wait.

Nodding, he sat back on his perch.

Standing still, Tressa looked up and down the block, trying to decide which shop seemed best.

"Tha' one, Miss," the jarvey said, pointing to the shop across from which they had parked.

In running her gaze along her selections once more, Tressa saw that the jarvey was likely correct. The lender he indicated was the largest, and had somewhat less of a jumble in his clouded window. Candle holders and a large, blackened silver epergne that supported a collection of walking sticks, sat by an abandoned dolly with sad, sad eyes. Best of all, the shop had the biggest set of three balls, all stained by the weather.

Settled upon her shop, Tressa, who was accustomed to guarding her face with a veil, righted her shoulders, ensured that her little boxes were tightly in her grasp, and crossed the busy street. The weather was warm but blustery, and the scent of the jarvey's clay pipe eddied around her.

Entering the shop, she entered another world at the peal of the shop's bell.

If the shop windows were piled with an odd assortment of goods, the inside was an impenetrable maze of items large and small, valuable and worthless. Bits and pieces of furniture and a staring stuffed owl, which certainly set the freakish tone of the place, sat cheek by jowl with things she had no inclination to identify, nor the needed illumination.

Pressing ever deeper into the murky stillness, she followed the clearest path, not sighting another soul. At last, though, she arrived at a barred window set in a rear wall. In a cubbyhole behind the bars, a small mole of a man sat hunched over.

Stationing herself with the bars between them—together with a small counter of sorts, obviously for doing business—she sought the man's eyes.

He was old, very old, and in the dim light, his hair floated up from his head like filaments of white silk. His dark eyes, however, were lively, and Tressa knew to watch his watchful eyes.

"Sir?" she said, clutching her two small boxes as if her life depended on it.

"My lady," he replied in a rusty voice. "And what do you have for me today?"

Obviously, she had no choice but to slip the boxes through the space provided in the bars and along the only polished surface in the whole shop, the bit of counter beneath the man's hands.

Across from her and under her gaze, his crabbed fingers received the boxes. But before he opened them, he moved a branch of candles closer by, then fixed a small black cylinder with a glass in it into the wrinkles around one of his eyes.

"'Tis to be my lady's jewels today, is it?" he inquired, undoing the boxes and carefully lifting out first the ring with its big yellow diamond, and then the two earbobs with their candy-pink stones, the ones fashioned like her nipples, Hannibal had said.

The jewels looked suddenly out of place in this man's wrinkled fingers, under his candles and affixed jeweler's glass, but most especially in the dusty, hushed reign of man over curiosities. Tressa could be sure every article had a story behind it. Tales of desperation.

"Well, well," the little, darkly dressed man said, still hunched over but lifting those astute, living eyes to hers, even the one still dressed with the glass.

He studied her again.

She was sure he could see her fingers as they fidgeted within her gloves, her face behind her veil.

"These are worth a pretty penny, they are," he said. "I'd not like to have the man who gave these to you come looking for them."

"He won't," Tressa said hastily. Behind her veil she licked her lips and composed herself. "He doesn't know."

"I've heard that afore, of course. More times than you have the years for, my lady."

Tressa didn't know what to say. Her mind raced to the possibilities of the other shops, even as she knew this one was probably the best. The most trustworthy, if one could apply such a term.

Still, the man sat as he was, his eyes on her. "Do you understand the terms, my lady? I hold the diamonds for a year, and if you don't retrieve them for the amount owed, I'm free to sell them."

Tressa nodded. "I see. But I won't be returning for them, so you needn't worry."

"You also understand, don't you, that I'll give you far less for them than they're worth. Far less. These are very fine stones, and I shall have to go to the right buyer when the time comes."

"As I say, do whatever you want with the diamonds. I only need a certain amount."

"I decide the amount." He named it. "You say aye or nay."

"Aye," she replied.

Letting the glass drop from his eye socket, the crabbed little man went on to display precisely how expert he'd become in all his years of doing business on Stump Street.

Almost afraid of the amount of money she received, Tressa exited the place, the shop bell ringing her way out, and with the money simply stuffed into her reticule.

She hadn't thought about how to transfer it home, safely and undetected or about the way her reticule would appear suspiciously overstuffed.

She peered at everyone in the street nervously.

With a jaundiced eye she looked at the jarvey, only to realize he was speaking to Hannibal.

Nearby, Hannibal's crested carriage waited, his footman recognizing her and swinging open its door.

Grabbing a breath and forcing a composure she did not feel, she approached the carriage, nodded and was assisted inside.

Part of her, the part that nestled the overly stuffed reticule into her skirts, was relieved. But part of her prepared to do battle with Hannibal.

And soon he came, obviously receiving a signal from one of his entourage. His quarry was seated within his fine carriage, awaiting his ire. And his expression, as he climbed in beside her, was full of it. His well-chiseled features, his general's eyes, were filmed with banked fire.

"How pleasant it is," he said as the vehicle got under way and his astute gaze ferreted out her reticule, "to find one's lady in such a place, fresh from doing the business that's transacted here. I hope you fared well in your transaction."

"Well enough," she replied, sounding more calm than she felt.

"It appears you did."

She would not discuss the amount that filled her reticule.

"Dare I ask what you've pawned?"

"I'm sure you dare anything, my lord. I have pawned the diamonds you gave me."

He paused. "It seems it is you who dare anything, my lady."

"They were mine to do with as I wished, were they not?"

"They were yours to wear."

"But they were mine nonetheless."

He reverted to the window, his demanding general's eyes freeing her for the moment.

Still, the carriage was thick with his disapproval—nay, more. With his barely contained anger.

She remained quiet.

"I knew you didn't like them," he finally said. "But I never imagined you detested them."

"And how would you feel, my lord, to wear diamonds fashioned after a very private part of your anatomy?"

"I'd be complimented."

"Well, I was not. Besides, our agreement is not the usual one. We are independent agents who are together out of choice. You need not give me the expected baubles, and I need not keep them."

"Obviously, you do not choose to keep them. So be it. I have more important points to make than the inordinate cost of your trifling trinkets. I wish to discuss your safety. You promised to leave the house only if escorted."

"I did not promise precisely." Tressa detested prevarication. She wanted to be open and honest with Hannibal, and she relented. "But I do promise now that in future I will do my best to leave the house as you have asked. Truly, I appreciate your concern for me, and I will comply to the best of my ability."

"As if that gives me any comfort," he muttered, again watching out the coach window. But only for a moment. His voice was soon laden with a demanding, cynical tone. "I suppose I cannot ask, in this independent arrangement of ours, precisely why you need so much money."

"You may ask."

"And I do ask, ma'am."

Tressa sighed. "I don't wish to anger you."

"But you do anger me."

"But I cannot reveal the problem in which I've recently become involved. Let me merely assure you this concerns someone else, and you needn't worry about me one iota."

"Let's see. Is this iota large enough to include clandestine trips via public hacks to moneylenders? Can this iota accommodate a reticule fairly bursting with money, which would tempt anyone to knock you about in getting it for himself? I think not, ma'am."

Tressa saw there was no reply to appease Hannibal. After all, he had his arguments.

She could only revert to her own carriage window and to an unpleasant, unwanted silence between them that ensued not merely for the short distance home, but through the night and into the following day. In that silence, she saw nothing of Hannibal.

By the next afternoon, Hannibal was calm enough to seek out Mudge. His mind had passed from his fright over Tressa's safety to the practicalities of solving her problem.

The biggest problem was that she wouldn't discuss it with him.

While Hannibal realized that Mudge's first loyalty was to Tressa—and he hoped that would always remain true—since that night they'd both caught up with Dan Quick outside the Crown and Feathers, Mudge had viewed Hannibal in a new light.

Their frequent encounters had become laced with openness

and mutual confidence. He and Mudge had a relationship of equals.

Hannibal liked it, and he didn't want to chance losing it.

In going to the Crown and Feathers in the afternoon when Mudge habitually had a pint with his fellows there, Hannibal acknowledged he was taking advantage of their near friendship. Still, Tressa's safety was of primary importance to Hannibal, and even Mudge's respect for him had to bend to that.

Hannibal's best hope was that the wise and capable Mudge would understand.

On a summer's soft afternoon, the Crown and Feathers was more light of company than during the rest of the day. In the commodious taproom, with its timber-framed walls, Hannibal saw the older man sitting at a heavy trestle table, talking with his friends. The colorful diamond-pained windows were thrown open.

The minute Mudge spied him, Hannibal saw his concern had been unnecessary. Mudge came to Hannibal with a slight smile on his lips, even warming in his eyes.

Mudge wasn't slighted one rap. Quite the contrary. Hannibal felt gratified.

"You needs me, me lord?"

"I want to talk to you. Privately."

Mudge shrugged, his eyes running to the few smaller, empty tables in the tap room. "Can be as private in the noise as in the quiet, I suppose. Will it do here, me lord?"

"Just so. Over there at that corner table. Can I buy you—"

"No, me lord. This is my treat. Just sit down and it'll come to us. I have a little say here, you know."

Indeed, on Mudge's repute at the place, Hannibal felt welcome as the house brew was set before him in a large pitcher. Pouring their own refreshment, the pair settled in quickly, with Mudge peering at Hannibal across the small table. Both of them were patterned with jewel-colored light cast through the nearby window. The summer breeze cavorted with Hannibal's unlikely topic.

"I understand your strong loyalty to Miss Dear, and I wouldn't tread on it. But I'm damned worried about her—"

"You see those two fellows over there at that table where I was sitting, me lord?"

Hannibal nodded.

"They're the footmen at Sir Percival's. Two more good men in my company works at Godiva's, the gaming hell."

"Yes, I know."

"So I have the whole of the story for you, me lord, from them. It ends with the delivery of a book in a brown paper parcel, just yesterday late in the morning. It's tha' story you're wanting to hear, me lord."

With the head of his cane, Hannibal rapped at the door of Sir Percival Pounce's residence on Green Lion Square. It was mid afternoon, just after he'd finished with Mudge at the Crown and Feathers, and his blood was up for the occasion.

Fortunately, the butler's was not. At first impressed by Hannibal's appearance, the stout middle-aged fellow grew taken aback when Hannibal swept in around him.

"Where is Sir Percival's study?" Hannibal inquired.

"The door's just there, my lord. But I should ask Sir Percival if—"

"Don't bother. I'll announce myself."

With that, Hannibal swung into the study. Sir Percival sat behind his desk, hard at it over a manuscript. Hannibal had heard of Sir Percival's writings—had been acquainted with him at Oxford—apart from what little Robert had conveyed to him.

Bounder, Hannibal wanted to say, *ill-mannered, ill-favored, illiterate bounder.*

"Sir Percival," he said instead, when the man looked up.

Aye, Hannibal found a mix of surprise and pleasure, quickly overridden by an unctuous need to bootlick, in Sir Percival's fleshy face.

"I'm not here on pleasant business, Pounce."

The man froze halfway out of his chair. "My Lord Braxton, I, uh—"

"You will have Lottie's box of meager jewels on the surface of your desk before Ambrosia comes down."

Hannibal moved back to the door, which he opened. "I shall have your butler fetch her and give you a scant moment. Take advantage of it, sir."

Sir Percival dropped his toad-eating smile and scrambled— just where, Hannibal did not see. He spoke to the now trembling butler and then turned back into Sir Percival's sanctum.

On the desk, square in the center, a small box inlaid with mother-of-pearl waited.

"Rather trifling for one such as yourself to take into your possession, is it not?"

Sir Percival turned his red-blotched face to the window and stared resentfully out. "I intend to have no more to do with this business, Braxton. I see what you're about. Frankly, I say good riddance to the pair of chits. They've been nothing but trouble since they came through the door."

Braxton was saved a reply by the careful approach of a girl who, on first appearance, looked no more than in her early teens. With ginger coloring and a pretty face, she could be none other than one of the sisters in question, Ambrosia, the one Tressa had befriended on her walks.

"You are," he said to be sure, "Ambrosia, I take it?"

She nodded, then bobbed a curtsy.

"My name is Braxton, and I've come on behalf of a good friend of yours—Miss Dear."

The girl looked about to collapse. "Miss Dear, my lord? I do declare. Miss Dear."

Sir Percival harrumphed. "Miss Dear is behind this, is she? I should have known!"

"Ambrosia," Hannibal said, "open the box on the desk and inspect the contents. I want your assurance that what you find belongs to your sister and only to your sister and that the contents are complete."

The girl did as she was bid, nervously looking from Hannibal to her tormentor. But since he refused to glance at her even as she turned over the box and quickly fingered through a few pieces of inexpensive jewelry, she was able to brace herself.

" 'Tis all my sister's, my lord. All of it and none other."

"Good. Now, Ambrosia, you will return to your chamber and pack your belongings. Call whomever you need to help you, and we will be on our way. I'll bid your good-byes to Sir Percival for you, as well as my own."

With Sir Percival no longer recognizing him, Hannibal was back in the entry within minutes. He'd issued his warnings to the man, and was anxious to be shut of the place. Since Ambrosia took a while to come down, he paced back and forth under the nervous watch of the butler.

Finally in his carriage, Ambrosia gave him the direction of her mother's abode, and Hannibal delivered the girl there. On seeing the blowsy mother and her place, the situation of untidy rooms she shared with her current lover, Hannibal had to wonder how long the circumstances would last.

None of that was his concern, though, and he drove on to the final stop in his distasteful duty—to Godiva's. He barged into the old harlot's sanctum as he had Sir Percival's.

He paid the bejeweled, maquillaged crone only the amount of Lottie's original voucher, and said he'd hear no more either from her or of her.

Like Sir Percival, Godiva ended without two words to rub together, and Hannibal left.

Again in his carriage, he felt for the first time Tressa's shame in having been given such outlandish diamonds, and only days within being known to him.

Hannibal felt subdued in spite of his victories. He certainly hated the demimonde. But he especially hated that Tressa knew about it and possibly saw herself as part of it.

Chapter Fifteen

Although Tressa hadn't seen Hannibal since the afternoon before when he'd found her at the moneylenders, she finally decided to dress and go down to dinner, just as she had last night when she'd eaten alone.

Naturally, every sort of idea had assailed her in the hours since seeing him, since arguing with him, and she'd nearly decided it was time she and Mudge left Pocket Street.

But first she had to finish what she'd started in helping Ambrosia. She'd definitely done the worst part in fetching the money from the moneylender. Now she had to decide how to pass the funds along to the girl.

This was a problem she had pondered as much as she had her differences with Hannibal. What's more, having the large amount of money in her reticule was unnerving.

Still without solutions, she put Ambrosia's problems from her thoughts and concentrated on dinner, especially on how she was dressed. Wearing one of her new gowns from Madame Henri, she felt dashing, even daring.

Using every advantage she could think of, she'd chosen a gown in a night-sky blue, the nearest shade to her eyes at night. Madame Henri had been right in dressing her in so much blue, because Hannibal liked it.

This blue gown was ladylike, as were all her gowns, but also touched with daring. The lowest neckline she could imagine set off the swells of her breasts and her shoulders. Of soft satin, with a short train, it was fitted close to the bosom and finished at the edges with silver cord and silver beading. Silver beads also trimmed her small, neatly fitting evening cap, making her honey-colored hair appear like purest gold.

Rosemary's satisfaction with her elaborate hair arrangement and her gown and cap helped Tressa decide she looked well despite her emotional state.

Going down to the sitting room at the rear of the house, she entered the chamber just as Bates was lighting the candles and putting the finishing touches on the table. Beyond the open windows with their balustraded balconies, evening creatures fiddled and sang their songs down in the garden.

Everything should have been perfect, but it was all wrong.

Without Hannibal, everything seemed wrong.

As the silver clock on the mantel below Doro's lovely portrait struck the hour and the mattress turned over, Tressa realized how far she'd come in her experience on Pocket Street.

She'd developed a tolerance for the clock.

Hearing Hannibal's footsteps, she lifted her chin and faced the door. He wouldn't find her downcast. She was, in fact, so pleased to see him she felt she could weather his worst mood.

"A good evening to you." He entered the room, but left the door ajar as if he had no intention of staying.

"Good evening, Hannibal."

As usual, he looked wonderful in dark evening attire. In this instance, though, he appeared as interested in her garb as she would have liked. His general's eyes, perhaps against his will, coursed over her. Yes, he liked the color she wore, the low cut of her neckline, her graceful address.

He told her so without words. His eyes, his absorption, told her.

But he also told her other things without speaking. Unlike himself, he didn't keep his gaze to hers. What's more, he seemed subdued and in a hurry to go.

"I won't be staying for dinner," he said, confirming her surmise. "I'm eating out with friends."

She nodded.

"I want to apologize, however. I want to say I'm sorry about the way I spoke to you yesterday in the carriage. To make it up, I've done the best I could by your friend, Ambrosia."

"Ambrosia? But how did you know?"

"To tell the truth, it was easy to discover the trouble she was having with Sir Percival and Godiva. As I say, I've seen to them and returned the girl to her mother. You needn't worry."

Tressa was so stunned she didn't know what to say. Ambrosia with her mother instead of with Sir Percival?

"I think it's a good idea if I leave you be tonight," Hannibal said, "let you have some time to get over being angry with me."

"But I—"

"I promise to take you riding tomorrow."

She blushed.

"I mean in Green Park. Sky. And after we ride, I'll see to it you have an account into which you can deposit the money you raised at the moneylenders."

"But I already have an account. Of course, it doesn't have all that much in it, but I've been saving."

"I'll be glad to add to it. I'm still hoping to make you financially secure in a way you can accept."

Tressa wished he'd sit down. She needed time to adjust to what he was saying. She wanted to spend the evening in conversation, and then . . .

But Hannibal remained aloof, although cordial, even when he stepped closer and withdrew a little box from his pocket.

"Now, don't have my head on a plate just yet," he requested, as her eyes took in the box. "This is not whore's fare. At least, I wish you would not regard it as such. In fact, it's trifling, too trifling to give any consideration. Merely part of my apology."

Tressa opened the box and concentrated as best she could. He was so subdued, so unlike himself.

She picked up the simple gold ring and examined the equally simple dark blue stone.

" 'Tis called lapis lazuli," he explained. "As I say, not much at all. But I do hope you like it. I know I do. I thought of you the minute I saw it. The color, you know."

Tressa nodded. Actually, she was amazingly touched by the simple ring, the meaning for them in the dark blue shade.

"Thank you," she managed. "I like it, too."

He seemed relieved, more and more himself. Soon he'd be free to go.

"So I'll leave you in peace," he said. "Enjoy your dinner, have a nice quiet evening and a good rest, and I'll see you first thing in the morning for our ride. Knobby's excited about going with us, although I must say he doesn't much like it that we're changing Blossom's name to Sky—if, that is, you still approve."

Again, Tressa nodded.

She wanted to grab him by his fine evening coat and shake him, to kiss him hard on the mouth. She wanted to demand he stay with her and tell her what was wrong.

But she couldn't. She was too craven.

She'd spend the evening the way she had her hours since yesterday, thinking about Hannibal and how she could lure him back. She had so little time with him left.

* * *

Since their school days, they'd been known as the Devil's Own, Braxton and his friends Nicholas Ware, the Earl of Sleet, and Cinder Sinclair, Viscount St. Cur.

The Devil's Pack and the Devil's Blood had also been used to describe them down through the years for their devastating good looks and heartbreaking disinterest in marriageable ladies, their extraordinary privilege and elusiveness, their solid front, and, although not so much anymore, their devilish behavior.

In Sin's small rooms in St. James's, a few candles burned low in their sockets late into the night. All three men, with their black hair, were noted for the way they wore their clothes on their splendid bodies. Tonight, they were incomparable in the most expensive dark evening attire to be had.

A bottle of the finest claret shone like liquid silk on the table where Braxton sat across from Sin. Nick, who was said to be as cold as his title, stood, of course. Always restless, he occasionally paced, his black eyes nonetheless attentive to their meandering discussion.

Sin lounged on his chair, deceptively languid, and, as some claimed, potentially lethal. His pale gray eyes, almost colorless, were always sharply observant, and as softly affectionate as they ever were.

"I'd say ol' Braxie is having troubles with his mistress. One night drunk as a don, and now not taking a drop."

"Yes, well," Nick murmured, "it's just as well he don't drink. He disremembers how to find his way home. In any case," he added, "don't we all have troubles with our mistresses?"

"I certainly wish mine to the devil," Sin said, sighing.

"On the other hand," said Nick, pausing to examine his silent friend, "our ol' Braxie might just be the first of us to fall in love."

Sin shifted uncomfortably, if also slowly. "As if any of the three of us would fall in love. In fact, as I recall it, we've all sworn not to. Somewhere over some ghastly open grave, as I remember. And shedding a bit of blood, too, pricked from our fingers with a damnable penknife stolen from the house master. Absolutely no women would ever come between us, we pledged.''

''And so far,'' said Nick, ''we've managed. No women in anyone's life. Except for our conveniences, if I may put it so crudely.''

''Yes, well, this one is a lady,'' said Braxton, drawing their eyes. ''She don't deserve to be a mistress, and now I've gone and made her one.''

Nick inhaled deeply, deplorably put out. ''Who is this lady mistress of yours?''

Hannibal knew he could tell this pair, and only this pair, anything he wanted and it would go to hell with them. And yet he didn't feel he could speak Tressa's name even in such intimate, trusted company.

At his silence, Sin's wicked pale eyes caught Nick's black gaze. ''I'd say ol' Braxie's in love, all right. Not that I know how to recognize love, but it's obvious he's gone and broken our pledge. Worse yet, he's keeping the first secret any of us has ever had.''

''And so,'' said Nick, ''the Devil's Pack begins to crack. Like all good packs, brought down by a woman—excuse me, a lady. I hope she's worth it, Braxie.''

Sin held up his glass. ''To Braxie's lady mistress. I hope for our sakes, Nick, she's soft on the eyes, even if she's taken a knife to our hearts and prized us apart.''

In a filmy, highly pleated nightgown, Tressa lay in her bed, fingering the ring Hannibal had given her earlier in the evening. Because she'd left her candle burning, she studied the deep-blue stone in the simple gold band.

She adored it. As she adored him.

Admittedly, she waited, listening for any sound the old house made in the night. Surely he'd return soon. It was nigh onto midnight, and she'd never spent such a restless time in her life.

She was hoping he'd come to her despite his having said he wouldn't. Even if he came in announcing he was foxed and then falling into a deep sleep at the bottom of her bed, she'd be able to sleep, too.

Where could he be? Dining with friends, he'd said.

Recalling the Dowager Lady Farronby's chatter about Society's doings—for the dowager had been at the pinnacle of the polite world in her day—a few things about Braxton arose in Tressa's mind, aside from his privilege and station.

The marquess had been connected with two gentlemen of his own ilk, the Lords Sleet and St. Cur. The Devil's Spawn, she'd heard them called, but surely only in their younger years.

Braxton was entirely dutiful now. True, he was dangerous in the sense that others could pin their wishes on him and he might not find those wishes of value. He certainly had no need for her heart, the love she would bear him for the rest of her days. So, to her, he was dangerous. But otherwise, the iron-eyed general was quite a—

Abruptly tossed out of her wandering considerations, Tressa heard Hannibal enter downstairs. Right away, she was up against a decision she hadn't made. Should she confront him? Should she wait and see if he came to her?

No, she'd not chance missing him. Not anymore.

Throwing back her covers, she dashed to her door and opened it in time to see him enter the corridor they shared. She measured him closely. He appeared, if a bit tired, entirely himself.

His gaze caressed her in her filmy gown and nothing else. He saw her breasts ripen beneath her gown, heavy with need for him. Her mouth blossomed, full and rosy. Her hair drifted down her back to her waist, a honeyed temptation.

He stiffened, nodded, barely pausing out of politeness alone. He hadn't imbibed much, if anything at all. She knew that by the clearness, the wariness, the general's control in his beautiful gray eyes.

"No doubt you were worried I might crawl into your bed and accost you. I know I've come to you inebriated before, but all of that's to change, my lady. I'm quite sober, and I'm ready for my own bed. If you'll excuse me."

His eyes lingered on her despite his curtness, his control. She thought he . . . she hoped he . . .

But, no. Gathering himself, he strode inside his chamber and closed the door.

The general ruled the lover. But why?

She was so obviously available, so apparently wanton.

Perhaps he was tiring of her. That happened to mistresses regularly. Mayhap he couldn't abide her independence, her bargain of equals, the trouble she caused. Possibly, as one of the Devil's Spawn, he couldn't equate her to his former females, to the females he would seek out in future.

He wouldn't settle. She couldn't settle.

She had to stay clear and protect him from her secret, her cursed name and nature as Bad Buck Devlin's daughter.

Talk about the devil's spawn.

In her room and still unable to sleep and restless beyond measure nearly an hour later, Tressa again threw back the covers. Inevitably drawn to a view of the street, she crept upstairs to the attic room at the front of the house.

Last time, Daniel Quick had been in the street and Hannibal had chased him off. She could be sure she'd never see Quick again, and recalled her relief. But with a trepidation that never changed, she approached the closed curtains. One watcher, one alone, could turn her blood cold.

Parting the drapes and peering down on Pocket Street, Tressa viewed the usual, peaceful scene. The tiny neighborhood slept as it lived its days, largely in harmony.

That a barrel-shaped man who represented all that was evil

to her would step into the light so she could see him made her look again.

Rub her eyes and stare again.

Yes, it was Joe Legg, her uncle's minion. She knew it, and he knew she saw him.

As before, when they'd met in their mutual, relentless watching, she at a window and he on the pavement, Joe Legg removed his hat in a parody of respect and greeting.

He was letting her know he'd found her, and he was proud of doing his dastardly job for her uncle so well.

How he'd located her she'd probably never know, but she'd been certain he'd track her down.

And here he was, tipping his hat, his cruel, taunting smile directed to the slight movement she made at the draperies. Frozen for a moment, Tressa jerked the drapes closed, and recoiled.

Joe Legg. It really had been Joe Legg, here on Pocket Street.

He'd reminded her again that he watched, that he'd always watch, that her uncle would always know where she was and what she was doing, that she'd better live according to their expectations, or there would be hell to pay.

As if she hadn't paid already. As if she wouldn't pay in the future by leaving Hannibal.

Hannibal!

Just as the sight of Joe Legg had breathed hell into her, the thought of Hannibal asleep in his bed breathed panic.

Down the stairs she sped, trying to be quiet, but clumsy and racing. In her bedchamber, behind her closed door and in the light of her single candle, she pulled her reticule, still stuffed with money, from the drawer in the nightstand. Her trip to the moneylender would become her salvation, and she placed the reticule in the candlelight.

She'd take with her only the clothes she'd brought, and she began putting them on her bed. Emptying her drawers and sorting through her wardrobe, she quickly had a pile, but not a huge pile.

It wouldn't take much doing.

She'd creep out the back way, using the same route to the Crown and Feathers she'd employed the day before. Instead of hiring a hackney carriage, however, she'd hire a room at the noisy, bustling inn and be safe until daylight.

Then she'd wait for Mudge. He'd stand by her.

He'd find her a room in a lodging house, somewhere she could hide until he settled her into another position in the City as a companion. He'd said he'd find her one when the time came, and it had come.

But then Hannibal came into her room. He entered quietly and closed the door behind him. As understanding filtered into his handsome features, they grew harsh.

He'd come to make love with her, for he wore his lightweight, black-as-blame dressing gown and nothing else, the one he'd worn when they'd first been intimate.

But, straightening, he retied its sash with its golden tassels and pierced her with commanding eyes.

"I find you, at last, sneaking away in the night."

She replied calmly. She was set on her path. "Blood will out, my lord. Surely you're feeling most satisfied."

All his coolness exploded into hot rebuke. "Blood will out is utter nonsense, and you and I know it, even if other fools don't. I am not *most satisfied* that you are leaving. You know damnably well I want you to stay."

Tressa continued packing quietly, efficiently. She had her portmanteau open on the bed, and she filled it from the piles she'd sorted there.

Hannibal paced, his dark silk wrapper hissing his agitation. "Have you been peering out the windows again? Have you seen someone to disturb you? Is that what this is about?"

Tressa remained silent.

He continued to pace, but slower. "Tell me your secret, Tressa. I can help you. I can protect you."

"I'll take the ring you gave me this evening, my lord, if you don't mind, but nothing else. Only my trunk will follow later."

"Of course I don't mind that you take the ring." The heat returned. "I gave it to you, by the devil, for you to keep. I gave everything for you to keep. What damnable good will a wardrobe of gowns do me?"

Tressa's heart palpitated sadly at this mention of the future. He'd suffer, too, if only briefly compared to her.

Still, she couldn't help softening. The general's hands were tied. She'd tied them, and he was frustrated.

Poor general. Poor lovely gray-eyed general.

Perhaps he sensed her moment of softening. Or perhaps something in him eased in that direction, too. In any case, he came to her. As she paused to peer at the ring to gather some strength, he took her into his arms.

"Tell me," he coaxed. "I can help."

She shook her head. There was only danger for him.

She could only run, only find someplace new and watch out the windows again, only do what was expected and protect this man she loved.

He stood with her, embracing her, placing his lips to her forehead and fitting himself to her. He was so warm and strong, so comforting. Almost elementally, they fell into a rocking motion.

Tressa had never experienced anything so dear.

"Tell me," he urged softly. "Tell me something about Lance Hall. Not about the secret, if you won't, but about your childhood, perhaps."

Lance Hall. After her father's death, it had become such a frightening place of cruel isolation that Tressa hadn't willingly thought about it since she'd left at eighteen.

"Up until this last generation, our family was a well respected one in Middlesex. Very fine, going back hundreds of years and many generations.''

''Very fine,'' he murmured, his mouth still against her forehead.

''The Hall, and Castlelance before it, were important places where important things happened, and I learned its history from a governess I liked very well. Since I had no one but my uncle and my Aunt Editha, and they weren't interested in me, the staff at the Hall became like a family to me. I had good friends that I missed for a long time after I left. By then, my Uncle Straith and Aunt Editha seldom spoke to anyone in the neighborhood, except politely if they encountered someone on errands or after church. But, by and large, we had little outside contact and lived . . . curiously. Darkly. Drably. In most ways, the Dowager Lady Farronby's invitation for me to come live with her in London was a happy relief. I certainly grew fond of her over the years we were together.''

Hannibal's embrace tightened. ''I'm glad you had her, at least. I've always thought having parents was a scourge, what with mine fighting day and night, tooth and nail. But I see now they were better than none at all.''

Softly rocking in tune with Hannibal's body, safe in his strong arms and with his lips pressed to her forehead and hearing his confidences, Tressa was tempted to tell him all. Instead, her darkest childhood fear, even darker than her fears of Uncle Straith and Aunt Editha, tumbled out.

''Up in the hills above Lance Hall, which is very old but also in good condition, is the ruin of Castlelance, our oldest family property. In what's left of the castle, there's one room solidly intact. But the reason the room is intact is because the walls are very thick. And the reason the walls are very thick is because, once, my family buried the enemies it had taken in a feud within the walls. The captives were cemented alive into the stones and left to die horrible deaths. When I have nightmares, I'm always in that room on a stone slab, my breath ebbing away and . . ."

Reaching the end of her most regular nightmare, Tressa felt relief at finally having told it to someone, and Hannibal obviously felt a relief at her having shared that much with him.

Never had she felt so at one with another being. Never had she felt so safe. And yet she wasn't safe. Even this strong male, with every advantage in the world, wasn't safe—because of her.

She couldn't bear it.

She might not leave tomorrow or the next day, but she'd get cleanly away soon.

After some minutes, their rocking motion slowed to a stop. Tressa recognized the emotional shifts taking place in Hannibal because they also occurred in her. Tender warmth became more than tender, more than warmth. Desire rocked, then rocketed, centering them on the inevitable.

In her filmy gown, she'd purposely revealed herself to him in the hallway when he'd returned home. For an hour, he'd remained in his room, but obviously had no more slept than she had.

He'd come to her naked except for his black silk dressing gown barely closed by the tie which rode loosely, revealingly, at his trim waist.

With every emotion running high in her, Tressa still desired Hannibal above all. As she'd readily admitted to herself time and again, he held more sway over her than anything in two worlds—the *beau monde* and the demimonde.

Hannibal led her across the hallway into the master's chamber, where the dark paneling and heavy furnishings contrasted with her own chamber's gilt and delicate yellows.

The old, thickly carved bed waited in the shadows, as freshly dressed as Tressa's bed. Rosemary kept the two beds crisp and fragrant, standing ready in a mistress's house.

At the bedside, Hannibal blew out the candle, leaving them

in the dark. No fire glowed in the hushed room, no light reached up from the street. Even the music from the garden was muted here.

In the dark, Hannibal became as palpably everything to Tressa as he was in her heart and soul and mind. For this brief time, here in the pitch black, nothing else existed, only his warm hands lifting off her filmy nightwear, only his warm breath like a whisper on her shoulder.

Reaching out, she found his silken dressing gown had disappeared in the unlit vastness. His warm skin, under her coursing fingertips, covered a firm structure of undulating muscle. She skimmed his profile, as hard and jutting as his male center.

And that, too, was hard and jutting—heated in the dark, pulsing and long in the dark, awaiting her in the dark.

Wanting to grasp him to her, to cling to him as long as she could, Tressa filled her eager hand with his rigid male flesh. She was greedy, wanting all she could hold.

But he was hungry, too.

When he could stand no more of her marauding hands, he swept her up against his solidity and tumbled her onto the mattress, then followed her down, hot and ready and wanting.

He plunged into her with his manhood, taking her as she wanted to be taken—in the dark, without a word, not even of love.

Without a thought for tomorrow.

She wanted to taste and smell him. The scent of his evening lingered in the light aroma of tobacco and claret.

She liked it that the room was night-sky blue and masculinely spare. She wished for no softness.

She opened her eyes and reveled in his driving possession, but she only felt him, hard and heavy and letting go of himself into her.

She wanted him to mark her forever. This could be their final time, she thought, and she wanted it to last wherever her spinster's life might lead her.

In the hush, the pads of her fingers made their indelible claim on him. Always, he would be loved. Always, the aging and nunnish Miss Devlin, who would grow more unlike Bad Buck with every year, would harbor this abandoned night with her well-remembered lover.

Chapter Sixteen

Last night, it had taken Sin and Nick, of all people, to bring Hannibal to the recognition that he loved Tressa. As the Devil's Own, none of them had expected to fall in love—certainly not Hannibal.

But he loved Tressa Devlin. And why not?

She was perfect for him. No, perfect in every way.

What an awakening! What a coil!

He wanted to please her, of course. He loved her. He wanted to keep her safe, to smooth her path, to press upon her everything he possessed, to cover her in his family's jewels and keep her otherwise naked and to himself.

He wanted to restore her to her rightful world. She deserved it.

He wanted everyone to bow to her as the Marchioness of Braxton.

He wanted to hie her off to Cannongate and show her the sea.

He wanted to treat her with every regard.

He wanted to erase any recollection of her having been a mistress rather than a proper wife. He wanted to marry her.

Unfortunately, all she wanted on this bright morning after their ride in Green Park was to have breakfast at the dashed tea garden. How could he deny her simple wish?

And so it was.

Just the pair of them. A long, surprisingly pleasant, walk to the decrepit old garden with its unacceptable mix of company, however smiling and polite they might be. He detested it that she knew of such a place as Cupid's Tea Garden, where low women strolled among the rest. It angered him that she had ever seen Pocket Street, that she had ever been a mistress, insulted by the ways of the half world.

But his powers couldn't give him everything he wanted.

Besides, she appeared so happy. Even behind her nearly transparent, flirtish veil, he could see the brightness of her eyes, her unexpected smile that burst upon him like the purest, softest light.

Like the purest, softest love.

By the devil, but he had fallen. And hard.

They sat at a table in an arbor smothered in summer greenery and lanced by trembling light. Garbed, now, in a walking dress—for she had bowled him over in a riding costume cut *à la militare* earlier in the morning—she frequently lifted her veil, giving him glimpses of her beautiful face.

Though he liked her in dark blue to match her eyes and highlight her creamy skin and honeyed hair, Madame Henri had dressed her in a dusty rose walking dress bordered with scallops in the forms of seashells. Seashells were recalled again in her close, secretive bonnet and hinted at in the accompanying veil.

But he was tired of veils and secrets and the tea garden. His newspaper lay on the fresh linen of the table. Her teaspoon rattled softly on her saucer. Plum cake went half uneaten on his plate.

"Why do you suppose Tia Toussand"—she brought up yet another irritation—"seems to make such a point of addressing you whenever we come across her? You are also of that impression, are you not?"

Hannibal shrugged. "Yes, I have the same impression, that she purposely seeks us out. Why she does so, I can't say. As I've understood it—and we have been introduced—her main interest in life is her own little social set, which is undeniably stellar, but is also comprised of people who have rather removed themselves from the normal rounds—people such as myself, I suppose."

"And why is she taken with people who are more outside the regular elite?"

"She's long had a running feud with Lady Jersey. They detest each other—which means, of course, that Sally keeps Tia from enjoying herself whenever she can. Having the power Sally has as Silence Jersey, she is not one to brook. I doubt Tia, who is in every way all that is top-of-the-trees, will ever make it much higher in the rolls, not with Lady Jersey having so much say."

"It seems," Tressa murmured, "that the half world patterns the polite world. All the insiders and outsiders, the private grudges and rows. Which reminds me, how well have you fared as far as the gossip is concerned, with having involved yourself with Godiva and Sir Percival and Ambrosia? And with this mysterious Miss Dear, of course."

He grunted, finally testing his coffee, which had stopped steaming in the bright summer air. "People of every sort gossip. I don't concern myself with it. Some of the tale will make the rounds, even in Society, but it doesn't bother me."

"You have the kind of consequence that allows you to do what you like and live above the tittle-tattle. You are most fortunate."

He didn't want to talk of commonalties.

He wanted to tell her how lovely she looked, how graceful

she was in any setting. He wanted to discuss the important matters concerning them, to ask that one crucial question.

But he warned himself not to act in haste. He wouldn't set her inadvertently against something that might come upon her as unexpectedly as it had he himself.

"So," she said, causing him to listen to the music of her voice, "I suppose I shall send Ambrosia a note. I want to make it clear that I shall always stand as her friend and that I'm happy you were so helpful to her. In fact, you say she lives quite close to the tea garden now, with her mother."

"Yes, but don't rest too comfortably on that head."

"What do you mean?"

"Her mother didn't seem too happy about Ambrosia's return to the nest—not that the nest seemed too happy, either."

"Yes, Ambrosia's conversations about her family were never happy. Her parents remain unmarried, and while she adores her father, he's a strolling player and seldom sees her. Her people on both sides are from the theater, and her mother still takes an occasional role to earn what she can."

"That accounts for their nearly proper use of the language, no doubt."

"Yes, I have mentioned to her on several occasions that, with her fine speech, she could support herself as a shop assistant, or perhaps go into higher service of some sort. But she looks down on regular work, and seems proud of her little round. I'm sure both she and Lottie, her sister, have been reared to view it that way."

"Mayhap, when her sister returns, Ambrosia will be more content to live with her."

As if talking about them conjured them up, Ambrosia and her mother, Mrs. White, appeared, strolling together on the gravel walk leading past their table.

Purposely, Hannibal had guided Tressa off the beaten path, and could have groaned. When the two females spied him and

Miss Dear, he read the writing on the wall. When his Miss Dear waved at the pair of females, they felt encouraged to greet them, tucked away in their arbor.

Mrs. White, who looked very much like her daughter, although with hennaed hair as opposed to Ambrosia's sandy coloring, was the blowsy, overly talkative sort with whom Hannibal never had much patience.

Picking up his coffee and letting the women converse was the single way he knew to endure. Unfortunately, it seemed he was to remain the center of their conversation. After effusive greetings, Mrs. White expounded on the wonderful help he'd been to her daughters.

Oh, and the payment he had made to that horrid, horrid Godiva!

"And I thank you, too, Miss Dear," she added, her thoroughly befeathered bonnet picking up the slightest breeze and rioting in the sunlight.

Ambrosia had less to say. But her eyes shone, indicating her admiration for both Miss Dear and Braxton.

"His lordship was most gallant in his rescue of my daughter, my dear Miss . . ." Mrs. White laughed. "Well, my dear Miss Dear. The way Ambrosia describes it, it was a scene fit for mounting on a stage—wicked Sir Percival and the gallant marquess. I can see it, I truly can."

Tressa's soft laughter encouraged Mrs. White to go on, all pudding-faced with sentimentality. "And now, my dear Effie— I mean Ambrosia—is at home with me again. I tell you, I can hardly wait for Lottie to return so we can be completely happy."

Hannibal shifted uncomfortably, which was better, he thought, than scoffing. He hoped it was his look that brought Mrs. White's flights of fancy down a notch or two. Soon he had her excusing herself and wishing them farewell.

"That was not nice of you, Hannibal," Tressa said, although not too disapprovingly.

"It was the only way to get rid of her. Besides, I was nice enough in paying off Godiva and assisting her daughters."

"Well . . ." She hemmed. "That is true."

For the next few days, Tressa wore riding habits, all of them in the military style, one after another as they were delivered from Madame Henri's. She did, in fact, love to see the light in Hannibal's general's eyes, especially when she wore smart riding attire. After all, his attire was invariably the latest fashion.

She also rather thought that Tia Toussand kept a close watch on Madame Henri's inventiveness, the playfulness expressed in her riding clothes.

Tressa was happy.

Oh, she knew Joe Legg had caught up with her and that he watched at night. It was likely he also knew a lot about her days, spent entirely now with Hannibal.

That was why she was happy and why she didn't run away. She wanted to see how many days she could eke out just with Hannibal. She'd come too far not to latch on tightly to what she could. Above all, she swore to be happy and enjoy it.

On yet another beautiful summer morning in Green Park, Tressa was sure that Hannibal noted, as she did, that Mrs. Toussand rode close on their heels. They heard her great horse blowing, the occasional jingle of his gear.

Tia Toussand was an exceptional rider, no doubt, and the style in which she rode, her fashionable costumes, made her a treat for the eyes. In the sunlight, her auburn hair flashed, signaling through the green foliage. Glimpses of her disclosed a smart rider in a perfect control, on her own and enjoying herself. Tressa was intrigued, just as Tia seemed intrigued by her, as well.

Coming up on the stables, but still on the bridle path and with the summer woods thick and warm and inviting around them, Hannibal reined in his own great Saracen and, surprising Tressa, climbed down.

He helped her dismount, too, but her veil hid the question in her gaze. Even so, Tressa knew he sensed her curiosity. Taking Saracen's reins, then Sky's, he grasped Tressa's elbow and began walking slowly in the direction of the stables.

With nostrils extended, the horses blew out their anxiety to press for their stalls. They turned especially nervy as Tia caught up with them on the path from behind.

Always in charge of her mounts, Mrs. Toussand easily rode out the bit of confusion that ensued. With a big smile and a tip of her mannish beaver hat, she acknowledged them.

She dared using another male prerogative, Tressa saw, impressed and closely observing the woman.

When Hannibal stopped walking, abruptly halting the mixed party of people and animals, everyone but him seemed taken aback.

"Pray, Mrs. Toussand," he said, "you must forgive my inconsideration on the bridle path."

Mrs. Toussand flashed him a grin. "My forgiveness would not have meant three straws had we all collided, my Lord Braxton. How go you? Is something amiss?"

"No, as you can see, we are quite well this morning. My purposes are to test you out, Mrs. Toussand."

Looking down at them, she appeared puzzled. "To test me out, sir? This should be fun."

Hannibal didn't smile.

"I should like to know how you might react to being introduced to my veiled lady."

"Your *lady*?" She emphasized the key word.

Beneath her veil, Tressa cringed. Her heart lurched.

What in heaven's name was Hannibal about? It had been so pleasant. They hadn't much time left. Why must he do this?

"You must trust me, Mrs. Toussand," he said, "when I say

lady. I should like to introduce you, but I will not do so if there's any chance of either of you being slighted.''

Taking a moment, Tia freed herself from her sidesaddle and slipped to the ground. ''I shall be pleased to have your lady presented to me, sir.''

Tressa felt worse and worse. Still, as one lady meeting another lady, she had to do so face to face. With nerveless fingers, she lifted her veil, tucking it back into her own jaunty beaver hat.

Tia Toussand was all amazement.

''Mrs. Toussand,'' Hannibal said, formally, ''if I may present—''

''Yes, I know,'' said Tia, interrupting Hannibal. ''Miss Tressa Devlin. But I had thought . . .''

''You had thought, what?'' Hannibal urged.

''Well, I don't know. Everyone knew, of course, when Miss Devlin was staying with the Dowager Lady Farronby.''

''Earning her own keep at the demand of her uncle,'' Hannibal announced, sourly.

Indeed, thought Tressa, everyone had to know that because of Bad Buck, the Devlins were pockets-to-let and Tressa had been earning her own way.

''And then,'' Tia went on, ''I'm sure most people believed she stayed there, seeing to the house for the new Lady Farronby—Harriet, my half cousin. As I recollect, Harriet said Miss Devlin was an absolute jewel. Harriet had plans to rejuvenate the house once their mourning was over, and I'm sure she said Miss Devlin would be the one to oversee the large amount of work to be accomplished. Harriet has been caught in the country, however, first with mourning for the dowager, and then with her most recent child. I know she was depending on Miss Devlin, and I had thought Miss Devlin at Farronby House, overwhelmed with work. Harriet plans to return for the Season next spring, you see. She intends to take the Town quite by storm, following in the footsteps of her deceased and very well-regarded, mother-in-law.''

Tressa was amazed to hear herself spoken of as if in a casual conversation. To think that few seemed to know she'd left Farronby House was astonishing.

As if reading some of Tressa's awkward feelings, Tia displayed her understanding. ''I do beg your pardon, Miss Devlin, for speaking of you thus. I was so surprised at seeing you . . . at seeing you with . . . well, here I am again, saying something unacceptable.''

''I understand your point,'' Tressa said, unable to dislike her.

If Tia Toussand was known for anything, it was her charm. Her bluntness, however, had put her on the outs with Lady Jersey, the very center of society. All the lady patronesses had hardly had two words for Tia since unless they, too, were willing to come under the fire of Lady Jersey.

Fortunately, Hannibal didn't abandon what he'd started, although Tressa still didn't see his reasoning. She remained embarrassed. But even in the face of the blunt Mrs. Toussand, she kept her bearings.

''I'm sure the two of you are wondering what I'm doing,'' he said, ''all but forcing this meeting. The truth is, Mrs. Toussand, that Miss Devlin is residing with me for the present.''

Tressa had everything she could do to keep her feet.

Her happiness seemed tawdry, and it crumbled about her.

''But you see, Mrs. Toussand, I have fallen madly in love with my lady mistress, and I should like to marry her—if she'll have me.''

In her shock, Tressa jerked her attention to Hannibal, barely able to keep her mouth from falling open. She rather thought Tia had the same reaction to such an unheard-of admission.

Her mind now blank, Tressa forced herself to focus on Hannibal as he went on, as confident as always.

''We haven't been residing together long,'' he said, ''and

we've been most discreet, of that I can assure you. But loving Tressa as I do, respecting her and wanting to marry her, I should like to restore her to her proper place for her own sake. Believe me, if I could go back, I would do it all differently. But I must go forward, and I think, Mrs. Toussand, you might be our best hope for restoring Tressa to at least some acceptance in her rightful world.''

In the building silence, Tressa seemed to grasp only birdsong and the rustle of green leaves. Their horses had relaxed somewhat and stood oblivious to the words so fraught with meaning.

Hannibal loved her. Wanted to marry her.

"Well, my Lord Braxton," Mrs. Toussand said, "you've set us quite a task."

"I take it that in saying *us*, you have accepted the challenge."

"I have. I'll also point out I've weathered your test very nicely. The fact is, I like your Miss Devlin. I like what I've seen of her, heard of her, over some years now. The Dowager Lady Farronby absolutely sang her praises. Surely such a fine lady as yourself, Miss Devlin, has come to this pass for a reason, and I love a good story better than anyone. What's more, I'll be honest with you and tell you my own reasons for accepting your gentleman's challenge." She flicked a smile at Hannibal. "But not here on a bridle path. No, we have too much to discuss, too many plans to make. The first requirement for our little project is that you come live with me in Berkeley Square. Of that, there's no question.''

Tressa's mind remained a blank.

Luckily, Hannibal somehow got her back to Pocket Street.

Oh, the packing. Again.

Tressa was to take only her new wardrobe, which grew with the daily deliveries from Madame Henri. That this woman's clothes, designed for mistresses in particular, would be viewed in one of the premiere houses in London would have been comical if Tressa had been able to see anything as comical.

She remained nearly blank, hardly functioning as she watched Rosemary fill the trunks Hannibal had sent over from Braxton House in Park Lane. She and Hannibal and Tia Toussand had had their fantastical meeting only hours earlier.

Now Tressa didn't know what to do. She should pack her old wardrobe and run. But where, in broad daylight, could she run? Even in the dark, where could she run? How could she think this through?

For now, she could merely do as Hannibal wished. Once she was clear again, she'd run—in this case, from Berkeley Square.

The sponges, Tressa thought, picking up the silken drawstring pouch from her bedside table and absently fingering it. She'd been unable to use them several times. Now she was more and more determined to stop Hannibal at the right time and employ them.

But perhaps she wouldn't need them anymore.

That was, in fact, the reason for moving her to Berkeley Square, so she would be sponsored. Chaperoned.

Yes, those were the true reasons behind their mad rush and Hannibal's absence. He, too, was busy complying with Tia's directives, and Tressa hadn't seen him since they'd returned to Pocket Street.

One of the few things he and Tia had decided was that they would be open about their intentions and doings from now on when they were able, but they'd fudge when they had to. They'd begin by claiming Hannibal and Tressa had been secretly betrothed for some time. Now they were seeking Tia's sponsorship in approaching Society with their engagement.

That was the beginning of their story—or so they'd decided.

Soon, Tressa and Hannibal and Tia would pull up into Berkeley Square in front of Tevor House. Trunks and trunks of clothes would be unloaded and duly noted. To live on one of the most exclusive squares in London was to know everybody's business and to have everybody know yours. That also would be used to their advantage when they could arrange it.

Just how they would get past the numerous other sticking points was yet to be discussed and determined.

If Tressa didn't run.

Yet later in the afternoon, with Rosemary and the trunks in the Toussand carriage and Hannibal and Tressa and the lively Mrs. Toussand in his, they were delivered into Berkeley Square.

Mrs. Toussand was still talking. "We shall admit Tressa disappeared from Lady Farronby's house unchaperoned, but we shall also say she was chaperoning Doro and Robert, which she was. We shall say that Doro and Robert were finally married, and shortly after, the pair of you were betrothed. What we don't mention," she added as the carriage rolled to a stately halt, "is the time elements. And now, you, Tressa, are here with me, readying to become Lady Braxton, which is also true. All true."

Tressa thought that if she was going to say something, now was the time. But a smartly liveried footman let down the steps, and Hannibal vaulted out onto the pavement.

He seemed compliant, even unguarded in his confidence in Tia's directives. For him, all would be well, as usual. Tressa, who couldn't be so confident, watched for her opportunity to run.

Inside Tevor House, which was especially known for its staircase, they sought out the drawing room. As if by rote, Tressa followed her hostess, vaguely aware of the fashionable decorations, the many servants bustling up and down the fine staircase with her—or, rather, Hannibal's—trunks.

In the drawing room, done in reds and golds, they were served tea. It was an elaborate occasion, after which the servants disappeared and Hannibal and Tia got down to business. Now the real strategy would be sorted out. It was all done behind closed doors and without interruptions.

"We must start at precisely how and why you left Farronby

House, Tressa." Full of energy, Tia walked the small space in front of the formal settee Tressa shared with Hannibal.

He lounged, his fine personage a match for any room, any house, any family in Berkeley Square.

On the other hand, Tressa could hardly gather herself for this important meeting. Mrs. Toussand had questions for her, and she watched this barely familiar lady mold, even remold, her life.

Hannibal wanted to marry her. He loved her. She had to run to keep him safe.

"You say," her hostess stated, "that you left under cover of night and went with Robert and Doro to Hannibal's house on Pocket Street so as to avoid the cost of living elsewhere. We, of course, will not speak of anything but chaperoning Doro and Robert. But what is essential here"—she turned to pace some more, her fashionable gown swishing with every quick step—"is how you broke it off with the new Lady Farronby. Luckily, Harriet is my half cousin. Although we see eye to eye on very little, we do have numerous friends and family members in common. I've heard her complaints about how you left and am prepared to deal with some of them. But in the end, she is key to our success. She was, so to speak, your last chaperone— from a distance, of course, and with you as her employee taking care of her house. But you lived respectably under her auspices and in close contact, as I understand it, through your correspondence with her."

In her daze, Tressa said, "Yes."

"Yes, what?"

"All of that is true."

"But under what circumstances did you leave? Usually one in your position would not leave at all unless it was suggested by the employer. And when one did leave, it would be with a letter of recommendation so one could respectably pass along to one's next employer."

"I had no letter of recommendation from the new Lady

Farronby,'' Tressa admitted simply. ''I gave her no notice. I just left.''

Tia's brown eyes engaged Hannibal's. ''This is worse than I thought. But,'' she added, ''I know Harriet. She remains essential to our success. If we can apologize to her and win her back, if she isn't too angry with Tressa to listen, if she can be persuaded to, more or less, vouch for Tressa again—to, at the very least, not talk about her . . .''

All three of them, Tressa saw, recognized that Mrs. Toussand's suggestion of ''winning back'' the new Lady Farronby would be almost impossible to accomplish. The woman had appreciated Tressa as the dowager's trusted employee, but Tressa and the new Lady Farronby hadn't been friendly. They'd been cordial, but Tressa had forfeited even that.

''I beg your pardon?'' Tressa asked, concentrating again on Tia as the petite woman resumed her pacing. Mrs. Toussand's carriage dress, in a soft coppery color that complimented her auburn hair and her lustrous pearls, kept attracting Tressa's eye.

Tia Toussand.

Tressa could hardly grasp that she sat in the lady's fine red and gilt drawing room. Tressa floated in a dream. Beside Hannibal, who'd said he loved her, she still tried to grasp the sudden changes in her life.

''So,'' Mrs. Toussand announced, jerking Tressa into following her again, both in her pacing and her cogitations, ''our first objective is for Tressa to apologize to Harriet. Whether or not Harriet accepts the apology, we move on quickly. Tressa and I will be seen together here and there, nothing formal, thus putting the *ton* on notice that she's seeking readmittance. We'll push on to a private presentation to the old queen, which will be easily arranged through some connections of mine, and then to a dinner party with precisely the right guests. We'll make it known the pair of you intend to be married as soon as may be. After the ceremony, you'll go off to Cannongate. I hope you're are prepared to retire there for some time to let this first foray into Society have its effect.''

"I," said Hannibal, "should like nothing better than to take Tressa to Cannongate and settle in for a considerable time.''

"Good. When you return to London, we'll have firm groundwork on which to build your entire acceptance. So, see," she said, already all triumph, "it can be done. It can be done. Your consequence, my Lord Braxton, can cover many, if I may be so bold, sins.''

Mrs. Toussand's brown eyes gleamed with a confident, teasing light, and Hannibal responded to her confidence with one of his rare smiles.

Tressa wondered how she'd escape Berkeley Square.

"And since we are in tune, sir," Tia added, facing Hannibal and including Tressa with quick side glances, "I want you to fully understand you have a genuine friend in me. Indeed, once I choose a friend, I'm known for my loyalty. You and Tressa can trust me with your secret no matter how we fare in our exciting challenge. I'm quite enthused and ready to start. I shall write another trusted friend, one who will know any possible plans Harriet has for returning to London any time soon. I do believe she is due a trip, in fact. She's still trying to get Farronby House prepared for next spring.''

At last, Hannibal stood up, inhaling deeply, as if he was pleased to be on some sort of path. "I have but one question, Mrs. Toussand.''

"Tia," the woman insisted. "We must all appear on quite good terms already, and must employ our given names.''

"Tia, then," Hannibal said, readily falling in when Tressa couldn't imagine addressing this person so easily. "My question is, why have you decided—within moments, actually—to help us? As you say, to be our loyal friend? Forgive me, but—''

"How like a man," Tia said, grinning. "You cannot, of

course, simply believe I'm a sympathetic person and have your best interests at heart.''

"I must admit I find it relieving, but also difficult.''

Tia laughed. "The truth is, I've been cultivating a group of friends for years. I'm sure you must have learned who some of these people are. Indeed, you can ask any one of them what sort of a friend I can be.''

"If I am to also tell the truth, my dear Tia, I must say I've already asked discreetly about you.''

"Oh?'' She appeared delighted and intrigued. "And whom did you ask?''

"Well, they aren't the most socially astute pair. But I also have friends I trust, and they've said much of what you've said.''

Tia grew even brighter.

Tressa could understand why this lively woman was so popular. She conversed with Hannibal as if they'd known each other for years and years.

"You must tell me, Hannibal, whom you asked about me. Truly you must. Could it have been Sleet and St. Cur?''

A smile softened Hannibal's gray eyes. "Who else, ma'am?''

"Ah, yes, who else?'' Tia was in alt. "And therein you have my second reason for helping you and Tressa. My first is, as I've said, you and Tressa yourselves. You see, I have a sympathetic heart with regard to your situation. But the second reason involves your friendships with Sleet and St. Cur. They are the most elusive of all fine gentlemen, and what a coup it would be for me to entertain them. Indeed, what a blow! Lady Jersey, my nemesis, would be pea-green with envy. As you also must have learned, my greatest delight is in turning Lady Jersey pea-green with envy.''

Hannibal actually laughed, obviously enjoying Tia.

But Tressa hardly managed anything at all. The day seemed interminable, filled with one careening turn after another.

Once again, Tia was openly, amazingly solicitous of her.

Coming to take Tressa's hand, she urged her to her feet, as if she were bidding her a good night.

"Now, Tressa, you look as if you are worn to a shade, and I can understand why. You must allow my staff to wait on your every comfort and have your dinner in your chamber. I know your woman's name is Rosemary, and she awaits you, as well."

"Thank you . . . Tia," Tressa said, seeing in her hostess's eyes the caution to use her given name.

Releasing Tressa's hand, Tia went on to offer hers to Hannibal.

So forward, Tressa thought. So like an equal.

Tia smiled up at him, small and full of energy by comparison, but equally as fine and, yes, confident.

"We will accomplish this, you know. We need only rest on it and discuss it a few more times, and it will come clear. While I intend to act as the most proper of gooseberries, I will leave you alone for a few minutes with your betrothed. On the morrow, however, bright and early, I expect you at my breakfast table so we can eat and then ride. We'll have more time and privacy to talk on the bridal paths."

She walked toward the closed doors, still speaking over her shoulder. "You'll give the announcement of your engagement to the papers tomorrow, and, you'll bring a family engagement ring."

"Oh, but I have a ring," Tressa said, extending her hand to display the dark little gemstone in its simple setting.

"Yes, I've seen that. But, good heavens, Hannibal," she said, grinning, "I should have anticipated exceptional diamonds from you for this exceptional mistress of yours."

Chapter Seventeen

When Tressa and Hannibal were left alone in Tia Toussand's red drawing room, Tressa felt suddenly awkward. It wasn't late, but the long afternoon sunlight shafted in, setting the red walls and heavy gilding alight.

Heavens, she thought, they had lived together, joyfully shared the same bed together as recently as the night before. But since that morning on the bridal path when Hannibal had told Tia he loved Tressa, that he wanted to marry her, everything had turned topsy-turvy.

He loved her.

"She's right, you know." He locked his general's eyes to hers. "You look worn to a thread, and must rest. This has been an amazing day, but a good one—a right one, I must also add."

Tressa didn't know how to reply. She couldn't judge what was good and right anymore. She was bone weary.

Coming to her, Hannibal gathered her into his arms.

"I disliked not spending the day with you on our own. I've liked being with you so constantly over the last three days that

I want those days to come again. Only I want them to be legitimate now. I want to marry you, Tressa. I want to show my regard for our days together. I want us always to be as we were on Pocket Street.''

Lowering her eyes from his, Tressa slowly shook her head.

So soft before, Hannibal watched, growing harder. ''Why do you say no that way? You've been happy with me. I've seen your happiness. I've felt, with my body, the joy in your body. You can't deny it.''

''No, I can't deny it.''

''Then why? It's this watcher business with Joe Legg, isn't it? It's the secret you keep from me so carefully, as if I were the enemy.''

''You aren't the enemy.''

''You treat me as if I am. I feel as if I am.''

Finally, he dropped his arms from around her and walked to a window looking down on Berkeley Square. Tonight, when Tressa sought a window from which to scan the same scene for a possible glimpse of Joe Legg, the elegant old square would seem different to her. It would appear laced with her fears of her uncle.

Hannibal folded his hands behind his back, assuming his imperious general's stance. He was righting himself, she saw, going on, pushing for his way.

As if he hadn't had his way all day long. He hadn't discussed a single aspect of his designs with her beforehand. He'd manipulated her and Tia, setting them up with a momentum that would sweep them on.

''So tomorrow,'' he said, ''will be a day for our announcement and your betrothal ring. The family ring, worn by my grandmother rather than my mother, is a very fine diamond. I hope you won't mind a diamond in this case.''

''I don't mind diamonds,'' she said, both heartened and disheartened.

"I shall come in the morning, as Tia requires. But I shall leave later so as to go to Lance Hall and speak to your uncle."

Shock such as she hadn't known even that day shuddered through Tressa. "You must not go to my uncle!"

"I can't like him, of course, and I never will. But if we are to marry, I should—"

"You will not approach my uncle under any circumstances. You must promise me."

He turned from the window to peer at her where she stood, in the middle of the rich carpeting and furnishings, twisting her hands in her sudden anxiety.

He softened. "So it is Straith who's behind the secret and behind Joe Legg. I'd thought as much."

Tressa didn't reply. While she met his gaze, she didn't say a word. She wouldn't discuss the secret, much less reveal it, especially to him. Above all, above even her own safety, she must keep this man she loved safe.

"I'll make you a promise," he said. "I will not seek out your uncle. Ever."

Relief, like the anxiety before, shuddered through Tressa.

"But," he added, "I shall also exact a promise from you. You will not go outside of this house on your own. You will not run away in the night."

"You know I cannot make such a promise."

"But I am afraid for your safety, and I need this promise as badly as you evidently needed the one I just pledged."

Again, Tressa was brought to a stand.

What could she say to his fears for her?

"I will promise, then," she said, "not to run away. I must still go, though, Hannibal. But I will not leave in the middle of the night. Somehow, I will let you know when I am ready to leave. I promise."

"You will allow me to drive you to your new situation—if you go at all."

"No, I cannot promise that much. Pray, you must believe I

will go. More and more, it seems, it will appear as if I have
jilted you, and I cannot like the talk that will cause. Once I'm
gone, however, I'll again live as Miss Dear, and you need not
worry that your name—''

''You will not go,'' he repeated, at his most commanding,
standing in the rich light and every inch in charge. ''We will
marry, and you will not go. That is final.''

''I'm not promising—''

''I know you're not promising. But just as you will be allowed
to operate on the expectation of leaving me, I will be allowed
to operate as if we are marrying. And so it shall be.''

How could Tressa answer that?

''If Tia can arrange a meeting between the new Lady Farronby and me within a week or so, I will stay that long. I would
like to have the opportunity to apologize. I have done her a
wrong. But after a week or so, Hannibal, the time it likely will
take Mudge to find a post for me, I must go. In the meantime,
couldn't we return to Pocket Street, just the two of us?''

''That's impossible. You are fixed here, and my intentions
with Tia must be given a chance to work. Tressa, give this
situation a chance.''

''I'll give you, as I say, a week or so, and then—''

''While you are here''—he cut her off—''I will mount a
guard outside to stand between you and Legg and whoever else
might be involved in this secret. And don't worry. It will be
done quietly and discreetly. You, however, will surely notice
and even recognize some of the players, so I shall mention
them to you. Unfortunately, I'd be identified by everyone, so
I cannot have my part, although I intend to be with you as
much as I can. But you will see Mudge and Knobby and Bates
hanging about. And my friends, whom you will not recognize,
have offered to take a part—Sleet and St. Cur.''

''Oh, I'm so sorry to involve—''

''Never mind that. Finally, I will write to Robert and Doro
to tell them that we are marrying and that you will be staying

with Tia until we do. I know they'll be happy to hear they can soon reach you at Cannongate as Lady Braxton.''

''Oh, but, Hannibal—''

He cut her with a glare as he strode toward the door. He had issued his order, had made what bargains with her he could, and that was that.

But she had one more demand of her own. ''I'll need a carriage tomorrow to go to Pocket Street and speak to Mudge.''

He gazed at her, his general's eyes cool, removed. He knew what he was telling him. She would ask Mudge to find her a position in the City.

But he would carry on as if they would marry.

Theirs remained a relationship of equals. He wouldn't go back on that, so he nodded, however distasteful her demand.

''A carriage. Bates on the back and Knobby inside. You shall have it.''

With that, he bowed, just as coolly and formally.

Tia had given them the brief opportunity to fall into each other's arms. They hadn't. Nor had Hannibal told her, as he had Tia that morning—so long ago—on the bridal path, that he loved her.

''I adore a rainy day,'' said Tia, gazing out the nursery window on the uppermost floor of her house in Berkeley Square. ''It keeps me from riding, but I make up for it with cards. I love cards on an afternoon like this one.''

Tressa smiled. ''You simply love cards.''

Tressa rocked, cuddling Tia's six-month-old close to her, resting her cheek on his down-covered head.

Little Thomas Toussand—one day the Earl of Tevor.

She'd grown to adore the nursery and the little creature within. Little Sandy, who, Tia said, looked like his papa. Little Sandy whose papa preferred living in the country with his current mistress and his own father, the Earl of Tevor, while Tia lived in the metropolis.

They had an arrangement.

Or so Tressa had learned over the near week she'd lived with Tia. In fact, in the constant stream of time they'd spent together, she'd come to know Tia well, and they liked each other better and better.

"It's been a lark, hasn't it?" her hostess asked, turning from the window to engage Tressa's dreamy eyes, "to ride each morning with your handsome, perfectly garbed Hannibal as escort in Hyde Park, to turn all those heads. We have become all the crack. I swear your Madame Henri is as good as any modiste in London, even mine. I've been wondering, in fact, if she might make something for me on the quiet."

Tressa rocked with little Sandy. He was asleep, and she lowered her voice in the spare, scrupulously clean nursery room.

"I could ask her if she would next time I . . ."

Next time she what?

Tomorrow might well be her last day with Tia. Tomorrow was her dreaded meeting with Lady Farronby, the meeting Tia had worked so hard to arrange.

Like Hannibal, Tia had every hope for success with the young matron.

Tressa was considering running again. But she wouldn't run. She'd promised Hannibal. Besides, Lady Farronby deserved Tressa's apology tomorrow, eleven in the morning, at tea.

Tia reveled in the prospect. They'd be on their way to initiating the rest of her plans.

Tressa concentrated on little Sandy's warm body tucked into hers, on his sweet hand grasping the hair at her nape.

She'd never held a child before Sandy.

She'd never much thought about what she'd miss in not having children. She'd been learning to use her sponges, and she hadn't made love with Hannibal since coming to Tevor House in any case.

She'd been seeing Hannibal, of course, regularly in company, but also formally, as if he were a suitor. The struggle between them, beneath the surface of their civilities, wore at Tressa as did all the rest.

Inhaling deeply, she sniffed the freshly laundered fragrance she associated with the child. The room had been whitewashed recently, and numerous nursemaids in equally fresh aprons were busy as bees in a hive. The rain kept little Sandy's nappies from quite drying.

Everyone adored him, especially his mother. Tia, for all her love of company, was an excellent mother.

Part of Tia's agreement with the senior Sandy was that little Sandy would be with her in London despite the senior Sandy's love for his country life. Otherwise, they had the typical marital arrangement—or so Tia claimed—separate households, separate lives, an heir between them, and nothing else. Nothing but discretion and cordiality when they were together.

An arranged marriage. Nothing like a love match, Tia had confessed.

Tressa couldn't help thinking about how different her marriage with Hannibal might have been. It could have been a love match, one of time spent together, lived together as lovers, with children, beloved children, filling the nursery. Children to nestle and rock with.

She'd never thought of it before, never realized . . .

She had to remain on course, however. These were temptations.

"I think it's best that Hannibal have at least a little time with you," Tia said, surprising Tressa. "He's grown quite . . . well, not precisely surly, but cross upon occasion. I realize he doesn't like Society—"

"Oh, but he does like your friends. He's told me so."

"Yes, I know he likes my friends. And he—and you, too— fit in very well. But men do need that sort of thing, and when I see him looking at you, I know he needs some time alone.

Perhaps a rainy afternoon with him would help you, as well, so that you're ready for tomorrow.''

A rainy afternoon? What was Tia saying?

Alone with Hannibal? Today? Where? Tressa's heart leaped.

When Tia moved away from the window, Tressa sidled over to it, rocking little Sandy while she stood. She hoped the scene outside might resettle her thoughts about this rainy afternoon.

The rain came down almost quietly, it was so fine. But it was also steady, soaking everything and everyone down on the square. Tressa didn't watch the square as closely as she wanted to, but she stole what moments she could to glance outside.

She'd grown conscious of the guard Hannibal had set on the house, and caught glimpses at all times of the night and day of Mudge, Knobby, Bates, and even of Hannibal's friends, the Lords Sleet and St. Cur.

When Tia, who knew nothing of the guard, had caught sight of St. Cur in the garden eating an ice from Gunter's, she'd nearly dashed out of the house to have a word with him. Tressa's chuckle at her excitement, however, had curbed her enthusiasm, and she'd restrained herself.

Because of their closeness to Hannibal, Tia still expected to meet Sleet and St. Cur. But Hannibal hadn't said a word as to whether or not he could produce them for her in her fine gilt and red drawing room. Tia believed she needed but a little time to have even them eating out of her hand. And with her charm and appeal, Tressa agreed she just might.

Tressa wasn't so sure she wanted to meet Sleet and St. Cur. They were, like Hannibal, the most handsome and privileged of gentlemen. But, also like Hannibal, they couldn't be comfortable to be with.

Unless they were in love.

Tressa still couldn't accustom herself to the idea that Hannibal loved her. Lately, across a card table or carriage, he was most attentive. His eyes followed her, as Tia said they did. But he'd made no moves toward her that were out of the ordinary, nor had he spoken to her of anything personal.

Little Sandy, sagging against her, prevented Tressa from taking another good look at the Braxton diamond that was so unfamiliar on her finger. Even that amazingly heavy stone had been given to her more as a part of their plotting than as a memento of an important step in their lives. Hannibal had handed it to Tressa at the breakfast table with Tia watching.

And, as to Hannibal's having told her he loved her, he hadn't. He had not, bluest of blue diamonds or no.

So, after one more glance out the window, Tressa turned away. No guard in sight, but no Joe Legg, either.

Only once in the near week she had been with Tia had she spied Joe Legg, and that hadn't been at night, but in broad daylight. He'd been standing in the square, beneath one of the shady plane trees, looking entirely out of place, but also looking at her as she climbed into a carriage on her way to Tia's dressmaker.

He still watched.

He still reported to her uncle.

He still stood as a reminder to keep the secret.

Even so, Tressa had to wonder what her uncle could be thinking. Didn't he wonder whether she'd told Hannibal at least something of the secret? She'd been so tempted, but she hadn't. Could her uncle believe that, as well?

She doubted it.

Hannibal, stepping into the room, brought Tressa from her fearful round of worries. Tia had gone off to speak to the head of the nursery staff, and Tressa still rocked with the sleeping baby in her arms.

Little Sandy had grown quite heavy against her and very warm, but she was reluctant to put him down. She'd have few, if any, opportunities to cuddle a baby again.

Unless this very man, who stood before her, peering at her so intently, had already gotten her with child.

It was possible; Hannibal had warned her so. What would he think if she were to have his child?

She knew the answer to that. He'd told her already. He would want the child, would do nothing, in fact, to prevent one. He'd left the prevention to her.

If only she could toss all her worries to the wind and marry Hannibal, could love him openly and freely and bear his children. If they could live by the sea at Cannongate, it would be all she could wish.

The temptation to think it was possible was mighty.

He'd definitely be in accord.

Hannibal examined her as she held the child. She wondered if his thoughts didn't concur with hers—to have a sweet child like little Sandy, a child that would be Hannibal's and look like him. Tressa thought her heart would break at the bittersweet idea.

"So here you are, Hannibal," Tia said, bustling into the small plain room with the rain softly drumming outside. "How odd to see a man in our nursery."

When Hannibal would have pulled his eyes from Tressa's and replied, Tia reached for the child, gently taking him into her own arms. Dropping a kiss on his forehead to settle him, she walked the baby to his cradle and tucked him inside. She spoke to Hannibal as she did so.

"You look quite well, of course, Hannibal. Even clothes for dirty weather look wonderful on you."

He wore nankeen trousers with his blue coat. A neckcloth, unstarched and fastened for summer comfort in a large six-inch bow, had been claimed by Byron to be as free of the trammels caused by starched neckcloths as possible. Instead of boots, Hannibal wore shoes with strings and gaiters—clothes fit for the most fashionable of watering places.

No wonder Tia remarked on his wonderful looks. Tressa thought she'd never see enough of him, even if they were gifted with a lifetime to share.

Unlocking his gray gaze from Tressa's, Hannibal thanked Tia for her compliment and said her guests were arriving downstairs.

"Yes, I was just telling Tressa I like to play cards on a rainy afternoon. But she"—Tia barely glanced at Tressa, then looked back at Hannibal—"has the headache, I'm afraid. As I will tell anyone, she is taking a rest in her room. But would you, my lord, like to carry her off to Pocket Street instead?"

Unlike himself, Hannibal hesitated. "To Pocket Street, ma'am?"

Tia chuckled. "Yes—if, that is, you can get her out of the house unnoticed."

"Unnoticed?"

He recovered somewhat, glancing from Tia to Tressa, who also had to smile.

At long last, he took the point and was all certainty again.

"Ten minutes, my sweet. No time to waste. Come out the side door and down the rear alley. I'll be waiting with a hackney. Come veiled. And hurry. *Hurry*," he repeated, already disappearing from the room, his hard shoes rapping on the corridor flooring outside.

Tia laughed. "I quite like seeing Hannibal in a dither, and I quite enjoyed causing it. Since I don't suppose I'll ever accomplish such a dither in him again, I intend to set it firmly in my memory."

Popping open a rain umbrella and escaping through a seldom-used door at Tevor House, Tressa cautiously entered the rear street—little more than an alley, really—and spied Hannibal at its mouth. He also carried an umbrella, a large black one, and strode toward her, leaving the waiting hackney carriage behind him.

Because she'd exited the house in less than ten minutes since being in the nursery, she still wore a lightweight afternoon gown, done in finest white muslin and ornamented with small tassels in the yellow shade Madame Henri called *jonquille*. *Jonquille* tassels also jiggled at her cap and along the edges of her plain white shawl.

An unbidden laugh bubbled up when Hannibal took her elbow and attempted to accommodate his umbrella with hers.

"If I'd known I was to come out in the rain today," she said, "I would have dressed differently."

He smiled around his squinted eyes. "Stout orange walking shoes and yellow duck feathers, no doubt."

"I didn't wear a veil, either," she said. "I thought the umbrella would do."

"The rain will do."

He still wore his trousers and gaiters, his string-tied shoes. Nothing, it seemed, could ruin his fine turnouts or make him look uncomfortable.

After helping her into the dilapidated hackney carriage, which appeared somewhat newer in the wash of rain and with fresh rushes on its floor, he closed the umbrellas and climbed in beside her. The conveyance was immediately under way, splashing so loudly in the rushing water as to cause Tressa to lift her voice inside the vehicle.

"I can't believe you found a hackney carriage so quickly."

"There's almost always a hack or two just up the block, even at night. I noticed that the other day when examining the situation with regard to keeping an eye out for Legg."

Setting the dripping umbrellas against the corner, he turned to gather Tressa to him as naturally as he had when they'd been together those last days on Pocket Street.

What had it been now? Tressa asked herself, glad to nestle into him. More than a week? She'd missed this the most, she thought, the closeness, the warmth of Hannibal—his strength and wonderful scent, his voice, his conversation, his loving.

What hadn't she missed?

She wasn't going to consider that. The heavens had opened

and not only delivered a day of warm summer rain, but an unexpected chance for them to return to the little paradise of Pocket Street.

Pocket Street could mean only one thing to her mind, and obviously to Hannibal's, as well. He jostled her happily—free, for the moment, of his recent constraint, if also propelled by pent-up emotions. Looking into her eyes, he spoke volumes without a single word. They were in accord. They would make love.

Dropping a kiss on Tressa's nose, Hannibal surprised her by releasing her and setting a foot on the seat across from them. His string-tied shoes were wet, the polish standing with raindrops that shed like silver, dripping on the fresh rushes. His knee-high canvas gaiters were also wet. Removing his gloves and laying them aside, along with his hat, he proceeded to undo the hooks and eyes.

He was starting to undress.

Tressa had seen Hannibal strip out of his clothes on other occasions. He simply revealed himself, confidently, without embarrassment. Now, he unfastened the hooks and eyes on his gaiters one by one, working upwards first on one calf, then the other.

She watched. Yet another hook vacated yet another eye, splitting open the canvas yet wider. His light drab trousers were at last let loose. Tossing the gaiters on the seat across from them, he turned to her.

Tressa recognized the light tricking Hannibal's gray eyes. He dropped his mouth to hers for a kiss, a long, drawn-out kiss warmer and wetter than the day. It shut out even the hollow clip-clop of the horse's hooves, the splash of the old carriage wheels.

A rain-silvered day, as warmly gray as Hannibal's eyes.

At Pocket Street, the carriage stopped and Hannibal climbed down and paid the jarvey. "You've got yourself two umbrellas, some gaiters and other things," he called up to the fellow. "Enjoy them."

"I will, me lord. Thank 'ee," the man returned as Hannibal sought out Tressa. He was smiling and already dripping with pewter rain.

Tressa wanted to remember him always just as he was, happy and looking for her to complete his happiness.

He tugged her from the old vehicle. Because they had no umbrella, the rain began its warm assault. Holding her hand, he propelled them toward the door. It opened, and they dashed inside the small entry.

"Bates," Hannibal said, now grinning and light of breath, "we thank you. Is Mudge in?"

"No, me lord." Indeed, the sturdy, good-looking Bates appeared surprised at having been at the door in time. "Just me here now, me lord. Mudge be at the Crown and Feathers having a pint."

"Good." Hannibal coaxed a bright coin into the man's palm. "We'll need our privacy, Bates."

The footman nodded and, already turning away, said he'd see to it.

By now, Hannibal was out of his wet coat and drooping tie. As he took off his waistcoat, Tressa moved to the large mirror over the gilded hall table and laid aside her shawl, gloves, and cap.

Some of the tiny *jonquille* tassels were stuck to the damp fabrics, and she concentrated on the fasteners of her muslin gown. It was like tissue paper, really, stuck to her skin and revealing her every curve. When the gown and her petticoats landed in a pile on the black and white tile flooring, she saw her shift beneath her short corset also clung to her.

In only trousers now, Hannibal stationed himself behind her, locking his gaze to her gaze in the dimly illuminated looking glass.

He desired her.

Fully.

For all that he worked at her corseting, his passion-fogged eyes wouldn't leave her alone. The clinging muslin turned to pink circles at her nipples. It shaped her breasts, traced even the plump shadowy undersides and the deep cleft between.

Letting the corset drop to the floor, Hannibal turned Tressa toward the staircase, where he sat her on a riser. She wore only her transparent light muslin shift and her white silk stockings, their garters embroidered with bluebells.

Of course, she also wore her two rings from Hannibal. On one hand, on the proper finger, the enormous blue Braxton family diamond; on the other hand, the little dark blue stone he'd given her and which she treasured.

Lady and mistress both represented on her fingers and both facets of her own self, she thought, nicely, comfortably riding together inside of her.

She was more mistress than lady, surely. She wanted Hannibal's loving. She relished it and readied herself.

This might, in fact, be the last time for them to be together, and that possibility made her more aware of the nuances—the few raindrops that still bejeweled Hannibal's black hair, one perfectly perched for her appreciation in his thick brows.

She wanted to kiss it away, to drink it with her lips, but she also wanted to leave it be, catching what light it could from the soft day.

Hannibal particularly enjoyed removing her stockings, and Tressa stretched one leg toward him, then the other. He'd slowed, also to fully absorb the details, to not miss a thing.

Hannibal treasured the arch of her foot. As she sat on the risers, he smoothed his hand up her bare leg and beneath the damp clinging shift, the single article of clothing that remained between them.

Lightly, caressing her with his eyes, he tested her with his fingers. He found her as wet as the day—as warm, as softly dewy and ready.

But they wanted to prolong their time together. His eyes spoke to her eyes, discovering their harmony. She waited in thick, warm anticipation, yearning for his wishes, his own delights.

This could be the last time, echoed in Tressa's mind. The suggestion made her throat thick and her eyes sting. But it also made her appreciate the moment, to emblazon its last detail in her mind.

Hannibal tugged Tressa to her feet. Breathless with need and yearning, she followed him through the dimly lit book room into the back sitting room, where he left her long enough to open the windows. The white balustrades of the small balconies dripped musical rain. The garden sang its pure joy in the afternoon.

Through the tall open windows, Tressa absorbed summer's color—blue delphinium, purple iris, yellow iris standing at the reflecting pool, doubling the splash of color in the mirroring surface, periwinkle, dotted with violet-blue blooms, the dear little faces of love-in-idleness.

The gardeners had tamed the place, but also enhanced it. Its neat order beckoned to her. She'd walk there with Hannibal when the rain stopped, when they were sated and rested again, when they were so in tune as to be one, when their minds, their hearts softly sang the same song.

Surprising her, Hannibal stepped out of the window and onto the balcony, fully displaying his nudity and obviously not giving it a thought.

He next surprised her even more. Like a native creature of the rain-silvered garden, he vaulted down off the balcony into the yellow snapdragons just below. Standing calf deep in the bright yellow spires, he turned to grin at Tressa, to coax her out onto the balcony into the rain.

"Come on, my sweet. Up on the balustrade and then down into my arms. I'll catch you."

In her shift, and without thinking he wouldn't catch her,

Tressa awkwardly climbed onto the wide handrail, where she perched, staring down at him. Naked and as natural as a jay in the garden, he lifted his hands to her.

How could she resist?

Without thinking, she slipped off the edge of the balustrade, and he did indeed capture her and lower her into the stand of yellow flowers.

"The gardeners aren't going to thank us for this," she said, a chuckle escaping into her words.

"Nor this," he agreed, breaking off the puffy blooms with their wet mouths.

Tressa gloried in the rain that poured down on her, that splattered her hands as she received the snapdragons from Hannibal. He went on, plundering the pink carnations and bringing them back to her like trophies.

His accumulating bouquet smelled so wonderful, so strong, especially the ravaged carnations, she thought she couldn't abide the assault on her senses—the splendid mix of color and fragrance, the slippery, wonderful feel of the warm rain on her all but naked skin, the amazing picture that Hannibal made.

She'd always enjoyed looking at him, and she decided she would finally fully study him in the nude. He had no modesty whatever and likely didn't note her first shy gazes.

But as he went along, pillaging the garden, stealing its colors and robbing its perfumes, then gifting her with both, she also gazed at him. His lovely male body was the opposite of her own, the long muscled limbs, the thick shoulders, the dark hair that was blacker than black in the rain.

He was a native creature.

His man's part, long and ready for her for some time, grew somewhat more slack, waiting for her and not so full and hard as it could be. Rain silvered that part of him, too, dripping from the ripe tip, which swung suggestively with his every move. The thatch surrounding it bore crystal-like beads.

When he looked up suddenly, he caught her staring at him.

Coming to her with delicate pansies in his big hands, he grinned in a way that made her cheeks bloom.

That pleased him.

Finally, slippery and wet, he handed her the last of her rain-drenched bouquet and smiled so even his eyes warmed.

"Let's take our booty into the summerhouse, shall we?" He rubbed the crumbs of rich garden dirt from his beautiful fingers. "We're both sufficiently . . . wet."

Grinning, he swept her and the blossoms into his arms and carried her toward the octagon-shaped structure. Inside, he set her on her bare feet at its center. Designed for a mistress, and in the middle of a mistress's garden, it offered privacy, while at the same time giving a clear view of the surrounding flowerbeds.

The low eaves cascaded with rain, causing a veil outside the windows. Inside, it sounded as gentle as a musical ensemble. As could be expected in a mistress's summerhouse, a large bed stood in the center on a natural fiber carpet. The bed was draped all in white, kept fresh and waiting like the other beds, even though Rosemary had removed to Berkeley Square with Tressa.

Plucking up a thick blanket folded on the end of the mattress, Hannibal came to her and laid her armful of flowers at the foot of the bed. He used the blanket to buff her skin softly as he also dried himself.

The silvery rain disappeared into damp shades that pleased her equally as much. It darkened Hannibal's hair, thick on his head, inviting on his chest, shadowy around the gentle sway of his enlarged but waiting shaft.

He was her wizard, her warrior, her creature of the shimmering garden, and she'd never forget.

He stood so close, his breath warming Tressa and becoming her breath. His eyes saw only hers.

She'd taken the time to insert a sponge before leaving Tia's, and that allowed a deep sigh to carry her soul to his. As she'd learned at Tia's, and particularly with Knobby, a child deserved the best nursery to be had. Such tiny, precious creatures needed parents and a name and a place. Children deserved legitimacy no matter what moments adults stole from life.

Hannibal skimmed a finger down the side of Tressa's face, along her jawline. He enjoyed the look of her, and she glowed with giving him pleasure in such a simple way.

"My heart," he whispered, "for surely you are my heart beating in my chest."

He reached to caress the breast that covered her own heart, softly clasping it, as if he closed her love into his palm.

"And just as certainly," he whispered, "I am your heart beneath your breast."

"You are my heart and always will be. I can feel it is so."

If they never exchanged wedding vows, even if they never said I love you, she and Hannibal were so deeply one that even time and space would never separate them.

She was content.

As he kissed her throat, she sipped what was left of the rain from beneath his earlobe, caught there in a crystalline droplet.

She drank his kisses from his mouth.

"Say 'my heart,' Tressa. Say 'my heart.' "

"My heart. Forever my heart."

Hannibal had once told her there was a difference between loving and bedding. That afternoon, Tressa knew it was so.

But he did not tell her he loved her.

Chapter Eighteen

From the moment Lady Farronby entered Tia's bright red drawing room, sharply at eleven o'clock of the morning, Hannibal knew the woman was not disposed toward relenting where Tressa was concerned.

Lady Farronby, who resembled Tia despite their distant relationship, had brown hair with a reddish cast, as opposed to Tia's vibrant auburn shade, and was also diminutive. But the similarities between the women ended there.

Tia was bright and witty, accepting, even unique.

Lady Farronby, who had to resent her cousin, was none of that.

When her ladyship perched on the settee within the crescent of furniture before the grand chimneypiece, she barely nodded as Tressa was brought to her attention. Hannibal could have throttled the priggish creature. No wonder she and Tia seldom saw eye to eye on any topic. Fortunately, Tia possessed the graces of the drawing room, and with an encouraging glance to him, pushed them all on.

There were a surprising lot. Not only had the required attendants, now balancing their teacups, arrived strictly on time, but Nick and Sin had shown their faces, as well. Hannibal had been talking to them a good bit lately, gradually revealing to them his very strong attachment to Miss Devlin.

She sat quietly, as lovely as ever, his beautiful companion of the silvered garden on the afternoon before, listening as Tia talked and talked.

As Hannibal could have expected, Nick paced to a window, resorting to the square below for some activity. Also astutely aware of the grand failure that appeared to be in the making, Sin lazed, deceptively languid, in a chair he'd placed as near to Lady Farronby as possible without causing the woman to shriek.

Hannibal recognized Sin's tactics.

The lady kept track of Sin nervously, the one crack in her icy determination to freeze out Miss Devlin.

Hannibal experienced a strong urge to toss the creature out.

Still, he stood—or, rather, paced and then stood. He'd hover over Tressa protectively, only to grow aggravated with their guest and turn away. But turning away inevitably brought him back to Tressa's shoulder to peer at Lady Farronby, which also seemed to unnerve the woman somewhat.

For all her spoken desire to entertain him and his pair of friends, Tia now wished—and he could be certain from the little glances she shot at him—Nick, himself, and especially Sin to the devil.

They were the devil's regiment this morning, all in blue coats, all in shades of blue with cloth-covered buttons rather than gilt, of course. Nick wore a Mathmatical, severe and grave in black taffeta, gray kerseymore breeches and the topboots he seldom went without.

In peerless pantaloons and high-lows, Sin sported a more relaxed knot, a *Cravate à la Maratte*. Of the finest and most white India muslin, it was unstarched, simply and plainly folded.

Hannibal had chosen the middle ground with pantaloons and tasseled Hessians. Because he'd wanted to be at his most impressive, he'd come in a cravat of the purest white muslin, starched and high on his throat.

Rather unusually, Hannibal could be sure of what Sin was thinking. With his languid pose and his pale gray eyes, he endeavored to unsettle Lady Farronby so much that she would capitulate, preferably in copious tears, and run.

Nick entertained the same positive feelings for Tressa's success, but he was far less readable to Hannibal, even after their years together. Nick, the Earl of Sleet, known to be as cold as his name, was actually the one who needed their personal ties the most.

For Nick, a drawing room where the business of high Society was hammered out was the least desirable place of any. Nick had to want to be there badly to remain, even somewhat removed in a window.

Thinking that Sin should step back and leave off his discomforting stare at Lady Farronby, who was growing pink and perhaps disoriented by his wicked doings, Hannibal realized Tia had broken off, and that it was the lovely cadence of Tressa's voice he heard.

"My Lady Farronby," she said, "I'm so happy you've come here today, if for no other reason than to have a moment with you in person."

Everyone went still—Nick in his window, Sin on the small chair he'd placed nearly under Lady Farronby's uplifted nose.

Tia became a listening statue, and Hannibal stationed himself at Tressa's shoulder, prepared to do battle.

"I must start by saying again," Tressa continued, "that I was very fond of your mother-in-law, and I always will be grateful to her for bringing me to Farronby House here in London. I feel doubly bad, then, for having done you a disservice in leaving Farronby House the way I did. I know you are in the throes of refurbishing the house for next Season, and I'm sorry to have deserted you when you needed me.''

Even though Lady Farronby remained unmoving, Tressa continued, sincerely.

''For me to have left without notifying you, indeed in the dead of night, was unforgivable. As Tia has said, I was thinking of myself and of Doro and Robert, not of your concerns. For that, I want to apologize most plainly in the hope you'll forgive me—if not entirely, perhaps a little.''

Now even Tressa went as still as everybody else, having said her piece, but having no hope of bringing Lady Farronby around.

When the woman cleared her throat, Hannibal found even he listened.

''I see,'' the woman said. ''And I do, Miss Devlin, wish you the best in your future despite the disservice you have done me in the past. Your family has been too close to my husband's family down through the generations in Middlesex for us not to have harmony between us.''

With even those crumbs, the occupants of the room relaxed somewhat, enough to walk the lady to the drawing room doors and stand in a loose crowd as they bid their *adieux*.

Once the doors closed on the back of Lady Farronby, those she left behind responded in kind. Nick bid a brusque goodbye and left, with Sin soon following. Tia claimed victory, as slim as it was, and Hannibal quit pacing at the rumbling sensation in his gut.

It was more than his desire for the luncheon they were soon to share that contorted in him.

Tressa remained calm, apparently feeling better for having been able to apologize.

''And, now,'' Tia said, ''onward and upward. In a few days, our presentation to the old queen, and then we're on our road. While Harriet's acceptance of Tressa's apology could have been more magnanimous, Harriet does nothing magnanimous. We can only be glad she'll let the matter of Tressa's disappearance and her complaints about her drop so we can put them behind us. I do feel most relieved, for Harriet, as I'm sure you could tell, can be the most sticky of sticklers.''

To have another visitor suddenly announced, this one unprepared for and obviously shocking to Tressa, set Hannibal back apace from his plans to eat.

Even Hannibal, who feared no man, felt the impact of the elder earl's entrance through the double doors to the grand red drawing room.

Grave and hollow-cheeked, tall and thin, in dark, almost worn clothing, Lord Straith walked toward Hannibal and Tia and Tressa where they again had collected in front of the cold hearth.

Looking into the man's face, Hannibal read nothing in the highly aristocratic features. But in the earl's flat, expressionless eyes, Hannibal saw no soul, only a blank, almost a bland determination to have what he wanted and to leave as he'd come, forcefully.

''Mrs. Toussand,'' Straith said, ''I know we have never met and I hope you will forgive my intrusion into your home, but I want to speak to my niece. It seems her surprising presence here necessitates a call on my part. Living in the country as I do, and having no conveyance of my own, I was required to take advantage of my good neighbor's offer—Lady Farronby, of course—to drive with her to Town. She informed my sister and me just last Sunday following church that she'd be visiting my niece here this morning. Since it seemed to fit in so nicely, I came along in the hope of, as my niece has, throwing myself on your generosity.''

Yes, Hannibal thought, the man had come in the guise of shabby gentility. His coat, with its light rust wearing at the cuffs, was perfectly kept. But, mindful of the fraying threads, Straith demanded everyone else be mindful of them, too. His elder brother, Bad Buck Devlin, had ruined the family for good, and its head came calling, using a threadbare coat to cover his steel.

This was no man with whom to trifle. Filled with suffering and hatred, he had over the years gone slightly mad with it. The secret Straith held over Tressa could only be an evil one.

Feeling as if he'd been brought to an unheard-of level of despair within an unheard-of amount of time, Hannibal suppressed his desire to show the man his own steel.

"Let me say, Lord Straith," Tia said, "that you, as my dear Tressa's family member, will always be welcome in this house. Since you wish to speak to her privately, I will, naturally, excuse myself. My Lord Straith," she finished, bowing her regard.

If Tia was harboring the strong emotions awash in Hannibal, she didn't display them. She swept from the chamber, only glancing back to question the fact that Hannibal remained instead of following.

But Hannibal hadn't been introduced. As he most definitely expected to be, Tia went on, the footmen in the entry hall closing the doors behind her.

Straith peered at Hannibal.

Tressa performed the introductions.

"Yes," said Straith, "I had thought as much. The talk of your betrothal has reached my ears. But, of course, I have not been addressed directly."

"And that has been my fault, Uncle," said Tressa, still calm as stone. "I asked Hannibal not to apply to you."

"Because you knew it would do no good." The man focused the flat willfulness in his eyes on Hannibal. "Indeed, this betrothal, sir, is impossible, not to mention any thought of marriage with my niece. I prefer to speak to Tressa in private."

Hannibal was being dismissed with no more than a snap of condescension. He'd never experienced such a slap in the face. And yet he hardly felt it.

Hannibal thought only of Tressa and wanted, above everything, to stand staunchly by her side.

What hideous secret could she share with this man? What could bind her so thoroughly for her to eschew not only a life with him but her own independence?

Tressa was so afraid of the man, despite her grave dignity, that Hannibal experienced her fear in his own gut, which twisted fully into a knot.

"Sir," said Hannibal, "I shall be blunt with you. I know there is a secret between you and Tressa, but not because she has told me. Nor do I know anything of what this secret is about. She has not told me that, either. But it's time this secret be revealed, especially to me as Tressa's soon-to-be husband. I swear to you, sir, I will do everything in my power to solve this riddle once and for all."

Straith did not reply.

He merely averted his head as if Hannibal no longer existed.

Looking at Tressa and receiving no indication that he should stay—in fact, receiving the opposite signal from her—Hannibal couldn't imagine what else to do but leave. He feared for her being alone with her surely mentally crippled, if not insane, uncle. But it would do no good for him to stand there, either.

The pair had gone silent.

How could such a villain have gained such a firm hold on their lives? Nay, on their very hearts and futures?

In a dream, in a nightmare, Hannibal left the room only to find Tia pacing just beyond the doors her footmen had closed on the two occupants within.

Evidently Tia'd had the same reaction to Straith.

"So, Tressa," said Straith, his tone, his gaze, deepening in the falseness he employed—false civility, false harmony. "Your aunt sends her best wishes to you."

Both her Uncle Straith and her Aunt Editha had invariably

dealt in falsity. How had she almost forgotten? They all but reeked of it. By merely speaking to this man, Tressa fell into the pattern that said all was well and always had been.

But Bad Buck Devlin was still dead, and the truth of his murder remained buried with him.

She must be as bad as Straith and Aunt Editha, joining the falsity by even speaking to her uncle.

"I suppose, sir, that Aunt Editha did not come to London with you and Lady Farronby."

"She did not. If you will recollect, she does not travel well— nor do I on such short notice. You have been irresponsible for too long—running away from your safe haven at Farronby House, living with this man, to whom you dare to introduce me, and now coming to this house, where you surely live all too freely. I hardly know you anymore. These wedding plans I've heard about, this unseemly ceremony Lady Farronby has described to me, as simple, as private, as understated as possible—there is but one word for it, Tressa. Impossible. I'm here to remind you of that word."

Tressa didn't reply.

Her uncle went on, all implacable power.

"The only good thing is that you have not told him our secret. If you had, it would be the worse for you—and for him."

Tressa stared levelly into her uncle's hate-distorted features. She had everything she could manage, but she was proud to do that much.

Hannibal was to be safe.

That was what mattered.

She could take her own chances, involving only herself, once more.

"I shall be here for one more day, Tressa, waiting on Lady Farronby's kindness in allowing us to return to Lance Hall in her carriage. You will be ready to go the morning after tomorrow. You have ruined what little freedom you've had in earning your own way here in the metropolis with your impossible behaviors. Now you have no choice but to retire to Lance Hall with your Aunt Editha and me. As distasteful as that will be for each of us, you've brought this on yourself. I'll not hear another word, ever, of your leaving Lance Hall again. Do you understand me, girl?''

At last, his great villainy got the better of his false civility, and her Uncle Straith had to take a moment and compose himself. He had to drag his drilling, now red-rimmed eyes from hers. He had to let his shaky voice regain its level tone.

He adjusted his carefully tied neckcloth with a slight tremor in his hand and dusted a bit of nonexistent dust from a rusty black sleeve. ''I shall see you in one day's time, Tressa.''

At the doors he didn't dare revert to her with final formalities. He simply left, and the footmen closed Tressa into the red drawing room, the last survivor of the morning.

None of the comfort and encouragement Tia and Hannibal had offered on the leave-taking of her uncle had any effect on Tressa. She appeared contained, as if their plans would go on and she would recover from her uncle's call.

But Tressa knew otherwise.

By early the next morning, she was at Pocket Street, having asked Tia for a carriage before Hannibal could arrive for breakfast. She wouldn't keep her trip to see Mudge a secret from him. She'd merely tell Hannibal she'd gone to Pocket Street to retrieve something.

She'd also tell Tia and Hannibal about her uncle's request that she return to Lance Hall and retire. She'd say he wouldn't countenance her match with Hannibal, and that would be that.

Tia, and especially Hannibal, would expect her to explain more, even defy her uncle, but Tressa wouldn't. She'd bid Tia a warm farewell and do the same with Hannibal, thus saving him from her uncle.

But she would not—would *not*—return to Lance Hall, as she'd tell them she would. She'd lie again, but for the last time.

In the middle of the night, for she only had one more, she would run away. She'd go to the City, where Mudge would help her with a position. She'd make a last try at escaping her uncle and grasping her own bit of freedom.

If some small freedom was the most she could have, even if Joe Legg located her again and sat day and night on her very doorstep, she would not go to Lance Hall—definitely not with a pretense of willingness.

With the carriage standing and waiting for her, Tressa mounted the short flight of steps at the house on Pocket Street and rapped at the front door. It was early, with a peachy-golden sky predicting another lovely summer's morning.

Even so, Mudge was up and about. Smiling, he let her into the small entry. Then he eyed the fine Toussand equipage as he shut the door.

"So unexpected, Miss."

"Yes, but I had to see you, Mudge. Yesterday morning, my Uncle Straith called at Tevor House."

"I must admit I've heard some of it. We're outside the house in the square, you know, most regularly. Usually me and Knobby puts in some time in the afternoons, with Lord Nick and Lord Sin, and even Lord Braxie sometimes at night. We make a nice little guard, Miss."

Tressa was taken with Mudge's apparent and growing affection for Hannibal and his pair of friends, especially since Lord Nick and Lord Sin were renowned for their great eligibility and their even greater elusiveness.

"Well," she said, not knowing how to answer the warm gleam in Mudge's wise eyes. *Lord Braxie?* "I'm glad to have such a fine guard, as you call it, keeping a watch out for Joe Legg on my behalf. And you say even Knobby, who's scarcely twelve . . . ?"

"Knobby stays with me, Miss. I keep an eye on him. Anyway,

Knobby and his lordship are at Braxton House now, living with the skeletal staff there so as to be in Mayfair again. Says it looks more acceptable for his lordship to be there, although he'd prefer rattlin' around here. Quite likes Pocket Street, Lord Braxie does. Won't sell the place, he says, but will return as soon as he can. For now, though, his lordship keeps an eye on Knobby over on Park Lane, and I has the lad here some, too. Doing well, the boy is. Happy as a lark.''

Tressa smiled.

''O' course, as to the guard, Miss.'' Mudge's eyes lit with the adventure he longed to seek in far-off, warmer climes. '' 'Tis Lord Nick who's had the most luck. Spied Legg, he did, late one night, prowlin' around Tevor House. Pulled his sword stick on Legg. Pinked him, too. But you don't need to worry, Miss,'' he added, seeing Tressa's eyes widen. ''No worry for you in it.''

''I'm glad to hear this, Mudge. And you, as well, seem content.''

''I am, Miss. Only place I'd rather be is where the salt-sea air blows in your hair, although that's not likely to happen anytime soon.''

Tressa chuckled.

Aware, however, that Tia's coach awaited, its horses as fresh as the morning, she told Mudge their business—that she must hide again.

''Aye, Miss. I knew tha' time might come now, what with the old lordship visiting. I'll get you safely away, though. Tonight, you come at midnight. Your old wardrobe is packed an' ready to be whisked away with you. I'll have everything arranged. But can you leave Tevor House on your own tonight? Can you avoid our little guard—maybe Joe Legg and possibly even his lordship?''

''I think by tonight there will be no guard and no Joe Legg. My uncle believes I've capitulated and am leaving for Lance Hall with him in the morning. As to Hannibal—*Lord Braxie*—

I'll be having a word or two with him after I return to Tevor House."

Mudge's wise old eyes reflected the sadness Tressa was endeavoring to hide.

"It could not last, Mudge," she said. "I can simply be glad I have you and can depend on your help."

"On tha' you can, Miss. No one will know your whereabouts but me and you."

Fearing that tears would flood her eyes, Tressa tugged at her gloves for no reason. She wanted to escape the little house. She was glad to hear Hannibal would keep it, probably because he had a soft spot for it, too.

"Oh, Miss," Mudge said, picking up a paper parcel from the hall table just as Tressa was about to bid him good-bye.

Tressa's heart turned over.

The parcel could only contain a book of Robert's, in which Ambrosia had hidden a second letter to her.

Tempted not to look at the message, not even to take the parcel from Mudge's hand, Tressa took it anyway. She had far too much on her plate to worry about Ambrosia, but the girl looked to her for help, help she had told her she'd give her.

Tempted to carry the package up to her old bedchamber, but afraid of how she'd feel seeing the room again, Tressa stepped back to the sitting room—not that she was any more comfortable there. The house on Pocket Street was the truest home Tressa had ever had.

Pocket Street, where Miss Lovelace had decorated with a nice touch that Tressa also had liked.

Pocket Street, where Tressa had spent her happiest days, with the people about whom she cared the most.

Pocket Street, where Tressa had learned about love, and where she would leave her heart.

Still, it was time to go.

At some point, the dust would settle and Hannibal would return to his life. He'd forget her. He hadn't said he loved her,

except that once on the bridal path. Even then, he'd only told
Tia so Tia would help them.

No, he would get over Tressa, just as he had his other—

It was time she stopped thinking of herself as a mistress.
Soon she'd be a respectable companion again, and the mistress
within her would shrivel as it should.

At the table in the sitting room, Tressa ignored the garden,
the silver clock, and even Doro's portrait. The painting would
go to Cannongate and be hung in a place worthy of it. Tressa
had accomplished something for Doro and Robert, and that
would always be equal to the rest.

Finally, with the paper parcel open, Tressa found Ambrosia's
message inside. As with the last letter, this one was blotched
and tear-stained, almost impossible to read, nor could Tressa
believe the mess into which the girl had fallen.

Because Mrs. White had not liked Ambrosia under foot, the
woman had ordered the girl out of her house. Because Ambrosia
had nowhere else to turn, she'd ended up back in the clutches
of Sir Percival Pounce. In taking her in, the bounder had admitted he was getting even with her by tormenting her.

"Oh!" escaped from Tressa's lips, bringing to her attention
the fact that Mudge hovered inside the sitting room door.

Tressa read on.

In returning to Sir Percival, Ambrosia was in worse straits
than before. The man watched her constantly, and she was
allowed out only in his company.

But never worry, Ambrosia reassured Tressa. Ambrosia's
sister, Lottie, had returned from Paris, and was willing to take
in Ambrosia. All that was required was Ambrosia's escape
from Sir Percival, planned for this very night.

It was to happen at Cupid's Tea Garden, at the Cyprian's
Summer Ball, where Sir Percival planned to thoroughly enjoy
himself drinking and carousing with other females.

When he was thus occupied, Ambrosia went on to say in a
very messy patch Tressa could hardly decipher, Ambrosia

would get away. She would run from the garden and catch a hackney carriage out front. In that conveyance, she would fly to her sister.

Anything of importance to her had already been removed from Sir Percival's house, and Ambrosia could well and truly wash her hands of the blackguard. She'd learned her lesson, she assured Tressa. She was even considering a position as a shop assistant, as Tressa had suggested.

But there were a few problems.

"I thought so," Tressa murmured, causing Mudge to shift his weight uncomfortably.

Ambrosia was afraid, of course. She needed encouragement in her designs, and the fare to pay the jarvey. Outlining how Tressa could help her with her few problems took Tressa through two more laboriously written pages.

Still, after reading the letter—which ended with Ambrosia's every affectionate and respectful salutation—Tressa thought it could be done. She'd have to think it through, of course, and tonight, with her return to Pocket Street and running away to the City, she would be quite . . .

Well, Tressa could not disappear merely to sit and worry about not having helped Ambrosia when she'd seen it could be done. She refolded the letter, her mind already at work.

"They say the rain day afore yesterday made quite a mess of the garden, Miss."

Mudge's words brought a sudden, surely surprising, smile to Tressa's lips.

The day before yesterday, the garden, the silvered rain, Hannibal traipsing about in the nude, rooting up flowers and handing her a very wet bouquet.

Since Mudge hadn't been at home when she and Hannibal made love in the summerhouse, they hadn't seen him. He'd heard about the mess in the garden, though.

So much to forget.

So much to clasp tightly to her and remember.

"Yes," she said, "it was indeed a heavy rain. But it isn't the rain you want to talk about, is it, Mudge? It's the parcel. And, no"—she tucked the pages into her pocket—"I don't need your help in this instance, nor must you worry. I can handle Ambrosia's request on my own. You do enough for me as it is."

She finished softly, as she got up from the table and gathered her things, "Stay faithful only in my one last favor, my friend, to establish me in the City. Then you may wash your hands of me and do as you will. I promise. You may even go off in search of warmer breezes." She gazed into Mudge's dubious expression. "And, pray, do not tell his lordship about the parcel and Ambrosia's message should you see him."

Oh, the deceits, the lies, the falsities. Would they ever end? Did lies end if secrets didn't?

Tressa would have enough time to ponder that question.

For now, she had to rush upstairs to the attic rooms. Rosemary had packed away some things Miss Lovelace had left behind, thinking to return them to her, for Rosemary liked Miss Lovelace.

In the trunk, Tressa located what she needed, a plain black silk domino and a black silk demi-mask. While she'd never thought to go to Cupid's Tea Garden at night, especially not to a Cyprian's ball, those accessories would suit such an occasion down to the ground.

Considering the time Rosemary had spent putting the accessories away in the trunk, Tressa laid them as carefully inside one of Madame Henri's discreet boxes. After retying the string, she plucked up the box and, in the street, passed it to Tia's liveried footman, who placed it on the seat of the carriage as if it were purest treasure.

Chapter Nineteen

Getting down from Tia's carriage in front of the house in Berkeley Square, Tressa straightened the red Cossack spencer she wore, the one with black silk frogging and a high black collar to match her dapper black hat. The skirts of her walking costume were also black, and Madame Henri had pronounced her very smart.

The under-butler opened Tia's door, and the footman followed Tressa into the entry with its very fine staircase. Tressa didn't feel very smart. She felt brazen, especially with her upheld chin and determination and the discreet box from Madame Henri's, which contained the black silk domino and demi-mask Tressa intended to wear that night.

Yes, words like brazen and nefarious would suit her this night. *And this morning, too*, she told herself, walking toward the breakfast room at the rear of Tia's house. She'd find Tia and Hannibal there having breakfast, at least discussing Tressa's trip to Pocket Street, if not worrying over it.

Little she would do on this day would be pleasant.

Tressa's entrance into the breakfast room caused a minor stir. The butler, who was serving along with another footman, came to attention as Hannibal stood up at the table. Across from him, Tia appeared relieved that Tressa was back.

But not for long, Tressa warned herself. After this encounter, these people she cared about most of all would be glad to see the back of her.

The footman on the carriage had taken Tressa's box up to Rosemary, so Tressa remained standing, not even moving to the mirror to take off her hat.

"I'm sorry to tell you this in this way," she said, briskly, over anything Hannibal and Tia might have said by way of greeting her, "but tomorrow morning I will return to Lance Hall with my uncle. He cannot approve of my marrying, and he has demanded I retire with Aunt Editha and him."

Tia's eyes narrowed. "So that's what the old rascal wanted in coming here all in state yesterday morning. And you have agreed to retire from life, to sacrifice even Hannibal?"

As much as she felt like lowering her eyes in shame, Tressa didn't. Coloring up somewhat, but keeping her gaze steady, she met her hostess's eyes. "I've appreciated all you've done for me, Mrs. Toussand, but—"

"Mrs. Toussand, is it?"

Tia was stung, and Tressa couldn't blame her. Facing Hannibal, Tressa did her worst. "I am, of course, calling off our engagement, my lord."

Having removed her gloves already, she had but to pull the large blue diamond from her finger and lay it on the table where it wobbled under its own weight. "If I might, though, sir, I should like to keep the other ring you gave me, the lapis lazuli."

With a vile epithet, Hannibal slammed his newspaper onto the polished table, causing the great blue diamond to wobble again.

"You will actually do this, Tressa? To you and to me?"

"It is done, sir," she replied. "I don't know, however, what I should do with the wardrobe."

He stared at her. She met his gaze.

As Tia got up from the table to excuse herself, along with the astonished butler and footman, Tressa stayed her with a hand.

"It is I who must go, Mrs. Toussand. I've said what I must. I should like, though, to leave the wardrobe with you. My uncle would not tolerate such a wardrobe. I know most everything is too large for you, but perhaps you could have some of it cut down. You've liked this and that, I know, and I wish you joy in it."

"There will be no joy for me in this, Tressa," Tia said. "But since you are leaving on such short notice, I will see to the clothes."

"Thank you," Tressa replied, glancing back at Hannibal.

In the mornings, especially, he looked so very fine, as he did this morning. He stared at her—nay, glared at her as if he despised her.

She had but this one last moment with him.

"If you don't mind, then, sir, about the ring—"

"Devil fly away with you and the ring," he bit out.

With the barest bow for Tia, he excused himself from the day's, even the evening's, activities, and stalked out.

"Pray," said Tressa, "you must excuse me as well, Mrs. Toussand. I shall leave in the morning with my uncle, and I-I . . ." Taking hold of herself, Tressa finished with every dignity as she walked from the room, "I shall always remember you."

Tressa spent the rest of the day in her room at Tevor House. She and Rosemary packed what they could, sending some to Pocket Street, giving some to Rosemary herself, leaving most for Tia to do with as she wished.

Frequently, Tressa fingered the ring Hannibal had given her.

Even though his final words had been harsh and had concerned the ring, she'd keep it with her always.

She felt physically weak and humiliated, but she'd accomplished the hardest part, and she pushed herself on through the evening.

Tia, Tressa knew, had in friends for cards. She and Hannibal, who would have been included had stayed away.

Tressa tried not to think about what he might be doing.

He could be doing anything. He could have already left for Cannongate. He could have chosen yet another mistress.

Tressa reined herself in, knowing she wouldn't be ready to consider such thoughts for a long time. She concentrated instead on going on. She bid Rosemary an early good night, withholding the knowledge that she wouldn't see the lady's maid anymore.

Here was another sadness she'd have to face at some point. She'd grown to like Rosemary very well, and was grateful to know Mudge would look after her.

Still, there was so much Tressa would sacrifice, all for the secret she loathed, the secret she'd been too young to agree to, but which had shaped her whole life.

She didn't have the time or energy to grieve that all over again. She dressed in a dark blue gown that would blend in with the black silk domino. Everything she wore would be dark, chosen to make her less noticeable rather than more.

Still, her mirror reflected her as so strangely unfamiliar that she turned to her reticule, checking again for the fares needed for the hackney carriages.

At last, as ready as she thought she'd ever be, she slipped out of Tevor House as she'd done before and caught a hired vehicle easily. A nearly full moon illuminated even the dirtiest, darkest corners of London.

By eleven o'clock, she reached Cupid's Tea Garden. Tonight was the Cyprian's Summer Ball, an especially big occasion, and she wanted to come and go before the unmasking at midnight. Still, she sat in the carriage for a moment, trying to get her bearings.

It was shocking, really. The tea garden was so changed from the friendly place it was during the day.

It was much more crowded, even outside along the flagway in front. People came and went, laughing, talking, evidently enjoying themselves, but all so different to Tressa's eyes.

More boisterous. Less polite.

This wasn't merely a question of gentlemen and their mistresses, this Cyprian's Summer Ball. There were gentlemen aplenty in expensive evening attire, and mistresses, too, appearing as fine as ladies. Mostly, though, there were other sorts. Low women, as she'd heard them defined, with painted faces and garish clothing. The men pursuing these creatures wore every kind of dress.

Even prizefighters, housebreakers and footpads invaded the garden after dark.

"You want me to wait, lady?"

Tressa, who'd gotten down from the hackney carriage, found herself addressed by its driver. Going to his perch on the vehicle, her unfamiliar garb suddenly distressing in itself, she gathered her wits.

"Yes, do wait for me," she said. "I shall bring someone to you, and I will pay both her fare and mine. But you also did say, did you not, that I should next be able to find another hackney carriage for myself easily?"

"Aye, lady. Just look around and see the hacks coming and going. You'll catch another easy enough."

"Good," Tressa said, turning away. "I shall be right back, then."

Emboldened by the fact that she was as familiar as anyone with the tea garden, Tressa paid her way and went inside. Along the walkways, people appeared extremely curious about her, but also recognized her as a lady—or something like.

Though there were a few rude comments and more than a

few bold glances in her direction, she sped from the colonnade at the front to the eating area at the rear.

Going directly to one of the arbors beyond the fountain, one similar to the private table she and Hannibal had shared at breakfast just before becoming involved with Tia, Tressa recognized it as the right arbor straight off.

Even through the throng and the diffused light cast by the flambeaux, Tressa picked out Ambrosia. The girl sat, as she'd described in her note for Tressa, with her party.

Tressa had never met Sir Percival, but she identified him immediately. He and his friends were costumed and masked, raucously awaiting the midnight hour for the unmasking. He sat in the middle of the booth, with another gentleman and three other females aside from Ambrosia. When he guffawed, Tressa recalled Robert's mention of Sir Percival's odd braying laugh. Yes, it was him without doubt.

As she drew nearer, she saw that Ambrosia peered about, searching for Tressa herself, her pretty young face full of worry. When Tressa got even closer, Ambrosia recognized her despite her heavy disguise, the black floating domino and the black demi-mask.

That Ambrosia was unmasked had been an idea suggested by the girl so as to make it easier for Tressa to recognize her.

The girl sat at the end of the table, where she could easily extricate herself from the arbor, yet another good idea on Ambrosia's part.

Indeed, the directives she'd given Tressa were proving workable.

Again, Tressa thought, it was going well.

Surprisingly so.

Just that quickly, in fact, Ambrosia sprang to her feet and, coming through what cavorting crowd was left between them, grasped at Tressa as if she would save her. Tressa quickly turned with her, and firmly took the girl's arm. Ambrosia shivered violently, but Tressa held on to her, forcing their way back through the revelers without glancing behind.

"All right, now," Tressa urged. "You've been a brave girl, and we're nearly out of here. We have but to reach the front of the garden where I have a hired carriage waiting. Hold on to me tightly. All is going well."

Ambrosia, whose tongue usually ran on wheels, was so over-wrought by the situation that she merely clung to Tressa, causing Tressa to feel all the more sorry for her.

The girl was, after all, very young, and she definitely could have had a better life.

As they drew closer to the sweep of the colonnade and just beyond that the gateway, Tressa felt Ambrosia's grip on her arm loosen.

"I'm so happy to see you," the girl finally gasped. "I kept hoping and hoping you would not fail me—not that I thought you would if you had received my message, but I couldn't be sure you'd gotten it."

Tressa patted Ambrosia's hand on her arm. "Well, I received it and I'm here. You've been courageous, and just past the colonnade, we will have succeeded. Although"—she glanced behind them—"I think we've managed it already. I don't see anyone following us."

When the girl also dared a glimpse back, a nervous giggle escaped from her throat. "No. No one is following us."

Around them, the crowd thickened. A tattered harlequin chased a bawdy shepherdess. Two young bucks argued as to which of them made a better Friar Tuck, and one of them knocked down the other right in front of Tressa and Ambrosia on the gravel path.

Stepping over the fallen man, whose nose already bled profusely, Tressa pushed Ambrosia on, each of them now clutching the other to the last.

Even so, they had accomplished it. Out on the flagway, with all sorts of people milling about and hackney carriages coming and going, Tressa was relieved that the vehicle she needed still waited.

Heaving a sigh, but still not saying or doing anything except ushering the girl to the carriage, Tressa noted the jarvey had parked a bit off the beaten path, probably to get away quickly.

Better and better.

At the hackney, then, and calling to the jarvey, Tressa all but pushed the girl into the vehicle.

Ambrosia peered out at her from the window and began to sob with relief. Tressa said she'd write to her one day soon through her mother.

That was all they could say, though.

Tressa turned to the driver and repeated the direction Ambrosia called to her over her sobs. Paying the jarvey, Tressa told him to hurry. The carriage sprang away.

Standing for a minute and watching the disappearing equipage, Tressa couldn't say if she'd ever see the girl again or even hear from her if she tried to correspond. But she did know she'd done right by Ambrosia, just as Hannibal had by rescuing her from the grasp of Sir Percival. That would always be enough for Tressa—to do what was right, as Hannibal did.

To help whom she could, as Hannibal did.

With her own tightening throat, Tressa set about locating a carriage for herself. She was still somewhat to the side of the busiest activity, still on the flagway but definitely in a shadowed area where the coachmen likely wouldn't see her hailing them.

Just as she was about to step off the flagway and forge back into the hullabaloo, someone grasped her from behind. He gripped her tightly, knocking the breath from her and scattering her wits.

Through her abrupt confusion, she felt his body pressed against her back. She sensed the barrel-like shape of the man. Joe Legg.

He clasped an odd-smelling handkerchief over her nose. She struggled, but it was hopeless. He was deceptively strong.

To think Joe Legg would have been so quick to take advantage of her without her guard seemed impossible.

Impossible. Falsity. Lie, lie, lie.

The words flickered around in Tressa's head, dimming until they puffed out like candle flames.

Naturally, Hannibal warned himself, standing at midnight outside the door at Pocket Street, he couldn't expect to have the barrier swung wide and see Tressa perched on the staircase waiting for him.

He simply wanted to be away from the big house in Park Lane.

He wanted to be at home. Oddly enough, that had come to mean this little house.

As that also indicated, he wanted to be where Tressa was. It only followed, then, that she had become his home, and that scared him.

"That means," he said to the lion's head door knocker, "that my home will abide in the house of the man I hate most in the world. Hell's fire," he grumbled, remembering he hadn't applied the knocker as yet. "Foxed."

No sooner had he rapped than the door swung wide.

"Mudge, my good fellow."

"Me Lord Braxie?"

"Who else, my good man? You look as if you're viewing your worst enemy."

"No, no, Lord Braxie. 'Tis just—"

"Aye, the lateness of the hour and no notice. But best let me step inside, my good fellow. 'Tis my home—I mean my house—and all that."

Braxton was surprised by the several lit candles and that Mudge—Bates, too, he saw as the footman came to greet him—was fully dressed.

Braxton inquired if something was amiss.

Mudge, never anything but confident, appeared anxious.

"Well, let's have it, man," Braxton ordered.

He felt, strangely, that he must clear his head. He wanted to lie down upstairs on Tressa's bed, with her fragrant hair just by on the pillows.

"Well?" he rapped, feeling clearer by the moment.

" 'Tis our Miss," Mudge said.

Hannibal grew immediately sober.

So much for self-indulgence.

"Beggin' your pardon, Lord Braxie, but she was supposed to be here long afore now."

"Be here? But she's asleep, man, in her bed in Berkeley Square."

Mudge's wise old eyes softened with hope. "You've seen her, then, Lord Braxie?"

Braxton shifted his weight. He'd been in the same clothes, he wasn't sure for how long, and his beard felt rough as he rubbed his cheek in exasperation.

He'd been drinking most of the day at Park Lane, drinking and dozing off only to drink again.

He swore that no matter what, he'd never take another drop. *Lord, just get me through this. Just let her be safe.*

"Mudge," he said, "you'd best start at the beginning and move us through this quickly."

The elder man sneaked a look at Bates, obviously assured of confidentiality by the young footman's nod.

"I was to help her run away tonight," Mudge admitted.

Hannibal crashed down his fist on the nearest solid object, the knob of the banister post.

Mudge pushed on. "But before she come here, she was supposed to help Ambrosia."

The man had reason to fear Hannibal's fist now, but he plunged ahead.

"She went to the Cyprian's Summer Ball at the tea garden to fetch Ambrosia away from Sir Percival again. Miss didn't tell me this precisely, but I put it together meself tonight while I was cudgeling over what to do—another parcel from the girl at Sir Percival's, the Miss taking something to wear from Miss Lovelace's trunks upstairs. Of course, if I'd thought on it sooner, I'd have stopped her or at least gone with her. Insisted, she did, tha' she knew how to escape the house on Berkeley Square and hail down a hackney carriage on her own.''

Hannibal groaned. He'd taught her those tricks.

Indeed, he regretted having taught the miss all too much.

"I should have gone anyway, though," Mudge ended, also regretfully. "Would kick meself over and over, I would, if I thought it'd do any good."

Hannibal realized he was pacing the confined space of the entry. "Anything could have happened to her, but it's still most likely only one thing happened—Joe Legg."

"Aye, I've had time to think on that, too, Lord Braxie. But she already agreed to return to Lance Hall with her uncle. Leastwise, that's what she told the old earl. Surely Legg wouldn't need to abduct her, knowing that."

"Surely he would abduct her. I doubt her uncle trusted her agreement to return to the hall. Legg was given an opportunity to snatch her, and he has. That's still the most plausible thing to have occurred, despite the countless possibilities, and that's the likelihood we'll choose to chase."

Hannibal knew that Mudge and Bates watched as he paced, mulling it over, grasping for the clearheadedness he needed.

"How did you come here, me lord?"

"How did I come here?"

Thoroughly awash, and frightened by the little trick that could be played on his memory when he imbibed too much, Hannibal covered the space to the door and opened it.

In the quiet street, the Braxton equipage stood with two horses and the small figure of Knobby at the leader's head.

In the pale lamplight, the boy lifted a hand and called to

Hannibal. "Have you fetched Mudge, Lord Braxie? Tell him I needs him now, remember?"

Mudge, who wedged himself into the doorframe, evaluated the situation. "So it's you and the boy. Who drove, me lord?"

"I'm not sure, but I have the feeling I did, and I'm none too good a driver. I recall the pair of us putting the horses to, and then—"

"I'll check the gear, me lord, and I'll drive, too."

"To Tevor House," Braxton ordered. Enough of this witless business. "We'll start at the most obvious place. Bates, you're in charge here. If Miss Dear comes, see that she stays. Don't take an eye off her."

"Aye, me lord."

Braxton knew Bates would do as he should. He was fortunate in his retainers on Pocket Street. He liked them very well.

With that, he and Mudge headed toward the boy and the standing carriage.

"I suppose," said Hannibal, "you also drive carriages."

Mudge nodded. "Been a coachman a time or two."

"Good. We'll make it to Berkeley Square, then. Spring 'em."

At Berkeley Square, as the carriage halted before Mrs. Toussand's still lighted house, Hannibal got down from the box, leaving Mudge and Knobby behind.

"You're as fine a coachman as everything else," he called to Mudge. As he turned away, he came face to face with Nick and Sin.

It had become a personal matter between them and Legg, especially since Nick had pinked the blackguard. So Hannibal wasn't surprised to see his friends in the square this supposed final night of Tressa's stay there.

After giving Nick and Sin a brief explanation of what was going forward, Hannibal and the two lords barged into Tia's house. They found her on her way up the fine staircase after having bid her company good night.

Another brief explanation, followed by a thorough but fruitless search of the house, brought Hannibal to his next stage in his considerations.

None of them were talking about the various possibilities regarding Tressa's fate—white slavery operating out of the docks, a footpad coming on her and violently stealing her purse, a jarvey waiting for victims with purposes of his own.

Hannibal kept his troops on the straight and narrow.

Tia, still bright at this late hour, spoke to them as they regathered in the entry after their search.

"I knew there wasn't something quite right about her this morning after her return from Pocket Street. Poor, dear Tressa. I simply must come with you to search for her. Where do you go next?"

Feeling pressure to leave, Hannibal also took advantage of whatever he could, like a good general.

"If you will, then, Tia, order out your carriage. Go with Nick and Sin, of course, to the hotel where Straith is staying and carry him down to Lance Hall. By force, if necessary."

His eyes found solid verification in Sin's pale gray gaze, in Nick's black angry stare. Hannibal knew he could depend upon them.

"Go easy on him," he warned. "We might need information from him. If he won't give you directions to Lance Hall, Tia will show you the way. You've been to visit Harriet, have you not, since she's married and lives in the neighborhood?"

"I have." Tia called for a wrap against the cool summer night and for her carriage.

Fortunately, Middlesex was a fairly short drive, and the moonlight laid bare the open road, the spill of undulating countryside.

Hannibal, atop the box again with Knobby and Mudge, was hardly conscious of anything but what they'd do next. Mudge had to save the horses somewhat and watch the road carefully despite the good driving so close to Town.

Knobby was all excitement with the little Mudge had evidently told him. They were off to save Miss Dear, their Miss Dearie-Dear.

With a few directions gotten by way of available inns, the trio located a hillock overlooking the valley that cradled Lance Hall. Above, on the highest hill, the first light of day marked the dark bulwark of the remains of Castlelance.

Having discussed it at length on the box, Mudge and Hannibal left Knobby with the now spent horses and the coach and walked down to discover what they could about the situation at the house. They didn't expect to find Legg there, but they ascertained what they needed to know about the lay of the land, the emptiness of the outbuildings, the genuine peace in which the attractive old residence rested.

The fact that the earl was away and that his return was anticipated by his small staff lent the only air of activity as the dwelling slowly came awake. Lady Editha, the lady of the house and the earl's sister, was evidently content with their retirement and spent a good deal of time on her own.

Back at the carriage in the growing light, Mudge and Hannibal discussed their thoughts on the matter. Both were satisfied with what they'd expected to find, but disappointed in what little they'd accomplished. With the scant information they'd attained from the nearby inn, plus their own deductions, they stood watching the boy and the quiet horses, visibly searching the countryside for clues.

"He has to be here," said Mudge. "He has to have her somewhere just by."

"He obviously took her, surprised himself at running across her out on her own. That was part of his waiting and watching—to catch her and take advantage of it." Hannibal inhaled deeply, his eyes narrowing on the hillside and the castle ruins above them. "After all his years of working for Straith, he's familiar with every inch of this district. He could be anywhere. He's settled in, waiting for the earl to come back later this morning, overjoyed with his amazing feat. I can almost feel his excitement.''

"Devil," Mudge muttered. "Like the very devil, he is. Can be anywhere.''

For encouragement, Hannibal looked to what they'd accomplished that night. All had gone surprisingly smoothly, and they were here now. The next step had to come equally as smoothly. If it did, Tia's carriage would soon arrive with Tia, Nick, Sin, and the earl. Nick and Sin would have more thoughts by now, and Straith would be theirs to bully.

Still, Hannibal felt as if Tressa were oddly close.

"There's a bit of smoke, me lord," Mudge said, "stealing up to the sky from the woods up there by the castle. Might be a campsite, me lord. Someone staying outside for the night.''

Braxton focused on the thin smudge, reaching like a dirty finger into the morning sky.

"The castle," he ground out. "By the very devil, why didn't I—onto the box and up the narrow lane, Mudge. Come, Knobby. But quietly. We don't want to flush our bird before we can catch him.''

Chapter Twenty

Atop the box again and keeping an eye on the finger-like smoke, Hannibal, Mudge, and Knobby drove steadily upward, reaching the woods mantling the castle ruins. Unfamiliar with their surroundings, and now in the greenwood, as well, Hannibal feared they might make a misstep. Still, Mudge tracked the rough, ever steeper, ever narrower lane through the thickening trees.

A memory stole over Braxton. Once, Tressa had recounted her most frequent dream—or, rather, nightmare. It was about being at Castlelance.

"Been a carriage through here just afore us, Lord Braxie. Can see the disturbances if you look close enough."

"Aye, I see, too. Quiet now, Knobby. We draw nigh. When we're there, you stay with the horses no matter what, like a good soldier."

The boy grinned. "Like a good soldier, Lord Braxie."

Sure enough, Mudge and Braxton located the campfire. A

shabby hired carriage waited with a pair of hobbled horses. Their quarry slept, rolled in a blanket by the smoldering embers.

Even when the horses stirred at Mudge and Braxton's approach, Joe Legg remained sound asleep.

Jerking him quickly to his feet, Hannibal and Mudge had the immense satisfaction of additionally jerking him from the arms of Morpheus, and then of shaking the man until his teeth rattled.

The mark of Nick's sword stick stood out on Legg's cheek, livid red.

"Show us where she is, man," Hannibal demanded.

Like all puffed-up bullies being nabbed, Joe Legg shrank back on himself. Braxton and Mudge, confident in their own large sizes, had to look very big and bullying, too.

"She's—she's in the castle."

"Show us," Mudge bit out.

Everything was going so easily, Hannibal found himself thinking. Too easily.

A vial tumbled from Joe Legg's pocket.

In Tressa's nightmare, in the castle there was a thickly walled room—thickly walled because it bore the bones of men buried alive as enemies.

Tressa had seen herself there, laid out on a bier, losing her life.

As Mudge picked up the vial, Hannibal clasped Legg's throat. "Show us the room, or I'll kill you and find it myself."

Because Legg was barely able to breathe, barely able to nod, Mudge unclasped one of Hannibal's hands from the man's throat. When Hannibal's eyes met Mudge's, his rage cleared enough to read Mudge's feelings regarding the vial.

"A bad potion, Lord Braxie. Something nasty, likely from India. Something too expensive and rare to be bought by the likes of Legg."

Hannibal, strengthened and enraged by fear, took an emotional leap he hadn't known existed. He'd have to live Tressa's nightmare—his own nightmare.

Without more to say, Mudge dropped the vial into his pocket as Hannibal shoved a still choking Legg ahead of them.

As they approached the crumbling castle, the undergrowth grew thicker. A path, thin as vapor, appeared, just wide enough to take a foot.

In her dream, Tressa had been losing her breath—or losing her life or something else beyond Hannibal's concentration.

He had to get to her.

In what counted for a corridor, they finally found a heavily barred door intact in a solid rock wall.

It could only be the room that was a grave dedicated to hatred and bitterness.

Hannibal could hardly bear it as Mudge lifted the bar and morning light flooded into the pitch-dark chamber ahead of them.

Edging into the bare room, Hannibal had Legg by the throat once more. "Couldn't you have left her a candle, you bastard?"

More sane than Braxton, Mudge again unloosened Hannibal's fingers and took his place as a guard on the man. Hannibal turned to face the figure lying on a stone slab and draped in unrelieved black silk.

As he drew nearer, he saw even her beautiful face was covered halfway by a black silk demi-mask. Her bright hair was hidden within the folds of the domino's hood.

Almost unable to go on, he grasped her darkly gloved hand. Pulling off the glove, then stripping away her mask, he saw she was pale.

But beneath the paleness, she felt warm to his touch.

"Thank God," he whispered, the close, stifling space muffling his gratitude like a black fog.

Hearing just that, Mudge repeated his words behind Hannibal.

But Hannibal was on the move again.

"We'll get her to the house. As to him"—he merely glanced at Legg, for fear of killing him with his bare hands—"leave him here and bar the door."

"But, me lord," Mudge protested.

"We'll let Sin and Nick decide his fate. I can only want him in hell."

Back inside the carriage, alone with Tressa, who was still unconscious and pale on his lap, Hannibal finally was able to take a long look at her. He'd removed the domino, and she was garbed in a dark blue gown that lent her every appearance of normalcy, aside from her stillness, her paleness.

He could have wept, but he didn't allow himself.

Slowly, he took the lapis lazuli from the finger on her right hand and placed it on her left hand, on her ring finger.

At Lance Hall, Mudge stopped the carriage in the drive, then climbed down from the box. With Knobby quickly at the horses' heads, Mudge helped Hannibal lift Tressa from the vehicle. By then, a butler had appeared in the door.

Obviously, the household was awaiting the arrival of the earl, and a footman appeared. Both men recognized Tressa and came forward, apparently anxious and full of unspoken questions.

"I'm Lord Braxton," Hannibal said, still with Tressa draping his arms. "I'm betrothed to your Miss Devlin, and she's been taken with a sudden serious illness. I've brought her home so you can help care for her. Her clothes, together with her uncle and more people to help, will follow in due course. My man, Mudge, will need your cooperation, and the boy needs assistance with the carriage."

With that, more retainers appeared, the word spreading in whispers, mustering the slight staff into yet another group ready for Hannibal's command.

Tressa was carried to a room that already awaited her. The sheets were fresh, the featherbeds aired. A warming pan waited by a fire in the mellow chamber. Flowers picked by the staff in their eagerness to welcome Miss Devlin scented the room, chasing away memories of the thickly walled castle chamber.

With Tressa fully dressed and lying on her girlhood bed, Hannibal sat with her until the second coach could arrive. Then he'd leave Tressa to Tia and forge on with what had to be done.

For now, though, he thanked heaven that Tressa was alive. He prayed she'd be fully restored.

He hadn't told her he loved her.

He'd said everything but that he loved her. He'd resented the fact she'd kept her secret from him, and had withheld what he'd had in his power to keep from her. His sorrow nearly swamped his strength, his will to go on.

But when he heard Tia's carriage in the gravel sweep, he stood up from the bedside. After a final look at Tressa's hushed pale face, he went downstairs.

In the great old hall at the middle of the house, he rapped out his orders. Mudge had accomplished a great deal toward setting up a meal in the dining room. None of Hannibal's growing company had slept in their beds the night before, and Hannibal's admission as to Tressa's condition further sobered the new arrivals, emphasizing their fatigue and stealing their appetites.

All were moved but Straith, Hannibal could be sure.

Hannibal simply could not fathom the quiet creature.

Straith, obviously snared, moved into the front sitting room, where he took his chair by the hearth and politely accepted the coffee presented to him on a tray by his butler.

Tia went on up to Tressa, and Rosemary, who'd evidently begged to be brought along, went with her. Hannibal had every confidence that all that could be done for Tressa would be done.

In the sitting room over fresh coffee, only the earl appeared comfortable. Hannibal, Nick, and Sin stood, waiting as Lady Editha came in and sat across from her brother by the small wood fire. Hannibal had requested that Mudge be present, and he entered, stationing himself by the door.

Only the day beyond the diamond-paned windows was cheery. Birds, always loud and evident in the country, set about their summer business. Trees crowded around the ancient house, offering green, shady relief.

Life went on, except in Hannibal's heart. In his heart, life hung by a thread.

"So," he said, once the servants withdrew, closeting in the six of them—he and Mudge, Nick and Sin, the earl and his sister—"despite your designs, sir"—he stood over the earl—"your niece is at home in her bed."

" 'Twasn't by my design, sir," Straith insisted in his low careful tones. "If Legg brought Tressa here, he has acted on his own. I did not tell him to do so."

"You told him not to let her escape you this time. Thus, when he had the chance, he grabbed her and brought her here—to that chamber at Castlelance."

At last, Lady Editha showed a sign of life. Tall and thin like her brother, hollow-cheeked and removed from living, she set her coffee cup on its saucer.

"I don't understand this, brother. Tressa? At the castle? Whatever for?"

Hannibal placed the small vial on the table that held the coffee things. Both Editha and Straith could see the vial clearly.

"What is this?" she inquired, obviously at sea.

Her brother ignored her. "I had nothing to do with that," he said levelly.

All confidence. All lies.

"If she dies," Hannibal said to him huskily, "you will also sniff from that little vial. I will see to it personally."

"If she dies?" Lady Editha cried softly. "Why should she die, brother?"

Because Lady Editha's cup and saucer rattled violently, Hannibal took them from her fingers and set them on the table beside the corked potion. Her eyes followed Hannibal's, full of fear and question.

Nick and Sin stood by, their eyes also on him. Mudge, still at the door, watched, too.

"What's going forward here?" the elderly woman asked. "I don't understand, brother. This has to be about ... about ..."

Straith's voice grew waspish. "Hush, Editha."

Hannibal forged on. "You will live here, Straith, for as long as I say so. But you will also quietly break the entail and sell Lance Hall to me for a pittance. I will become your sole support. You will be my prisoners, and after a short while and following my marriage to your niece, you will announce your leave-taking. You and your sister will travel to the West Indies, to a plantation of mine, where you will live out the rest of your days in some comfort—if, that is, you continue to act your parts. If you don't play your parts, there will always be the vial."

Lady Editha sprang to her feet, nearly overturning the table that had been at her elbow. "This is about the secret, isn't it?"

"Editha!" Straith warned.

She peered at him. "We never should have done it. What has killing him brought us?"

"Editha!" Straith ordered. "Sit down and shut your mouth!"

Editha stood only a moment more, but she'd said enough. The secret.

Straith and Editha had killed their brother, and his daughter had somehow known and been forced into a living hell of secrecy.

Hannibal didn't think he could stand to hear much more.

Nick sent him strength through his steady black stare.

Don't let them finish you, Sin encouraged with his pale gaze.

"And so it's done," Hannibal pronounced. "My friends here, Lord Sleet and Lord St. Cur and Mudge, will be your jailers, Straith."

Hannibal looked to them for confirmation.

"You'd best become accustomed to us," purred St. Cur. "We have our road ahead of us. How nice it leads through such a pleasant place as Lance Hall can be."

"And you, Mudge," Hannibal finally said. "Are you for being a jailer in the West Indies?"

Mudge smiled a wicked, wise old smile.

Carefully, Hannibal opened the door to Tressa's chamber. Tia and Rosemary had her dressed in a nightgown, certainly a remnant from her earlier days in the house, and sat by her bedside.

Tressa didn't look any different than before, however. Their eyes worried, Tia and Rosemary stood up.

"I'll stay with her a while," Hannibal said in a low voice. "Mudge has something to eat set up in the dining room."

"You'll let me stay until she's well, won't you, Hannibal?"

He smiled at Tia as best he could. "At the very least, I expect you to wear ruts back and forth from here to London."

Also smiling sadly, the lady took Rosemary with her and left.

Alone in the chamber, with Tressa appearing as comfortable as possible, Hannibal finally reached the point where he could do nothing but wait. They had the support they needed. The puzzle had been solved, and Tressa was where she belonged.

With him.

Although everyone else was exhausted and would be looking for their beds, he was surprisingly clear now. He wondered if he'd ever sleep again. He couldn't at this point, not with Tressa as she was.

He would never sleep really well again if . . .

He was determined she would grow better, would come back to herself and to him.

She had to.

Sitting in the wing chair by Tressa's bed, he had an open view of her. Except for her extreme paleness and stillness, she seemed as if she slept, her head on the pillows, her hands clasped on the folded-down sheet, her nunnish little gown framing her lovely face, her hair fragrant on the linens.

"I love you so," he said to her, "and I'm so sorry I didn't tell you sooner. But I'm telling you now, Tressa, and you must listen. As I've been taught to be a better listener by you, you must hear me now. I love you, and I'll never be happy without you. So you must stay with me. Stay with me."

He filled his lungs.

He leaned forward in his chair to see if he could read the least change in her—a deeper breath, the twitch of a finger.

Nothing.

"I remember your telling me that night beneath Doro's portrait in the attic on Pocket Street about Robert and Doro. I hardly heard you then. You spoke of their future happiness, of their *daily* happiness, and I barely understood. I had the arrogance to believe Robert would get over Doro and find someone else. A simple replacement, I thought. No need for happiness, I would have said. He'll find what happiness he can in a mistress he chooses with his free will, not in a wife who is a necessity. How arrogant I was. And now I see how, without you, I will still go on—but without happiness, my heart. Only with you will I ever be happy. Pray, you must stay with me."

In the silence he said the last he could say.

"You've been so brave, my heart. Be brave now. With whatever effort it takes, stay with me. Say I am your heart, too."

Riveted to Tressa's quiet face, Hannibal saw the frail movement of a lovely eyebrow, the lifting of her thick, light-colored lashes.

Obviously with great effort, she smiled at him with her sudden unexpected smile. Or rather, with a slight rendition of it.

Rendition enough!

"My heart," she pledged softly.

Lance Hall
October 26, 1816

Just after the ceremony and in her wedding gown, Tressa broached the open doors of what had become their favorite sitting room at Lance Hall, the one where the large oak tree just outside had turned to golds and browns.

The one where they were most private, the safest from the busy and large staff, where they took the most freedoms, argued almost like brothers and sisters.

Inside the pleasant chamber, Tia had taken on Nick and Sin. They were fully rigged out for the wedding, and one never would have thought such fine people in such fine garb, so handsome and pretty in themselves, would argue over who had taken the gate in the orchard the most easily while out riding that morning.

"Why don't you just admit," Tressa said happily, "once and for all that Tia is every bit the bruising rider each of you is."

Tressa glanced from Nick's savage black stare—now as tame as a pussycat's, if also a little dark from his disagreement—to Sin's far more friendly, if less predictable, pale gaze.

Lately, Tressa had wished she were a portrait painter, for she had the most excellent idea for a picture of the three gentlemen who filled her days.

Hannibal would stand at the center, dressed in his best black silk cutaway coat and breeches. If she had a favorite turnout for him, it was his riveting groom's attire. At any rate, he would stand at the center of this portrait, just as he stood at the center of the trio of men, their stable, dutiful general.

Sin, with his pale-gray gaze and his cynical smile, would lounge, naturally. Seated on a chair to the left, his long legs would stretch to the middle of the picture, and, like Hannibal, he'd face straight out toward the viewer.

On the right, then, just easing out from the shadows, Nick would observe the viewer with his cold, unsettling black stare. Drawn to being with his brothers beyond blood, he'd still be reluctant to stand for his portrait.

It would never come about, even if Tressa were able to paint.

And so, too, neither would give an inch in their argument with poor Tia. She was not yet to be acknowledged as a bruising rider, crafted in their own neck-or-nothing styles.

"So," said Tressa, having settled little, "Hannibal says all is in readiness and we should come down. Although I must admit I'm nervous at giving this maiden speech of mine as the new Lady Braxton."

Tia hooked her arm in Tressa's. "You'll do wonderfully. And we, *all of us*," she added for the two fellows who stepped into place behind them, "will hang on your every word."

In the great hall at Lance Hall, refurbished like most of the house and lit by the bright autumn morning, Tressa found both a unique scene and one she'd known to expect.

The now large household, still made up of faces and families she could recognize from her earliest childhood, gathered at the bottom of the tremendous Elizabethan staircase. At its top, where she would stand with Hannibal and their little group in the blaze of light through the heraldic glass behind them, she would address the collection below.

She and Hannibal had decided that, with all the changes, she should reassure everyone as best she could. Stepping up to the old oak balustrade so she could look down and see everyone— and more importantly, so they could see her—she smiled. So many of them, and of such wonderful help over the last few months.

Tears of gratitude welled in her eyes.

"There's so much to tell you," she started. "Over this last week, I've endeavored to speak to each of you personally, and I think I've managed to do so. Just to be sure, though, I say thank you from the bottom of my heart for your loyalty and assistance. My new husband"—she glanced at Hannibal and smiled—"the gentleman who knows all my secrets"—she grinned and got dozens of grins back—"also thanks you."

Applause broke out, surprising Tressa. After Hannibal stepped forward to bow, just a bit, she went on.

"Having said that, I want to assure you that life here at Lance Hall will go on as it is despite some changes. As you know, his lordship and I will be leaving for Cannongate, our home in Devonshire. But you will have a new couple to tend to, a lady who also needs your assistance. My husband's cousin Robert Wexby and his wife, Dorothea, will be coming to live here. Since Dorothea is with child, you will soon have another charge, as well."

Again, cheers sounded. Tressa saw not only smiles of relief that life for them would indeed go on, but a recognition that she and Hannibal would ensure their livelihoods as best they could.

"I'm sure most of you have heard about Mr. Mudge's letter to us."

Now even a few huzzahs broke out. Mudge had become a favorite at Lance Hall, even though he'd been gone for weeks now.

"Let me say that Mr. Mudge is fine, and that after only the first leg of their journey to the West Indies, he is returning with my Aunt Editha. As you know, my uncle, Lord Straith, died at sea. Mr. Mudge is returning, and we will welcome him back. And my aunt, too. This also means that the house will go into mourning for a while—but not into deep mourning, I can assure you. Not with Mr. and Mrs. Wexby taking up residence and their not having known my relation."

After a brief, relieved sigh of quiet, Tressa went on to finish.

"Let me publicly thank those who, first, sat by my bedside, and then enlivened my long days and nights of recuperation. My husband, of course. That goes without saying, but—"

Again, applause rustled through the crowd, this time with Sin stepping up to encourage a heartfelt round of hurrahs.

Hannibal smiled and nodded. When Sin moved back, Tressa went on.

"But also I must mention my gratitude to Mrs. Toussand, who played so many hands of cards with me that I've become a middling player."

Tia, ever popular, was duly recognized.

"And then my sincere gratitude to my dear and faithful Rosemary."

Rosemary got a hearty round. She was, after all, one of their own.

"And thank you to our new Mrs. Effie Bates." Tressa searched the crowd below for Ambrosia's pretty and pleased face. The girl stood in the fresh bloom of her pregnancy, also newly married to their new under-butler, Bates.

That couple, too, received a fine recognition, as did Knobby, who stepped forward and swept a bow at Tressa's introduction.

"And finally, my thank yous to my new brothers, Lord Sleet and Lord St. Cur."

Here, a chant of hip-hip-hoorays rang through the old hall, building and building into a happy hurly-burly.

But Tressa heard only the words her husband whispered as he grasped her hand and kissed it for all to see.

"Well done, my heart." Turning to the noisy mass, he called, "Enjoy the celebrations! Everyone!"

Epilogue

Standing on the outside steps on Pocket Street at midnight, Hannibal fiddled with the lock and key. "What with Mudge's return day after tomorrow, this is our last chance to have the house entirely to ourselves. After a month in Town and with the Season at its height, I'm not missing this chance."

"But to leave Tia's ball as we did—"

"Nick and Sin will shine for Tia."

"Yes." Tressa chuckled. "They do tend to turn Sally Jersey quite a nice shade of pea-green."

"And we, too, my heart. Tia claims our reinstatement in society is complete. Anyway, if anyone understands my need to have you to myself, it's Tia."

Hearing the soft, satisfying click he'd been seeking, Hannibal finally had the door unlocked and shoved it open.

"The house has been closed up for some little time," Tressa said as he struggled at the hall table with the tinderbox. " 'Tis a bit dusty, I would think."

"Neither dust nor tinderboxes," he grumbled, finally getting it to spark into the cotton wool, "will keep me from my purposes." Lifting the lighted candle, he turned toward the shadowy staircase, his eyes searching upward. "We start at the top of the house, in your little nun's bed in the attic, and work our way slowly down. Not a bed shall be missed, nor the big brown chair in the book room, nor the summerhouse. We shall be hard-pressed, indeed."

"Indeed," said Tressa. "Perhaps we'll get us another baby from it. Two in three years has been very nice, and I should like another."

"I shall do my best."

Hannibal took her hand in his and, with the candle in his other, charged the stairs, ball clothes and all.

"Whatever happened to Joe Legg, do you think? You've never mentioned him, Hannibal."

"Frankly, I don't know what happened to Joe Legg. Since I wanted only to kill the man, I left him to Sin and Nick. They merely said he wouldn't see England again. But, pray," he added as they reached the backstairs, "the last person I wish to discuss is Joe Legg. Do you think we're up to a turn on the back stairs? By the very devil, how I did want you that first night on the back stairs."

"It sounds too uncomfortable. Indeed, stairs are uncomfortable. And so are little balconies with stone handrails. And coaches. And the library at Tia's with company in the next room. Heavens, but—"

"As you say, they are all out. You simply must stop looking so beautiful, my heart, and then I'll stop . . . well, I guess I'll never stop wanting you."

At last, they reached the little corridor in the attic just outside the room Tressa had occupied three years earlier.

"Poor Mudge," she said. "First, his aborted adventure to the West Indies—"

"He said it was a living hell."

"And now so indispensable to us and the children, even to

Aunt Editha. He has to leave here and visit Lance Hall for a week at a time and listen to her mad prattle. Hardly anyone but he can understand her anymore."

"Speaking of prattle," Hannibal said, finally inside Tressa's tiny chamber and pulling her into his arms, "no matter how much we care about each one, there will be no talk of a single friend or family member, including the boys. On Pocket Street, it's just we two, my heart. Here no one exists but us—for two whole days."

"And nights, my heart." Tressa spoke softly, welcoming her husband's initial quick kisses. "And two ... deep ... dark ... nights."

She puffed out his hard-won candle flame, casting each of them headlong into the other's hungry embrace.

Put a Little Romance in Your Life With
Betina Krahn

DO YOU HAVE THE HOHL COLLECTION?